Bishop's Endgame

ALSO BY MICHAEL FROST BECKNER

HITLER'S LOKI
Berlin Mesa

SPY GAME
The Aiken Trilogy
Muir's Gambit
Bishop's Endgame
Aiken in Check

A NATION DIVIDED
Volume I: Episodes 101–104
Volume II: Episodes 105–108
Volume III: Episodes 109–112

Bishop's Endgame

Book II
The Aiken Trilogy

Michael Frost Beckner

Los Angeles
2022

Copyright © 2022 by Michael Frost Beckner

All rights reserved.

Published in the United States by Montrose Station Press LLC, Los Angeles.

LIBRARY OF CONGRESS CONTROL NUMBER: 2022901282

ISBN 9798985597431 (hardcover)
ISBN 9798985597448 (paperback)
ISBN 9798985597455 (ebook)

Printed in the United States of America
FIRST EDITION

Jacket design & interior art by Andrew Frost Beckner
Book design by Michael Grossman

For my children

Acknowledgments

"Come play with us in Mustique, Michael. Now I won't have it otherwise. We have Yellowbird this year, so there's gobs of room. And before you say no, there will be a dear friend guesting with us who would love to meet you. I think he has some good stories for you. We'll count on you?"

Of everything I pursued later in authoring this novel, it was that telephone call from my many times gracious hostess, and all-around fabulous delight, Lady Diana Heimann (daughter of Great Britain's chancellor of the exchequer under Churchill), by which *Bishop's Endgame* was born.

The gentleman with whom I "guested" looked nothing like James Bond. He did, however, bare a close resemblance to Ian Fleming as I remembered that novelist, gaunt and glowering from his photograph on the backs of the James Bond paperbacks of my youth. He was introduced as having served in the "foreign service," a gentleman—with *gentle* pronounced "hard"—of that generation who extolled the medicinal virtues of gin—with tonic for malaria, and straight for everything else from hangnails to hepatitis, colic to cancer—and made you believe it. Like most British spies I've met, he listened more than he spoke. When he did speak, it was only to suggest I turn what I was guessing at inside out to look at it another way; to consider another topic while never following up with comment on the first. He'd asked that I view events through a lens of what didn't happen and compare that to what wasn't apparent. Never a "Why?"; just a "Tell me now, what does the invisible link look like? That's your crux of the matter."

An afternoon with this gentleman required twice the time for me than for him, as once these one-sided conversations ended, I'd spend an equal amount of the evening walking the entire thread backward to discover the secret he'd walked with into the room at the conversation's outset that I'd somehow revealed to myself by its end. The gin helped. And in that way, he silently divulged intelligence he'd never specifically detailed, I'd never coherently imagined, but I somehow could now identify with clarity and take to heart as my own.

Cooling off one afternoon at Basil's Bar on the edge of the island, were it not for the company of my impenetrable companion, I would have dismissed the leather-skinned Dutch expat, scruffy and garrulous, more drunk than sober, without a second glance. As he made his way to our table, I thought my British spook would repel him with the flat edge of his steely glance. Instead, my companion grinned. I watched him rise to his feet.

Surprised to see each other after "so many years," the two men reveled in a shared past from their former careers. Where my British friend remained inscrutable behind his smile, the Dutchman joined our table with uncomplicated zeal. Introductions made, the Dutchman announced, "Do I have a short-hair curler for you." Dared me to "take it back to your friends at Langley and damn them to call me a liar. They know me, and they're stinking liars if they deny it."

He'd been kicking around Southeast Asia as "international press" during our Vietnam conflict. Had heard about a CIA operation being considered that would finish the North Vietnamese, and with them, the war "with one great big bang." Our spooks, he said, were serious when they'd first bragged about it. Made it a joke a few weeks later when he tried to run it down.

Deadly or funny, it was the most dangerously stupid spy story I have ever heard. Gin or no gin, I'm no fool to think this chance encounter at the beach bar was coincidence. I don't think the two other players in the arrangement cared at all if I saw through the happenstance of their charade. They couldn't have possibly thought I'd verify the story with anyone but liked taking a shot at embarrassing the Agency if only by distant proxy through me. And, an operation proposed yet abandoned, whom that I might tell, so many decades later, would possibly care? I put it from my head and got on with the business of "guesting" under the sunny Caribbean sky.

But a story that difficult to believe is a story impossible to forget.

A year or so later, invited unexpectedly as a guest to an OSS Society (the Office of Strategic Services, World War Two precursor to the CIA) dinner in Virginia, I had the fortunate distinction to be seated at a table with General John K. Singlaub. A he-man if there ever was, Singlaub had, in 1944, parachuted behind German lines to coordinate Resistance attacks during D-Day; helped found the CIA; served in Korea, along the Ho Chi Minh Trail, and in Laos, Nicaragua, and Afghanistan. The clandestine-services veterans seated with him were playing a kind of "Can you top this?" trading stories of the dumbest operations and in-field blunders they could remember. As fate will, its broad eye aimed my way and winked. When the tall tales came round to the general, I listened to him repeat my Dutch acquaintance's story as the worst idea ever approved by President Lyndon Johnson for CIA Vietnam operations. He looked at me and said, "Bet you could make one hell of a movie out of that one."

Conceived is one thing. Abandoned, a better thing.

Approved?

Acknowledgments

From that single word, Operation ATROPOS (my name, not theirs), and van Eijk (my Dutch friend's name, not his), *Bishop's Endgame* was born. All of you have my double thanks—for getting this story to me so that I can tell it now, and for never having implemented the hideously stupid plan back when it would have caused a nuclear war.

As for the setting of this novel—its recent crises notwithstanding—Malaysia is a peaceful, welcoming, magnificent country. The social trouble, political unrest, and radical Muslim terrorism depicted in these pages are pure invention created for drama and suspense and bear no resemblance to the politics, social fabric, and religious tolerance of that nation. I have a deep affection for and gratitude to Malaysia and all of its people.

Of those Malaysians on my two journeys to and through their country who deserve special thanks are the owners and staff of Pangkor Laut and Tanjong Jara, particularly Dr. Yip, who spent two days with me in the jungle, sharing his deep knowledge as a naturalist and his life story, coming of age on the peninsula in the more tumultuous times of the second half of the twentieth century. Thankfully, of all the wildlife he tracked and revealed to me, we never saw a tiger, but the number of bird species I added to my life-list increased by ten. The last two I've never been able to top: a mated pair of rhinoceros hornbills.

In Kuala Lumpur, at the Carcosa Seri Negara, I would like to extend that same special thank you to my valet and personal assistant Vicky, who never left my side no matter where I wanted to go—especially when I purposely had no destination in mind other than a mental dart thrown at a map, or when I knew my destination exactly and ignored his words of caution while he doubled his vigilance. Vicky's affability and sincerity paid dividends with every introduction he provided me to scores of strangers from all walks of life, races, and religions whom I spoke with and for whom he served as translator. Tireless, ingenious, and fearless, possessing the most impeccable manners of anyone I have ever met (even when extracting me from unintended dangers I'd gotten myself into—once with student demonstrators, another time with some rough types carving a village canoe with machetes and hatchets)—Vicky introduced me to the former commando, retired miner, and tiger artist who is the basis for Lucky-Boy.

The real Lucky-Boy remains nameless at his humble request, but in *Bishop's Endgame*, Vicky appears written as himself to *his* humble delight.

Thanks are also due to a certain American individual from the US Embassy named Scott (no last name given) who didn't work for our State Department and knew, in detail, indicators, plans, mechanisms for events capable of provoking a Malaysian civil war; the measures the Malaysian government would take; and three rapid-reaction scenarios that could be employed by US military and "other on-station direct action forces" to protect American diplomatic staff, their dependents, and US travelers based upon escalating levels of local and national unrest. I've attempted to remain accurate to my briefing and where I've fallen short is most likely my own mistake gussied up with dramatic license.

In an effort to examine cultural stereotyping before converting my Malaysian experiences to drama, I studied two books in parallel: Graham Greene's *The Quiet American* (1955, Heinemann) and Edward Said's *Orientalism* (1978, Pantheon). I'm glad I did, and I hope the best qualities of awareness, even when portrayed in opposite, colonial relief, show through my words.

Additionally, for my understanding and ability to write on sign-function and identity perception, I have relied upon and am indebted to Jacques Maritain's *A Preface to Metaphysics: Seven*

Lectures on Being (1939, Sheed & Ward), his "Sign and Symbol" from the *Journal of the Warburg Institute, Vol. 1, #1* (July 1937), and his *The Range of Reason* (1948, Scribner's); and the brilliant and comprehensive *A Theory of Semiotics* by Umberto Eco (1976, Indiana University Press). Using these theories as a springboard into the core theme of this book—the search for identity and identity perception in a world where false identity is paramount—this novel would not exist without the excellent work of Demian Whiting's "On the Appearance and Reality of Mind" from the *Journal of Mind and Behavior* (Winter 2016, Vol. 37, No. 1); *The Case Against Reality: Why Evolution Hid the Truth from Our Eyes* by Donald Hoffman (Norton, 2019); and *Reality Is Not What It Seems* by Carlo Rovelli (Penguin, 2014) ; Erik Parens "Genetic Differences and Human Identities: On Why Talking About Behavioral Genetics Is Important and Difficult" from *The Hastings Center Report* (2004 January-February, Vol. 34, No. 1). When I scratch the surface of these subjects, it is with the knowledge of these authors, thinkers, scientists, and experts guiding my hand.

There is one more piece of HUMINT that informs this book: another telephone call I received, the fear it overwhelmed me with in the voice of a loved one telling me they had a brain tumor. It's a fear you cannot do a thing about but receive and join it, and it's followed by the deepest kind of sadness, knowing that your portion of that awful fear will never be close to the horror of the one who has shared it with you. While this experience equipped me with the ability to write the symptoms, thoughts, and emotions, my understanding of the medicine and the science needed research. I am especially thankful for the excellent writings of Peter Black, M.D., Ph.D. (with Sharon Cloud Hogan), in his *Living with a Brain Tumor: Dr. Peter Black's Guide to Taking*

Control of Your Treatment (2006, Griffin) and Henry Marsh's *Do No Harm: Stories of Life, Death, and Brain Surgery* (2016, Picador).

For the parallel conditions of Wernicke's aphasia and hypergraphia that accompany the tumor in this book, *The Midnight Disease: The Drive to Write, Writer's Block, and the Creative Brain* by Alice W. Flaherty, M.D., Ph.D. (2004, Mariner) was indispensable and served as a brilliant guide in understanding these afflictions.

As always my special thanks to Kara, Joel, and John; Heather and Rebecca; Charlie Lyons and Murray Weiss; and Andrew most particularly: couldn't do it without any of you.

A final shout-out must go to the two FSB thugs who interrogated me for three hours in Vladivostok under the false belief I worked for the CIA. (Thanks for nothing, Langley, telling me they'd have no idea I had a nominal association with you.) It played out for me almost exactly as I've written it down to my *Star Trek* inspired escape. But don't let me get ahead of myself. As manic and delusional and obtuse as he can be, the story is always better when Aiken tells it.

Bishop's Endgame

"Semiotics is concerned with everything that can be *taken* as a sign. A sign is everything which can be taken as significantly substituting for something else. This something else does not necessarily have to exist or to actually be somewhere at the moment in which a sign stands in for it. Thus *semiotics is in principle the discipline studying everything which can be used in order to lie.* If something cannot be used to tell a lie, conversely it cannot be used to tell the truth: it cannot in fact be used 'to tell' at all."

— Umberto Eco, *A Theory of Semiotics*

This day May 10, 2001

*DISPATCH MID-FLIGHT ABOARD UNITED
STATES MARINE CORPS F/A-18 (AIR WING
CVW-9), USS JOHN C. STENNIS (CVN-74)*

*Russell Aiken, Clandestine Services Officer, Directorate of Operations
(formerly legal counsel, CIA Office of General Counsel), the Central
Intelligence Agency, United States of America*

> *Jack and Jill*
> *Went up the hill*
> *To fetch a pail of water.*
> *Jack fell down*
> *And broke his crown,*
> *And Jill came tumbling after.*

When I draft a CONPLAN—the concept form of an operation before I legalize it as the final OPLAN—I keep this nursery rhyme forefront in my mind. The perfect example of my task ahead. "Jack and Jill" spells out the mission, puts the deception out in the open, and uses plain language to distract from the luggage of the lie to create a sympathy in the reader.

Anyone who reads "Jack and Jill" comes away from it with a kindly aspect for its twin protagonists. Forever after, when you recall the pair or repeat their legend, your allegiance carries forward. We like Jack and Jill. We regret their mishap. But we see no reason to assign malintent or affix any blame.

Jack and Jill: how a Russell Aiken CONPLAN gets approved for operational planning. Hand in hand, the cutie-pie pair skips you past the big lie I've gotten the government to sign off on. A deception operation staring you right in the face.

The nursery rhyme was a seventeenth-century psychological propaganda operation run by forces of British Parliament against King Charles I to inflame the English population against the monarch. The little ditty covertly informed the populace of how Charles betrayed them by raising taxes on liquid measures. He ordered that the volume of a Jack (1/8 pint) be reduced while the tax increased. This meant King Charles received more cash as his subjects received less ale. Hence, the lines "Jack fell down and broke his crown" (most pint glasses in the U.K. still have a line marking the 1/2-pint level with a crown above it) "and Jill came tumbling after" (reference to a "gill," or 1/4 pint) reflected the drop in volume handclasped with the tax hike consequence.

"Jack and Jill" ginned up popular support for the parliamentary overthrow of the Crown. And the thing missed by all and sundry? The endgame is never about Jack and Jill. Not about Jack's bloody boo-boo. It isn't about the pail. It's not about the water—or beer, as Charles learned when they lopped off his head.

The operation is the hill. Lives or dies there in plain-view, signed-off secrecy. And the endgame is as drastic and impactful as the beheading of a king over lost booze by a primed populace incensed at receiving less buzz for their buck. Or as meaningless as the dish chasing the spoon to Malaysia is prelude to the cow jumping over Manhattan.

No one ever dug a well at the top of a hill.

PART ONE

CONCLUSIONS

"A widespread neurosis began to be evident, faintly signaled, like a nervous beating of the feet, by the popularity of crossword puzzles."

— F. Scott Fitzgerald, *Echoes of the Jazz Age*

1

Harker piled cold Thai noodles from the buffet table onto his plate and spoke to my shadow on the wall.

"I am not going to let some old, dead triceratops and his Barney Rubble golden-boy gone rogue topple my Agency over some useless secret to some forgotten Malaysian conspiracy of thirty-three fucking years ago. Guess what—?"

I don't need to guess. Barney Rubble never had a triceratops.

He had a saber-toothed tiger and a pink prehistoric lobster grass-clipper.

But…

…were I to stoop to Harker's level and engage in guesswork (inappropriate for this deadly game we're players in), I'd say, if he means anything, he means Baby Bop. That strange green little tri-top who hung out with the big purple T-Rex crooner of "Wheels on the Bus" fame. Squeaky-voiced like our Jessie, with whom I watched that cloying sing-along as I'd rope my tie around my neck before I'd head to headquarters and, at the end of my gibbet, kick out the legal paperwork that keeps the illegal business of the CIA in lawful accord with our Constitution.

Jeremy Harker III executed a kind of King of Pop spin and singled me out, eyes behind gunmetal glasses, small and brown, that might as well have been the nubs of two bullets inside the cylinder and me staring up the dull muzzle of his nose.

"Not going to happen while I'm director of Central Intelligence," he said.

Let's be honest, Mads, he's acting director. And not very well at that. His main focus these days Arthur Murray lessons twice weekly at a Tysons Corner mini mall.

"Dance and golf have a symbiotic relationship," he tells me ten days ago as I collide with him and his missus. They heading out of the dance studio as you, I, and the kids headed into the India Clay Pot for curry.

The both of us—Harker and I—somnambulists in our belief that Southeast Asia rested safely folded at the back of the "been there, done that, bought the concert T-shirt" drawer of our Agency lives. But a spymaster's murder, the loss of seven agent networks, and a coded message out of Malaysia from a longforgotten agent ooh-gahed *our klaxon and—moving too fast to your won't-be-bothered-by-foreign-civil-war suggestion I might want to "Grab a fun T-shirt and those Patagonia fly-fishing shorts Jessie picked out for you last Christmas"— I pulled that drawer off its rails.*

Tumbled concert T-shirts stared at me like a penilik nasib's *sooth-saying portents. Their words, the exact timeline to all that would transpire:* U2: Rock the Vote, Journey: Frontiers, Wham! The Dark Side of the Moon, *and* The Rolling Stones: Bridges to Babylon. *My mood not on doom, I missed the prophetic headlines, grabbed a shirt from the pile, and raced for Harker's aircraft.*

As USUAL, I stumble ahead of myself. It's ten years and two children since my aborted suicide. Passing fifty after blowing through every Stop sign of my forties, I strove to do right by my family only to discover striving became the thing I did most and best and I missed the effortless love staring me in my face. I neglected to cherish the gentle affection I received, and I never shifted a backward glance to understand why.

"Scratchy…" Jessie's enjoyment of rubbing her hand up my cheek against the day's stubble, then down, "Smooooth," and I'd tuck her into bed.

Lots of love, the three of you. Though I now know you, dear Madeline, had more to give.

You tell me I'm maturing and better-looking than ever. I appreciate that. You point out that my eyes are still youthful and deep. My vision remains better than perfect at 20/15—I can read a freeway sign a quarter-mile away like a hawk sees its dinner mouse from the sky—and my once unsettling crooked smile has lost its serial-killer leer *(your tease, Mads, not mine)* to become fully bemused, drawing people to me who want in on the joke, you not knowing that the joke is "bemused" has nothing to do with amusement and everything to do with my daily and constant ritual confusion.

I've lost fifty percent of my hair without noticing until after it was gone. My body—*Corpus delicti*—when I look in the mirror sags a bit too much everywhere and surely can't belong to the me I remember I wanted to be and imagined I would. When I lie in bed to work a crossword, I stare at the backs of my hands. The skin so wrinkled and loose. My index finger creased and crinkled as an elephant's trunk. When did the two or three brown spots decide to show up and ruin an enjoyable puzzle? It's ten spots. I'm lying. As usual.

What was the Muir First Rule of Thumb—or Stare Decisis, binding precedent, to my legal mind? "Don't trust a lie I tell unless you can make it true."

WHERE AM I? My mind keeps running away from my fingers as I type at Mach 1, claustrophobic among the clouds. Ah, right. Our Malaysia problem. The *acting* director (*acting* because the new president, dumb as they make him out, is not so dumb as to make Harker's position permanent) Nureyeving from the buffet. Nervy and making me nervous.

The nerve of him.

"You're sitting there like an idiot," Harker said to me, jolting my attention back from its verbal gear-stripping, back to the DCI's (Director Central Intelligence) Seventh Floor Conference Room.

Harker's room as of fifteen weeks and four days ago when he foxtrotted in as acting director of the Central Intelligence Agency and, first order of business, added the daily buffet he'd been whining about since the day in '91 Nathan Muir turned Operation SIDESHOW (Harker's plan to let Tom Bishop be executed in China) into Operation DINNER OUT (Muir's plan not to). The day when former Director Folger made the mistake of ordering in lunch as a way to keep Muir a pinned butterfly in a bell jar. This allowed Muir—retired with prejudice that morning from his forty-plus years as an ops officer and agent runner—full access to Agency headquarters.

Stare Decisis: Never let Nathan Muir flap butterfly wings inside Langley if you don't want a tsunami on the other side of the globe.

"Huh?" I said.

"To repeat. You are sitting there, Aiken, like an idiot."

"Yes, 'sitting,' sir, but idiot—no. Ing. Sir," trying my hardest not to sound idiotic, which I always achieve—one or the other. I fixed him with my blandest stare.

Ballroom dancing is officially a fad.

I hate fads.

I hate Harker.

"Yet you are the only one, Aiken, who can get this job done."

"I'm not sure I follow. This 'what-job'?"

He hates me. Entirely.

If I hadn't indemnified the Agency from the Charlie March murder ten years ago, legally hiding the secret of that former and still-pretended hero of the CIA's treason; if I hadn't secured the now deceased Muir's early retirement after proving he engineered March's assassination hands-free, legalesing our way *out of the way* of Executive Order 11905, which specifically forbids the Agency from engaging in political assassination, I wouldn't be here these past ten years, papering dubious operations of doubtful results in the CIA Office of General Counsel.

Yes—sorry, Mads. I'm sure you caught that—Nathan Muir is dead.

I'm sorry I couldn't tell you. It remains classified, but there's no way to unwrite those words any more than God can unwrite an event. So, if you want to read further, you must trust me it's happened—he is dead (Muir, not God, I hope)—and he was murdered. Trust that this meeting I was "idioted" in determined the culprit, and the culprit is who we've expected would kill him these ten long-and-misplaced, happily-sad spent years since promised and sworn to on our very own doorstep, July 4, 1991.

"Tell Nathan when you see him: if he did this, I'm going to kill him."

Patricide.

Or, in reproductive respects—or I suppose, "disrespect"—when Tom Bishop pulled the trigger, Muir murdered himself.

2

"I'm sending you to Malaysia. The job: you sort out this Bishop mess."

"Not something I care to lawyer for you, Acting Director."

"And this isn't your campus law society. You don't get a vote."

"Conflict of interest," I pointed out. "Entirely in my favor."

"You're not getting me, Aiken. I'm putting you in the field. Your dream job. 'Transfer Request to Clandestine Services': *Approved.*"

He gave me his *Gum-Gum with the Flavor-Flavor* Chiclets-teeth smirk.

Approved. My-my, glad you could get to it. After twenty-eight years.

But my interest was piqued and, gray ambitions whoofed off in dust motes from the cover of my life story, I heard myself saying, "That transfer permanent—not just this one field trip? I'll have that to do this. Otherwise, I walk, and you can keep your Malaysian disruption, Muir's burned foreign networks, and your Tom Bishop thorn snug in your paw."

I clapped my hands and spread them palms up like a Vegas dealer to the eye-in-the-sky cameras—nothing to hide—God's and Androcles' honest truth.

Never in a million years Harker goes for this. Pension time, here we come. Not a moment too soon.

Harker's smile shrunk to a furious butt-pucker as dry and loathsome as pumice. Harker did the impossible. He bobbed his head yes. "Permanent," he said, using the same inflection a cobra uses to spit.

I had stopped applying for the lateral move across directorates five years ago after Harker hadn't even bothered to deny the last one. I was hit by a high-velocity thought. The only reason Harker would hold on to my transfer request would be to one day use it to ruin me.

A "The-thea the-thea the tha-that's all, Folks!" fade out for me.

"Thank you," I said, best of enemies. "I'll draft the paperwork to that effect as soon as we're finished here. I look forward to a long and healthy career in the Directorate of Operations." I gave him my most open-faced smile, but I'm as good as pulled-pork Looney-Tuned sandwich-pig dead.

Harker slurped a noodle. Tiny drops of peanut sauce flicked off its tail and only now does clarity arrive too late and too violent in its revelation of how this whole disaster worked its way into Harker's best day ever: get rid of the last two (me and Bishop) of the three reminders (Muir, third, dead, off the chessboard) of his DINNER OUT/SIDESHOW blunder in which Muir prevented the execution of his CIA officer son and his son's Crown Colony Hong Kong-British activist wife by rendering an unsanctioned CIA rescue of the pair from China.

Beside me at the conference table sat Harker's deputy director, Meryl Hofmeyr. "For you, hmm." She slid me the pre-drafted transfer paperwork.

Yeah, one f and no e. Explain that to two wiener companies. Hoffy, Oscar Meyer? Jessie devours them both when I grill.

"Is a hot dog a sandwich?" I mumbled, grasping for bricks, sticks, or straws.

Can't stay away from the crosswords at cross purposes. Always been this way. I hear words, speak them, write 'em, read 'em, and especially think them across and down.

Sanctified and forgiven.

Or not, depending what I've deified. Words? Concepts? Constructs? God? Is it He in the detail or the devil? Far as I'm concerned, the devil never even lived. It's all God, and God only exists in cognition, and cognition can only be deciphered through language that pins meaning to slithering life. My ouroboros. The Word was with God, and the Word was God.

Don't nod, Mads.

Crosswords at cross purposes and the letter boxes, ependymal cells fill the grid of the four ventricles of my puzzled brain. The impenetrable black spaces ever-growing. F–U–N—as Arthur Wynne, inventor of the first crossword, chose the word to begin the neurosis I alternately chase or hide with every word I hope-hype-type.

Meryl, like Harker, is one of those whom Muir dubbed the "Young Turks." Those CIA wonks who came in after the fall of the Iron Curtain to clear out the Cold Warriors. To look forward. Modernize. To www-dot everything possible with Spiderman-slung accuracy. You met her once. Said she reminded you of a Teletubby. Laa-Laa. The yellow one. And not merely the look, the up-the-forehead curl of her bangs, but the funny little encouraging squeaks and hums she makes while you're speaking with her; whirs she peppers her speech with as if trying to encourage herself to sneeze. As lifelong president of the Contrarian Society, Meryl Hofmeyr contemplates in those deceitful myna bird calls how to gain personal power and professional control from opposing what she's pretending to haw to with the fatuous abandon of Laa-Laa bouncing her oversized orange ball.

"I'll write myself an OPLAN," I said.

"Ah-ah-ahhh—Russell." Meryl chuckled. "Now that you *are* Ops, mmm, you'll see we don't really do this that way. *You knooow,* an OPLAN for the tiniest of whats? A Pony Express delivery? Officer to officer, hand to hand, no foreign involvement to finger the baton you're trading off?" she *tsk-tsked* her tongue. "Not truly an op in need of a plan, now, seeing it that way, no?" She bore into me with a stern look.

I puttied my face with smugness, thinking verbal tics might be better named *Tic-Tacs*, their confectioning of language squarely identified as confection.

"Russell, Director Harker just tossed you *off* your law books. You'll take a vacation from 'on the record' with this one."

"Get out of here, Aiken," Harker said. "I've got as much need for you remaining in this room as I do a big third tit."

Didn't know Harker sized his other two.

"Go home. Pack your toothbrush. Kiss your kids and make love to your wife. In two hours, your butt's on my Citation X to Malaysia."

Does Harker know five percent of women grow aberrant breast tissue in their axilla—their armpits—and in rarer cases the scapula, the thigh, and the labia majora? So, nippled or not, a woman can grow four to ten boobs. How's that for a fun time? Harker—who has none—claims two and claims he doesn't want a third because he hates me in his sight. Now that anyone can get 'em, tits might be a fad too.

I hate fads and the tit growing inside my skull.

Should've been a doctor if I'd known there was so much comedy in the human body. Once, a guy had five testicles. Proven fact.

"Splendid," I said. "Of course, sir, your aircraft can't make Malaysia in the time required. Short on speed by about fifty mph, time loss multiplied over distance."

Silence around the table, which included Bill Carver (deputy director, Forensic Investigation, Office of Security) and three of his CIA detective investigators who put together the case against Bishop, plus two senior East Asian analysts who work the Malaysia Section for the Directorate of Intelligence. Had I gone too far? I'm sure I'd kept the tits and testicles comment utterly benign in my head. 99.99 percent sure, as benign goes.

One of the Malay Section boys came to my defense. "He is correct, sir. Also, your jet's a bit short on range. Just saying."

"This isn't your concern, Dr. Zhou. You fucking figure it out, Aiken. Just get there."

I got as far as the door. "One more thing. With or without an OPLAN, won't I need orders cut for Bishop? Or a warrant? Something to get him back?"

"Bishop is rogue and running from a murder. Paper won't cut it with him. You're the only person in the Agency he trusts. If he shows himself to anyone, it's going to be you, and it won't be about coming back."

Or end as non-lethal as a paper cut.

Six days ago, all of Muir's former agent networks short-circuited. Blacked out like bright-burst flashbulbs across the globe. Over fifty of our foreign agents. Arrested? Dead? Running scared…? No idea. Just gone.

Five days since Tom Bishop reappeared in Kosovo after vanishing rogue two years ago on the first anniversary of the death of his wife.

It's four days since Nathan Muir's murder.

It's three days since Bishop was given both Harker's "all is forgiven" and my last allowed CONPLAN, which sent him back into the field and into a budding Malaysian civil war.

Two days since Bishop went rogue. Again.

And twelve hours since it's been settled that Tom Bishop murdered his father, Nathan Muir.

Four minutes since I vomited.

Not from drinking. Had my last drink a decade ago, outside my 1938 Tenleytown townhouse moments before entering with Muir's Sig-Sauer pistol, where I failed for the second time in as many days at suicide.

I've thrown up because I'm flying faster than the speed of sound in a coffin-like rear cockpit of the F/A-18, getting this all onto my ThinkPad, after riding wicked Harker's wicked-fast (but not fast enough) Citation X from Washington to US Naval Forces Central Command, Bahrain (via a Paris refueling), where a package awaited me. I collected it and choppered out to the USS *John C. Stennis* aircraft carrier, where—without so much as a cup of coffee—they catapulted me from the deck, hurling me hurling into my threat-turned-reality dream job, sonic booming to a Thailand airbase and an unwanted, unwarranted, betrayal by brother.

And he's not even my brother! That's how close I consider Bishop. You know? It's like when you have a brother—which you don't and neither do I—and you say, "He's not just my brother, he's my best friend." Well, if it works that way, it's meant to work the other way too. With me. And Bishop. That's the trade-off. No traitors allowed.

Can't trust anybody these days, Mads. Can ya?

I have two more barf bags in the right calf pocket of my borrowed flight suit. After that, I guess I could use these Mickey Mouse-sized flight gloves they gave me. At least the Citation offered a headset and Harker's DVD selection. Here, all I have is the roar of the afterburner and the Model T-like, impossible to engage, crank of my afflicted mind.

Everyone chases stupid. Me included.

Learned as a kid. Remember vividly. Fifth-grade science. You drop a penny off the Empire State Building (better: New York's Twin Towers, the Observation Deck), it could penetrate a skull if it hit someone below. Will go through the roof of a car.

Ergo, why make bombs?

Simply drop one million pennies on your enemy.

We exit the Tysons Corner India Clay Pot and, "Look, Jessie, a penny. 'Find a penny pick it up, all day long you'll something-something-something.'"

Forgetting simple rhymes the least of my worries, my point is:

Everyone's dropping pennies constantly in parking lots and on the sidewalk anyhow, so why not drop 'em on your foe?

You think I'm joking?

Okay, sure, a penny dropped from the Twin Towers hits the Fifth Avenue sidewalk at a velocity of 64.4 mph and, okay again, yeah, that's not gonna penetrate a skull, but drop them from a B-52 Stratocaster, I mean Stratofortress (still have Led Zeppelin T-shirts on the mind), and from an altitude of 12,000 feet—packed in heavy clusters to burst on impact, the velocity is 600 mph. 880 fps. A single 950 lbs. CBU-87 anti-personnel cluster bomb goes for $14,000 a pop. One million pennies are the equivalent of 555 cluster bombs: $7,777,777 million. A million pennies? What bargain hunters enjoy. Government cost: *cha-ching* $10,000.

Dad's record collection: Sinatra–Basie: *"Pennies from Heaven."*

And those who survive the copper rain of death? They fill their upside-down umbrellas, hats, pockets, and shoes with the Abe Lincolns they begged from our American generosity every day of their lives. Depending on the size of the air raid: retirement money for the speedy scrabbler; US destruction is foreign aid at work.

Instead, Mads, the payload I'm delivering is $10,000 in tens, twenties, fifties, and hundreds, and ten 10g PAMP gold bars of Swiss origin. Bishop demanded ransom. And before I forget "myna bird" is wrong. It's the Tickell's Niltava, which in Malaysia looks *both like Laa-Laa and a winged Tic Tac—not that I remember why that's important now—but what I couldn't say while I picked out the all-too-eloquent Grateful Dead: Blues for Allah Tour T-shirt from the spilled drawer on our bedroom floor: There is little likelihood I'll be returning home in anything other than a sealed box.*

3

WITH THE COLLAPSE of the Soviet Union, the concept of First, Second, and Third World nations ended. Not the nations themselves—obviously—the designations. Word came down from the United Nations this was US-imposed, political/military-industrial complex Cold War, internationally intentional *trigger-branding*. In the UN rush to eliminate "Third World" as a horrid American expression coined to shame other nations, they invoked the 1918 post-WWI, PTSD term *trigger warning* and implemented a safe set of designations: Developed, Developing, Under Developed, and HIPC.

You don't know what that last one stands for, do ya, Mads? You're not alone, most common folk don't bother. That was the point. Alternately pronounced Hi-P-C to discourse-shame the suspicious to silence (it's PC, after all), or Hi-Pic to distract with a techno-vocab Apple computerese vibe like that newfangled iWant Pod thing Jessie begs for. But you can read about those silly HIPCs over your latte or your bottled water at the gym in CNN closed-caption peace and not know to bother a wit about them because even though in those countries they're still dining on a twigs with mud sauce single daily meal, they are now HiPic in with the "I" crowd, and Heavily Indebted Poor Countries is never spelled out because that would be a trigger warning. Instead, it's enough to know and feel safe that HIPC means the World Bank's got their back and indigenous children always smile in their advertising.

Under the paternal gaze of the United Nations and their curative new designation, one particular country—where Malay-Muslim, Indian, and Chinese workers, women and men, leave work arm in arm and hand in hand day after day, officially recognized by the government as a cultural sign of friendship, misrecognized by the vast influx of foreigners as gay—Malaysia awakened to a world beyond the jungle economy of tin mines and coconut oil, to a city of glass and steel, silver and gold, banks, gas companies, hotels, and office towers. According to the UN report on Malaysia, once freed from the stigma of US imperialist "Third World" designation by World Bank globalist grant, the tropical state immediately and successfully petitioned a move from HIPC to Under Developed—

UN signing bonus

—allowing the ICC Banking Commission to announce international regulations met, making Malaysia a Developing nation—

Somebody say Kool-Aid? Just add water and ice!

And throw wide the door to legal influx of illegal Chinese Communist and Saudi dark money. The Malaysian government filled its coffers with appropriate loans and inappropriate promises, and the UN, having authored Malaysia's new non-triggering designation, took credit for the fastest-growing economy in Asia. They broadcast Malaysia as the third highest GDP per capita in Southeast Asia, behind Singapore and Brunei. This launched government–private partnerships in three remarkable endeavors that all came to gleaming fruition by 1998. Their brand-new international airport ranked in the top-ten worldwide in service, efficiency, design, and amenities—the only Cinnabon below the equator—built by the Malay-Chinese industrialist Tan Sri Dato' Lim Kang Hoo. A sparkling new Formula 1 racetrack designed and run by racing enthusiast Malay-Muslim entrepreneurs. The Petronas Twin Towers: tallest skyscrapers on Planet Earth.

A new national stadium soon followed. A new philharmonic hall. The XVI Commonwealth Games were held in Malaysia—the first in an Asian nation and the last of the Games of the twentieth century. And the Ferrari, McLaren, and Team Stewart F1 drivers were given the first elevator tour of the Petronas Towers, zipped up the Japanese-constructed Tower One and descended the Korean-constructed Tower Two, before flying off to the brand-new five-star luxury resort island of Pangkor Laut, owned by a Muslim princess.

And that's not all who came to the party. UN-woke Malaysia was arisened-and-shined (some morning words still shouldn't be mis-tensed) enough to generously allow the seventeenth son of the fifty-two children of a Saudi construction magnate—who once went over the Hindu Kush to take control of the Afghan heroin trade, and did—one Mr. Osama bin Laden, to host his al-Qaeda summit in Developing Kuala Lumpur to evaluate ideas for his latest venture: worldwide terroristic Islamic jihad.

The summit transpired January 5 through to January 8, last year, with impeccable turn-down, Michelin-star in-room dining, and exceptional top-to-bottom service with a smile.

The UN did not tell us about this little convention until later. Only after we inquired did the Malaysians share video, but not audio, and the video *somehow* didn't reveal lips for reading. While unable to prevent the August 1998 bombings of the US embassies in Nairobi, Kenya, and Dar es Salaam, Tanzania, had those lips been read, the seventeen sailors from the USS *Cole* in Aden would not have needed flag-draped coffins for their trip home last October.

Turns out, this al-Qaeda group of KL conventioneers left some staybehinds who infiltrated the Malaysian political process. Under their Malaysian proxy "Ramadan Moon," al-Qaeda has disrupted the recent elections.

Classic Harker: "Who gives a shit about Malaysian-Muslim politics? A couple bad apples on the last guy's watch? We have powerful Muslim friends in the Middle East. They don't want the radical extremists any more than we do, and they got the means and proximity to take care of them. So, before any arm of this agency charges off in the wrong direction on some kind of Asian crusade against *Middle Easterners*, I'd remind you: Muslims came to Jesus's cradle first. The Wise Men tossed him their gold and Frankenstein—"

Yep, said "Frankenstein."

"—and guess what, boys? 'This is the Messiah who God— which *could also be* Muhammad or Allah, their pick, not going to meddle—called you with his star to follow to the barn-born Baby Jesus.' I'm not diminishing the magnitude of any of these past attacks, but Malaysia's way down my 'let's be worried' list."

CIA had dealt with terrorist bombings for decades. Real, hard-working terrorist groups. To Harker's way of thinking, bin Laden was no Arafat—"sales staff, not boardroom"—making Ramadan Moon world terrorism's "stockroom schleps." This, he points out, isn't only his POV. Through Operation CYCLONE, the Agency paid him and his mujahedeen to fight the Soviets while in Afghanistan, and *twice* the White House has backed Harker's opinion. When presented with plans to take Osama out after the embassy bombings, Clinton judged the first plan an 11905 assassination and moved instead with his Justice Department to indict the pesky sheik. A sort of ring-his-doorbell-and-run strategy. The second, which promised now-indicted bin Laden's capture, the president deemed more trouble than bin Laden's arrest would solve as the terrorist small fry presented no imminent threat.

Al-Qaeda had not made any formal declaration of their goals such as all prior terror groups always did and we kinda require of them. They had the least interesting terrorist leader, an awkward, thick-wristed quiet giant who didn't make for copy because he had nothing to say. Didn't even look angry. A trust-fund brat. He'd helped fight the Soviets, for God's sake, er Allah's. So, like Harker, from the newsroom to the boardroom, from Hollywood to the living room: Americans didn't give much thought to al-Qaeda; ninety percent of the population had never noticed hearing the group's name. What America *did* know of terrorists, we were busy celebrating.

The New Year woke bright that January as we sentenced a *real* bad guy, Ramzi Yousef, to life in prison for the bungled World Trade Center bombing—as if that would work. How you gonna take down two 500,000-ton skyscrapers with a passenger vehicle?

World, American, and therefore Agency "focus" laser-guided in on Kosovo. War crimes and war criminals, and the increasing presence of our *one true enemy:* Russia. Russian arms sales became Russian advisers became straight-up Russian shock troops backing the Serbs busy cleansing the Muslim population. Blood as soapsuds. For all of this, al-Qaeda was low priority, Ramadan Moon ant-belly lower still.

Now that Ramadan Moon has blasted Harker's theory to hell and busted out in violence, Harker faces the Malaysian Crisis from the following set of criteria:

1. *Harker lives to avoid trouble; Bishop and I are more trouble to Harker than Muslim shoot-'em-up fire-bombers in Malaysia.*

2. *Dead, Nathan Myrrh (Harker's three wise men still stuck in my head) seems to have had a hand in the creation of this current problem.*

3.   *Living, Tom Bishop seems to have fooled us all into sending him to Malaysia to worsen it.*

4.   *Trapped in clouds between life and death, I am being sent with $10,000 and ten gold bars—at Bishop's request-slash-ransom. A pistol to be acquired upon landing at Harker's order:*

5.   *"Resolve the Bishop–van Eijk problem with sole discretion."*

Van Eijk, you ask?

Dand van Eijk.

Yes, D–A–N–D, Dand. It's a real name—Ask Jeeves.

A Dutch colonial in Malaysia. Recruited by Nathan Muir, Vientiane, Laos, 1968. Codename: TITAN. The last of Muir's vanished agents, van Eijk materialized out of the misty past seven days ago in Kuala Lumpur as the first canister fell and the tear gas flooded.

Since this van Eijk matter concerned Muir, Harker summoned me from the green-glass goblin of our New Headquarters Building Legal Department to write all the ops paperwork and the motions needed to prevent the New Jersey State Police from access to the Muir murder scene.

All that my involvement was supposed to be. And yet, this afternoon I raced home, I kissed our sweet fifth-grade Jessie and our infant, Nate. I made love to you, my footloose *bless-your-heart* fancy-free wife of fourteen years. Then, halfway out the door, you pulled me back and fucked me once more, hard.

"For good measure," you said.

You kissed my cheek and sent me out the door with "It was all bound to happen. All of this."

"An Islamic coup d'état attempt in Malaysia? Or are you spouting Hinduisms?"

You laughed. Crinkled your nose. "I don't even know what any of that means. I meant between you, Nathan, and your imagined twin brother."

"Not the way it's happened," I said.

It sure wasn't, was it?

I yearned to tell you then: Nathan Muir is dead. Tom murdered him. Instead, I've saved it until this writing, safer on digital paper when you receive this file before I meet Bishop and my death.

"Your only problem, Rusty, is you believe that the story isn't about you."

"I'm not the one who's Muir's son."

"There's a lot more than biology to being a parent or a child. So, before you guys kill each other—tell Tom 'hi' from me? I've missed him. You might want to grab something lightweight for your return. You'll be off the clock. Grab a fun T-shirt and those Patagonia fly-fishing shorts Jessie picked out for you last Christmas."

Is it the T-shirt I picked? Psychedelic skeleton with red-rosed rib cage and crown? Or is it your fatefulness (yes, your "prescience," without the word with the th*)? Effortless how you make every moment of life symmetrical.*

Even bopping around the motels.

"Okay," I said. "And remember: don't expect any calls until I'm back in the States—I'm not going to be able to telephone you or the kids."

"We're all going to be fine. Just you remember one of Nathan's Thumb Rules: Don't write a word you can't take back."

And I just vomited again.

I don't know how happy Bishop will be to see me. My unspoken orders are to deny him the 10k cash/100 grams of bullion, pass Monopoly "Go," but save the dime, skip the dice roll, and shoot him as he's counting the money, which I know means that as soon as he sees the gun I have yet to receive, he will kill me first.

I'll stop vomiting now. What's the point?

I'm reminded of Colonel Grivas—Greek Freedom Fighter, Cyprus, 1953—ready to execute a twenty-three-year-old Nathan Muir and traitor Charlie March, asking, "Would you like a blindfold? A last cigarette?" Muir took him apart instead.

There is no Nathan Muir inside of me, I'm afraid. I am not Muir's son, and my dad was a pill-popping truck driver burned up on a sunflowery highway in Kansas.

Kiss the kids: the blindfold.

Make love to Madeline: the last cigarette.

Baby Nate: the real shot in the heart.

Transferred from the Citation X to a Navy F/A-18 with LR tanks and a midair refuel, 700mph at 40,000 feet, I've two and a half hours of free time/alive time to outrun the morning to Asia and to chase all the demons of the past and the present into the open.

Madeline, honey-bug, let this serve as my testimony to my life and the lives of the two men who've impacted it the most—which must be your life and the life of our two kids. I hope then—blindfolds off, cigarettes tossed—you'll understand me, and I will understand you, and you can come to some reckoning of what you have done to us and to my heart when, as usual, I wasn't looking and had forgotten to make sure it beat in time with yours.

With my electronic signature—*Russell Aiken, legal counsel to the Central Intelligence Agency, United States of America*—the genuity of all that follows may, sadly, be verified.

4

1 P.M., MAY 2, 2001. Last week. KL. Kuala Lumpur. 92 degrees Fahrenheit, broken clouds, 77 percent humidity. All documented in the report. Nothing atypical about that open-source stuff. And the satellite stuff? Secret stuff? Same. Our Malay Section boys thought, What's atypical about political volunteers preparing a rostrum for their candidate's speech? Our boys thought so little about what the satellite showed them they went downstairs to the New Headquarters Building food court and had Whoppers at our very own CIA Burger King, where the cashiers and cooks carry clearance. The fries are excellent and more secure than McDonald's any day of the week. Though, this secret BK doesn't offer the Spicy Chicken Sandwich. That's the only thing I'll eat at Burger King—and why wouldn't they have it? Security risk? I do the vetted and cleared New Chicken Quesadilla advertised in television commercials by that balding nerd Jeff Bezos, trying to promote some outlandish worldwide web bookstore, shilling for Taco Bell. CIA Taco Bell is two vendor counters down from BK, a Sbarro snuggled between. But in the "Land of Burgers where Whopper is King," our Malay Section boys went blind to the KL rostrum our one-eyed satellite watched and they bit into their flame-broiled beef, which by then was too late.

I've looked at the satellite imagery. I've looked at on-site surveillance of the location. The cobblestone-brick pedestrian square with the palm trees fronting the Central Market chosen for the shade cast by rows of those frond-fanned giants. I've looked. I agree with the fast-food paper-crown analysts: nothing indicated how this positive scene would resolve so badly.

The Colonial British built the Central Market in the late nineteenth century. The Colonial British bulldozed the Central Market in 1931. Identifying a need for a Central Market in 1933, the Colonial British rebuilt it in the art deco style it still enjoys today just in time to hand it over as a gift to the Japanese occupiers of WWII when the Colonial British abandoned Malaysia in justified yellow-menace fear.

Art deco is a style the Japanese adore. Though as unsuccessful in building it for themselves as they are at adapting to the obviousness of the fork, they preserved art deco buildings everywhere they conquered. Good sports too. Where Hitler demolitions the entire medieval quarter with its Michelangelo bridge in Florence, Italy, the Japanese allowed the Kuala Lumpur Central Market to flourish throughout the Second World War, where the wet market of live fish and animals, butcheries and bakeries and ovens much suited their conversion to a headquarters and torture chamber for the Japanese military Kempeitai Secret Police.

I mention the ovens? Like Much Ado about Adolf, they didn't use them for food.

The art deco brushed steel, English-lettered: C-E-N-T-R-A-L M-A-R-K-E-T was respectfully allowed to remain until, world war won, the Colonial British threw out the Japanese, sluiced the abattoirs, and set the building back to wet market and animal slaughterhouse.

Painted turquoise and white with crenellated bands and fauxgothic adornments, smoked-glass checkerboard windows, the place looks a lot like Miami. The wet-market concept abandoned, the Central Market is, today, a celebration of national diversity as a handicrafts, furniture, souvenir, batik traditional clothing bazaar. Malay, Chinese, Arabic, Indian, Thai, Indonesian: all given equal and loving prominence as the exotic aromas of each culture waft from the food festival upstairs. Signs read in Malay, Chinese, Hindi, Jawi Arabic. You'll even find English in the corner of the market where ripped-off American electronics and pirated Hollywood movies are sold with impudent impunity. The Central Market is proof positive Malaysia is "developing" in the boldest and brightest one-world way. God bless 'em and Harker can dance away to *Moulin Rouge* one month before its US theatrical release.

The activists decorating the rostrum were the perfect mix of all of this. They were doing no wrong. At the end of a major avenue, theirs was the perfect spot for their candidate to end her march, climb onto the rostrum, and give a speech. They were all full of energy and expectant joy.

Some low-band (Malay N-word equivalent) Indians and poor Chinese day laborers milled about, wearing the ratty hats they make and sell from the fiber of the gomuti palm. Seated or squatting, they watched from the market's front steps, inured to the clinging heat. They smoked tobacco and clove cigarettes and they talked. Some drank fat bottles of Harimau (Tiger) Beer; some drank tea; some strong espresso-like traditional coffee; some played the illegal gambling dice game *judi belangkas*, a form of craps, getting away with it by not playing with any money exchanged or on hand. (A respected professional *diandalkan*, or "count man," with a photographic memory, tracks all of it for a later backroom settling.) Old men chew the betel nut. A nervous Muslim woman brings her daughter for a Hindu fortune before her wedding and never tells her husband. And all of them, no matter how engaged, were second- and third-glance curious of the activist youth.

True, the activists had permits to assemble. True, their candidate's election commission documents had the appropriate election tax stamps. They had their personal documents—national ID, party registration, driver's licenses, student identity cards, worker/employer identification, pocketful of miracles—what else d'ya need?

Everything until there's something they can find you without.

They were the opposition party to the current decade-long entrenched, monarchy-backed regime. Their populist candidate, first elected to the Dewan Rakyat—Malaysian House of Representatives—age twenty-one; elected to the Upper House, the Dewan Negara, as a senator at thirty; now age thirty-two, less than a week from polling day, led the race by a wide margin. But this youngest candidate to ever run for Malaysian prime minister had the audacity to be a lifelong female. Gender-stuck even after clitoral mutilation. The nerve of *her*. Polls be damned, everyone believed this last factor insurmountable against the quiet rise of fundamentalism.

Cloves pop in cigarettes. Dice roll. Beer bottles jangle. Red saliva is spit from betel. Fortunes are told and money is lost to Cary Grant cries of *"Judi, judi, judi."*

The suspicious eyes of the day laborers tracked the young men and women putting finishing touches on a huge banner depicting their candidate: Nurul Mawar Musa. Head covered as true and faithful to Muslim custom, she looks toward a future depicted as a blended society. Men, women, and children, their costuming suggested the three major religions—Islam, Hindu, Buddhist—intermingled with happy, coexistent intellectuals, students, artists, scientists, laborers, farmers, families. Their big bright banner read: "VOTE POPULAR DEMOCRATIC FRONT."

A gust of hot wind blew a roll of yellow crêpe paper off the platform. An Indian, shirtless, hoisting torn trousers with one hand, chased the unspooling streamer and smiling toothlessly returned it to the pretty young Malay woman who appeared in charge. Off the rostrum and looking puzzled, the young woman inquired of the Indian if he'd seen any members of the press around the market or heading their way. Frankly, she was surprised none had yet arrived.

The Indian told her. He had seen the reporters: stopped at Royal Police roadblocks that, scant minutes ago, had sprouted at the mouths of the connecting streets.

The Malay woman thanked the Indian. She returned to the rostrum, handed off the crêpe paper, announced this concerning development. They continued decorating, braiding the yellow streamer with green and white. The young woman plugged in the microphone.

"Test. Test. Test."

A group of tidy-uniformed female market workers—two Chinese and two Malay Muslim walking four abreast, hand in hand—emerged. Others followed them in pairs and clusters. Everyone interested in this new, dramatic female candidate. Food carts assembled and sold sweets, rambutan and lychee, spiced meats, coconut milk and other drinks to combat the rising heat. For more than two decades, Malaysia's social fabric embraced a philosophy of live and let live.

This was exemplified in the approaching tramp of marching feet. In voices raised with song by the candidate and her supporters. All ages, all ethnicities, all religions. Not yet in view, their passion preceded them with increasing volume only to be drowned out by the deep growl of ominous engines, a growing echo from the opposite direction.

Inside the Perdana Putra—the building in the lagooned and fairy-tale-marvelous Putrajaya, where the prime minister keeps his offices—Prime Minister Dr. Mohamad Aziz gave in to self-doubt and ordered the Federal Reserve Unit (FRU) of the Royal Malaysia Police to attack.

Three FRU troop trucks lurched into the square; screeched, skidding to a stop: front and two sides of the rostrum. Paramilitary riot police piled out in a whirl of helmets, gas masks, and shields. Batons, rifles, tear-gas launchers. But, for the stomp of their boots, the clatter of gear and guns, the FRU troops made no intentional sounds, and no expression whatsoever crossed their faces behind their rigid plastic masks. They surrounded the platform.

Had the plaza denizens, the market workers, and the PDF party organizers been the only witnesses to what was about to transpire, CIA notice of this event would have been postmortem. Our turn at the word *trigger*—as in "overpassed triggering event"—to all that has since erupted, brutal and grave in KL.

"Overpassed:" CIA C-Y-A lingo for "fuck-up failure to notice."

Our Malay Section boys, on it since they finished having it their way with the Whoppers, returned to their video feeds halfway through the ensuing riot.

Doh!

They now believe—in concert with interdepartment psych analysis—that the location for the end of Mrs. Musa's march was selected by the candidate with a foreknowledge of what she would confront, based on her desire for confrontation formed by memories of Operasi Lalang and a subliminal but burning need for revenge.

Operasi Lalang. In translation: the "Weeding Operation." October 27, 1987. One hundred and nineteen citizens, perceived political opponents to then Prime Minister Mahathir Mohamad, were arrested and detained without trial by the FRU under the false argument that racial tensions had reached dangerous levels in the country. Mrs. Musa, at the time an eighteen-year-old student of no political belief, found herself caught in the roundup. In her best-selling memoir that propelled her into the senate, Nurul Musa described her unlawful incarceration in stark terms, describing degrading interrogations, beatings, and the implied worse.

In a Muslim country, you mustn't—if you're a woman—ever identify what that "worse" is. Men of certain religious convictions who had nothing to do with the crime other than being family pledged to love and protect the woman—husbands, cousins, brothers, fathers, sons—would find need to punish her for defiling herself by immodestly admitting such a thing out loud and dishonoring the men of her family. Those of strictest faith would save that woman's honor by killing her for the fact it occurred at all. Conversely, since everyone knew exactly what befell so many of the girls caught in the "Weeding Operation," the modesty Mrs. Musa showed by not explicitly writing the details of the truth made her a populist darling to those otherwise stone-throwing, sword-wielding, bomb-hurling, vest-wearing, explosive-truck-driving, missile-launching, bury-loose-women-to-their-head-in-sand-then-drive-over-it-until-the-sand-is-red-and-flat one true primordial *fitrah* faithful.

In the truth and religious aspects, Mrs. Musa knew before any of the rest of us figured it out that her campaign, her movement, was against this metastasizing evil not only in her own Malaysia that she loved with purity of devotion, her religion she loved even more, but globally. Extremist jihad descending on heavenly horseback with fire and sword. The beauty and love, the power of peace that her religion gave her and gave all the people of faith, the religion running through her body and soul, called her to participate in the world with all Peoples of the Book and even the polytheistic others… to a liberal degree.

Therefore, we mind-read, Mrs. Musa selected this location, this day of her final campaign speech, for its proximity to the

United States Embassy located approximately 150 yards from the Central Market Plaza. She desired our attention.

Here, two US Marines in combat rig manned sandbagged emplacements on either side of the heavy bollard gates of the American compound. I have read their reports. I have written their indemnifications, which will give them appropriate commendations and non-political future postings, one of them on our list for Agency paramilitary recruitment. Certain heroes can't be trusted in the light of the public eye but, cared for, can become heroes utilized in darkness.

I make sure to take care.

But do I care enough?

Have I ever done enough?

You? Jessie? Now Nate? Love in high fidelity on a Beatles T-shirt, and my inability to focus. Growing confusions grow inside me. A microscopic expanding universe of star-shaped glial cell constellations en masse under the heavenly dome of my skull.

ADJACENT TO the Central Market—Jalan Hang Kasturi, 50050 Kuala Lumpur, Wilayah Persekutuan—the Malaysians have a Burger King of their own. Their staff, though not honored with intelligence service security clearance, take their jobs with seriousness equal to ours. In fact, every meal that passes over their counter must appear perfect in every detail to match the menu photographs. Nothing sloppy is ever served here. This is where the political activists had, earlier, purchased their lunch. So, while our Malay Section boys wiped ketchup stains from their ties, it wasn't slopped tomato condiment discoloring those young activists' clothing. It was blood and it flowed in profusion.

5

ALL MORNING, the two military guards outside the American Embassy, KL, had been, to the lax attention of their duties, riveted to the activity around the rostrum. They focused on the pretty Malay organizer who, "un-mummified"—their word, not mine—by Muslim Khimar, allowed her long ponytailed hair to swing in counterpunctual rhythm to hips embraced by snug, high-waisted, bell-bottomed shiny rayon slacks. Her bare arms, tan and toned, appeared from billowy sleeves that fell back to her shoulders as she extended her shapely body to its utmost to hang the braided crêpe-paper streamers.

These guys were Marines. Young—twenty and twenty-three years of age—and they'd never been anything but exemplary in behavior, manners, chain-of-command. Perfect haircuts you could see reflected on their shoes every dress inspection. But they were male, and afterwards humiliated to admit that the one had said to the other, moments before the FRU riot police arrived: "Get a load a'that ass. God, I'd love to tap that tight thang. Give her the time of her life and I'm talking the two-hole."

Because the two Americans were intent on their ass gazing, they saw the entire confrontation. The riot police surrounded the rostrum, menacing and silent, trapping the young political activists. Two Royal Malaysian Police squad cars, lights spinning orange and blue, a siren whooping, arrived and released eight officers. Tailored uniforms with enough extra brass and polished leather to provide a Hugo Boss Beer Hall Putsch brown shirt menace. They mounted the platform.

Shouts and threats. Equipment seized. Papers demanded and handed over.

The activists did what their candidate, Mrs. Musa, had insisted. They squatted. Raised their hands over bowed heads. The FDU tore down the posters. Knocked over the podium. Whacked a few skulls.

A United States Marine is not unique to agitate at the sight of a young woman in a crouch, her hands over her head, pounded between her shoulder blades by a cop—once to loosen her up, twice to lift her head, allowing a reach-around to choke her with his stick and wrench her to her feet—even if said Marines had had only just swapped vile misogynistic comments about her. The violence enraged them, but what could they do? Embassy guards carry strict orders not only preventing them from leaving the US soil the Embassy compound represents, but forbidding them from engaging or interfering with the host country population in any matter, direct or indirect, in body, conversation, and mind.

A young Hindi man reached to help the choking, struggling Malay woman. He took a club in the jaw for that. Spit blood. Spit teeth particles.

Corporal Latrell Jackson—the twenty-year-old jarhead with the ass-fuck comment—choked with fury. "Fucking motherfucker, fucking fuck Bumis."

Benjamin Newman, sergeant, three years older, said, "Stay frosty. Listen—Look!"

Beyond the Marines, coming around a curve in the road and heading straight for the rally point, came Mrs. Musa's merry mob. Bullhorns bellowing. Enthusiastic activists chanted their candidate's promises as slogans. Young girls at the front of the parade—Malay, Chinese, Indian—carried the red , white, and blue tempera banner: "Tomorrow is OUR Day! WE are Malaysia!" Their numbers were somewhere between two to three hundred strong. Men and women, young and old, waved party flags in fists or billowed national flags on high poles in sync in the manner of American high-school tall-flag performers at the Pasadena Rose Parade. Others carried posters, framed photos of the candidate. Upon seeing the FRU form a quick cordon—feet horse-stomping as trained—Candidate Musa's parade halted. They were in front of our embassy. Made sure to stay clear of the sandbags. The US Marines. The machine guns.

For a moment, nothing happened. The two forces stared each other down. Then a whistle, shrill and unsportsmanlike, and the Royal Police officers hustled off the young woman and her fellow activists from the rostrum.

A moment of caught breath for the Malaysians of both sides, it seemed to suck all oxygen from the dust-thick, hot charged air between them. An "It doesn't have to go this way" acknowledgment that it "absolutely will" moment of stillness.

Sergeant Newman deposed in his affidavit that, at this time, he radioed Lieutenant Reeves inside the main entry doors with the sit-rep. Advised it was his belief that the embassy was in imminent danger of collateral damage from the impending riot. He requested orders to redeploy his and Corporal Latrell Jackson's guns inside the compound gates.

Lieutenant Reeves reported to Embassy Internal Security. Namely Paul Sedaka, CIA chief resident. (The Agency does not, currently, believe Malaysia requires a chief of station at that attendant pay/benefit grade—just a cost-efficient chief resident.) The lieutenant advised Sedaka of the external conflict, non-US involvement, happening directly outside compound walls. Crisis mode. Sedaka and his team temporarily superseded the Ambassador in authority. Security protocols, tight, calm, we-won't-be-fooled-again post-Saigon post-The Who: activated.

This is where it got sticky.

A cry rose from the candidate's supporters like a backdraft explosion as they watched their bloody and broken comrades from the rostrum slammed into police vans. The single voice of hundreds together as one. The first rank of riot police clacked canisters into tear-gas launchers. The parade crowded into a mob. Nervous dark fingers pulled up collars, scarves, bandanas. They wouldn't much help. They never do.

Lieutenant Reeves, holster unflapped—against regulation, but he was concerned to the point of agitation, and he never drew his sidearm, just prepared—arrived behind the gates as the mob stampeded. "Sergeant, secure weapons. Withdraw the perimeter behind the gates." He brushed aside the local-employ gate operator and hit the button.

The two Malaysian forces met. The clash was vicious. Blood, fractured bones, wailing from hatred indistinguishable from wails of pain. The clink-clatter of tear gas hitting asphalt. The hollow pop of the canister percussion valve. That higher-pitched, unique, strangulated squall—involving choking gas—belonging only to lungs hit by poison.

Flags trampled. Rocks flew.

Fists and fingers clawed and gouged.

Batons swung and they cracked and they cracked and they cracked.

Lieutenant Reeves and his noncoms pulled on and cinched tight gas masks. The sandbags tumbled. The sidewalk filled. The tumultuous mob condensed, balling together as happens in riots— clenching knots that explode into flayed humanity. Nothing involved or would involve the embassy. Two of the three Marines relaxed.

Not Latrell Jackson. He'd been eleven years old in 1992 when South Central Los Angeles burned with the LA Riots. More Americans died of violent trauma in that US city those few days than died over the entire two previous years in Operation Desert Storm. Think about it. Four times the Americans dead in Los Angeles than in Kuwait and Iraq in full-blown foreign war. Latrell had hidden with his mama in the bathroom. Inside the bathtub she bleached on Saturdays. Always smelled bad, like the children's lavatory at church. When Mama fell asleep, Latrell crept to the window. Peeked outside. He watched three paramedics work on Tirus, the little boy from across the hall. Tirus had managed to wander outside and catch a stray round. They stabilized the boy and were moving Tirus onto the gurney when three gangbangers from the next block came into the alley. They murdered the child and executed the paramedics against a wall.

Laughed at the crazy fun of it. *Pow. Wow. Pow.*

An off-duty highway patrolman, along with his partner, called-in spur of the moment, happened upon the scene. Happened upon the laughter. The two of them put the gang-bangers down with shotgun and AR-15. Happened to drive away a moment later.

Latrell Jackson would claim that he was seeing Tirus when, this crowded, lonely day, through the bug eyes of his gas mask, he saw the skinny "Mowgli" boy, who now approached him.

We don't know the Indian boy's name—certainly not Mowgli—and I'm sure we never will. Latrell saw him frozen amid the storming tide surging uncontrollably around him. Saw women fall with bloody heads. Men stomped, mangled, blinded, noses pulped. Teens protecting smaller children from streams of high-velocity, handball-sized rubber bullets. But it was this vision of Tirus, as an Indian child, holding out a skinny arm at Latrell—a kind of beckoning wraith in the smoke—that burned into Latrell's soul. A ghostly child made even more supernatural as the crowd parted around him, fearful of the strange kid stake-still and planted in the heart of their own violence.

"Lieutenant, there's a Bumi-kid out there! Got no one! He gonna get killed!"

Latrell circled his arms like a rolling tide, waving the boy to come to him. The riot swelled. Screaming. Crying. Coughing, gagging, choking. Saliva spewed rage. Latrell abandoned his weapon. He threw himself into the gate. He shoved both arms through the bollard posts. This time, he would save Tirus.

Lead bullets mixed in with the rubber twanged and thwacked. Killed a half-dozen. Wounded more who died later. The gas swirled.

"C'mere, kid! I gotcha! Over here, baby!"

Tears streamed from the boy's eyes swelling shut. He coughed and trembled. He lurched toward the Marine. Jostled, he staggered. Hitting a knee, he pushed back to his feet. He was shoved again but remained upright. He managed the sidewalk, and choking, clambered the cascaded sandbags. His clothes were a diaper-*dhoti*, raggedy tunic, and swaddled turban denoting Sikh. I've seen a video capture from the gate cameras: he embodied a fabled character out of Kipling.

Problem, that. Should have been a sign for someone who knew better how we ply upon our own people's racist expectations. But no one did, not that sweltering day, not now, only in the worthless shade of fabulous retrospect.

By this time, Sergeant Newman stood adjacent to his corporal, also urging the boy to the safety of Latrell's strong arms.

"Don't touch that kid!" Lieutenant Reeves said, in accordance with the Rules of Engagement.

Lieutenant Reeves seized Sergeant Newman, pulling him from behind. He went willingly into his officer's grip. And Newman—like a good Marine—took initiative. He peddled them both backward, shouting, "Corporal Latrell, secure the hostile attacking the gate!"

"Grab my hand, little guy—you'll be okay!" Latrell said.

Lieutenant Reeves screamed over Sergeant Newman's shoulder, trying to escape the sergeant's—don't mess with a former Ohio State tight end—plow: "Dammit, Corporal, I said stand down!"

Lieutenant Reeves spun off Sergeant Newman's back. He lunged forward. He grabbed Corporal Latrell Jackson's shoulders. He's signed his name to his deposition that states:

"The Indian boy's right hand linked with the left hand of Corporal Latrell Jackson. Double horror eyes. One or two seconds only. Then they were torn apart. The Corporal and I fell. He landed on top of me. I could already see it in Corporal Jackson's fist—the wadded envelope."

Corporal Latrell Jackson surrendered the envelope to Lieutenant Reeves. Both testify the boy backed away. Both testify to the appearance of his sudden sly grin, and they exchanged a look like, *Did we just get played?* The boy turned and, running, dissolved into the crowd.

Lieutenant Reeves tore open the envelope. A sheet of A4 paper. A single page of code. Strings of random letters filled the page held in the Marine's hard black hands.

PAUL SEDAKA, forty-two or -four—there is a file jacket and health insurance discrepancy—was the next individual to hold the coded page, received directly from Lieutenant Reeves. It is out of the question that the message was compromised between the gate and Mr. Sedaka's possession.

"Thank you, Lieutenant," Sedaka said and made his way to the code room.

Now, I like Sedaka. I like him because I'm a sucker for misfits and Paul Sedaka is a classic misfit. Vastly overweight. Eyes that never quite made the full switch from blue to brown, they have a muddy gray aurora around the irises. Heavily-pored. A constellation of moles peppers his right cheek, the rich brown color his eyes should be in an otherwise paste-colored face. He dresses in Hong Kong wash-and-wear copies of Brooks Brothers suits he's proud of at an $89 price point and is a man who lives under the eternal misconception he is owed.

And I know that man. We are always owed.

Has Sedaka or have I ever frowned? Has he ever had a dreadful thing to say about anyone? Has he always been shit upon? I've given his personnel file a thorough go-through—and yes: he has always been shit upon. I did. Wrote his pay-grade rip-off chief resident contract that he should never have signed, but guys like him always do when I hand 'em my pen. He's the kind of guy I call the falling-striver. This was Paul Sedaka's moment to shine and strive without falling and he came into all of our lives as a meteorite: surprising and flaming bright. I expect he will, a piece of atmosphere-burned space rock, vanish after his moment, flashing the night sky with his brilliance.

Sedaka's cipher clerk—shirtsleeves allowed due to poor air conditioning, sidearm required—turned from her computer as Sedaka said, "I have an urgent decipher. I want it sent to Acting DCI Harker, a written acknowledgment returned."

"Yes, Mr. Sedaka." She gauged him with worried eyes. "How bad is it out there?"

"The beginning of the end, I'm afraid. When you finish, see I get a copy on my desk. Top Secret/Eyes Only."

Mowgli's letter entered the flow of the Great Game.

Through the window, Sedaka observed the destruction of the once celebrated Malaysian social contract of "live and let live"; and Dand van Eijk, who'd written the code, pulled a frightened, forgotten old spy's "live and let die" into immediacy.

6

Turn the calendar back four days. Back to Princeton University. Back as it was this May and every other: a sudden cannonade of color boomed at winter's monochromatic ranks to blast the soul with a charge of front-line flowering vitality. Your vision is bombarded with nature's explosion; blossoms named to Muir's deception-loving amusement with perfect horticulturist paradox. The delicate "plum blossoms" of the white blooming Japanese apricots outside McCormick Hall. The purple and white profusions of the saucer magnolias outside the graduate college, their flowers spending their bloom distinctively shaped as teacups. Enchanting yellow florets spangle sleek arms of cherry dogwoods without a hint of fruity red or hound. Spring is renewal, and its arrival this year early to the campus only added to Muir's enjoyment of the place he understood and had chosen to meet the expiration of his life.

I can hear Pete Seeger turn, turn, turning of this Ecclesiastes loam:

> *To everything there is a season*
> *And a time to every purpose, under the heaven:*
> *A time to be born; a time to die;*
> *A time to plant, and a time to pluck…*

I spoke to Muir's personal secretary of thirty years, Gladys Jlassi. She seized me with her eyes and said, "'Death will find you even if you hide in fortresses built up strong and high.'"

I took a stab. "Your Quran?"

And punctured her heart. "Quran 4:78."

She fell into me with anguish, and I experienced my usual ineptitude at women's tears. I folded her into my awkward arms. Gladys's nobility of faith was equal to her heedfulness to the lamp lit now to Muir's legacy that, she told me, would be hers to keep trimmed and burning and guarded.

I've spoken to his closest students, aerating grief from their adoration, adoration aerated from their grief and the range of observation between the students and Gladys ran as unique as the veins in a rose petal and as varied as the flowering plants in the university's many gardens Muir had grown to love. The one thing all his students pointed out and agreed upon was that this year, Professor Muir embraced spring early. When gloves, scarves, and caps were still necessary for his "ambling rambles"—as he'd taken to calling his walking lectures when he wasn't referring to them as "rambling ambles"—all agreed it unusual and not to his traditional pattern. A pattern that always hinged upon the first white fragrant flower spreading its petals outside his 1879 Hall window. This year, Muir was out the door at the earliest appearance of the buds themselves. Students noticed. Gladys remarked. All agreed it was from high spirits. One last kick left an old horse to colt out of the barn one final time, if only to spit in someone's eye.

I must admit, I sensed this battening of his personality. Both the battening of securing, making fast in preparation for difficulty or crisis, and the battening of profuse feeding, almost a gluttonous need to devour as much of nature as his senses would allow. This I saw: I saw when I saw Nathan Muir for the last—

A horrifying bone-cutting saw I will not face.

—happy and thriving, meaning blithely sarcastic and healthily gruff. This was two days after Muir's seventy-second birthday, making it Friday, March 23, 2001, two weeks after the birth of our son. We'd named the baby Conrad. Named him after Madeline's father but decided to give him "Nathan" for a middle name. We chose to call him Nate.

"Better nickname than Connie," Muir said. "Why would you call a boy that?"

"We're not. I mean, call him which?"

"Well, that's the best decision you ever made," said Muir.

The pair of us were bundled against the returning chill of afternoon. Seated on a goldenrod-adorned log in the Class of 1946 Garden on the west side of Maclean House, a kind of natural bench, the place was quiet and hidden with visible and choked approaches. The spot for a twilight spy or two killing time.

I said, "Were you ever called 'Nate'?"

"Not on your life. Do him and Madeline a favor and call him 'Conrad.'"

"We prefer 'Nate.'"

"Glad you came all this way without wanting my opinion." He unwrapped a Coffee Nip candy and popped it into his mouth.

He added, "Man and woman, the animals, we come, spend our time, and we go. One trip round the block where everything counts, look twice if you're smart, touch as much as you can, physically and otherwise—done and undone. The only thing that lives, dies, and returns for the perfect, unjudged do-over is nature."

"Is that an observation, advice, or an augury of doom?"

"You certainly still have the disease of language. Rusty, you've never needed an oracle. Common sense, yes. Oracle, no. Want my advice?"

"Therapist hasn't done me much good."

"Never will. They're in business to stay in business. I'll solve it all for you right now. Won't charge you a penny. Russell: be more tree-like."

He rubbed his hands. He studied me a moment. He gave me a smile that brought back all his youth and none of his tragedy. It brought back all the perceived betrayals he'd never done me, hard as I'd complained, and he'd insisted were for my own good. I smiled too. No crook in it—at least I tried my best. I'd never seen it before—this mood in him. Happy resignation? Knowing sadness with a leer, king-sized at that? Teasing as always—and my puzzlement increased as my better-new smile expanded.

Muir tapped me once, twice on the shoulder and pushed to his feet. I gave him an up-from-under look, expressing my disappointment with his advice. He fixed me in a direct stare, not needing me to speak to articulate my inner dialogue.

"You'll get it," Muir said. "I have zero doubt in you anymore. No more the tromped-on tiger-striped cat, you. But here's one that's easier. You want it in English or the French?"

"You hate the French."

"I do. But it's how I first heard it when I came back here after Korea."

After Jewel. After he'd killed her—his first wife—and their unborn son and let the traitor Charlie March recruit him to the CIA.

"'Un lâche fuit en arrière, loin de nouvelles choses. Un homme de courage fuit en avant, au milieu de nouvelles choses.' It appeared later in my mentor's book—"

"Wasn't Charlie March your mentor?"

"Wasn't that my cover? My real mentor resided here. That oft quoted remark—"

Never heard it quoted before or since, in English or French or Pig Latin.

"—came out the next year in a book. I've always felt he coined it for me after I confessed him my Korean War, and I take that coin from my pocket and hand it to you."

"Who? I can't read French! Whose book? What's its title?"

Muir gave a scoffing laugh. "You figure it out, Dumbo. Want a coffee?"

We'd been talking already for two hours, but I jumped at the chance. I've been telling myself since Gladys found him dead and telephoned me that I half suspected once we parted I would never see him again.

"I could use a cup of coffee." I stood, ready to press on.

Muir pressed a Coffee Nip into my palm. The cellophane crinkled. He sucked them day and night since he'd quit smoking while facilitating the deal with China, brokered through Great Britain, to allow the Chinese cancer team who were willing to treat his son's wife in Taipei with the experimental BRCA1 and BRCA2 gene therapies that, successful, extended Elizabeth's life two years beyond her terminal diagnosis.

A time to kill, a time to heal

A time to weep, to laugh; to mourn, to dance

Time, time, time… Life, life, life: does writing it make it real? Does it ever or even matter? Is nature more alive than we are, or better? Why can't we renew like he said we can't? Life has one objective: not to die.

Words. Letters. Alphabets.

Be more tree-like?

CONDITIONAL TO ELIZABETH'S treatment was a formal apology by the Agency for the Suzhou Prison raid. It officially erased from the records that China had ever taken a British subject unlawfully into custody (Elizabeth Hadley, Tom Bishop's wife) and instead could use Hadley's gifted cancer treatment as "proof" of their National Revolutionary Compassion. Bishop was a different story. As the spy who executed the raid, his in-and-out of China was agreed to be relegated to the shadows as long as he abided by a persona non grata in China, Hong Kong, and (unofficially but Chinese-demanded) Taiwan. Bishop accepted by signature—a promise made but never kept, as he and Muir worked their old business slipping Bishop in and out of the Taiwan capital for the length of Elizabeth's treatment, strictly adhering to their own agreement never to meet, for such an occasion would precipitate Bishop making good on his death sentence. As a final part of Muir's deal, he facilitated Chinese access to commercial satellite manufacturers Hughes Electronics and Loral Space & Communications Ltd., which, to the horror of the Pentagon but with the blessing of the White House, allowed the "accidental" transfer of military technology to our communist enemies.

Muir waved all of it away to me earlier that afternoon. "Big splash in a puddle. Chicoms would have developed every last one of those gizmos on their own within three years. A dozen of their kids we scholarship could've done it in two, and one of them, back in Beijing, who works for the Company now—much to the Chicoms' inscrutable imbecility—they put on the project, so we still have a grip on it from the inside out."

He didn't need to sell me. No price could be put on two more years for Elizabeth (never once a moment when one of the three of us wasn't at her side); for her graceful forgiving of her father-in-law; for the hope of Tom's future forgiveness of Muir—and of Muir dropping his deadly tobacco habit.

Secondhand smoke is the springtime blossom for cancers.

I unwrapped the candy and knew our conversation and company were over.

Because we run abnormal risks of life and death in this business, every parting has an element of the last goodbye. Muir studies my face. I memorize his. I pretend he touches me with his hand, but he hasn't at all. He was already a corpse, and they never offer receipt.

Only nature is reborn.

A tiger-striped bee tumbled on the stone paver at the place Muir poised his feet. Muir left the garden before the bee, careful not to step on it. The best of case officers, he went before me to make sure his former asset's way would be clear. The bee did a gymnastic backroll fly-away. Too late in the day, cold coming on, it would die before returning to its hive—plunge out of the air mid-flight like airplanes, sometimes, when the passengers are the *enfants perdus* at the onset of unwanted war.

7

TWELVE HOURS AFTER the van Eijk coded message came into Sedaka's possession in Malaysia, Muir gave his final amble-ramble.

Thirty-six hours before his murder.

"Myth, as it exists in a savage community, is not merely a story told, but a reality lived," he said, guiding his 400-level Philosophy of Mythology students between golden daffodil beds away from classroom constriction.

The syllabus describes his course: "Theoretical approaches to the study of philosophy, myth, and ritual in ancient systems, their impact on contemporary issues and thought." Forty-one years Pied-Pipering the rats of the rest of the world to oft deserved doom, Muir led these youthful charges under the arpeggios of harmless mythologies to something both the elitists (who know better and intend to keep it that way) and the hoi polloi (who don't want to know and intend to keep it *that* way) would unite over in their contempt for him. For with the spell of ancient time's ancient legends, Muir covertly escorted his students thrice weekly to modern uncomfortable truths of who mankind has always been and what we all should be while we pretend to be someone else. Or, as Merlin said to Wart, led them to "Learn why the world wags and what wags it."

And we all know how King Arthur finished, learning what wagged the tail of his wife.

Mads.

"I am reminded of the Montagnard tribes of Laos the CIA tried to recruit into our Vietnam conflict," Muir said, apropos of nothing but only everything he was.

He continued his students along Princeton University Avenue to the corner before the roundabout, and right-faced into Prospect Garden down a path laid by Edith Wilson—wife of Woodrow and the secret US president from 1919 to 1921 when Woody was in a stroke-induced semi-coma state—past landscapers pulling the early tulips for next year's replanting and filling the seven-foot-wide beds with a variety of flowers from the eight thousand specimens the garden displays.

The afternoon was still warm. Butterflies, hummingbirds, and bees went around their pleasant business as Muir's coeds filed onto the lawn around the base of the fountain. He sat on the edge, his back to the modernist bronze pipe-playing centaur rearing on hind legs and twisting with exuberance, rising from abstraction to figuration.

Muir said, "Hello, Dimitri," calling the statue by the artist's name as he did each time he sat there. He turned to his students and added, "The hero, Achilles, was a student of centaurs. To both he and Herakles, centaurs represented a perfect combination of the physical and the intellectual. Also lust, which Bullfinch, Frazer, Burkhart and the other classicists underplay or fail to admit.

"And...where was I? Yes—"

IT WAS ON *YES* when computer engineering and physics senior Amy Kim, seated close to Nathan as she always sat, read his secret signal. Three years and a thousand legends back, Amy's graduate adviser had forced her—unnecessarily, to Amy's manner of thinking—into Muir's PHI 200 Philosophy, Epistemology, and the Modern Mind lecture hall. Muir knew this, having selected her for recruitment, and since her first day of her first course, Muir made sure shy and terrified freshman Amy Kim sat "right at the front, where I don't have to look for you and you won't stand a chance to turn invisible or into someone else—which you've tended to do your whole life. While those traits will come in handy one day, they won't while I'm speaking. Am I clear on that, Miss Kim?"

Scared stiff, Amy nodded under the startled, glad-not-to-be-singled-out gaze of fifty classmates, and Muir arrowed her heart with his brightest Willy-Pete white phosphorescent grin and said, "Or anywhere else you'd have the chance to turn off your mind to me—which I'll never let you do, as that would be terminal for your future."

He embarrassed this young American of Korean descent (I've never heard Muir use any of the "Asian American," "African American," "Native American," "Mexican American" phraseology: always "American of X descent"—he'd have it no other way) to no end for two years while she enrolled in every course Muir offered.

Amy assisted Gladys in his office. She forced Nathan to take her to church. She built him a computer he never used; he gave life to the origins of physics from his ancients: Democritus, Leucippus, Aristotle. And Amy Kim fell in love with Nathan Muir—not the old man, but everything she discovered she could hear from his youth that he never said out loud. The sorrow and the nobility, the grief and the love that would howl from his eyes when he thought no one was looking—especially not her—when the light hit them right.

It was on his *yes* that day, she said, when Muir shifted his gaze to the water and frowned. Amy, kneeling rather than seated—there's a Korean word for this posture; she always took it; Nathan would know it—craned forward off her heels to identify what had bothered him.

A wren. Dead and sunken under the centaur's rain at the bottom of the fountain.

Muir tossed Amy another secret look, accompanied by a gesture with his one real foot. It would take Miss Kim a moment to comprehend his request. In her interview, she forgot all about it and our investigators—with no idea she'd been handpicked for recruitment—deemed her statement, overall, as tremendously unimportant as those of the rest of Muir's heartbroken students.

I only know about the bird because Miss Kim called me about it; for some reason, Muir had given her both my cell and my home number. Oddly predictable, I suppose.

"Yes," he said, continuing his last ramble. "The Montagnards. The Montagnards were great enemies of the North Vietnamese and the Vietcong, and yet, for all our overtures to arm them, our offers of support and training, they rebuffed us. This made no sense. Their enemies were our enemies. They fought them every chance they got. But any explanation the CIA tried to get out of them came back incomprehensible. Fragments of ancient poems and proverbs. Their decisions always alluded to their mythological system."

You'll recall, Mads, it was these lecture notes I was puzzling on when I came home for our kiss goodbye and received Miss Kim's phone call.

Muir never says anything frivolous. Everything is operational. Everything, even if—especially if—he believes other lives are in danger from it, these are his Hansel and Gretel breadcrumbs *even if* only a dead bird remains with the Happy Prince to never taste another crumb or find another ruby.

The foot move, Amy explained, meant she should bury the wren, which she did, surreptitiously, in a hole in the grass by the centaur fountain. I thanked her for her last memory of the old man, but never having met her, let alone heard of her (and, admittedly, resenting Muir's special interest without telling me), I asked Amy why she felt the need to tell any of this to me.

"Two things, Mr. Aiken. It wasn't floating."

"Ms. Kim, the dead bird was waterlogged."

"Okay."

"What was the other thing?"

"After the lecture, when we were leaving the garden, he gave me your phone numbers. Doesn't it seem coincidental?" Her grief for Muir rang through her bird call loud and clear.

"Yes. Most probably it was. He made it seem that way, but not everything Nathan did fit a specific intent," I added, contradicting my own distractions of a moment before.

"I noticed that his tie clip had fallen off," she continued, as if I'd not spoken. "And I asked if he wanted me to look for it. He said, 'Miss Kim, you saw its design?' I said, 'An arrow.' He gave that sexy smile of his and said, 'Its clasp broke this morning. Shouldn't have worn it.' He started moving away. I heard him chuckle. He glanced back. Said, 'Must be what killed the little cock robin.' It was a wren, though."

Sexy?!

"'Cock Robin' is a nursery rhyme. Kid kills his best feathery friend with an arrow. Just Muir's kind of joke."

MUIR'S TEN STUDENTS that last day were those at Princeton University who knew him best. His "bestest network," he'd referred to them fondly that last time we met. All of them came around to pay their respects to Gladys, whom they loved for the love she showed their revered professor. They asked Gladys if it were true—had Muir's parents conceived him in the Prospect Gardens? Had he been born in this brownstone, where he lived and where Gladys had found him killed?

She assured them each in turn that it was true—"Professor Muir would never lie"—before she told Bill Carver, our chief investigator on the murder: "It's one of his myths, but carrying it along is the last subterfuge Nathan asked of me."

"When was that?"

"Years ago. He always planned ahead, and it's been my job to follow his plans, each as I catch up to them. Conceived in that garden he liked to play grandpa in and born in the townhouse he bought when we got here." And Gladys laughed, a brief flash of pleasure before she remembered him dead in his chair in that townhouse with his brains splat on the wall behind him.

I know Muir's entire history. Moral and immoral. More, even, than Tom Bishop, his own son. Nathan Muir's father met his mother on the ship back from Italy—1925—she a college student, he a cowboy, both returning from decidedly different half-years abroad. *Amore, Roma.* His conception was on the shuffleboard deck in the dead of night. The middle of the sea. Between the here and the there off the gameboard of any nation. How he was conceived, and how he chose to live, and how Muir picked that corner he'd always talked about, the corner where spies decide to fight death and die fighting and firing back, all begun in the ten triangle:

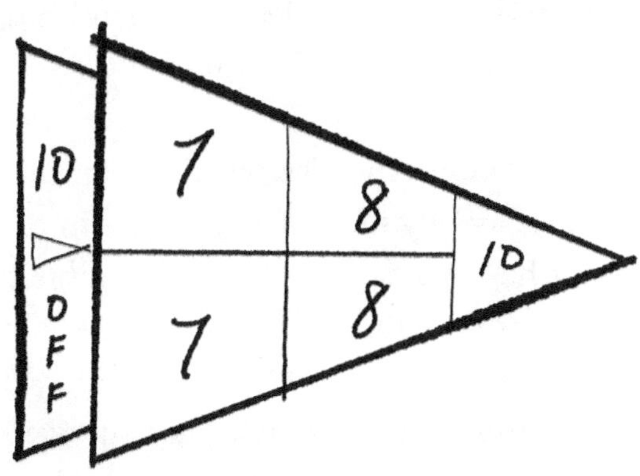

Hate him. Love him. Born and died.

Once, shortly after he'd moved to Princeton, Muir had a little housewarming. For a moment, the two of us were alone in his study. He selected an item from his desk. He offered it to me, and I took it. Three inches in length, it was large for an arrowhead. If authentic, it had to be ceremonial. Hand-chipped obsidian. On one side, etched. A grid not unlike a shuffleboard court, but more sectors, numbers without discernable pattern, and three random letters: *A* and *V* together at the bottom of the arrowhead, *R* right below the point.

"Am I supposed to know the significance, Nathan?"

"It's a party favor. Everyone's getting one."

We matched eyes, fencers at opposite ends of our lane. I waited. He snatched it back. I knew he'd meant the opposite.

"Tom is to have this."

He and his son had not been face to face for a decade. To do so would be fatal for Muir, as has been borne out.

"I'd be happy to get it to him." I offered my hand.

Muir mocked the gesture with a laugh.

"You will, after I'm gone. It'll be right here waiting for you."

Muir returned the arrowhead to the desk. We rejoined the party. As my life and my brain filled with new things—children and the other—I soon forgot all about it.

THE LECTURE CONTINUED and I've written from my recollection of his notes, because as I fly to my fate in KL, I'm of one hundred percent belief that he meant this last amble-ramble for us: for me and for Tom, and for all Muir's CIA networks—now lost to the wind and gone to destruction; for Dand van Eijk, who is the only of his agents from those networks who has survived this sudden and decisive removal of Muir's spies around the globe.

Van Eijk begging to come in from the cold of a hot Malaysia.

The fading afternoon sunlight reflected mellow off Muir's rugged, well-lined, torture-scarred cheeks. It danced after honeybee fur, sword blade glints off gold-rimmed glasses he'd worn for the past six years, once his vision dimmed, the edges blurred, and forced Muir's sight toward memories—mythic of themselves—of which he wanted to avoid. So he bought glasses to see and not to see. He loved his students. He loved what he taught. He'd begun confusing ancient mythology with the mythology he'd danced into competition at a level Harker and his Arty Murray ballroom slugs would never find expression of inside their hearts and wet-sole bellies. Muir's heart danced: so much more at the end.

"You can imagine how perplexing American Intelligence found these Montagnards. It wasn't until someone came along"— someone, Amy Kim knew, was a personal pronoun for her idol— "learned their myths, then couched the American requests in context of their figurative forms. Suddenly, the CIA couldn't give the Montagnard enough claymore mines and M-16s and they went off a'poppin' Vietcong and NVA like a permanent Halloween."

He paused—this is when Muir dipped his chin, directing Amy to retrieve the dead bird. He cleaned his glasses with his tie as a distraction to the other students while she buried the creature.

"I'm not sure their culture ever recovered," he said. "Which brings us back to our old friend Prometheus, who, as you recall, stole fire from his father, Zeus, gave it to mankind, and for this was chained to a rock on Mount Caucasus. An awful business. Each day a vulture fed on his liver, each night the organ renewed itself so that with dawn the vulture could return to its eternal feast.

"Now, First Rule of Thumb for the course: If myths are not merely stories told, but realities lived, I want you to consider over the weekend what reality of Greek life did the Prometheus story of theft and sacrifice inform, and moreover, how does that reality play out today—our own Western culture having been founded on that of the Greeks. There's no right answer, only thoughtful interpretation. Of course, Second Rule of Thumb: That doesn't mean this won't be on the final."

As HIS STUDENTS laughed in his garden of lies, van Eijk's Malaysian code, without any of the matching keys to the five one-time pads it turns out to have been elaborately encoded from, finally was deciphered by the cryptographic computers at Langley. The jumble of letters swirled across the silicon tongues of five different languages around electronic palates of letter concepts and became human words in equivalent English. The decoded document, printed, was slipped into a TOP SECRET envelope, and the envelope hand-carried to Acting Director Harker, practicing his golf swing, sans club, behind his new deeply polished and richly deserved (in his own mind) taxpayer purchased $22,000 desk and—invisible golf with invisible balls—the real ball got rolling.

Like the green marbles I find from time to time, my whole life, in odd places. I think they're ghostly, from my dad. I'm scared, Mads, if they are. I found so many before our Nate was born. There is no way to explain a green marble on my pillow, or in my coffee mug at Langley, or the dozens of other odd places they've turned up over the years—the last on my seat at the movies—underfoot like sidewalk pennies. But now they have stopped.

The ball started out small. Within days, it was the size of the one that chased Indiana Jones out of the temple. Now, I'm afraid, it's the entire globe I'm flying around, and this is all Muir. He walked home having closed his opening gambit.

He followed the afternoon sun out of the garden into urban twilight shadows, having dismissed his students for the last time with these words: "Since there's nothing I enjoy more than a mystery, I'll leave off with this clue. You'll find it in your Aeschylus… 'Of my own will I shot the arrow that fell short, of my own will. Nothing do I deny—'"

He posted his last known letter at the postal box on the corner. Walked down the block. Let himself into his nineteenth-century Gothic brownstone. He collected his own mail from the Persian runner on the floor beneath the mail slot as his black Persian cat scampered over and, purring, rubbed her back against the hard edge of his prosthetic foot and ankle.

"'—I helped men and found trouble for myself.'"

8

WHEN I SEE TOM BISHOP, I'm drawn first to his eyes. They are the kind of eyes that miss nothing, reveal nothing, ask for nothing in return, and whatever faith they once held has long since been replaced by vigilance. I picture him in Kosovo. I see him seated inside that battered Yugo ninety-nine hours ago, Muir's murder yet to be commited, wrapping up the loose ends of a personal war he has fought alone and in secret—reasons off-policy and known only to himself. This is what I know:

1. *His plan for Nathan Muir's murder is already— somehow—set in motion.*

2. *Arms crossed, not liking that he's not driving but knowing he couldn't have gotten to this cow-track outside Pristina without his asset, Miroslav Popovich [in CIA custody/already interrogated], he watches the windshield wipers smear across the windshield. Even though it is only sprinkling, they cannot clear the glass:*

    2.1. *Because the wipers are shitty, narrow gauge, low-grade rubber;*

    2.2. *Because in a war zone there's always dirt and dust and concrete powder, and with ethnic cleansing, human ash floats in the air and never altogether descends to ground until the gunfire ends and the butchering stops.*

Does it ever stop? Anywhere?

Miroslav's windshield was caked. The dampening rain and crappy wipers weren't ever going to wash away the sins of Kosovo. Tom Bishop's vision was smeared and fuzzy-looking, and he was fuzzy-looking too after two years rogue in Yugoslavia.

"Here?"

"I think, yes." Miroslav's hand shook as he lit a cigarette.

"You don't have to come."

"I thought I could."

"You got me this far."

Bishop bumped a fist on his shoulder. He slapped closed the crooked door of the Soviet-made, plastic-lined tin box of a car. Tom Bishop entered the Djakovica Woods.

Eerie quiet. Absent the sound of birds. Absent the rustle of wind. The drizzle seemed afraid. A dead and haunted place. Bishop moved down a random trail, random in that unlike a path made by animals—narrow, straight, and true—this path was wide and meandered between mossy stones and through brambles as if made by lost children.

Only nature renews to live again. Creatures are scheduled to die. Ask the centaurs. Ask me.

The first skeleton wore the rags of an old woman's housecoat. Patches of hair remained white clumps on her yellowed skull.

Bishop bore silent witness to the jumbled human remains littered everywhere. Most of them wore nightgowns, pajamas, sweats. What they had worn when pulled from their homes at night as clever cowards always choose to pull. Many were small and some were noticeably young. Surely most had been raped.

Bishop moved forward, face stoic, inured to what he saw. He'd seen it too many times. He stooped. He picked up an ID card: a girl's smiling face, not yet sixteen.

Nearby was a pile of IDs. Fifty or more. Photographed faces of women and girls of every age—most smiling, happy, hopeful. Innocent. Most in hijab as all were of the Islamic faith. More cards were strewn across the forest floor in a widening circle, like plastic leaves blown from a pile, never to decay but willfully forgotten, purposefully unraked. From the ID cards, one fact could be established: no men or boys were murdered in those woods.

Bishop found their skeletons elsewhere. Culled from their families, they were led to a plateau beyond. Made to clear trees and construct defenses across the region as slave labor for their Serbian captors, they were marched back months later to die outside the forest where their women and girls had fallen the previous summer.

Who knew Serbs so sentimental?

The last trench the men and boys of the Djakovica Woods dug was the long pit they were machine-gunned into. Nazis bulldozed over the rotting holes of their murders; here, kerosene was used. The top layer of bodies burned. Thick ash and skeletons preserved the lower level of bodies and allowed a mummifying and slower decomposition.

Tom Bishop climbed into the charnel pit. He took care to avoid the thick, tangled, and thorny vines of wild roses that had found and fertilized among the ash and bones and rot. Red roses poked through rib cages, open jaws, and shattered craniums—wild rose blooms budding, blossoming, dropping petals as if mortal wounds still bled and would forever each time nature renewed.

Miroslav put Bishop in the woods for two hours before the UN's blue-helmeted French patrol arrived and took Miroslav prisoner. They never asked him a single question. They already knew where to find Bishop in those woods. And there's a crime in that. They prepared arms and deployed into the wild.

Bishop moved among the dead.

Each time he discovered a particular style of black workboot, he lifted it. He checked the left sole. He checked its stitching. Forty-odd pairs of boots into this task, Tom Bishop found what he hunted: a left boot with blue stitching instead of white. One-handed, he opened his Spyderco tactical folding knife. Bishop cut the stitching. In the hollowed-out heel, he found six folded scraps of paper. Each side: a crudely drawn map of a village, a town, a crossroads, or fortifications, minefields, numbers of Serbian troops and defensive capabilities. Numbers of civilians— alive. The number of those who'd been exterminated. One struck me: a school in Djakovica. Used as an interrogation center and torture chamber.

Madeline, it appeared no different from any school anywhere in the world; it might as well have been Jessie's elementary.

I saw them all. Expertly drawn. Clinical in the face of the horror they represented. They are all addendum to the retroactive OPLAN I wrote three days ago, giving Tom pretended prior authority to have run this dead agent rather than be charged with espionage and the death of his man. I saved Tom Bishop through application of:

50 U.S. Code § 3122. Defenses and exceptions.

> *(a) Disclosure by United States of identity of covert*
> *agent*
> *It is a defense to a prosecution under section 3121 of*
> *this title that before the commission of the offense with*
> *which the defendant is charged, the United States had*
> *publicly acknowledged or revealed the intelligence*

> *relationship to the United States of the individual*
> *the disclosure of whose intelligence relationship to the*
> *United States is the basis for the prosecution.*

I wrote it with a false tone of hope for the success of an operation already long failed. For an agent long dead and rotted. I did it now because I knew in my heart, I'd been wrong to deny it back when Tom had recruited this Kosovo Muslim agent with his Nathan Muir-style yellow-brick-road promises.

Back then, he'd said, "The guy's doing this for his wife and daughter. C'mon, Aiken! You'd do the same. Wouldn't you?" But I didn't do it, not then, and the agent and his family died in the woods two months later, that guy marched back and shot, and I, too late, "Yeah. I would." But I hadn't written the OPLAN when he needed it, Bishop went off the reservation, and here we are two years later, fatally (or do I mean fatefully?) fetching him back to our breast.

I've written it now because I had no idea what Bishop would use this "Get Out of Jail Free" card to do. My new OPLAN of a week ago indemnified Bishop and got him home.

It didn't save anyone, and I won't save Bishop, and I cannot save myself. Such and nothing more. Well, one thing. It did kill Nathan Muir.

As Bishop's eyes went to the empty sockets of the young man who'd carried the intel, there was a flurry of movement above the pit. Bishop spun with his handgun and—the statements and official report already submitted to NATO and CIA extolling the restraint shown by those Frenchmen serving UN protocol—they didn't gun him down.

Bishop let his gun dangle. They took him prisoner because—shit—someone finds a mass grave of the people *that* someone's been assigned to protect, not to mention the women and children strewn in bones through the forest like some hobgoblin's dinner delight, not to mention they knew exactly where to go, *of course* you take Tom Bishop prisoner.

They beat the shit out of Bishop, dragged him unconscious to their trucks, but, no, they did not kill him.

US ARMY CAMP BONDSTEEL, Kosovo, is daylit at night. A seven-hundred-acre permanent facility for an as-long-as-we-want-to war. For a war we're not in—Muslims, who cares? Isn't that what Harker babbles? Clinton did a fantastic job spewing dirty work on the fronts of our boys' tunics, or Monica's, and George-Bush-the-sequel has taken the race baton on the track.

Run, Forrest, run!

They pulled Bishop into the office of the commanding officer, US 1st Armored Division's two-star General Calvin Lewis. The night drizzled with little interest or notice. Lewis leaned forward, elbows on his broad, puce-colored Army-steel desk.

"The French have filed a formal complaint with KFOR Command."

"Command, huh?"

"That's right. They don't appreciate an American operating in their sector. They want action on this. What I know about you, I'm not necessarily against that."

"General Lewis, I've kind of lost track who's on the leash end of our Army's collar these days. Last I checked, your commanding officer is some Italian guy? Or no, wait, the Norwegian fellow."

"Show some respect. General Thorstein Skiaker is NATO's chosen KFOR commander. A formidable soldier and leader."

"Guess I missed out when I was in the Corps. We Marines only took orders from US officers. I'll take my chances with that complaint."

"You're lucky they didn't kill you. They'd have been in their right. If you were in my Army—"

"I'm not."

"No. And no one knows who you are."

"Let's just say a guy who's going to die free and take all of you with me if I can."

The general waited for more, but Bishop waited him out. The general held the papers that Bishop had found in the dead man's boot.

"Explain this, and then you'll get the hell out of here."

"Need to know, General."

"I need to know."

"By whose authority?" said Bishop.

"Jeremy Harker."

Bishop's expression darkened.

"He's DCI these days since you've been AWOL."

"AWOGS."

"AWOGS?"

"Absent without giving a shit."

"Keep it up. I have full authority to incarcerate a civilian."

"I'm with Harker's outfit, pogue."

"You'd be surprised how fast this Permanently on Garrison 'pogue' can lose paperwork."

Bishop cocked an eye. "No desire to see monkey-mouth again. You go for it."

But with Harker in the mix, they both knew he wouldn't, and when the general realized he couldn't stare Bishop down (as is a general's understood prerogative), Lewis slumped backward into his chair behind the desk.

"I got to take a shit more important than you." The general waggled the intel one more time. Droopy eyelids, scowling jowls.

"Lookit, Bishop, I do have to account for these in my report, and sure, fuck the Norwegians, fuck all the Eurotrash—this isn't a partnership here. We fund NATO. The little portion they're required to pay but don't: that, we hold in debt. For what? Fuck if I can tell ya. 'Nam—ten times as dumb as this one, at least it made more sense to me."

"It's easier to discern your place in things when you're in the field."

The general met his steady gaze. There was more to Bishop than he'd wanted to credit.

"1st Armor only sent two units to Vietnam. Company A, 501st Aviation and 1st Squadron, 1st Cavalry. I was 1st Squadron. You?"

Bishop gave a polite shake of his head.

"Need to know?"

Bishop nodded yes.

"Then I don't want to know," said General Lewis, pulling a bottle of strong plum Skrapar raki from his desk and two shot glasses.

He cracked the seal and poured. They both drank, although Bishop only took half.

"The man I found that message on was part of my Kosovar network. Those are all Serbian positions. Long gone. He gave his life trying to get those papers back to me. He thought if he could get them to us, we'd get him vengeance for his wife and daughter he was forced to leave behind in the Djakovica Woods." Bishop drank the other half of his shot, a silent toast to the dead. "The whole time he worked as slave labor he made these maps, these charts, this war crimes genocide testimony, always with the hope he'd escape and meet up with me. We met this morning. Too late."

General Lewis poured himself another. Offered Bishop, but Bishop waved it off.

"Maybe later."

"You realize, Bishop, the Agency has had you on their casualty list for over a year."

"When they pulled their support of my mission, my work for them ended."

"A copy of your OPLAN has made its way downstream and will cover you and the rest of my command with the KFOR and the UN, if it comes to that."

Like I said, the OPLAN was retroactive. A mere but important detail, and Bishop knew there had never been one. Consequently, he saw at that moment my hand reaching out for him. He showed no reaction, and General Lewis continued:

"Furthermore, your Director Harker has requested I convey the message 'All is forgiven.' He has requested your return to Washington and my Army is to provide transport."

He corked the bottle. Tossed it to Bishop. "For the long ride home."

"Thanks, General."

This time Bishop's smile was genuine.

"Your plane leaves in an hour," the general said. "Dismissed."

Bishop was ordered straight to a DC safe house we keep at the Willard Hotel. We know now he rigged it with the Army transport NCOs to misfile his CIA Travel Orders with the military TDT (Temporary Duty Travel) orders of his fellow passengers. A generous spreading around of the Skrapar plum raki along with $500 among his Army travel buddies got Bishop out of mufti and into US Army combat utilities. He deplaned at Joint Base Andrews as a common soldier without a second look. Walked right past the NCOs set for his arrival and left them in a daydream, waiting for him to arrive on the next flight in nine hours. In the Army, waiting on initials is elevated to an art form.

Carver's investigators have gone back. They've tracked Bishop's journey by traffic camera. They've tracked it by independent video along his route. There's no getting around it. Bishop was making speed, not taking caution, and didn't care what we would uncover after the fact.

This bought Bishop the time he needed to rent a car on his cover ID. It allowed him to drive to Princeton, where Bishop paid a last visit to close a final, unnecessary, and cruel debt to Nathan Muir.

9

ON NATHAN MUIR'S DESK is a framed photograph of Tom Bishop graduating from high school. His mother, Sandy Bishop, poses at his side. She beams. Loves her boy. The photograph is taken from a distance, taken clandestinely, the shooter uninvited to the shot. It is the only photograph in Muir's townhouse, but plenty more were being taken now that the shooters were reversed.

Cornstarch, touch-passed from the medical gloves Bishop wore, was on the desk. On the telephone. On the photograph. On Muir's corpse behind the desk—his pockets torn open and inside out. Bishop had worn the gloves to conceal his identity. He didn't know that touch DNA transferred from fingers and hands during the act of pulling on surgical gloves is absorbed by the cornstarch donning agent. It can be extracted from the starch and latex proteins left behind. Although the miniscule amounts of touch DNA that can be collected and verifiably analyzed by law enforcement is so inconsequential as to be useless in a court of law, those miniscule amounts and the analysis tools available to Bill Carver are quite enough to secure a definite identification for our secret judgments.

It is conclusive. The cornstarch and latex touch DNA collected from Muir's brownstone belongs to Tom Bishop. Nothing I can say or do will change the fact. He came back from Kosovo. He went straight to Muir's townhouse. From the desk, his photo, his father's body, he went to the wall and removed Muir's honorary Ph.D. from Princeton. He opened Muir's safe hidden behind the frame and left it empty.

Documents? Cash? Gold?

Gladys said some of all that was in there, but also stressed these are things Muir would have gladly thrown wide the safe to give his son.

Gold, Frankenstein, and Muir.

And something else was missing. Gladys recalled it from Muir's office at Langley. Investigators contacted both of Muir's last two wives, Veronique and Tracy, who confirmed he had kept it in their home safes but would remove it once or twice a year, like some kind of relic. He would disappear with it, sometimes for weeks at a time.

A pewter flask.

It wasn't his. The ex-wives and Gladys agreed on that. May have belonged to Muir's father. Or Muir's grandfather. Or maybe not. I know Muir never collected things or fetishized items, possessions, accolades. But this flask was precious to him. It was missing and I was furious. Not because Bishop stole it, but because as Muir's one true and discreet confessor, I knew nothing of its existence.

Gladys described it to me the day of the murder—before anyone but I could identify the murderer. It was a "captive top" flask, the kind with the small hinged arm that keeps the lid from getting lost. On the flask is an enamel insignia, regimental in design. Beneath it, a monogram: "D.V.E."

Dand van Eijk. The last survivor of Muir's networks. The crypto-crier from the Malaysian wilderness.

Why the fuck did Muir have this agent's flask for all these years?

It was gone, but presumably it and the gold weren't all Bishop wanted. Drawers. Cabinets. Bookshelves. Chairs and sofa: all ripped-slashed-dug searched. Perhaps Muir beat him to what he sought; in the fireplace we found the remains of dozens of books, all identical, burned upon the grate. Along with a pine log or two, the fuel was a set of green journals. I've kept my prior knowledge of the green journals secret, but I recognized them immediately. Journals I'd found and rifled through at Muir's Captiva Island beach house a decade ago after my interrogation of Muir over Charlie March's assassination before I stole Muir's gun to fail at killing myself. They contained the story of his career, written in basic substitution code. Here, again, Bill Carver and his team have done incredible work reconstructing them, literally pulling the encoded writing out of the ashes.

The last we know of the events surrounding Bishop's patricide is that, while Nathan Muir was already dead, the phone rang, and Bishop listened to the message record on the answering machine.

"Muir, Jeremy Harker. I'm calling from your old Campus. Sorry to disturb you in your retirement, but something's up. We need your help. Call in as soon as you get this. It is imperative."

There is a background sound. It's fried chicken crunching— because I was there when Harker made this call from the phone installed on his precious conference room buffet table and he's not one to have the manners to finish chewing before dialing—"Thanks."

Bishop left him dead. Brains against the wall behind. Mouth stretched in eternal grimace.

As I'VE ALWAYS done for Muir and Bishop, father and son, I legalized the Kosovo operations. I made sure they read and verified bold and heroic and took the rough men standing on the walls and the men abed from Shakespeare to Kipling, Orwell to Cornwall-Le Carré to Nicholson-screaming-Sorkin, and sorted them into justifiable matter night-night or not, and the Quiet Old Lady Whispering "Hush."

Or as you aped so aptly, "What happens in bed, stays in bed."

I'm old enough now not to dwell in what I do and who I answer to when doing it right, meat-of-the-center cut of purview, growing uncuttable in the center of my gristled mind. I write for a living the darkest part of patriotism's underbelly. I write the lowest part that drags us through the dumb mud and the shit. And if I could remember the thing about the scuttling claws and Michelangelo, I'd write and indemnify that too.

My CIA commas kill or save. "Kill Dad." "Kill, Dad." My mind's on the "dad" thing but replace Bishop's father (or mine, for that matter) with any country or movement or political/terrorist/bystanding group/civilian, and karate-chop-slash *Hi-ya!* That is exactly everything I do for the CIA; exactly/everything my life matters to my clogged gray matter. So, there's this guy, Karl Kraus—he's why this is a paragraph rather than split like karate boards. A misanthropic Austrian Jew—dies of an embolism in 1936 before he ever gets to see himself and his theories on language borne out or train-borne away—*Arbeit macht frei*—whatsit…? *"Everything's futile when the house is burning."* This is about the Japanese invasion of Shanghai. Okay? So, Karl writes:

"I know that everything is futile when the house is burning. But I have to do this as long as it is at all possible; for if those who were supposed to look after commas had always made sure they were in the right place, Shanghai would not be burning."

I *do not* want to find Bishop when I land in Malaysia.

I don't want Muir to be dead by:

1. *Events.*
2. *Friend.*
3. *Brother.*
4. *Son.*

By commas, euphemisms—ding, dong, bell here-we-go-again Orwell—*Politics and the English Language:*

1. DYING METAPHORS.
2. OPERATORS OR VERBAL FALSE LIMBS.
3. PRETENTIOUS DICTION.
4. MEANINGLESS WORDS.

The puppetry of discourse; text to animate us all long after we flail, falter, fail, fall, comma, comma, coma [sick], period. Dead—
Me.
Line fault for missing everything.

AFTER MUIR WAS DEAD. After Bishop was gone. Harker called a second time. "Jeremy Harker, again. We must hear from you, Professor-Sir whatever-it-takes to beg, Muir-you-fucker… Please, as soon as you get this, call. *Muir, come in—gimme some a'that luscious hate.*"

At 7 a.m. the next day, Gladys Jlassi pulled her green Plymouth Neon to the curb. She went to the door. Locked. She rang the bell. Muir would always be dressed—cotton oxford starched and billowed and blinding white, his chinos that luffed some, and oxblood loafers on the aggressive tread he always wore "because," he'd tease, "one day my bestest network'll catch on I'm faking it and I'll have to run with the wind"—ready to set sail to campus. This day, Gladys used her key. Muir's cat, who always comes running at the bell, did not appear.

Within twelve minutes, four police cars, a detective's car, a coroner response vehicle—all-attendant first-responder personnel: clustered in small groups on the front stoop and sidewalk talking, drinking coffee, waiting. Gladys always carried her "retired" CIA credential. Yes, A: she'd called them; B: she'd denied them the crime scene once "murder" was determined; once the townhouse was clear of perpetrators who'd not remained on premises, Gladys held them off with a dozen or so phrases she remembered from some of my better CONPLANS that crossed her desk on their way to OPLAN permanence she shouldn't have read, and I love her for having read them. In Agency parlance: "To err is human, to cheat is divine."

That's when Bill Carver and his crew—four unmarked sedans—rolled up. I'd called him after she'd called me. He's a large specimen of a man both on the horizontal and the vertical. Was an MP, never a civilian cop. His high-and-tight curly black hair reflects Army over Agency. His mustache is blacker than his face but flecked with gray he fights his wife about dyeing or snipping or, forbid—she tried it once when he was innocently enjoying his PBS "limey mysteries"—plucking. Carver has the driest sense of humor and is the sharpest dressed of any man at headquarters. He's always tolerated me. Since most of the Agency despises me, I have a soft spot for Bill Carver.

"Bill Carver, CIA Office of Security. Detectives Powell and Clausen?"

Detective Powell did the pointing. "Powell, Clausen." Handshakes and suspicion, and Detective Powell continued, "As you people asked, no one's been inside since our first officers on scene made sure the premises were clear."

"Thanks," Carver said.

Powell shrugged as if he could take it or leave it.

Clausen scowled. Fuck the CIA. He could just leave it.

"Here's the way this works. We go in. We secure any sensitive material. When we're ready, you may join us. Join the investigation adjunct to my team until such a time as I determine this death carries no national security risk and the entire investigation is handed back to you."

Carver's posse from the other three sedans, having gathered equipment, galloped for the house.

Clausen said, "And, generally, what's the time frame on something like that? Ballpark."

"Ballpark: generally, something like this—never. Feel free to stick around outside."

Carver left them to reverie, walked inside, and looked at Nathan Muir. He'd always liked Muir and this friendship had been reciprocal. Muir let Bill and his wife, Nanette, have a week on Captiva every July with their kids and grandbabies.

"Some shit way to go, man," he said.

Carver signaled the photographers to begin.

I arrived two hours later.

I stared at my mentor's corpse. I remembered there was something in his study I was supposed to... Something. I was supposed to do something with something. I racked my brain for the memory, but I'd been losing memories, sand to a bottomless hourglass, for seven months. I divided the room and the destroyed furniture into sections. I turned on the points of the compass. I stared at each section as a kind of snapshot. For the life of me— undeniably of the life in me—I couldn't bring the lost moment or Muir's instructions or the item into focus. The last thing I did, I opened his desk drawer and shuffled around its contents.

If the arrowhead had been there for me to notice, I'd like to believe I'd have remembered.

I turned my attention back to Muir. Carver's team was ready to remove the body. I stepped aside. They laid out the bag. Opened wide the burrito flaps. They carefully transferred Muir's corpse onto it. It was the last time I would ever look upon his face. I fought the crazy urge to kiss his forehead. I reminded myself he'd caused me much pain. I told myself he wouldn't want that—better, he'd call me ridiculous to act on such an impulse. Carver's team adjusted Muir into the bag.

Muir gave me the strength to become everything I'm proud of in myself and this is the final goodbye? But, hell, his head's torn apart from Bishop's bullet. Not something you kiss.

Motherfucker, Bishop. What I can't get, and you'll have to tell me before you kill me, why did you torture him?

It was bloody and it was vicious.

Was it simply for the safe combination? If it was van Eijk's pewter flask, what's the point of tearing up the rest of the place? If it wasn't—God, Muir, where's the clue for whatever else was/wasn't in your safe? What could you have had that you wouldn't—as Gladys agrees—given your blood son, prodigal but home?

They zipped him inside. They grabbed the straps.

"Wait." I shoved one of the techs aside. I wrenched the bag from the others and dropped with it to my knees. I ripped the zipper and looked into his ruined face one more time. I don't know when I'd begun to cry, but as I leaned down, I saw my tears splatter his bloodstained, shattered brow.

"C'mon, Aiken. The tears—you gotta make my job harder with your contamination?" Carver finished with a grunt.

With my lips I did what I was never able to do with my own father. I kissed him goodbye. His blood thick and sticky in my hands, I held our lips connected.

"Enough, enough, enough," Carver said.

He placed a large hand upon my shoulder. Gentle. Meant to comfort. I shrugged it off, hard, and the next thing I knew I was outside on the front steps, doubled over the black-painted iron railing, gasping for air.

AFTER ALL Muir did for Elizabeth at the end—they'd made peace—Tom Bishop had lost his right to take his father's life.

Mads, you said after Elizabeth's funeral, Bishop had lost the last thing inside him that made him human.

"He's lost his fight," you said.

"His fight to save her?"

"No."

"His will to fight?"

"No. You always get everything wrong. He has plenty of that. I'm afraid of that."

"You're not making sense," I said, and you said, "His place in the fight. His why. Rusty, fighting is all he has left—senseless, brutal, slugging fighting without purpose. It's the 'his' part I mean. He's lost himself—hisself from all he fights."

For an entire year, I watched your words proven right with the weight of Homeric prophecy.

I miss you already, Madeline; I don't care whose son he is.

I right knew then (ugh—this brain), *knew right then* I wouldn't tell them Bishop had done this. They would find it out on their own or not. Naively, I swore to myself and to God inside me and in heaven, wherever that is or isn't, I would never see or speak to Tom Bishop again. In my heart, he was now as dead as Nathan Muir.

Why is it, Mads, I play the fool, mixing up everything handed me, to become the king of sorting it out wrong?

10

The Central Intelligence Agency safe suite at the Willard Hotel in Washington, DC, is the same room where Julia Ward Howe wrote the "Battle Hymn of the Republic". We'd launched a few of Bishop's operations from that room, and he'd once told me that bit of irony and I'd asked if anyone in the Agency knew. Bishop shook his head. "It's not the knowing, brother. It's the caring."

Harker will know if he ever reads this or survives this crisis, but it points out the lack of curiosity embedded in his CIA since he and his Young Turks came into power. Herein lies the problem.

After my return from Muir's murder scene, I met Jeremy Harker at his car as the bellman opened the town car's rear door for him. Harker gave me a dirty look, as if I should have beaten the bellman to it.

This is three days ago. Nobody held the back-seat cockpit hatch open for me today.

"Good morning, Acting Director," I needled.

Harker snarled, "Good morning, Aiken," through his *Dash and pep—that's Chiclets! Try 'em!*

You know his teeth. But did you know that his veins run with the blood of men who fired muskets into ranks of redcoats at Bunker Hill? He lets everyone else know. Constantly. One of those unfortunately not-so-rare birds who believe personal patriotism is defined by an accident of blood and nested to a family tree rather than a vigorous, diligent, and ever-active support of liberty. Sort of what our job here has gotten so off-track from. Muir's going-away present to Harker upon retirement—Muir had a career's worth of mementoes he left behind with specific instructions of how and to whom Gladys distribute them—went a photographic enlargement of Los Angeles from 1919. Why Muir had it, Gladys seems to remember, is it was taken from a film shot by Muir's grandfather, a Hollywood second unit director, as stock footage.

The particular frame showed demolition teams running from the blast of an explosion employed in the excavation of what would become the Los Angeles 2nd Street Tunnel. Dramatic. A bit funny, the fleeing dynamiters smashing bowler hats on their heads to hold them, one fella is falling as he's thrown from his shoes. Muir's grandfather sold the footage to Roach Studios to use as rear-screen projection in a Laurel and Hardy short. The reason Muir pulled this frame is the pigeons that took to the sky in terror released their bowels. A bird turd version of my pennies from heaven.

Muir added a little tin plaque to the frame.

Harker received it from Gladys, sneered at the image, and, stumped by the plaque, had his secretary call janitorial and send it straight to the trash. The first I saw of the photograph was when Diego Cuellar, chief of Seventh Floor Janitorial, poked his head into my office door. His grin was curved as a dog's wagging tail. He asked if I thought Muir would mind if he took the photograph home.

Like me, like Muir, like Bishop, Diego is an Angeleno transplant. I didn't get the covert humor he was reacting to until I read the plaque that had mystified Harker:

"2nd Street Tunnel, 1921. Just A Hole."

I laughed out loud. Diego joined me. As every Angeleno knows, the 2nd Street Tunnel is commonly known as Bunker Hill Tunnel and still every time I run into Diego he always says, "How's our Bunker Hill A-hole?"

Harker stumbled out of the Lincoln—seemed like another dance move—into the driveway planter where the daffodils bloomed. He came around the car, stomping the mud from his Ferragamo lace-ups as the vehicle scooted out, then barked: "He here, then?"

Why then? Then *doesn't mean anything: then acting director.*

He handed me a briefcase with a wire leash I secured to my sleeve-cable. Now they'd have to cut off my arm to get it. Then.

"Arrived this morning. Waiting on us. How'd it go with the president?"

Under the awnings, in through the doors.

Harker said, "Could have been worse. Bush the Second"—more madness of King Harker—"has given us a week to sort this out, then"—we split, passed through the revolving door. Once inside—"full disclosure before the Senate Select Committee."

Across the short lobby to the elevators.

"Any explanation why Bishop slipped his Army escort?" he asked.

"Said food was for shit."

"He would… Does he know about Muir?"

Now at this point, remember, I know but *they* don't know that Bishop killed Muir. "I don't think so."

A husband and wife joined us waiting for the elevator. We fell silent. Harker gave them a tight smile that held as much humor as a bird beak. The elevator arrived. The husband and wife entered— he, holding open the door expectantly polite. Harker waved them on. I hit the button for another car.

"Anything more on Muir's journals?" he said.

"I spoke to Carver twenty minutes ago." We entered the next elevator. Alone. "They've recovered the remains of forty bindings. Muir's career spanned forty-one years."

Harker punched the top-floor button. "So one's missing. Year?"

"Carver's working on it."

We watched the numbers flash. We ascended.

Into the corridor. Our suite at the end of the hall. I knocked.

"It's Aiken." I pulled out my keycard. "What happens here if Bishop fails us?"

"In seven days, I face Congress. In eight, every single bleeding heart in Washington gunning for me is going to have the ammunition to shoot this Agency down. Aiken, you're Muir's palsy-walsy, Bishop's paranoid paramour. End this: fucking fix it. I don't earn enough to give a damn about Malaysia and towel-heads hoping for a last-last-Last Crusade they can finally do dirty into the end zone."

The Crusades were the Christians, but there's no brakes on a bigot's mouth.

Then we're inside the room. Tom Bishop arcs across it— "Think fast"—a paperback. Stephen King's *The Girl Who Loved Tom Gordon.*

"Different. Suspenseful, though."

Guy's never caught anywhere without a paperback, a magazine, or an article in his pocket. Must be nice, free reading while you wait around with a sniper rifle.

"Suspense is overrated," I said. "In fact, when I read a book, I like to keep the author in suspense."

"Read it."

"Who's Tom Gordon?"

"Know nothing about baseball?"

"Nope. Er, yes-I-don't."

He gave me a funny look I avoided. In principle, I'm against single word responses. Always. "Then this will introduce you to a life-saving sport."

A safe house: good for debriefings, clandestine meetings, or those stifling waits for a knock on the door, the ring of a phone. I've told you that stuff about safe houses before—only this time, this one: luxurious. Bishop stood at the windows. Exactly where he'd said Julia Ward Howe watched Union reinforcements marching to Antietam and claimed God guided her hand in writing the "Battle Hymn of the Republic."

Glory, glory, Allahu Akbar.

"Here comes the rain," said Tom Bishop, and ten seconds later it started pattering the glass.

"The weatherman my wife and I watch predicted fair skies," said Harker.

Bishop turned with the overwhelming presence of a planted flag in enemy territory.

"I like to say it's the only business where you can be completely wrong most of the time and still make a fortune doing it on TV," Harker chortled with false geniality.

"Save it, Jeremy," said Bishop. "I've come a long way and I'm tired, and you're already the boss of being wrong all the time."

I unfastened the briefcase and put it on the Lemon-Pledged coffee table. I studied Bishop in the glow, trying to see where murder had changed him. It hadn't one bit, and as his eyes missed nothing, he captured that gaze of mine in the fresh, clean tabletop with the citric zest of a condemnable smile.

Sadness welled inside me. For all of us. How much more satisfying the constant disheartenment by Nathan Muir alive than the pointless pain of loving him murdered? How crushing to hate Muir's son for killing him and still adore him as the best friend—better than Muir—I have ever had? He is both the bullet and the fatal wound. I stepped away from the briefcase to watch the rain outside. As if falling rain would do something different this time.

"Food better here?" Harker asked.

"Just tell me what you want," said Bishop.

"So, you've spoken to Muir recently?"

"No."

"Not since you got back, then?"

"No."

They had spoken. We just didn't have the ECHELON intercepts yet. That's the NSA system that pulls every call and records trigger-word convos. ECHELON: a two-acre supercomputer underground in Fort Meade, Maryland.

"When did you last?"

Speak. Then.

Harker worked the combination lock on the security briefcase.

"Two years ago. The death of my wife."

Snap! Harker opened the briefcase and looked over its lid at Bishop. Smiling. So tolerant.

"You'll be happy to know, your two years AWOL in Kosovo will be conveniently removed from your service jacket, provided you cooperate from here on out."

"I don't give a damn about my record. Make your point."

Harker tilted his head as if to say, *Good idea, why not?* and as if still talking about the weather. "Nathan Muir is dead."

"Really," said Bishop.

"Murder, as it turns out."

"Is that why I'm here?"

I gripped the sill, digging my nails into the wooden frame, cracking the paint. Feeling like a pussy for the lump in my throat and wishing the lump inside my skull would use its power to erase these moments from ever becoming memories.

It'd be fair. I didn't tell you, Mads, and you didn't notice, but a few weeks ago for three days I'd lost your name. It's why I called you "dove" all week.

I wonder—what else have I lost so thoroughly that I've no idea I ever thought or experienced it?

"You're here because you still work for me, and I want you here." Harker flashed impatience.

"Am I a suspect?"

"Did you kill him?"

"Did you?"

"I must say, Bishop, the man was something of a father to you."

How vast becomes the little a fool insists he knows.

Now was the time to glance back at Muir's son, to confront him with my eyes, but his sole focus was Harker. My eyes dusted the air.

"I expected you'd feel a bit more at the news," Harker said.

Bishop's hard face challenged me to unmask his paternity. "More a father to Aiken. Take *his* pulse."

"Whatever. Sit down."

Harker had said it—the *sit down*—yet it was only he who did the sitting. Bishop remained afoot. Ready to go or ready to kill.

I willed myself calm.

"Suit yourself, then," said Harker.

Bishop took an unstudied military at-ease behind an armchair.

From the briefcase, Harker produced a stack of stapled reports. "Aiken?"

He handed me a signature page to acknowledge the expanded bigot list adding Bishop to the need-to-know.

He said to Bishop: "I want you to look at something."

I signed.

The reports were all marked EYES ONLY//TOP SECRET//NOFORN. I saw the first on the stack as I signed again and took out my official stamp. I inked it with my I'm-responsible, numbered and indemnified, ink that cannot be duplicated… unless it goes wrong. (Not the ink: the lurching world.) Like it was about to.

The first file was MEDUSA.

"Tehran." Bishop knew Muir's MEDUSA network. "I see. Or not. What's next?" He answered himself because he had the stack. "DIANA RED… Hong Kong: he built it; I ran it. Long time ago. D-RED hauled my ass outta the fire lots. Excellent product."

Why'd you kill him? Why do you hold everything so precious in a world of lies yet think your judgment knows best?

Why don't I?

He came around the armchair—he was interested now—and he plopped into it. He went through the files. "DESERT HYDRA, TROJAN, ACHILLES 4," said Bishop.

"Karachi, Cyprus, Kiev," said Harker. "And I don't have the reports yet but count our Tel Aviv cell and the Bogotá listening station as well."

"Muir's networks."

"All of them blown," Harker said.

They stared at each other with gunslinger eyes.

"This why he was killed?"

YOU did it.

"Maybe," said Harker. "Probably. The first two blacked out three nights before his death. The rest followed over the past two days. Over fifty of our foreign agents, countless assets under them: arrested, dead, running scared? Vanished. We have no idea."

I was amazed by this revelation, but at fifty-two—and lying pretty much throughout about all the small things of a modest life— I only write out loud to you, Madeline.

Nights of silence—door, "dinner?" Nothing, TV, a crossword, bed—sometimes the kids. But I'm usually home too late for much of that. Unless it's a half-hour deep sigh of Barney with "Camptown Races" who never did nothing for no one—although songsmith Stephen Foster, in rejecting the publishing of William Steffe's revival-tent barn burners, allowed his "Glory Hallelujah!" hymn to get into the head of this little lady Howe who had this room and transformed it into our national song. Like the al-Qaeda Ramadan Moon gents we're up against, Steffe and Howe were guided by God's hand in hotel rooms. Just a trivial difference between writing songs and chopping heads.

And while I've got your attention, I'm sorry I stopped going to the doctor. I was paying out of pocket. I'm sorry I lied, but to use the insurance would have triggered my removal from duty. It's just the occasional memory lapse, the mind-wandering confusion, and the dizziness on stairs, and headquarters has escalators and elevators, so I'm not worried about stairs, and time is time is time and benign is benign is mine. I'm cool; I got this shit. I'm going to stop growing.

"Jeremy, if I'm not a suspect in Muir's murder, what can the loss of his networks possibly have to do with me? You know where I've been."

"No one knows where you've been."

As the Oedipus tattletale Tiresias, Harker would have been remembered only for his blundering into doors. He'd a'shared the Greek's tits, though. Seven times. Or did blind Tiresias have his tits seven years?

Harker unclipped a photo from another file. A dossier photo. Bishop studied it while I pretended I wasn't peering over his shoulder.

Black and white. Taken unobserved. The man pictured in bush jacket, fanning his Panama hat, standing in full figure at a bar, a talon finger on the edge of a beer glass, caught turning as if his name has just been called yet he can't quite figure out by whom. His gaze is almost hopeful, somewhat sad, forever incomplete.

Bishop flipped it away.

"This is bullshit."

"You don't recognize him, then?"

"No."

Harker studied him, hunting for the lie. "He'd be in his late seventies by now. You positive you don't know him?"

"Jeremy, I have never seen this man before in my life. Why would you suggest I have?"

I know Tom Bishop's eyes: he recognized the man in the photo. He knew Dand van Eijk. Zero doubt.

Harker handed him the rest of the dossier. The written part. The part that can be acknowledged, knowledged, known, and understood. Signed in brown ink—which there was a lot of on the jacket and the pages inside.

"His name is Dand van Eijk," said Harker.

"Dan?"

"Dand."

"Whatever. I don't even need to be here. I'm out."

Bishop stood. I shoulder-handed—a control Muir'd taught me once—my false and fallen brother in place. I felt him relax into my hand. Trust. Safety. Faithful connection.

"Dutch colonial in Malaysia," Harker continued. "Recruited '68. Codename: TITAN."

Bishop opened the file, glanced through it. Cared as much as a fly.

Unpack it, Mads: every time a fly lands in its nonchalance, it cares entirely, as death is that much closer to a fly in stillness. And the three of us knew it in that room: I had landed Bishop.

"He wants to come in, Bishop. I want you to deliver van Eijk to my open arms."

"From what I hear, Malaysia's about to go up in flames."

"You're watching too much TV. This isn't the Balkans. This is a country with thirty billion dollars international investment. Malaysia leads the Asian recovery. Our analysts believe it's a simple case of pre-election jitters. Nothing more."

"Our analysts make mistakes," I said, unable to help myself.

"Who's Dandy's case officer?" Bishop said.

"His case officer was Nathan Muir. And it's not 'Dandy.' Dand *is* a name."

Bishop looked askance at me.

Totally in agreement. (Not that I'd encourage him with a back-atcha wink—I corrected by rubbing my eye.) In the chocolate box of dumb names, Dand is the gold-leaf-infused, Himalayan-salted caramel-chocolate truffle centerpiece dumbest name possible. Dand? A European brand name for a cheap train set. Dand? Crappy, un-homogenized Swedish milk in a box. Dand: a strong mint tooth powder handed out to hobos at YMCAs of the 1950s. Dand: that's what makes the druff. Or a tricky Hindu gymnastic pushup which it actually is.

The muscles in Bishop's face tightened. "Someone must've taken him over after Nathan retired."

Harker click-clacked his teeth. "Truth is, no one knew he existed. Muir had this file archived. For two days, Personnel insisted we never had an agent Dand van Eijk in Malaysia or anywhere else—"

"Dand van Eijk. Dand van Eijk!" I suddenly parroted. It sounded like something I *did* remember. Or could. "Daaannd vaaan Eiiijk."

I've begun to stammer. But, yes, you've noticed. Occasionally, getting words out becomes like a stick shift on a bad clutch. Not to any noticeable extent to others, though—thank God.

"Aiken. What's your goddamn problem?" Harker said.

I shook my head, the name right out with it. If they'd asked me at that moment to repeat it, they'd have gotten *Um v-v-vay Ihhshisk.*

"Get off his case, Harker. I won't tell you twice."

Suspicion grabbed on to the swirl of all my other emotions. Does Bishop know about *It?*

Mads, did you get word to him? That couldn't be possible. There's no way to guess what's growing inside my head. But his tone said he knew something—not that my behavior was strange or out of character, right? But he undoubtedly knew something.

"It wasn't until Accounting discovered we've been paying van Eijk steadily all these years—month by month by month by month—that we back-stabled this."

"Numbskull Nancy?!" Shit. Another blurt at my long-ago lover in Accounting.

Harker said, "What? Aiken—shut up." A glance flashed at Bishop. *"Please."*

"Nothing. Sorry. Didn't mean to speak, Actor, Sir, Directing— *Acting Director.*"

Bishop flicked eyes at me I made sure to miss. He reconsidered the van Eijk dossier. Record of more than thirty years spying for America. Bishop ran his finger down the page. Stopped at the paragraph headed "CLEARANCES." Beneath the heading were several designations. His finger and my I-spy-with-my-little-eye stopped at: IMMILFOR B-R577X.

"He carries an IMMILFOR B?" said Bishop.

Replace IMMILFOR B for "umbrella" on a rainy day the weatherman didn't predict, and you got buildings raining down on you. Harker dropped his gaze, uncomfortably.

Pennies from Heaven.

"On that and his codename alone, he can order up an American military strike without on-site confirmation-verification and you don't even know who he is? What the hell did he do for Muir?"

A million-penny fortune raining from clouds to fill umbrellas.

"Your job is to find out. Three days back, van Eijk got a coded message into our embassy."

"KL?"

"Kuala Lumpur. Yes. The man is afraid for his life."

"He should be," Bishop said. "Civil wars happen, it's guys like him get shot no matter who wins."

"This isn't about Malaysia. Van Eijk claims to know what hit Muir's networks. All of them."

Bishop looked at me (I looked away) and he said what I was thinking: "Why me? You can't possibly trust me. Why not send one of your Young Turks. Send Aiken."

"Hey, don't lump me in," I said (looked right at him too—damn!), voice sere and crispy.

"Please don't," Harker said, protective of his handpicked trolls. "Van Eijk asked specifically for you, Bishop."

There was inevitability in Tom's eyes. He dredged his decision from the bottom of the lake of his heart. Perhaps too many bodies rose. I don't know. I will find out.

Boom the cannon and watch my carcass come to the top.

"That's right. It's Tommy Bishop—he'll come in to and no one else."

"Jeremy, I don't know this man."

"Well, he knows you." And moving in with his pitch(fork): "Look, Bishop, we have our differences. You're old school—Muir's school. Cold War. I've never pretended to understand the way you dinosaurs operate, but I've given you rein, you can't deny that."

He looked at me. "Aiken, jump in anytime."

I placed my hand on the reports, knowing the murder, knowing more than Bishop about the man who tricked us all into this from his flower garden of mythology, a lid off a daffodil. Talk about reins—I pictured the reins on Fred Flintstone's work brontosaurus as the words slid deftly down the tail of my tongue: "Tom. For most of us, me included, men and women like Van Eijk are just codenames in a file."

After all Muir did to make right with Elizabeth, Tom didn't even go to his own wife's funeral. Why am I not turning on you?

I said, "You, you know agents."

The answer sneered at me, ensnared. My need to see where this was going, the blast footprint, cone of damage, the road to salvation, the answer to life's crossword and Muir's life and death superseded need-to-know for anyone but me and Tom.

I said with more confidence than I'd felt in a hard month, "Tom, it's your gift."

Okay: halt, stop, pause—whatever. Comma? Gift is a trick word. Why I used it. We get in—meaning in-tray delivered—studies on word weight. Gift has an 8 hard weight out of 10 when used/heard. We get this from interrogation studies, and are instructed to use them in our legal renderings where possible. Gift *is a magic word*—mom, daddy, birthday, trust, Christmas, winner. *Remarkable: magical:* gift—*"It's your gift." I say it and you brighten reading it. All 7s and 8s.*

I'll give you some 10s somewhere down the written road and you'll see how they make you feel. They're better than awards. (Slapped your ass with a 9.)

And, no, love *is weighted somewhere between 2 and 4. Overused and depleted of meaning. Don't like it? Blame the Beatles or me, as is your wont. Blame your "wife" (wife can only ever be safely trusted a 5-6, but* girlfriend *a 7-10, depending where you are on the dating-slash-sex glide-path).*

"It's your gift," I told him. "You cut through the politics and you're everything to them—brother, lover, confidant, friend…" (7s).

"Not with these networks. Except for Hong Kong, Muir never let me near 'em."

"C'mon, Tom," I said, not knowing I was sketching the chalk outline for the fallen of our duel. "This is a chance to make good. If not for the Agency or van Eijk, for yourself. For your own lost network. We all feel terrible about Kosovo."

Harker jerked his head at me. I think impressed. Harker said, "For Muir, then."

Bishop closed and squared the file. He looked me in the eye—last time I've seen him—and there was emotion there when he said to me: "All right. If you say so, Russell, I'll go."

"Thank you," said Acting Director Harker, and to me: "Bring in Sedaka."

11

I UNLOCKED THE DOOR to the adjoining suite. Sedaka stepped out, smiling wanly, travel-wearied and bumble-footed in a rumpled Brooks Brothers fake. Bishop took his measure as the fat man moved in with outstretched hand.

"Paul Sedaka. And to answer your first question: no relation, can't sing worth a twat… Good to meet you, Mr. Bishop."

I briefed Bishop, my held-on-to, hoped-for twin as he shook Sedaka's hand. "You'll travel together to Kuala Lumpur. Sedaka's been read-in on van Eijk and will accompany you every step of the way. He will provide support in every facet."

I gave them tickets on a Malaysia Airlines 747.

I went home. Made Kraft dinner for Jessie, shook up a bottle for Nate.

You were swinging back from LA.

They buckled into their last-row first-class seats.

Sedaka said to Bishop: "Look, you and I both know, Harker's set me on you as a watchdog. Worried you might try to give ol' Sedaka the ol' slip a'the leash."

"Just want to get in, get our man, get out. What you think you know about me: you don't. Let's keep it that way."

"Good, good. That's what I like to hear. How I've arranged it. Hit the ground running's what I always say."

Bishop didn't comment.

"You've not been to Malaysia before but trust me: you'll love it. I do. Every bit. How I'd love to show it off to you. But tomorrow van Eijk goes to the Batu Caves," said Sedaka. "So that's where we go and that's all you'll see."

Bishop squinted.

"Hindu shrine," Sedaka said. "Very famous, very crowded. If it's safe, he'll leave his mark by the Indian god Ganesh. That's the—"

"I know Ganesh."

"Good for you. A little Eastern culture in a man's a right thing. So, van Eijk will be waiting for you in what they call the 'Dark Caves.'"

The flight attendant stepped close and leaned in the more companionable first-class distance. "Champagne? Guava juice? Orange?"

"Oh, never turn down the bubbly," said Sedaka and took two. "Bishop?"

"Keep it. The plan?"

"Right. Not much more to it—you grab him. I'm waiting in the car, and bingo-bango-Oingo-Bongo."

"Boingo."

"Righty-*o*, and I bounce the two of you onto the afternoon flight out. Whatdya think?"

Bishop leaned back. Shut his eyes. "You need to do something about your teeth."

From a chill, rainy May in DC to May in Kuala Lumpur—102 degrees with 85 percent humidity. The Kuala Lumpur International Airport: architecturally stunning, and as modern in convenience as advertised, each terminal boasting unique innovations in service and technology, and an interior transportation system straight out of a Disney World Tomorrowland—and, lest we forget, the Cinnabon—a winner of multiple international awards, it is near perfect. Once you get to the terminal and inside.

The runways are a disaster. Same problem that plagued the previous airport for over thirty years: arrivals have trouble getting to the gates. The tower blames the ground crews. The ground crews blame the pilots. The pilots blame their airlines, and the airlines blame the lack of training in the pool their government forces their airline to draw from, and the cheese stands alone. Jetways hang like open-maw serpents, and half of all arrivals deplane on the tarmac.

Bishop and Sedaka's flight was one of a dozen jetliners clogging the taxiway and apron. The two CIA officers collected their bags off the baggage truck. They passed through a temporary security checkpoint.

The queue into the terminal building and customs control stations inside moved so slowly Bishop could feel his weight sinking his black Danner boot soles into the softening blacktop. Sedaka would walk right through on his diplomatic passport while Bishop traveled with cover. The disguise was simple: the unkempt all-weather gray suit and wheeled duffle of a world-weary American mid-level executive. No reason for more than a passing glance, provided Sedaka's incessant chat didn't mark them companions. The heat was interminable. Sedaka—lover of Malaysia—voiced a robust and nasty complaint against the country and everyone in it into Bishop's face, breath rank with the sour grapes of champagne fumes. Bishop allowed a half-dozen passengers move in front of him into the halitosis cloud. He'd rather suffer the heat than suffer Sedaka.

Stare decisis: Only time you let your passport out of your hand is for the stamp.

When we learned we could not have kids and adoption led us to Vladivostok and Jessie, Muir—who'd found out I'd be traveling to his old enemies' state (as even in retirement he always discovered things about me regardless of whether I wanted him to know, or wanted to know he knew)—briefed me that the FSB (which was the new moniker that the KGB hid behind, though to remain scary let everyone know they were hiding there) would come at me knowing I'm CIA in the first minutes I landed.

"Headquarters briefed me," I informed him over the telephone. "You've been gone awhile, but you'll be happy to hear my cover identity is clear and protected, not in any of their systems or on any watch list. They have no idea I'm CIA."

"They do a better job than they used to."

"Yes. We seem to be getting by without you. Whatdya know?" He should've been in my kitchen to see my triumph.

"I know that I didn't mean we were doing the better job, Rusty. So listen to me because this is important. The only time you let your passport out of your hand is in the booth for the examination of your visa and the plunge of the stamp. It will be the only moment you and their immigration officer will be face to face, locked in and alone."

"What's this locked-in booth?"

"At Vladivostok, it's a single-lane walk-through. You go in, there's a door directly in front of you. It will be down. The door behind you slides down. A light goes on to your left, revealing the immigration officer behind glass—young, stern, handsome, dressed in parade ground authority. He does his business, the door before you whisks up, and you're on your way."

"Bullshit. If they suspect I'm CIA, he just walks out and I'm trapped."

"You're already trapped, Dumbo. You're inside their country. A gigantic police-state prison. The last thing they'd ever do is trap one of our officers in one those boxes. Since you haven't had a chance to commit espionage, let alone get a jaywalking ticket, all they can do is send you home. They ever did that, we'd stop coming in through airports, and that would make keeping tabs on us a hundred times more difficult."

"Guess I hadn't thought it through."

"What I'm here for. Gotta protect my next generation. Start your kid out young, she'll be twice the recruit both you and Bishop ever were."

"You've got mail. An invitation never to meet her."

"We recruit at Princeton too. I won't have her attend anywhere else."

"You'll be long dead and it's not the Agency, it's the part of 'we' that includes you."

He chuckled. "Listen, I'm serious about the passport. Don't let it out of your possession to anyone else from the moment you land."

I told him I'd remember, and I was remembering as I stood the first hour, then well into the second, in the long line to what I presumed was this booth-kiosk Muir had exactly described. It looked like a Parisian Sanisette self-flushing street toilet. I was thinking about that when a gorgeous platinum blonde, dressed like a Muir fantasy stewardess—as opposed to the Aeroflot flight-cum-gulag attendants I'd been trapped with since Tokyo, two decades older than this young nymph (her glistening lipstick framing perfect teeth that parted for the tip of her tongue to wet high-gloss lips)—primed her fuse and torpedoed straight at my peacoated hull. I swear it: she did this in slow motion and against a wind machine.

"You look a little lost, sir. Is there anything I may do to help you?" Hollywood American-English Russian accent.

I wasn't lost. I reminded myself I was headed to the pay potty—glad I didn't blurt that—and blurted, "I'm a little lost. This wait—not that I mind at all…"

Her perfume smelled like the sheets in a suite at a luxury hotel on an exclusive Caribbean island I wanted to take her to and tangle in.

"Hey, Rocky! Watch me pull a rabbit out of my hat." "Again?" Mads, she was the original Natasha Fatale.

She had one hand electric on my left biceps and held out her other, fingers rolling open like the soft foam of a cresting wave. I deposited into the warm center of her palm not only my passport, but my folder with all my legal documents for Siberian travel, hotel reservations and confirmations, adoption paperwork, and various other permissions I'd spent the past six months acquiring in preparation for bringing Jessie home.

God, I was so tired; relief was surely in her hands.

I put my wallet on top. "If this helps."

She didn't say thank you. Didn't hang around. I didn't see where she'd come from, and she didn't swing her hips as she'd done bearing down on me as I watched her walk to an unadorned, solid white wall. A door appeared, opened for her without her touch or break in stride, and sealed behind.

Within moments, the line ahead of me moved at a normal pace.

Had I failed Muir's one request? All depends on how I chose to look at it. I weighed my list of successes against the little hiccup of losing my identity kit and everything essential for my visit.

1. *I am CIA and I had held out longer than—I'm sure—any untrained civilian would have against such a full-frontal attack.*

2. *I'd played it cool. Nothing I'd said compromised my cover as a junior lawyer at a DC dotcom Dulles Technology Corridor startup. (I'd argued for senior—hell, I am a senior attorney at Langley, for Chrissakes, why can't my*

> *cover identity be senior—? until Meryl Hofmeyr bopped into my senior-lawyer office and told me with a little burble that Deputy Director Harker didn't believe it was believable for me to be senior anything.)*
>
> 3. *I'd get to see my nymph again when, unable to crack my cover and identify my CIA employment, she would return it all to me—maybe even with an apology. (But, most likely, no trip to the Caribbean.)*

Another forty minutes passed. I was almost to the passport auto-toilet. Now I was nervous. Uncomfortable. Now I needed a toilet, or my trousers would be pee-coated. I was two bodies back from the guillotine door when the secret panel opened in the white wall. I prepped my cocky—don't Freud the word, please—face, which went from devil-may-care insouciance to devil-in-the-details slap-happy stupid as it wasn't Natasha returning with my paperwork but Boris Badenov and his uglier twin, Baddy Borisnov.

High point: I did get to see what was beyond the secret door. About ten feet inside a tight corridor is a metal door, vaguely institutional, that opens into an interrogation room. Before I went into it, I witnessed another guest escorted out. Young guy. Dressed like an airport town car operator. Trying to control uncontrollable shaking. Handcuffed. Under arrest.

My interrogation lasted the rest of the afternoon. I'll admit, the room was a bit claustrophobic. But it wasn't a cage, and I wasn't buried alive, and I quickly found out all I had to do was tell the truth about what I was doing in their country.

"You fight us in Cold War, you engage us in nuclear arms race, you crash our great Soviet system propagandizing our youth!"

A KGB/FSB v. USA-CIA b-i-t-c-h session. I played perfectly dumb in an off-kilter folding chair.

"I don't know about all that. I'm just a web company lawyer." I waggled a finger at my paperwork. "It's not written there, but I got a promotion five hours before we took off. *Senior* lawyer, now. Nice, huh? Anyhow, like I said, I don't know from Adam any of that other stuff. You've studied my paperwork. It's all approved. All in order." So dumb, in fact, I blurted something stupid. "I'm just here to take one of your Russian orphans off your hands, and raise her the America way with my wife."

Won the Cold War, crashed their economy, killed communism, corrupted their youth…now we're stealing their children. Nice going, Dudley Do-Wrong.

That was the first time Boris hit me in the face. The only reason the second punch didn't follow directly from the first is Baddy—and here's a little tip: the one dressed sloppier, appearing sleepier than the other, who lets the other thug talk, he's the one in charge. Baddy spent thirty seconds reprimanding Boris, finished with something that placated the hothead, and sent him off to collect—I hoped—my passport and papers. And wallet.

Baddy and I stared at each other. Long silence. He with a bored-enough glare from his naturally sanguine face, I with a *What can you do about help these days?* goofy arched-eyebrow lip bite.

"I'm looking forward to visiting Siberia," I offered.

"No one looks forward to Siberia."

Boris returned. The two FSB agents conferred. Baddy took my paperwork, checked through it, each page very slowly, until he pulled one.

"Incorrect hotel voucher," he pronounced.

"Your embassy in Washington provided it and your state-run travel office approved it."

Baddy pursed his lips.

"Incorrect hotel voucher." Boris clanged the gong.

"Okay. I get you think that, but I assure you: after your travel office approval—which included the hotel's faxed response to both the Russian Embassy and the Russian Travel Bureau—their approvals of that approval, approve the hotel voucher. All contained therein."

Therein. *Nasty compound-word deception indicator. Proceed with caution.*

I'd wasted so much time in this airport I could never get back and yet here I was desperate to buy more. I wasn't going to let these bumpkins cause me to fail Jessie.

—cause me to fail, Jessie.(?)

I pressed my case with urgency. "And to ensure the process was correct thus far, I went back to your embassy, and they approved that approval. Those stamps are there as well. I got an art museum of stamps."

"Incorrect hotel voucher."

"Fine. You're sticking to it. Okay. So what? How do we fix it?"

Baddy: "Cannot be fixed."

"What does that mean?"

"Without hotel voucher, it is impossible for you to be in Russia."

"This is something your embassy knew?"

"Yes."

"And your travel bureau?"

"Yes."

"And Aeroflot."

"Yes."

Fucking robot. And I suddenly knew how I was getting out of there.

"As soon as we landed, I couldn't be here?"

"Impossible. Without hotel voucher, you cannot step one foot in Russia."

I went back further than any CIA training. I was back with my dad—he in his recliner, me on the den rug, feet up behind me, watching Star Trek *on one of those rare nights he wasn't on the road selling drugs or whatever he really did for a living. My mother and sisters were at Girl Scouts, and Dad and I had the TV and its Zenith Space Command remote to ourselves. We'd beamed down to the K Class Android Planet where Captain James T. Kirk faced death and the destruction of the* Enterprise *from the planet's supercomputer Norman. AI far superior to human intellect, unfeeling and unreasonable, purity of logic and the truth of numbers.*

"There is no way around that?"

"None. No hotel voucher, you cannot set foot inside Russian Federation."

To my horror, Kirk admitted the folly of humanity. Something to the point of "Norman, as a human, everything I tell you is a lie."

I entered a space of calm and control, I imagined Natasha watching from somewhere secret, one of those round black bomb balls sparkling in her palm. I could almost smell her tropical perfume.

"But I am here."

"You can't be."

"I am. Sitting here. In Russia. In this room. With you."

With seconds left to save the Enterprise, *Kirk spoke three fatal words: "I'm lying now."*

Boris was suddenly nervous. He leapt to his feet. No towering over me, just a threatening pile in front of my face.

"Incorrect hotel voucher makes what you say impossible!"

The lie was the truth; the truth was a lie. The springs were ready to pop out of the ears of that one.

Norman screamed robot-voiced terror: "You say lie, but lies are truth! Does not compute! Illogical!"

Boris cocked his fist and let it fly that second time. Baddy was almost there himself. He wanted this over before he, like the Norman supercomputer, self-destructed.

"No hotel voucher: you cannot be in Russia. You are in Russia: with no good hotel voucher," he snapped.

I swiped a knuckle over my bloody nostrils. Pulled myself up my chair. "Which is, according to you, impossible, but my being here on Russian soil makes it—"

Dad chuckled. "Reminds me of you, Rusty."

"Kirk…right, Dad? I remind you of Captain Kirk?"

He laughed, enjoying himself. "Whatever you say, kid."

"Shut fucking mouth!"

"Shut."

"Who is contact at Hotel Vladivostok?"

"Oh, yeah. Sure." I pointed at the paper, fingers of my other hand pinching my nose. "Dat's his dame right dere. Super nize guy."

They said nothing more. They returned my passport and papers. My wallet. They pushed me through the secret door into the now empty customs/immigration lobby. My footsteps echoed as I walked to the narrow kiosk and rapped on the door. It whooshed open. I stepped in. It shut exactly as Muir had said it would and there sat his guy in the peepshow light.

Outside,was my new driver, the first already on his way to that place nobody looks forward to.

A COMMOTION greeted my arrival at the Hotel Vladivostok. Heavily armed state police dragged out a terrified mullet-headed young man. Pleading, crying, struggling. Sad. Ugly. You waited for me in the lobby. Jessie—at that time still Iskra Iessejovna Rybakov (translation: Spark, daughter of Jesse the Fisherman)—a miracle in the flesh, holding your hand, and staring up at me with joyous eyes.

I crouched. I spoke her name and mine and Jessie giggled and hugged me. I looked at you, moist-eyed, as happy as the day I married you.

"You see that commotion coming in?" you asked.

It took me a second. "That? Oh. Yeah."

"He was our hotel contact. He's been the best help. He has the best English."

"Nice."

"No, it's not nice. You saw what they did to him!"

"He must have done something."

"What? Honestly, Rusty. He's the guy they trust to do the hotel vouchers!"

THAT NIGHT, a cockroach climbed on my face. It went in and out of my mouth, and later I broke down in that little Fiddler on the Roof *birch grove near the abandoned airbase they'd stashed us in near Jessie's Siberian orphanage. The dawn of our court appearance. A Russian babushka strolling by stroking a hen cradled to her ample bosom.*

I said out loud to the air: "I can't do this. I don't want this hopeless, broken child."

Next morning, after the proceedings, the judge took me aside. Through our interpreter, he confided to me that had we not adopted Jessie, she was slated to be a pleasure girl at the military-run granary at age twelve. Most are dead by fourteen. Disease. Murder. Suicide. Or just screwed to death. "Na zdorovye!"

12

SEDAKA MOVED through passport control with travel-worn ease on the strength of his US diplomatic passport. For Bishop, it was another story. A modern airport, brand new, the latest HD video camera pushed its lens into his face from its wall corner mount.

Matched with his passport.

Stamped.

Returned.

Sedaka took Bishop's suitcase with his left hand while guiding him forward with his right—

CLICK! CLICK! CLICK! The two of them nailed a second time in a series of still shots. Bishop taking off his suit coat and swinging it over his shoulder, perfectly obscuring his face at the precise right time.

He led off at a rapid pace. "Your car's out front—curb, lot, where?"

They passed through a security choke and made their way outside, past a pair of undercover Malaysian Special Branch agents who moved in behind them.

Bishop indicated the cars at the wide, palm-clustered flame-back woodpecker hammer-squawking roundabout: "Which vehicle is your ride?"

Sedaka said, "Mercedes. The white one. I pretend it's a taxi, gets me free parking."

They buckled in. Sedaka checked his watch. "One twenty-seven. Gives us an hour and three—ah, twenty-eight—make that two minutes to get to the caves. You ready?"

Bishop's eyes shifted to the side-view mirror: the two Malaysian Special Branch agents climbing into a yellow Honda.

"Drive," he said.

Sedaka pulled into traffic. Bishop watched the yellow Honda follow.

About this time, Harker and Bill Carver were the only occupants in a Seventh Floor briefing room, four doors down from the director's buffet, er, conference room. They faced a television mounted in the wall displaying traffic-cam footage.

Harker said, "One of our own, then?"

Carver hit a remote. "Yes. If Thomas Bishop's still ours."

The image: a Volvo sedan.

Carver said, "This is the intersection leading to Dr. Muir's home."

"Not sure he was a doctor—officially, that is."

"Get real, Harker."

Then, image closer: through the rental-Volvo windshield, Bishop recognizable behind the wheel.

"These were taken fourteen hours before the body was discovered," said Carver.

"Did he kill him, Bill?"

"It is a possibility... We've traced a CDR through 60 Hudson switching. From a Camp Bondsteel payphone in Kosovo to Muir's home. Sixteen hours later, Muir is dead, and Bishop is in his safe."

"The autopsy, please."

Carver pulled a file from his briefcase. He handed it to Harker. Harker opened it. Scanned pages.

More to himself than to Carver... "So Bishop kills Muir... and probably wiped out the networks—now presumed dead—from

Tehran to Bogotá to Tel Aviv, right on down the line. And I've turned him loose on the last survivor: van Eijk."

He reached for a telephone. "Jackie, get me a priority line to Paul Sedaka in Kuala Lumpur."

KLIA EXPRESSWAY. Modern and stunning. Eight straight fast lanes that run the length of the country; lush green coconut-oil plantations on one side, the brand-new Grand Prix racetrack on the other. Sedaka drove in light, fast traffic.

"Eight years in Southeast Asia Analysis, I am considered the Agency expert on Vietnam. The war and all that. Mr. Apo-calypso-now at your service... You know what? I like you, Bishop. I do."

Bishop didn't remark. It didn't matter. No care for nonsense. Been in so many cars with so many guys who babbled to cover. Stupidity or betrayal, it goes either way. If you're Analysis, you go with stupidity, which is process and you move your chess pieces accordingly. If you're Field, you're all about results. Lock down betrayal and play straight to the endgame. It makes your mind faster and hand more quickly responsive on the draw when folly slips, and you kill the timer with a gunshot. Bishop pulled his duffel bag from the back. Popped the wheel-system from it. Dropped those pieces over his shoulder. Re-clipped the handles into a shoulder strap.

Sedaka said, "Anyway, in '98 when we reopened trade with Vietnam, I was assigned here to declassify Top Secret operational files stored in our embassy since the war."

Bishop opened his duffel. The Spyderco knife came out to cut.

"Infiltrations, covert actions—a bullshit goodwill Ho Chi Min chim-chiminey-cheroo. You know: no secrets between old enemies?"

With the blade, Bishop split the corner of his passport. Specially treated, the identification page peeled free.

"'Course they didn't show us jack shit. Still, Colonel Sanders got his triumphant chicken-strut back to Saigon." Sedaka hummed "Pomp and Circumstance," in love with his pompously circumstanced self because who wouldn't be?

Bishop shouldered out of his suit jacket. He pushed it inside out, cut into the right shoulder. From the inside padding he extracted a folded sheet of paper. A new passport photo page: a new number, a new identity. Bishop removed its sticky backing. He smoothed it into place where the old page went.

Sedaka sighed, like the weight of the world was first class delivered to his pudgy—no relation to Atlas either—back: "It probably sounds strange to you—'specially with all the tension surrounding these elections—but this place gets under your skin. In your blood. Said it before, I'll say it again: dig in before it disappears. I love it here. The Orient: and all its romantic, irrational, fallen, exotic, childlike, haunting, illogical, inferior, dishonest glory. Honest-to-God-go-figure. I figure: I'll stay just as long as Langley lets me."

"Sounds like illiberal, logical, capable *you* have made a career speaking on another culture's behalf."

Sedaka grit his teeth. Malaysia had also gotten into them as well. Nasty yellow. Gray edges. Bishop averted his gaze.

"It's *teh tarik*."

"Not a dentist. Can't help. Don't care."

"You will. *Teh tarik*: traditional 'pulled tea.' Milky. Popular—quite. Black tea drink. I take it with ginger. Can't live without it and worth the discoloration, as any Malay will tell ya. Nothing you can do about it. Spend any time here, you'll be on it lickityspittle-split. We'll find some. You'll try it. Least I can do."

Some car rides never seem to end. Sedaka's phone chirruped. He cracked the clamshell and answered, "Hello…? Hellooo…? Sorry, I can't hear a word you are saying." He clicked off. "Damn service out here. This country's for shit."

Bishop noticed a highway sign as they passed beneath it. "Pull off at the next exit."

"Actually, that takes us into the city. The caves are another eight kilometers. If we're to meet my plan—"

"Plan's changed. We've grown a tail."

Sedaka wrinkled his brow. "Someone followed you from Washington?"

"Someone's following you. Your passport and the way you grabbed my bag marked me at the airport."

"Please. I think not. Look, first of all, the Malaysian Special Branch has a lot more pressing business these days than following American diplomats."

"You're not a diplomat. You're a spy."

"And second—oh, give me a break. They don't know I'm anything other than a cultural attaché. By the way."

His phone rang again. He answered: "Helluuu! … I can't hear you!" He disconnected, said to Bishop, "But, second, I think you should at least show me the professional respect of accepting I know my tradecraft."

"They're in the yellow Honda three cars back."

Sedaka's eyes darted to his rearview mirror. He saw the two undercover security agents inside. He scowled.

Raja Laut Road is a crowded four-lane boulevard. A thin swath of exotic flowering shrubs forms the center divider rising from which is a long section of high-speed monorail track still under construction. It was plastered with political posters. Some for the candidate of earlier—"PDF: POPULAR DEMOCRATIC

FRONT"—but most were big and bold depictions of a stern older Malay in regal headdress with the caption: "A STRONG MALAYSIA = A FREE MALAYSIA. RE-ELECT PRIME MINISTER DR. MOHAMAD AZIZ."

"Make a left."

Pissed off, Sedaka snapped, "Bishop, I have been specifically tasked with getting you to van Eijk, and I will not let your paranoia stand in the way of my orders from the top."

"Left."

Sedaka glowered but moved into the turn lane. The yellow Honda glided past.

"Ha! Look at that. What did I tell you?"

"Make the turn."

Sedaka did. "Come on, give it to papa, what'd I tellya?"

"The gray Isuzu minivan pulling in two cars in front of us. Been stair-climbing cross streets. Just took over."

Sedaka made a derisive noise in his throat.

"Take a right at the next corner and hit the gas. Shake 'em both."

Sedaka made the turn onto a smaller lane, sped up. Entered a winding alley crowded with open storefronts and foot traffic. *Men in Black* and *A Bug's Life* beach towels; *Hello Kitty* backpacks and sixties-style bubble umbrellas; reused water bottles for sale as new with various degrees of liquid clarity. The alley fed into a giant square. It teemed with angry student demonstrators.

"Good try for a minute anyway," said Sedaka. "Want me to reverse? Flip a U-ey?"

"Stop the car. We're on foot from here."

"No. Too far, Bishop. This is where I absolutely draw the line."

Sedaka ratcheted the gearshift into reverse. He looked over his shoulder. Bishop switched off the ignition. The car stalled. "Goddamn you!"

For an instant, Sedaka was unhinged. Crazy-eyed. Bishop was already out of the car. Sedaka grabbed his cellphone. A car behind him honked. "For the record, my friend! You are responsible for this vehicle!"

Bishop shouldered his duffel, set off toward the demonstration.

"There's going to be hell to pay! I hope you're reading me!"

"Five by five, Papa," a Bishop over-the-shoulder toss. Moving off. Down the alley, away, and gone.

A chorus of horns. The driver of the car behind leaned out. Shouted in Malay. Sedaka turned, about to snap back, only to catch sight of the yellow Honda pulling into the alley three cars back.

Eye contact. Sedaka glared. The security agent in the passenger seat spoke into a radio. The horn chorus now an orchestra.

"Shit," Sedaka said. Wheeled. Hustled on Bishop's trail.

Once the Colonial British cricket fields, today Merdeka Square was packed with white-shirt, black-tie students. Sedaka pushed his way into the crowd. He was the only Caucasian in a sea of at least one thousand dark-skinned, angry young men. No females among them, their girlfriends and wives with mothers and aunts all wrapped in scarves, dutiful in their parlors, draperies closed when no male family is present.

The security men from the Honda approached from behind. Across the square, the gray minivan stopped. Two more Special Branch officers cleared that vehicle. Radio contact all the way around. They moved in from the far side—textbook.

Sedaka isn't. Textbook, that is. He's just bitched, bothered, and bewildered. Turned in circles. Lost. Sedaka's cellphone bleated at him again. He whipped it to his ear.

"THIS HAD BETTER BE GOOD!"

"It's Director Harker. Tell me you have Bishop." Sedaka stopped dead in his tracks.

"Yes. Absolutely, sir. I do—of course—I have him."

"Listen to me," said Harker. "Under no circumstances is Bishop to make contact with van Eijk. Got that? You are to detain him and take him to the embassy—"

Sedaka was jostled from behind. He lost his phone. He instinctively stooped to collect it. Couldn't find it—oh, well, bother—shoved before he straightened up. Hard knees: his on the pavement, theirs to his back and neck. Spit upon. Punched. These are students. They're angry. Less than half of them go to school, they're smarting too much from social justice, Islam-style. Sedaka started to go down—and if he did, well, there'd be no more "walking hand in hand with the one he loves" [decipher] as pavement smears don't generally have hands—which was the exact moment one of the Malaysian Special Branch officers from the yellow Honda grabbed Sedaka under his arms and out from under an intended head-stomp.

The two men's eyes met. And Sedaka—no relation—dazed, said, "I'm doing the bloody well best I can!"

<h1 style="text-align:center">13</h1>

From the moment Sedaka lied to Harker, Bishop was off the grid.

Three days.

The amount of time it took headquarters to figure out he had murdered Muir.

Same time it took us to figure out the destruction of Muir's former worldwide networks was Bishop's play all along. And Bishop, anticipating we'd gotten there, after three days, well, he checked backed in. All according to his long-range private OPLAN; a little hidey-ho back to the grid with a call to ask for the ransom I was now delivering. In the grand scheme of ransoms, it wasn't much amount-wise and no one bothered to question it—Bishop was only ever about principle, even Harker understood that, and so what? The big game-move for Harker was for the two of us to kill each other and who cares about Malaysia and who cares about yet another sideshow terrorist outfit, this without even so much as a pronounceable name: "Al-Qwe-ada? Al-Key-da, Al-Ka-eda—hear what I'm saying? And what's their mission? Their platform? Their ask? None. Until they get their shit together, which they never will. They're the JV team, and this Agency's focus has to be the big leagues—PLO, Hamas, Hezbollah, Islamic Jihad. Not even Iran plays with these Daffy Duck Al-Quackers."

And yet, Mads, they sure did a bang-up job on our embassies and blew up our missile destroyer in Yemen's charming harbor. They've also, through their Ramadan Moon sidekicks in Malaysia, brought me face to face with the best friend I'd ever had and his murderous pistol. Pro ball enough for me.

Two days later, plus an equator date change, Bishop and I met at the Christian Cemetery. Above the river. Center of town. Tombstones and trees pruned to keep them miniature. A sacred place tended by dramatic-looking, red-turbaned, bushy tea-dye-bearded Sikhs with faded military patches and rough rimmed war eyes. I'll remember those eyes forever—which won't be much longer. There were the cats, feral, but for some reason, as my experience of feral is meanness, malnutrition, and cruelty, these were all healthy bones and lustrous fur, orange and black, known to join nearby mourners who came to sit in the mornings. Poised tall and regal with skulls boxed like panthers, they appeared as distant and ancient.

I'd been slipped a pistol. A sweet, subcompact Sig-Sauer and one magazine of .380 ACP cartridges.

Three hours earlier, I'd landed at the COPE TIGER joint exercise, Korat Royal Thai Air Force Base, and thrown myself onto a UH-60M Black Hawk and—"Where to, sir?" some jackass named Nick Albro mouthed—rotored into Malaysia, where Albro knew I was going or he wouldn't have been on the bird asking. An American attaché to Thailand—meaning one of our non-official cover operators—Albro provided the gun. Whole thing a little demeaning 'cause, face it, the .380 is a ladies gun. Shape my hand like a pistol and point a finger: bigger and more menacing. Maybe the idea is for me to get the upper hand when Bishop laughs at my draw.

Albro asked, "You know what this is for?"

I said, "Nicky Boy, there's a Russell Aiken Stare Decisis—"

"Starry-what?"

"Legal term. A principle set on past precedent."

Sure, I could say Rule of Thumb, but I have my own precedents.

"Stare Decisis Numero Uno: Don't sign for anything you don't know what it's for."

No paperwork—I'd signed for nothing—I *that'll-show-you* shut my eyes for a rest.

BISHOP PANTHER-STEPPED through gravestones toward me from a Mercedes-Benz Unimog—a light-armored utility 4X4 short bed with Malaysian Royal Police light bar and markings. There might have been another person inside the vehicle. But if I had glimpsed someone, Bishop did not want them involved and they'd ducked out of sight. I was dizzy from the secret sharer inside my skull and could not be sure of much at that point. If the passenger did exist in flesh and blood, she was a beautiful, frightened woman in her thirties. Better than graveyard ghoulies. Or the orange cats beginning to approach me as if I had a pocketful of silver-sided, olive-oil-slick sardines.

Bishop was dressed in a formal black suit and tie, handkerchief, and all. Out of place for field operations, but, sadly, very much attired for a funeral. I watched him trudge uphill toward me, but in my mind's eye, I still saw the imagined woman. My dizziness subsided but her memory image grew in clarity.

In that, she is real. More than Bishop, more than I. The angel bearing reality.

And had our eyes met? Ever so briefly? Last moments loom large. Malay at first glance but with second thought, I allowed her face more white than peninsular brown. While her eyes and wide cheekbones would only ever be noticed as Asian, her nose-jaw-chin combination was Western, the nose narrow and delicate with an aquiline bridge, the jawline pronounced, chin strong, almost Native American in its prominence and familiar American nobility.

An ageless cat brushed my leg and my mind screamed *Kick it!* but I picked it up for a last living comfort, scratched its ear and it scratched me, drew blood, and dropped to scamper off and report to the others the dead fool still bled.

"Tom. This is a disaster."

"Our stock in trade, brother."

"You want what I brought?"

"Don't want to kill you to get it."

He waggled a pistol he'd acquired, aimed the barrel at God in the sky. He always shoots to kill.

"I'm not going to judge you for what you've done," I said. Tossed the black canvas satchel between us. "It hurts too much."

"Russell, you're judging me entirely. My mistake was believing all these years you were the truer man."

"When have I lied to *you*?"

"We both know you're doing it right now."

I pretended that I didn't see his heart was broken and that, observing his physical wounds, somewhere in the past two days of his Malaysia walkabout he'd suffered violent torture.

I said, "That better man now's you?"

"Seeing we're facing off in a graveyard over an escape kit, no.'"

The Sikhs walked, all at once from every corner, to the safety of their stone shack.

"Neither of us have any penance inside us. And I've got nothing to go home to," I said, fumbling with my gun to do my job and balance accounts with his father.

"That was slow and stupid. Not how you do it, Annie Oakley."

"Slow and stupid wins the race."

Bishop walked to the middle between us, his gun still pointed to an empty heaven above. Mine was aimed at him. He didn't care.

"You know how that story finishes?" he said.

"What story?"

"'The Turtle and the Hare.' You were his Greek student. You went to college—"

"Latin and philosophy. Not Greek."

"I was Class of Vietnam. Never had any options."

"When you reach for that bag, I'm supposed to shoot you," I said. "I mean it."

"This isn't my first rodeo."

He reached. He took it. I didn't shoot. He turned his back on me. His gun was still raised like a duelist. He said, "The next race—after the one where the turtle—"

I couldn't let him get away with this: "Tortoise. Turtles swim."

"—after the *tortoise* beat the rabbit, he went up against a snail. Knowing he'd beat a snail, he took himself a big lead—"

Bishop opened the driver's door of the police Unimog and placed the satchel on the seat. He exchanged words with the woman who was or wasn't there. I felt a river of sweat down my back. I fought dizziness. I understood I would not get off a shot—by choice—but in the end he would have no choice.

I don't care that Nate is not my son.

If you love me and the other guy doesn't love you—

I've proven a good father to Jessie. She needs me. Us. Her brother. A chance.

I'll start going back to the doctor—what's losing my hair at this point, anyway? Better than losing my mind, right? Radiation isn't the worst—the hands of my wristwatch never hurt counting down my time on this earth. The sun blasts everyone with radiation every day. Especially in steam-sweltering Malaysian graveyards.

The woman—imagined of my tumor—peered up, proven real in flesh and bone, but my brain still played it tricks and I saw my eldest sister unh, err—my *middle* sister—my whatsername—

Fuck! My own sister's name. I can't remember.

Panic. Hold the gun steady. Shoot. NO! This fucking brain! Shout: "Tom!"

The Eurasian woman who couldn't have been there sistering on my mind snapped to my gaze as Bishop spoke to her through the rear gate, but I'd lost focus on her thinking about everything else I was going to lose, which began with everything I'd already lost and never got over.

Dad. Not Muir. *My* dad.

The one who never came home from that truck wreck on the Kansas highway, burned to death among the sunflowers, the day, and the man we lied about to allow us to live off the insurance. Muir-pulled harp strings.

Bishop slammed the door. The woman ducked from sight. I flinched like he'd already shot me.

He faced me again and shook his head. His father's mocking of me my whole life built into Bishop's last simple smile. "You gonna finish this, or am I?" but he'd already fired his gun. At me. Unfairly before the word *or*. Interrupting my question with a bullet's answer.

This gives me some clarity as the slug digs into me and I hit the ground. I recall Muir's admonition to be more like a tree; but as my thoughts fade to nothing, I am reminded all people are grass and wither.

Maybe Harker is smarter than all of us? Do any of us care about Malaysia? I can't find a reason. All I can think about is time. Time never surrenders, never treaties, never gives us a truce. It is relentless and it carries all things belonging to time with it where it chooses. Without compromise.

I told you, Madeline, Malaysia would be my final landing platform. My first rest on my way to my eventual permanent resting place. My vision fades, my mind awhirl, my last sight: Tom Bishop standing over me, staring into my eyes as my vision goes black and my last jumbled thought—"Hello, Dimitri," says Muir to the centaur, as President Merkin Muffley says it to Soviet Premier Dimitri Kisov in my Dr. Strangelove *recruitment before they annihilated all life on Planet Earth.*

PART TWO

ILLUSIONS

"So let not this present life deceive you."

—*Quran*, "Surah Fatir": 5

14

Well, Mads, that's it for me as the centaur of attention. A long set of uneventful flights to a resting place among the cemetery gravestones and their sentinel senile felines. But now that you know where I end up, wouldn't it be appropriate to go back three days and let you judge the path by which Bishop came to the end of me?

After having evaded Sedaka at the Dataran Merdeka student riot, Bishop stood a small figure beneath colorful and exotic idols dancing around Lord Murugan, philosopher-warrior god of Hinduism, perched atop the cave's awesome black mouth. To understand awesome, understand this: Bishop stands six feet, three inches—six-five when he's thinking about it. The golden Murugan towered 140 feet above him, and the limestone pile enveloping the cave stood a good 300 feet above the divine totem. Duffel ditched, business suit replaced by rugged, vaguely athletic tactical clothing, Bishop faced out and looked down the treacherously steep, double-wide stairway leading from the parking area below. More strange effigies decorated the railings every tenth riser landing, their demigod grimaces spread either in encouragement—"Hey man, you'll make it to the top"—or in prescience that they already know your fate and you're never going to reach the top of anything no matter how many stairs you climb. This is where Lord Hanuman, the monkey king, creator of all mischief, scares the crap out of worshippers when bursting to life: his furry minions lunge from the railing for purse straps or carried food offerings. These chattering gangs of macaques scamper off, shrieking cosmic laughter.

The monkeys and the gods knew to stay the hell away from Tom Bishop.

A constant stream of worshippers in casual and traditional garb climbed toward the shrine from the parking blacktop filled and filling with buses. As a clot of them filed past Bishop into the cave, he joined with the group and made his way through the entrance chokepoint.

Once inside, the Batu Caves reveal themselves as a vast central gallery double the size of Notre Dame. No rose window. Instead, shafts of fading daylight pierce jagged fissures in the ceiling, a ceiling festooned with huge stalactites that collect condensation that falls *ploop, plop, pip, polp-poolp* as Hindu holy water. Subtle and unnerving, each droplet represents the unbrokeness of present and past in unending chorus.

Plop-ploop-plip hitting and echoing over the prayers of the faithful who, fanning out from the main entrance, make their way into smaller twisted grottos, intricate along the sides where altars and strange half-human half-animal effigies await burnt offerings. Wreathes of bright flowers and incense left to cut the stench of rotting fruit tribute. Uplifted tribute uplifted with the echo. The echo: contemplate gods and heaven and Vishnu to infinity.

The shrine continued to fill.

Poolp.

Plop.

Plip.

The ticking heart of religion and spirit.

Bishop purchased incense. He bought a tapered candle from a beggarwoman. The woman had a sweet face if you allowed for the missing eye and its open cavity as the lid had remained with the knife that plucked the eyeball. He lit the incense as he perceived the custom.

Smoke curled.

The echo mesmerized.

Bishop waited his turn before the elephant-headed man-deity Ganesh. He stepped forward and noticed a chalk line scraped along the wall.

Child's play; a spy's pay.

He stuck his incense into old wax and palmed the chalk stripe away.

Thunder rolled.

Bishop headed for another side grotto. A line of worshippers waited to enter with candles. Near the front, Bishop noticed a stunning woman. Malaysian features: luminous almond eyes, cheekbones makeup advertisers die for, rose-petal lips, but her skin was light and her nose and her jaw—well, I've already gone into that. She was something like a Vietnam War baby. The kind the Chinese, years later, pimped throughout Asia after the American GIs returned to their Vietnam playgrounds: Thailand and Malaysia and Singapore. An "I'm gonna wash that whore right outta my hair—just this one last time" indifferent sex-tour sensibility to screw their own countrymen's oft-sprung, offspring left-behinds. Those women usually stayed in their fuck dens or handled their money well enough to own their whorehouses. The hardness of heart condemned to and required did not exist in this mixed-race vision. There was something untouchable about her that shone through her secretiveness as something recently shaken.

She stared at Bishop long enough to acknowledge and to be acknowledged as an individual equal under the Eye(s) of God(s) but unequal in the eye(s) of society, then abruptly broke eye contact. Bishop brushed it off. They were the only two whites in the shrine, that bright flash of wavetop on a dark, windy lake that catches the eye in a storm; he told himself that's all that had attracted them to each other, and his gaze sought another.

A man. Dutch colonial. CIA-payrolled agent. Dand van Eijk.

He must be there—no other reason to abandon the ID-card-cast forests of Kosovo if van Eijk wasn't. Dand van Eijk would be inside the Dark Caves. The dead Muir promise.

Of my own free will, I shot the arrow.

The chalk line trailed off in the same direction as the woman. Bishop moved with the jostling crowd. Thunder boomed again and the woman did not look back before she disappeared into darkness.

THE DARK CAVES are a twisting of corridors. Smoke hangs dull and sweet in the air. The wax of a million candles, once burned, covers the limestone walls and the floor. One thousand more candles glowed and flickered as worshippers affixed fresh flame offerings in ancestors' melted pasts.

Bishop moved through the crowd. Purpose glowed in his eyes. He searched the faces: Hindi, young and old, all caught in a hypnotic state of religious ecstasy.

More thunder.

Cue lightning.

Wind funneled through the corridor cast dancing light upon the mysterious woman. The slight curl of her hair intercurled by the smoke, her face as familiar to Bishop as a dream. Or a memory being made that instant. Their eyes met again. This time held. There was something strange about her. A desire to know her. A growing fear that "never to know" (instead of "forever, yes") would ever be enough.

He moved her way.

She placed something among the candles. Downcast eyes lure. Nothing lurid. She desired Bishop to see that. The crowd shifted. Bishop lost sight of her. He reached the place she'd stood. He noticed what she'd left for him.

A broken stick of chalk among the candles.

The rain hit, hard and tropical. The Hindi chanted and swayed.

As I swayed: my first collapse at Jessie's school a few hours before the MRI introduced me to my tumor.

Crevices in the ceiling allowed broken showers. Candles guttered. Candles hissed out.

Bishop caught another glimpse of the chalk-stick woman. Far ahead. She ducked into an adjoining natural corridor. The intensity in his eyes was frightening as he stalked her back toward the main cave ahead. A wild wind whipped through the corridor, extinguishing every remaining flame. Darkness swallowed Bishop. The crowd surged. They pushed him; rainwater mixed with the slick sweat of their limbs. He fought his way after the woman, blindly forward.

At the cave's mouth, the downpour cascaded in a wall of cliff-top runoff like liquid glass framed in an oval of leaden daylight; glittering and pounding, it was broken by two Malaysian Special Branch officers. They rose into sight from the gray of the stairs, lifted by their riser-to-riser ascent like the strange, mythical gods. Handguns out, they moved across the dirty wet floor of the cave searching for Bishop.

The officers identified him. Radios lifted. Spoken into. Swift movement.

Pat-splash, pat-splash, sandal dash. The chalk-stick woman passed them without notice, headed to the mouth of the cave. She looked back at Bishop, once. Her eyes guilty. Terrified, as if seeing her imminent death returned in his glance.

They rushed Bishop. Seized him.

"Mister Tommy Bishop, you are under arrest for espionage," said the first officer.

The two pinned him between them. They hustled Bishop for the stairs. The long, steep stairway, 272 steps, slick with rain, empty except for the woman, *pat-splash-splat-pat* yellow zori butterfly wings, halfway down—feet fluttering fast, bright against the gray shadows brought by the storm—her whole lithe figure careening for the parking lot.

Bishop let his captors guide him onto the stairs and rainwater parted at the steel-capped toes of his boots. His captors' feet moved, steady at first. All cops, world over, lock into pace. Bishop matched their pace. He leaned forward. He subtly increased their speed. By the time they understood that his pace controlled theirs—and too fast at that—the two officers shared a look across the back of Bishop's neck, and it was too late.

"Un lâche fuit en arrière, loin de nouvelles choses. Un homme de courage fuit en avant, au milieu de nouvelles choses." Damn Muir, but I'd gone home from his garden goodbye and found it. Jacques Maritain, The Range of Reason, *Muir's philosophy mentor at Princeton. An identity of Muir I'd never known.*

Bishop leaned fully forward, and ain't gravity a concrete bitch? When she grabs, hers is not a grip you can break. Bishop twisted his torso as he threw his weight forward, adding momentum to their fall. The three men went down hard onto the concrete stairs. The first officer, who'd made the "Tommy" accusation, lost his grip. He plummeted. Head over heels. In deed dead, indeed. Alliterate that to the sound of skull clunking stair, obliterating bone.

Bishop tucked into the second officer. Rolled with him tangled, five stairs, ten: *WHAM!* Their bodies slammed into the center railing.

The first officer came to rest thirty-some stairs below. Blood gushed from the crown of his broken skull. His last thoughts ran away red on the rainwater.

The second officer pushed to his knees. Went for his gun. Bishop lashed out with his feet. He caught the man around the neck, vised him between his ankles. He gave himself a violent flip. They tumbled ten more stairs. The officer's gun skittered to the bottom. Bishop rose, shaking his limbs, fighting against the clenching pain of his fall. He tore keys from the man's belt. His every fiber focused on the parking lot.

A fast glimpse of the chalk-stick woman boarding a bus.

Bishop looked to his adversaries. Neither moved. One dead, the other didn't want to be. Didn't have it in him to continue forcing the issue with the American spy. He knew where Bishop would end it and he wasn't brave. They shared a look.

Bishop winked, because there is a side of my false brother that is cruel, and then he plunged downward, scooping up the officer's gun as he reached the bottom. Bishop shoved the pistol into his waistband. He unlocked his cuffs.

The bus turned out of the lot in front of him. Bishop's eyes met the eyes of the chalk-stick woman, her glum face framed in a window, her head now covered by a fashionable purple scarf as hijab-lite, then the bus was past.

"A coward flees backward, away from new things. A man of courage flees forward, in the midst of new things." Jacques Maritain, I do not forget you.

The surviving officer pulled himself to his knees. Beaten and forlorn. A monkey cocked its head. Gibbered at the Special Branch officer. The man ran his hands through his wet hair. He shouldered off all offered help. His eyes searched for Bishop as the bus pulled from view.

But Bishop was gone.

<h1 style="text-align:center">15</h1>

A STARK SELF-ASSESSMENT. I am not one who overly obsesses on nonsensical flights of fancy or frivolous abstracts. As Dr. Henry Higgins said—his fictionality notwithstanding—"I'm an ordinary man." Duly, then, I owe it to myself to conclude this "symbiotic" dance-golf bullshit of Harker's because I hate loose ends and I don't want to leave this earth with it stringing along my conscious eternal conscience.

So I braced him. A couple days after our India Clay Pot/Arthur Murray encounter (but before the Malaysia *mishegas*), riding the escalator inside the green glass goblin New Headquarters Building atrium, four stories of planters overflowing with shopping mall foliage, off the CIA gift store and the CIA art gallery. Harker joined the ride below me. It's a long escalator, and slow. I turned to face him.

"Acting Director, I was thinking about what you said the other night."

He gave me doubtful eyes over frameless glasses. "Bet that didn't go on too long."

He insulting me or himself?

"About golf. And dance." The remora that defines symbiosis—be it sucking on his golf shaft or soft-shoeing away with a hand cupping dimpled white balls. His lip curled. He didn't say anything, so I continued:

"Would that be mutualism: both dance and golf benefit? Commensalism: only one benefits while the other is neither helped nor harmed? Or parasitism: dance or golf—take your pick—one's killing the other inside?"

"Don't jerk me off, Aiken. I've had a long day."

Too late I realized we'd arrived at the top of the moving stairs and my heels hit the part where they're stairs no more and the moving stops. I tripped, dizzy. Harker huffed air in mockery and chasséd past me.

"Guess a little golf would help me," I said as I reconnected with him.

Harker stopped. Pushed his glasses up the bridge of his nose with the middle finger he liked to show me.

He said, "Just when I think you're moronic enough, you prove me incorrect. Dance is about fleetness of foot."

"Ness," I said.

"Ness what?"

"Footness. Fleetness of footness? It's the correct way to say that. Middle English—Cha-Cha Chaucer, I believe."

He squinted. Had I stammered or punned? He cleared his throat. "I see. Learn something every day."

I gave my pathetic look. Muir liked to remark, whenever I'd give him the opening, it wasn't something I needed to give. I always kept my patheticness available. Harker ditched it and walked on. I fell into step.

"The two are symbiotic." He clipped his words. "Listen, because I'll only say it once."

"Great, because I start my golf lessons this week."

Golf is a fad. I hate fads.

"God help your club."

I can Jeremiah that into such a crossword.

He said, "Your golf bag is your dance program. Consider this: there are clubs built for specific situations—teeing off, putting, or the sand trap—and there are dances that do the same."

"Sure," I said. "I'm starting to see it." Ever were it possible to see through mud.

"At Arthur Murray, we laser focus on the 'interrelated system of dancing.'"

"I'll tell you this, sir. I've been opposed to less."

He cocked his head a solid second trying to decipher a code not meant entirely for him. Too far into his twin passions, he missed mine and went on.

"Every club you carry in your golf bag is perfectly mated to a style of dance," said Harker.

"Like swing. Golf swing, swing dancing."

"A golf swing isn't a club."

"So there isn't one for swing?"

"There is if you would stop interrupting."

"Go on. I won't speak," I said. "But is your driver the same as driving the golf cart?"

"Your driver is your waltz." He waited. I blinked until he went on. "Both your driver and your waltz are reserved for single, special moments where grace, posture, balance are most singularly on display."

"A wedding reception."

"Quite."

"At a golf club," I added.

"Alright, Aiken. Are you—?"

"Yes: if 'interested'? I am. Distinctly."

Harker smiled to himself. As I think about him, I realize he doesn't smile at others. Nothing makes him happy enough to share. But Harker makes Harker proud. "You think you're clever, but, you having brought up swing, this will seal my point: swing is the 5 iron of dance. Both are the most utterly versatile for any dance or golf situation you ever will find yourself in. Bringing us to the putter."

"Tap dancing," I declared.

"We don't teach tap dancing," he said as he might have said they didn't teach retching.

I gave my chin a wipe. Took another stab. "Because I meant 'foxtrot.'"

Harker cocked his head. "But that's exactly right. You are getting this..."

"Thank you." I clutched him. Hand on the shoulder, hand to the hand. "This game, golf, is gonna be fun." Handshake as dance posture.

"It's not a game. It's a sport." He shivered away from me.

I grinned. I pistol-pointed. "You got to go—you're in a hurry, I know—but I always thought golf *must* be a game. At least according to the dictionary. Grab one and look up *sport* and look up *game*. You'll see what I mean."

I turned, as if to leave. Took one slow step away, patient, enjoying an imagined zinging of trout line—

Fishing is not *a fad if it feeds you.*

—relishing with sweet expectation the bite next to come.

"Wait a minute, Aiken. What exactly do you mean?"

Jesus and I have an altogether different definitional disagreement between us. The meaning of "a fisher of men."

I turned with childlike innocence and secret spite. "Well, see, Mr. Acting Director, a sport has opponent-bearing conflict on result. Active offense and active defense actively impacting one another. Games don't have that. A golf tournament: no player ever interacts with the other in pursuit of victory. Croquet is more a lawn sport than golf." I pantomimed a roquet chuck with the appropriate tongue cluck. "Your play affects your opponent and vice versa. The Olympic Games are called games for a reason... Track and Field?"

"Ha! Olympians don't play sports?" Harker's eyes gleamed. "What about wrestling, water polo—?"

"Judo," I added.

"And boxing, fencing—"

"Fencing, Acting Director, sir, *exactly*."

Touché.

I waited until he discerned what he'd done before saying, "Who better than you to prove the dance-golf game-sport paradox?"

One last bit about fishing. It's unique in sports as the opponent never signs up for the opposing team.

SOAKED TO THE BONE, Bishop perched on the bus's wide wooden rear bumper. His hands gripped the web canvas of a luggage net. He hurt inside and out. Espionage is thought of as a game. The Great Game, as Kipling introduced it to the world. But at Bishop's level, it will always be a contact sport. Your moves, their moves, the target's moves: all impact.

The bus headed onto a rural highway leaving the city. The storm abated. Passing a row of storefronts, Bishop witnessed Chinese shop owners sweeping sidewalk glass from shattered windows. Other Chinese scrubbed at spray-painted graffiti. A crescent moon, the star of Ramadan.

Somewhere in the evening, a mullah called the faithful to prayer.

The bus drove into a poor Malay village cast in strange orange light from the falling sun. A group of shirtless men worked on a canoe. The jungle encroached, insects screaming and insistent, then an open-walled mosque pavilion. Whisked by, a glimpse between columns: the devout at prayer inside. Colorful *sarong* and black *congcok* caps bearing down on the floor.

The farther into the Malaysian interior the bus tracked, Bishop noticed, with each hamlet and clustered shack village, an increasing number of posters and flags depicting the same white crescent and star of Ramadan on a green field. He'd been in Kosovo—saving Muslims. None of us really knew who al-Qaeda was and why to pay attention, and Bishop, that day, that time, probably even less. This was an offshoot: a political party formed to celebrate bin Laden—one step ahead of the bread line's triumphant six-shmuck summit. I mean, give me a break; or better, give one to Bishop. Just a simple flag and basic posters and simmering hatred by a political party with little hope for power at the ballot box.

Yet sometimes you hear a piece of radio music you're disinterested in but don't care enough to change the station. A sax, a trumpet, or a clarinet punch through with unfamiliar beauty and passion. A rhythm and harmony you don't know, know you never will, but nevertheless want to hear more as you feel its tug. The mullahs, loudspeaker prayers in wake after the bus, were that strain of music; for one fleeting second in passage, Bishop felt the tug and knew as Ulysses the sirens' call. And Bishop knew before any of us: the call to those who were listening was beauty deadly, strange, and irresistible.

THE BUS CLATTERED over a Marston Mat steel bridge. British Army-engineered perforated steel planking. The bus stopped under a bare-bulb streetlamp. The chalk-stick woman stepped off and the bus door sighed shut. She looked around. No one in sight. She self-consciously adjusted her headscarf. The bus shuddered into the black night. She stood a moment alone in the lamplight. Tangled green foliage dripped with water. Strange birds cried in the hot night. She hitched the waist of her loose cotton dress to keep it clear of the wet and the mud. She walked down the dark jungle road.

Bishop watched her every move from within the thick undergrowth along the riverbank under the bridge. He let her get some distance before he scrambled after her. He deliberated a brief operational inventory that ended with his acceptance that, if it came to it, he would kill her.

Bishop took to a narrow animal trail. Perhaps compacted by miniature deer chevrotain, or maybe those Darwinian cast-off bearcats who'd just had their Malaysian national day; scritched out by ubiquitous monkeys who'd left the path strewn with gnawed and half-eaten decaying fruit. He didn't worry much about snakes. Back in the Boy Scouts, Bishop hunted and sold snakes to pet stores and how different can a cobra be from a rattlesnake? Of course, the idea of a 350-pound, 20-foot reticulated python dropping a crushing loop around him from the gnarls of a parasitic strangling fig handily knocks the crown off the California kingsnakes he'd formally marveled at for size. He'd leash-looped a seven-footer back in his Griffith Park days—five feet the barest necessity for the private collector who'd financed the hunt. No, the only creature Bishop concerned himself with meeting was the Malaysian moonrat. Large as large housecats, the moonrat possesses the most malodorous defense mechanism of any animal on the planet. Bishop required his jungles smelled a certain way and moonrat wasn't that way. Moonrats make getting skunk-sprayed a perfuming by comparison.

Jessie's first Christmas. She asked me for perfume.
"Which one?"
"It's called 'Tester.' It's on every counter."
God bless the child.

But as Bishop swiftly and silently negotiated the muddy, root-seething trail that ran parallel to the vehicle road his quarry quick-walked, he was the only jungle animal to be seen while the eyes of the moonrats and the pythons and the mouse deer, salamanders, spiders, and monkeys, a pigeon and its mate, pink-necked and green, blinked and watched and watched and blinked, concealed and prickling with fight-or-flight, some less than a foot as he passed. If Bishop noticed, he ignored them; the largest predator, he was the most dangerous game. He knew, if he looked, they could not meet his eyes.

People are funny in their inability to see the wildlife that thrives all about them. We grip and develop our living spaces and lay our roads and never know there are animal roads that parallel, intersect, cross—lop-top your agapanthus, your roses, gobble up your dogs and cats—every city, every county, country, everywhere; Bishop knows to find them, use their trails to hunt man. Even birds highway the ground, and Bishop learned in the Scouts how to follow crows across asphalt.

He closed the gap between himself and the chalk-stick woman. She abruptly turned from the road onto a driveway, unaware of the beast who stalked her. Two tire trenches hardened into the clay like fossilized trilobite trackways entered the jungle on the other side of the road. Bishop waited for her to follow their trace runs and disappear into the gloom. He dashed across.

Pulled the pistol from his waistband.

Mist rose from the wet ground and rose from the dripping leaves with returning humidity. Bishop took comfort from the shadows that embraced him. He could hear the splash of the river, hear the creak of the black-barked banana trees, which grew a clustered fruit nothing like bananas. The driveway ended in a small clearing, the tracks disappearing into an old wooden garage converted from the original *rumah dapur* kitchen annex. A handmade *rumah melayu* native-style house loomed in the twilight. Constructed of stained and sealed dark timber, mortice-and-tenon joints, dovetails, and pegs instead of metal fasteners and nails; intricately carved and latticed hinged sidings meant to be flung wide to catch the breeze; a thatched and gabled vernacular roof, ornamental adornments on the corners and at the peak: the entire structure perched high on pilings half over the river that twisted around the property to bounce singing in rock and root splash, the *quick-quick-quick, ow-oo-ah* of frogs, and the *tut, we-ow knock-knock-knock* of the nightjar swooping for insects over the water.

At the top of the wide, heavy stairs and across the veranda, the front door shut, and the chalk-stick woman locked herself inside. Bishop watched, waited. A single light bloomed within.

Warm. Safe.

Target.

Bishop checked the first bullet seated in the chamber. He knew he had arrived at the home of van Eijk. For whatever reason, she'd stood in for his contact; she'd subverted Muir's designs by false witness. For her sake, he hoped he would encounter van Eijk at home. He jigged the lock with his knife and stepped into the dim interior.

The smell of furniture wax mixed with Malaysian cooking spices and mingled with incense flooded Bishop's nostrils. This was a traditional *rumah ibu*. One single large room. Patterned Malaysian blackwood flooring. Heavy Asian chests and chairs and tables. Rough-hewn support beams to divide the living spaces—day room, kitchen, bedroom—mosquito netting over a low, wide bed. A somberness hard to exaggerate in its rejection of luxury.

The woman stood before the mirrored doors of a carved armoire. A light bathed her golden from above. Her face shone moist from the heat of the night. Her expression was one of deep weariness, as though she carried the yoke of a heavy life on her shoulders and accepted being an ox rather than the humming-bird she'd been promised by her mother in the Malaysian lullabies of her earliest youth. She opened the armoire doors. Touched the purple knot of her hijab where it lay upon the hollow of her throat.

Bishop prepared to announce himself before she removed her head covering, but her hands slipped the dress straps from her shoulders before he could speak. It billowed around her ankles. Her naked back and the rest of her glistened with perspiration.

Guilt and shame assailed the man. When hidden behind the precision-ground ocular and objective lenses of the highly cali-brated sniper scope, paired to long-range anonymity, Bishop could always buffer his work with impersonality; while he held no compunction in close killing, gratuitous humiliation was foreign to his nature. The right-here right-in-his-face right-now hypoc-risy of his code inflamed his honor and brought a sour taste to his mouth. Where the chalk-stick woman was simply naked, Bishop stood bare in the unwashed ugliness of his soul.

Oblivious to Bishop, the woman studied herself—the purity of her humanity and the purple wrapper of humility before God. She yanked the hijab and her hair fell, and Bishop focused on his gunsight blocking out the woman whose form it framed. She lifted a silk robe from a hook. Something cheap. Old. Clutched to her breast like a treasure.

The chalk-stick woman turned to the wall panel that opened onto a balcony above the river. She unlatched it and stepped into the evening. She stood nude in an easterly breeze as it wafted across the dark water rolling to wherever. Skin cool, she ran her arms through silk sleeves and loosely bowed her robe.

The was no sign of van Eijk, no indication a man had ever been here. Bishop didn't want what would happen next to go badly for the woman, but he wouldn't let himself care if it did.

The bullet was seated and, Bishop always imagined, warmed as he warmed to its decision.

She returned to her armoire and hung her dress. She shut the doors. This time in the mirrors she saw not only herself but reflected in the gloom behind her: Tom Bishop aiming his pistol at her back.

She cried out and grabbed the front of her robe. Acknowledgment shot electricity between them; the ignominy of what he'd stolen with his eyes burned him with disgrace.

"All I want's van Eijk."

She steadied her breath. "Van Eijk is gone. He's never coming back."

"I don't believe you."

She locked eyes with him in the glass, defiance burning through her fear. "What you believe won't make it different. Van Eijk was my father and he died more than twenty years ago."

16

I NSIDE THE MALAYSIAN Special Branch Headquarters, Sedaka burned with fury. He faced the sinewy, eyeliner-wearing Colonel Josef Ibrahim, whom he liked less than he respected, which was to say: he held the eel-faced Malaysian behind the desk in utter contempt.

"Bishop was going to do exactly what I said he would, but the second I made contact at the airport, your assholes were all over us."

"My officers followed procedure. Once you ran—"

"Bishop made them. Of course we ran."

"One of my best men is dead!" yelled Colonel Ibrahim.

"'Best'? You're lucky it's only one." Sedaka wagged a finger in the colonel's face. "Now back off. It's the only way I can help you people."

"I will not have you CIA running free in my country."

Sedaka remained in his chair. "From where I'm standing, that's what you've got right now… unless you let me take care of Bishop my way."

"I have zero faith in your way."

"Then, Colonel," said Sedaka, "you need to make a decision. Do you desire what Bishop is after or not?"

He indicated a gaudy oil painting of Prime Minister Dr. Mohamad Aziz holding a dove that hung on the wall behind the colonel. "Certainly, your precious prime minister does—only way to hold on to power. Keep the world at bay after he loses tomorrow's election and throws this wretched country into civil war."

Sedaka waited for contradiction. Ibrahim's little black eyes filled with malice. An Orientalist expert on the Vietnam War and at nothing else that might help him save his skin if the trouble aimed at Bishop turned sights on him, Sedaka plied his face into a false mask of satisfaction.

BISHOP AIMED the gun at the woman in the robe. "So the message—causing everyone so many problems—was from you?"

"No."

"You sent the message. You serviced the drop. You were at the meet. So here's the life-or-death question: what do you know about the burned networks? Our vanished agents all over the globe—the answers that the van Eijk code promised?"

"I don't know anything."

Bishop thumbed back the pistol's hammer.

He was good at this. He'd put more years into this than van Eijk had already put in the ground. Spent the past two rogue, on his own and dead inside, getting even better. He buried worthless shame.

He wanted to kill—something, someone, anyone.

This one.

Where had life gone?

Why did cancer take Elizabeth? Because so much care had been given, love poured out, and wasn't that a more extreme protection than cancer's curse to keep her safe?

He missed Elizabeth. He wanted a second chance with his wife. He wanted a second chance with a father who he believed hadn't wanted him... but had stalked his every footstep. He wanted to shoot this woman for all of it: if he couldn't bring his dead wife to life, or get responsibility out of his dead father, he'd put a live woman to death.

She stared at the gun. "Go to hell."

Bishop struck, grabbing her robe with his free hand, shoving the barrel of his gun under her chin.

"Don't send me to places I'm all too ready for. What do you know?"

She shut her eyes.

"What do you know?!"

She shook her head, as if denying him would make his hands release her clothing, make him disappear.

"You're fucking crazy."

"Answer me. You were at the meet. What made you run?!"

"I got frightened!"

"Why?!"

She opened eyes ablaze with revulsion. "Look at yourself in the mirror. Look at yourself! Who wouldn't run from you? God, I just want you people out of my life."

For an instant, Bishop didn't move. Then he did a strange thing. He released her and lowered his gun.

"Who's running you? Who put you up to this? Tell me that."

"I never met him."

"Who?"

"His name is Nathan Muir."

Bishop didn't bat an eye. "How did he contact you?"

"A package. It came by regular postal carrier."

"To you or your father?"

"I told you: my father is dead."

"Muir knew?"

She twitched her shoulders. "It was addressed to my father."

"You kept it anyway? Didn't throw it away? Didn't turn it in? Participated."

She didn't answer. Nameless to him: those eyes, the robe, the river. Her naked body he'd taken in and couldn't erase.

She gave Bishop a helpless look. "His instructions threatened to expose me…"

"You said it was addressed to your father."

"Guess Nathan Muir knew about the daughter left behind."

"What about your mother?"

"It wasn't a greeting card."

"The money van Eijk's received from Nathan Muir all these years—money you've been collecting? It's CIA money."

"I didn't know that. I never heard of Nathan Muir."

"Doesn't make it any less a theft. Where did you think the monthly payout came from?"

"A trust." Then foolish: "My inheritance."

"All you've inherited is me. Who fed you this nonsense?"

"The sisters who ran my boarding school. My family lawyer. Everyone. My mother died when I was six. How was I to know? What else was I to think? Orphan kids don't have time to balance the family books."

And her gaze turned inward as the bitterness of words aimed at Bishop ricocheted back into unintended memories unrelated to him or to Muir or to her current situation—whatever they were, they were not to be betrayed.

"What else do you do when you're not messing where you don't belong?"

"I work for the government." Her shoulders slumped. "If they find out I've been taking CIA money all these years, I'll be arrested and put to death."

With that she expressed the crux of their predicament better than Bishop, so he let it sit with her. See how she liked that for a better companion. He watched her sink further into herself.

"Let's start over." He twitched his gun. "Sit on the bed."

"I'm not going to do that."

Bishop snatched her arm and forced her there with a shove.

"Muir had you put together the message. The message that went to the embassy, from your pretend-alive dead father. The message that summoned me."

"I didn't know what it said. It was already written. Random letters. A code."

"He sent it to you, and you sent it off to the embassy. Through some Indian kid."

"It was the instructions. The threat of exposure. I found a street kid. Can't be traced back to me. A crime of espionage is worse than drugs—not even a trial. I told you: that's how things go here, and in my job—"

"Where do you work?"

"The Ministry of State. I'm a social economist for the government."

"Your name—what're you called?"

"I won't tell you."

His eyes appraised her, her returning spirit.

"What else did Muir's instructions say?"

"He said you'd come for the package. To give it to you. Only to you."

"You ran from me."

"There was a copy of a photograph I was to show you. To prove the package genuine."

He didn't want to shoot her anymore but kept the weapon in hand and ready in case he changed his mind. She seemed to sense this and thrust forward from the bed in a move to step around him. Their bodies were close. He could smell the tang of her sweat and the fresh renewing clutch of the jungle that came from within her, less floral, more a scent of savory herbs. To nourish. To heal.

"Move. I'm getting it for you."

He forced the impression of her invading his senses from his mind. He stepped aside. The woman lifted open a chest at the foot of her bed. She withdrew a journal identical to those I'd seen burned in Muir's fireplace, seen before that, boxed at his home in Captiva. She opened the journal and removed a folded copy of a photograph. Bishop's high-school graduation. Like the one splattered bloody on Muir's desk at Princeton: Bishop smiling, proud, hopeful, spied upon by his father-photographer. She forced the two items into Bishop's dirty hands.

"I'm done. Take them and go."

The journal was embossed "1968," Bishop opened it and flipped through the pages. Encrypted with a substitution code.

He asked the chalk-stick woman, "You hungry?"

"What?"

Bishop went into the living area. He found a writing table. She marveled to watch him sit.

"You need to leave!"

"Can you cook?"

"I won't cook for you."

"Do it." He placed his handgun on the table with a dull, uncompromising clunk. "I'm going to be here awhile."

Bishop pulled a stone from his pocket. Flat and shuffleboard-shaped. The arrowhead I was supposed to get to him after Muir's death. I'd been unable to remember it the day Gladys found Muir murdered. Bishop considered the numbers etched into its surface, the three letters. A-V-R. He found a pencil in the table's small drawer. He studied the first string of code, referred to the arrow-head. After a few moments, using the numbers as his counting guide, he'd picked out all the A's on the first page, and one V, which he decided began the word *Vientiane* since it was the first word of a two-word heading and the name of the city from which

Southeast Asian CIA operations had launched from in '68. He penciled beneath the second word: L-A-O-S. The letters fit, the A's in the right place. This gave Bishop seven more letters— I-E-N-T and L-O-S. He rapidly filled in these letters across the rest of the page.

Van Eijk's daughter gave up watching him. She went into the kitchen and, with a quick curious glance to the night outside, began to organize a meal.

Bishop mulled over the R on the stone. Below it was two numbers: 11 and 15. Beginning at the first letter of text below the location heading, he counted in eleven letters and put in an R. From there he counted another fifteen and placed a second R. Where the first R was placed, Bishop already had an E-V-E-R-_-T-_-I-N-_: *everything*. He added a Y, an H, and a G to his code key. The second R-word was three letters _-O-R. Most common construction: F-O-R. He added the F. Bishop had worked with this style of code many times before. The key stone made the work easy and quick. His initial assumptions of its usage proven correct, he soon divined the usage of the other numbers on the arrow-head and within five minutes had deciphered the first page. Upon reading it, he knew the page had nothing to do with the CIA or the Vietnam War.

"Hey."

Her rice pot clanged into the sink. "What?"

"Listen to this. Tell me if it means anything to you."

She scowled at his familiarity. Snatched a towel. Bishop read:

"'I've done everything I could for you, Soumountha; was that not enough?'"

Bishop glanced at his captive. Her back stiffened, dishrag and rice pot poised in midair over the stove.

"Well?"

She swiveled her head over her shoulder, and he witnessed in her face the same internal struggle he'd seen after she'd made the greeting-card crack.

"Go on."

"'Soumountha could tell that Koumphan—'" He peered at her again. "Are these actual words or have I screwed this up?"

She let her head bow, a kind of assenting nod. "Not words. Names. Ancient names."

Bishop's lips curled into something that wasn't a smile and not yet a smirk. "Figures with Muir… I'll keep reading and you'll tell me what the hell he's talking about.

"'Soumountha could tell that Koumphan was exhausted and near his end. She begged him to return to the palace and find someone to heal his wounds. He told her that he could never return to his kingdom without her. Even though he might die, he would never abandon her and live separately from her. It was impossible.'"

Bishop looked from the journal. He watched the chalk-stick woman walk back to the bed and sit.

"Keep reading."

Her eyes glistened with tears; her face pinched by their betrayal.

"What is it? What does it mean to you?"

"Just read it."

"Sure… 'Hearing those words from her husband, Soumountha wished he had never chosen to fight against Sinxay.'

"'Sinxay lectured the dying Koumphan—'" Bishop read, and the woman joined in from memory: "'You are a thief, taking Soumountha and not marrying her, as normal people would do. Was this how you were taught by your parents and ancestors?'" Bishop reached the end of the page.

The woman continued reciting. If her tone mocked, it was only a mocking of herself. "'Is this the tradition you have chosen to follow? You seem to be ruled by moha, which can only lead to undesirable consequences.'"

"What's that—*moha?*"

"Should be familiar to you. A Buddhist term for 'delusion, confusion, and dullness.' The opposite is *prajna*—insight. Wisdom." With a fingernail, she scooped a tear from the corner of her eye before it fell and flicked it away.

"This some Malaysian creation story? Your people's mythology?"

She went to the kitchen area. She turned her back on him once again. Bishop came up behind her. She shuddered but didn't turn and he wouldn't touch.

"It's something important to you." This was as kind as his voice had yet sounded. "What is it, Chalk Girl?"

"This story is an epic poem from Laos. The *Sang Sinxay.*"

"Why do you know it so well?"

Bishop watched her twist the dishrag between fists. "It was the one book I had growing up in the convent school that belonged to me. It had been a gift of my father to my mother. It's Buddhist. My mother's religion."

"Did your mother give it to you?"

The young Malay woman turned, her eyes narrow, accusing. "The estate agent—our family lawyer I mentioned, who brought my money and paid the convent school—the man who handled all my legal paperwork my whole life. He told me it was my father's when he gave it to me."

"What was the lawyer's name?"

She sneered. "The one I was told? Or his *real* name we both now know?"

"What name did you know him by?"

"Bucknell. Mr. Linus Bucknell, Esquire."

"Those are Muir names. Family names." Bishop furrowed his brow, concerned.

She said, "That bothers *you*?"

"In our line of work, we don't use real names for cover legends." He sighed. "Muir gave you your father's book, but it was your mother's religion."

"That's what he said—'your father's book.' Inside, it was inscribed from my father to my mother."

"Brown ink?"

She cocked her head. Pursed her lips to contain the *fuck you* before it became a *fuck me* at herself.

"Was there a date?"

She ignored the question. Went back to preparing the meal, mechanical in her every motion. From the refrigerator she took a *redang* spice paste she'd prepared that morning along with a plate of beef short ribs. The plate shook in her hand. Bishop watched her work a carving knife, hacking the rib meat into cubes.

She plunged the knife into the cutting board. "How is it possible this man Muir would know in 1968 to write that story in the green book, present me the storybook years later when I'm a kid, all for you to come to my home—now, decades after all that—and throw it in my face at gunpoint?"

"Guess you had to know him…" Bishop trailed off, regretting his words as she shouted:

"I thought I fucking did know him!"

She tugged the knife free. Turned. Its blade flashed. Bishop stepped back. She didn't attack him, and he didn't think she would. He knew the signs in a person when their world collapses; were she fighting anything, she was fighting demons from her past. Demons she'd never known had always surrounded her. Demons of a past she was unwitting handmaiden too.

"Muir wasn't a lawyer for your estate or anyone else's. He was a spy. His cover job: a doctor of mythology. Though he never cured anyone with his damn fairy stories."

"Is that how he roped you into this, as your teacher? Teach you to be a CIA terrorist?"

"No."

Her eyes sparked at the turmoil escaped in his voice. She ran her gaze over him. Recognition dawned. "He's your father."

"Put down the knife or get back to the food."

"Why you seemed so familiar in the caves. I couldn't tell that from the photo."

She softened, perhaps at a sense of shared faithlessness, perhaps at a scrap of humanity he'd let slip at the identification of his bloodline. Perhaps at the aura of tragedy that hung about him she'd missed until this moment, and she waited.

"I look more like my mom," Bishop mumbled.

"No. You don't. You're everything like him."

"Believe me, Chalk Girl. Muir and I are nothing alike."

Bishop retreated to the desk. He flipped through the rest of the journal. The rest of the entries, although still in code, were clearly not from a fairy tale; the dates and times throughout were a record of operational information Muir had some reason to want him to find. Bishop set to work decoding the dying secret of his father.

17

FOR THE HOUR or so it took to prepare the beef *redang*, the woman did not speak again. After bringing Bishop a plate and a glass of wine, she retreated to a small kitchen table to eat by herself.

Bishop sipped the wine. It tasted unfamiliar and strange.

"I poisoned it," she said.

An awkward silence as he processed the many implications.

"Tasty."

She rolled her eyes and ate.

"Muir acted as your estate agent. So you interacted with him. Often?"

"Twice—sometimes three—times a year."

"Anything particular you remember? Especially the last time you saw him?"

She took a moment to choose her words. "You're not going to kill me, and I don't feel like telling you private conversations with my lawyer."

"Spy, yes. A professor, yes. Lawyer? Sorry, Chalk Girl—"

"Stop calling me that."

"Don't like it, tell me your name."

She took a large swallow of wine, spirits for the dispirited. "What's it matter what he said? Just lies like everything else he told me."

Bishop ignored her sorrow as anything akin to his own and waited.

MUIR'S PRINCETON MENTOR, Jacques Maritain, a preeminent twentieth-century thinker in metaphysics—the science of mental phenomena and of the laws of the mind—built upon the works of Aristotle and St. Thomas Aquinas in his philosophy of the First Principles of Things—being, knowing, substance, cause, identity, time, and space—to construct a theory of reality that extended from a child's first conception of being to culminate in the consideration of the nature of God. Bishop's captive, then, was experiencing through Muir nothing less than a metaphysical crisis.

She didn't know Maritain. If she'd ever held a book of Aristotle, she'd never opened it. She'd been taught in the convent she'd been reared in that *"The things we love tell us what we are"* and that *"There is nothing on this earth to be more prized than true friendship,"* but as far as she knew, these were Mother Superior pabulum, not Thomas Aquinas truths. Anyway, they were far from her mind that night.

She rose with her plate. Scraped bones into the trash. She rinsed the plate and, with another searching glance out the window into the night, placed it in the sink. The power shut down, plunging the room into darkness. She moved quickly in the direction of the door. Bishop gripped his gun, thumbed back the hammer with a *click*.

"Not one more step."

She stopped but grabbed something off the entry table. He took slack from the trigger.

"Drop it."

"They're matches. Out here, power goes off at ten. I don't control that."

Bishop lowered back into his chair. He replaced his pistol on the tabletop.

"You want to keep fooling around with that notebook," she said, "then I need to light candles."

Bishop followed with vigilant eyes as she went about the age-old ritual of lighting nighttime fire in this time, this place, with a long wooden match to candles placed around the room. He found himself paying attention to her fingers. Slender and elongated. The manicured nails of an office worker, alluring without being so decorative as to render her hands useless. She passed him and he stole a glance at perfectly curved and naturally swaying hips. Hips he'd seen unclothed.

Bishop disgusted himself. He looked away, feeling base. Shitty.

He needed to focus his thoughts: unprejudiced, unemotional. His captive was naturally intelligent, and she was educated; possessed of a curious nature, she moved boldly into risk, held herself unafraid in subjugation. Independent in spirit, solitary in lifestyle, distrustful in nature. She'd been trapped into this by Muir with threats but, Bishop sensed, Muir maneuvered her more as allied to his objective than as an opponent.

Why?

Bishop knew himself the cause of her immediate stress, but a deeper tension radiated from her. Apparent since his first sighting, it suggested outside influences she suspected or anticipated, maybe counted on, but concealed. He might employ a Pride-and-Ego Up or Down technique to break her. He'd used both CIA interrogation methods to numerous successes, but as quickly as he considered the option, he went back to Muir's purpose in all this: for all his father's flaws, his misguidance, disappointments, and betrayals, Bishop sensed Muir wouldn't have sent him to her only to make the woman his prisoner—an interrogation resource to develop, dismantle, and discard. Muir had wrapped up too much real life in a lifetime of lies with her. In fact, Muir's methods in all this indicated the older spy's staunch protection of her—both from the CIA and something, possibly those invisible forces nagging at her distraction, far worse.

She brought the last candle to Bishop's desk. She touched flame to wick as the matchstick curled and puffed out. Bishop contemplated her face.

"Don't look at me like that."

"Like what?"

Dismissal and disgust clenched her jaws. "Don't."

Once more back to the kitchen, she gave in to useless tidying. Somewhere faraway in the night, a mullah called the faithful the fifth and final time. Bishop watched the woman move her lips, reciting portions of the prayer.

"A convent-school Catholic who lurks in Hindu shrines, a Buddhist mother, yet she flirts with hijab and whispers the Rakat Salat-Al-Witr."

"My religious disposition is none of your damn business."

"Right now, this book and your disposition are all we got going to get us through this dark night of the soul."

"I know what you're trying. There's no us. That this has anything to do with your soul or mine is bullshit. If you're smart, you'll finish that book and take your CIA sickness out of here."

"You know something I don't?" He did that intolerable thing Muir could do and made his eyes twinkle. "I know you're dying to tell me."

He watched the blossoms of yellow candlelight, dancing all around her house, quiver across lips now bunched to hold back a scream that had been threatening since he'd first caught sight of her inside the caves.

"The more you cooperate, the more likely that wish I'd go comes true for both of us."

She blew a sigh that might have represented her weariness with his ongoing threat, the undiminished heat, her shattered past, or the whole profane condition of man.

"Is the Quran something you learned in spy school?"

"Some earmarked for smarter jobs than mine learn it. Me, I spent the past three years living among Muslims. Friends taught me to appreciate it. Most of the time, the place we were trapped, it was all we had."

"What happened to your *friends?*"

She didn't hide her sarcasm and Bishop stared because he didn't want to play into it. She'd turned the tables, provoking him into revelation.

Pride-and-ego? Up or down? In for a penny, in for a pounding.

"Very bad things."

"Must make you proud," she spiked. She took his wineglass and plate.

"Charitable of you to serve me dinner." He floated the words gently behind her.

She scraped his bones then stopped. "Last time I saw him? Right here. In this room. Right the hell where you're sitting. With his own set of papers. Papers for my parents' house, which he gave me along with my mother's robe—I didn't even know she had a robe, let alone a house—and I wept for missing a family I never knew except from a lawyer who said he'd be back to check on me from time to time but broke his promise and vanished." The words emerged from a cave deep inside her: dry, untested, and brittle. Nourished on dust for years and she didn't like the way she sounded. "Mother, father, lawyer: the three who connected me to who I am, all gone to be replaced by a pair of pretty oh-so-dead eyes and a gun. So fucking forgive me if *you* don't understand how hard I search for God."

She grinned without a shred of pleasure, a sardonic misery Bishop knew too well. And he knew, if he waited without speaking, she'd fill the silence to stay out of that cave she'd surprised herself in escaping. She tossed the wine he'd only sipped into the sink basin, followed by his plate.

"As a multiconfessional state, Malaysia has always been complicated," she encouraged herself. "What has always been celebrated as tolerance is now weaponized for politics. There's official efforts in my department to disguise radical Islamist activism as a voice of poverty striving for economic inclusion in our recovery through religious education. A laundering method to funnel money to extremism. Soft math for hard corruption hiding behind God."

"It'd be my guess the God number is infinity. Hard to ledger that."

"What's that supposed to mean?"

"'How temporary is man, how infinite is Allah'—Quran says something like that, right? Money never buys God; it usually pays for the opposite."

Bishop turned back to the journal. He'd opened her a little— or maybe she'd opened him and the part of that he wanted to shut down, but she wasn't finished.

"I believe the way I was raised because Christianity is what I know. The deeper I know it, the deeper I believe it. But the people I work with, the majority of the country professes Islam. My friends are afraid now. No one says anything, but you'd have to be blind to miss it. People are silent. Fewer hold hands. Everyone fears the harmony might change with tomorrow's elections. Probably why you people have inserted yourself—exploiting our problems like you do all over the world. Exploiting our fears to American advantage."

"Not my end of the business. You expect there to be violence?"

"No. I expect the true message of the Faith—peace above all things—is stronger than political incitement."

"If you're wrong—what will you do?"

"Survive."

THE CANDLES BURNED. Black-speckled clear wax dripped. Smoke floated into the darkness of the chalk-stick woman's house, and the woman, now on the bed behind the netting, lay turned away from Bishop, knees pulled to her chest, pretending she wasn't the loneliest creature in the jungle.

Bishop deciphered Muir's diary from the year Bishop had been seventeen before his mother had signed the release to let him go shoot long distance in Vietnam. As Gunnery Sergeant Beckett had taught at the Camp Pendleton range: one shot, one kill, no exceptions. Muir had written the journal the same year he'd stolen the opportunity to take Bishop's picture at his graduation from US Grant High School, Van Nuys, California. Tom Bishop was the only kid without a dad who'd made Eagle Scout that year and then, fulfilled his lifelong—*long* as a seventeen-year-old views time—desire to enlist in the Marine Corps. Beckett made him a sniper, but the ability to kill without remorse: the father he'd never known had already, at a blood level, brought to being from mind to heart to fingertip and full-metal-jacket release.

18

At a downtown telephone kiosk bathed in the glow of the Petronas Twin Towers, Sedaka placed a call and was connected to his party.

"Bishop has become a rogue elephant, Director."

"This is a screwup of Old Testament proportions," said Harker.

"Sir, I am running some leads, and I can assure you—"

"What about van Eijk? Bishop *didn't* get to him? You know that for a fact?"

"Categorically. When we didn't show at the rendezvous, van Eijk returned to the dead drop, left his mark. He's still out there, sir. All I have to do is—"

"Nothing," said Harker. "You will do nothing. Do you understand that? Is there any part of nothing you're confused by?"

"No, sir. Nothing."

"Nothing what?"

"Nothing, sir?"

"Fine, then. Return to the embassy, draft your report, then bend paperclips until I can get someone out there to make a field decision on the entire operation. Wait for Nick Albro. He takes care of things."

Bishop's candle guttered, almost gone. He decoded the final page and closed the diary. Beside it were sheets of notes he'd written on the woman's stationery. Fine paper embossed with her name, "LARA VAN EIJK."

Bishop looked at Lara. Asleep, peaceful, in her robe. Bishop recognized it as the kind of garment from Vietnam back when wholesale killing seemed a promising idea to a bunch in Washington and Langley who weren't there and weren't getting killed. This particular robe: a US Navy souvenir kimono. They sold them plain, and soldiers and their war-girlfriends personalized them with embroidery or fabric paint. Few made it back to the States. Most were pornographic in imagery and comment, a decorative road map to lust and infidelity. If they weren't left with girlfriend or mistress or main-squeeze hooker, if you tried to bring one of these home, they'd be confiscated and destroyed for the American serviceman's own good. The kimono bonfire burned daily at Tan-son-Nhut Airbase.

He missed Elizabeth.

Bishop looked at his gun, self-loathing overtaking him. This went on for forty minutes until it was gray outside. He didn't move in any of that time but lived in memories of other dawns and the dead in his mind. And then he went to Lara. The mosquito netting had wafted open in the night. Her breasts showed. He gently pulled up the covers, careful to avoid touching her. He closed the obscuring netting and didn't think of his dead wife. He stepped back.

"Lara…?" he said, and then, a little louder, angry inside himself because it couldn't be Elizabeth and never would be again: "Lara. Wake up."

Lara flinched. Her eyes glared at the sight of him.

"Hoping I'd be gone?"

She hid her misery that he hadn't stolen away in the night behind a frown.

"You'll find I'm full of disappointments."

"You know my name." She rolled away from him. Stared at the intricate louvered wall panels. "Thanks for rummaging through my things. Should I check my purse, my underwear drawer?"

"That's uncalled for."

"You're what's uncalled for."

"Your name's on your stationery. I used it up making notes. I'll pay for it when I leave."

"I don't want any more CIA money."

"It's my money."

"Just go. *Please.*"

She brushed past him to the kitchen.

"What are you doing?"

"Making coffee."

He watched her fill the kettle. He watched her face lift to the window over the sink. A slow right-left-right scan of the yard for something. For someone. Bishop pulled the tilt bar of another window, opening the slats. "Who're you expecting?"

She clenched her eyes and gave an exasperated "No."

"What's 'no'? No *one*?"

"No one. You didn't let me finish."

Their eyes met to check the invisible box they could both see between them. Check mark: lie.

She lifted a jar of Nescafé from her cupboard.

Back at square one. Bishop aimed his pistol. "Who the hell you looking for? This is last night's bullet, and it still wants its dance."

"Can't I look out my own window?!"

Bishop pushed her aside. Made another scan of the yard, the edge of the jungle, the rutted car path, and the *rumah dapur*. No movement. No unnatural shadows. Unbroken birdsong and insect rattle, buzz, and natter.

"Anyone you need to call? Work."

"Election Day. It's a holiday."

"No boyfriend? No lover?"

"I'm sure you discovered all the aloneness you needed searching my house."

She found two pressed-glass coffee cups and spooned two helpings of instant crystals into each. Bishop walked back to Lara's writing table. He'd threatened her into preparing last night's food. But the wine? This coffee now? They denied her overt and insistent declaration that he leave. These were covert enticements to stay. And as far as enticements go, the passing of cups, sharing of drink, was psychologically the strongest enticement to cooperation between captor and captive and usually worked the other way around. Hence her "poison" deflection over dinner.

"And where do you get off looking at my tits when I was sleeping? Pervert."

Deflecting again. Bishop looked at his notes.

"Lara, you told me your father died when you were a child. He was around when you were a baby, though—right? Not saying you have any memories of this stuff here, but…"

She turned. And this is the moment it happened for her. The moment Bishop closed the trap because she grasped that he'd learned something about her life she didn't know.

"You were born when? '66? '67? '68? Looking at you, maybe—"

"If you say 'older,' I'll scald you with this."

But she brought over coffee. He took the glass.

"Thanks."

She watched him sip before dropping the guard he'd been waiting to hit the floor and said, offhand, "Why?"

Bishop picked up the journal. "This was Nathan Muir's desk diary during the time he ran CIA operations for the Vietnam War. But Muir traveled here—Kuala Lumpur—to attend a baptism on February third, 1968. I'm guessing yours."

"Ask Nathan Muir."

The light caught his eyes in such a way, looking into them Lara saw an endless tossing sea.

"Asking's no longer an option."

"He's dead?" She held back a second. "I'm sorry."

"The less you know about my problems, the better. I need one more piece of information, then, as promised, I'm out of your hair."

"You trust me to just leave?"

"Said it yourself they'd kill you over your association with people like me... Unless you're lying."

Lara pulled the flaps of her Vietnam robe farther over each other. She retreated to the safety inside her coffee cup.

"The church where you were baptized? Where is it?"

She didn't answer. He drank coffee. Followed Lara with his eyes as she returned to her mosquito-netted bed. She sat and fixed him with a strong and level look.

"You don't get to do this. Come into my home, hide in the shadows, raping me with your eyes instead of announcing yourself. Threaten murder while you make me cook. Question my beliefs while I feed you like your slave. You tear apart the entire fabric of my life, then it's 'good luck, hope they don't kill you'? You may be a male of this fucked-up species of ours, but you're no man." She drove the knife of her revulsion into the deepest part of his heart. "You're no better than your spineless, lying father."

"I'll light a candle for all the sins of my blood and confess my gender when I get to the church. You want out of this, you tell me where the church is: that gets you out. You have my word."

"I had your father's word—*hung my whole childhood on it!*"

"Stop lumping me in with him."

"Want a fucking lump?" She hurled the coffee cup at him, the hot liquid splashing his chest and across his cheek as the mug glanced off his shoulder. He barely twitched.

"I'm a person, you son of a bitch."

"Noticed. And you were baptized. The church. Come on. February third was the middle of the most important military campaign of the Vietnam War."

"Fuck you and fuck Vietnam."

He answered her intensity with deepening calm and sharpening focus. "For the man in charge of all CIA operations to leave his post to attend a baptism in Malaysia—Listen to me, Lara, your father did something for Muir back then. Something important. Something that if it didn't cost your father his life, it definitely tore apart your family."

"Did his little book say that?"

All he had to do was lie to her. Make up a story to mollify her; she was already a chapter he was closing. Shut the book on Lara van Eijk. Be done.

"Did it?"

Just make up a lie. Tie up Lara van Eijk with its bow and get the hell out.

"No. I don't have that kind of answer for you. But for Nathan Muir to go out on a limb for anyone, they'd have to have had extraordinary meaning."

"To the CIA."

"Your father to Muir. To his personal code. His mythology. His meaning. And passed from that man—your father—Muir felt a life obligation to *your* care and safety. Whatever he and your father did…? Well…they spun the globe and it's come around again. That's why he sent the book. That's why your Sinxay story opens it, why your baptism is his calendar's central anomaly, and why I must find out what this puzzle is because things are happening in the world that Nathan saw but I don't. Yet. That's how all the numbers add up and that's why you'll give me what I ask."

Dead silence. Without a memory of having crossed the room, he'd somehow drawn close to her during his speech and squatted in front of her. Bishop couldn't fathom what she meant to Muir, but he saw—now that he'd begun, against all better instincts, to look at Lara as a person and look anywhere other than into her eyes—that her garment wasn't a soldier's slut's kimono but a lovingly handcrafted *áo dài*. Translates simply into "shirt long," and men and women wear it nowadays, even in public. But with the period stitching, and that Lara wore it privately as a robe, Bishop understood, it held meaning not only to her parentage but to Muir.

I remember the importance Nathan put on his first wife's Korean wedding dress. I don't know if Tom knows the story at all, but I do. Muir told the story of Jewel to Elizabeth—you'll remember, Mads, you were with us—and we both know Elizabeth told Tom everything she learned about Muir to thaw the implacable glacier of his vengeance. I think…Tom must have known about Jewel's Korean hanbok *wedding dress she died over and he must have seen something of that in what Lara was wearing.*

Maybe while Elizabeth lay dying, the globe was already spinning Bishop to this clutch he'd made without thinking, a hand now on her shoulder, warm beneath his wide palm. Their faces a foot apart. Lara was shocked. She thrust both hands into his chest to push him back. Once. Twice. He didn't budge. May as well have been a wall. His hand did not move from her shoulder.

"Stop playing games, Lara. You recognized my father's handwriting as soon as you opened his package and read his instructions. Went through the little green book. So, the lost girl, family lawyer, *Great*-fucking- *Expectations* charade would've been shattered before you went to the Batu Caves to lure me here."

Provoked, Lara, shook out of his grip. "I did recognize his handwriting, as I'm sure he knew I would. And I was an orphan, you fucker, while your Nathan Muir deliberately killed my childhood Mr. Bucknell-protector fantasy without giving a damn for what it would do to me once you—his fucking son—showed up to rub my face in it."

"Give me the church, Lara, and you'll never see or hear of either of us again."

Her eyes gleamed, feisty and unapologetic. "If I refuse? You'll kill me?"

"Don't refuse, and you'll never need to find out."

Her revulsion was real. He'd earned it. He carried loathsomeness in all its forms everywhere he went. Her face hardened with decision.

"I *do* know the church. I remember it. He took me there once on a day trip from the school. I guess now, he did that to make sure I'd know it when you got here."

He felt her hand close around his other fist, the one hanging between his knees. The fist that held his pistol. She locked eyes with him. Lifted and pressed the barrel into the tender skin directly behind her chin.

"The way I see it," she said, "you've got two choices: pull the trigger or I take you where Muir wants *both* of us to go. I have nothing else to lose."

BISHOP HAD NOT been with a woman since the last useless attempt in the hospital bed in Taiwan over three years ago, when Muir called the number they shared and neither father nor son acknowledged that meant anything personal—private, shared phone number—and Muir said to his bright boy: "It's close, Tom. Just grab the ticket waiting for you at the airport. Use your

Canadian cover kit. Taipei immigration has been taken care of. You're clear."

"If I see you, you're dead."

Bishop crawled into Elizabeth's hospital bed. Elizabeth shivered convulsively. But she smiled. She warmed. She said, "Make love to me," but he couldn't. Four nights running.

A new Serbian front opened, threatening Tom's Pristina network, and Miroslav initiated contact. Tom Bishop slipped out of Taiwan the next morning before the light was full, and I came in for my turn at the bedside watch. Elizabeth saw my sadness and she said to me:

"Russell, it isn't easy to love your best friend when he spends his life playing stranger on purpose. Some of that's why we love him, though. Isn't it?"

She asked that I tell Tom those were her happiest nights in Taiwan, having Tom beside her, holding her warm life and nude in the bed. She'd said, "All the things God takes from us, from the world, and from the children I wanted to help I'm not going to get the chance to, God gave me Tom Bishop. Silly, unhappy, yearning Tom: God is the best spy ever. Let him know: Tom didn't need to make love to me to love me."

Doctors with first and doctors with second opinions gave all of us assurances Elizabeth had *at minimum* two weeks left. Kosovo was cooking and Bishop's network needed him. Elizabeth had urged him. "In Kosovo you are protecting Muslims from genocide. Save the lives you can—it's what brought us together, saving lives. I'll be here when you return."

But the doctors were wrong. Bishop had been gone only two days before I got word to him after my conversation at Elizabeth's bedside. It took an additional twenty-four hours for Langley to deliver the message, and another twenty-eight for Bishop to drop everything and race back.

Elizabeth Hadley died, and he'd not been there. Bishop had missed the death of his wife. That man, the one who didn't say goodbye to his wife, didn't hold her hand while she went, the man he saw in the mirror when he stood scared and naked before it dressing to leave after being unable to make love to her that last time he'd held her, that man returned to Taipei, Taiwan, watched from afar his father take care of the paperwork, realizing his wife had given that unforgiven man emergency power of attorney in Tom's absence.

He continued spying on Muir when I joined the old man to accompany Elizabeth's body to the mortuary. Bishop slipped onto the flight we all shared home. Later, Muir gave me the ashes and the number to call. Tom Bishop never answered. I gave up after three days. A good secret soldier, having kept his Kosovo network alive, Bishop had already vanished into killing. Death over closeness.

BISHOP STOOD in the rectangle of hot sunlight that poured into Lara's garage. His pistol held loose along his thigh, he monitored her every move as she worked her way around an old, tall vehicle, pulling off the heavy plastic tarp that had covered it for some time. Dust billowed and gave form to the shaft of sunshine beating on Bishop's sweat-dripping back. Lara dragged away the plastic to reveal an overexaggerated military-style, right-hand-drive green British Land Rover.

She exhaled, catching a hard breath, and stared at it.

"Thanks for the help."

"Thing's older than me."

"It's a '56—so not by much."

She wore jeans shorts and a floral-patterned batik blouse, the classic tropical design perfected over five hundred years.

A wraparound, belted front allowed for as low a décolletage as necessary—not for seduction but for air conditioning. Its bottom edge hung free over her rear while the sleeves ballooned where they ended past the elbow. The entire point is to allow maximum airflow, but after five minutes of concentrated exertion that point was nullified, and she appeared to have just stepped out of a shower taken in her clothes. Lara's face flushed and glistening; she wiped damp hair out of her eyes, tucked it behind her ears.

Bishop stalked around the Rover, peering inside, looking for any sign of a weapon.

"Thing run?"

"I turn over the engine when I remember. I take it out a couple times a year, but they banned right-hand vehicles a while back. I keep it registered but don't like to risk the citation." She pulled the keys from her pocket. "Muir told me it belonged to my father."

Bishop opened the driver's door. "What kind of name is Dand, anyway?"

"The kind they named my father."

He noticed an old decal in the corner of the windshield. Like a license, or parking pass, insurance, or something.

"What's this?" He tapped the decal: chipped, faded, depicting a snarling tiger over crossed swords.

"It's a permit."

"For?"

"A tin mine my father owned outside of Ipoh." Hearing herself say it, her expression wilted, disappointed. "But I guess we don't really know that. It's just a story Nathan Muir spun for me."

"Did he have a story for what your father did for a living?"

"He said he was a financier. I chose my course of studies because of it."

"Did you ever research your parents on your own?"

"When I was at university." Lara grabbed her scarf from a workbench where she'd put it. She covered her head and tied it, saying, "I never discovered anything. All I had was his word. I didn't know about the car or the mine until Muir moved me back into the house."

Bishop opened the driver's door for her. She climbed in and engaged the engine as he sat on the left-side passenger seat. Lara reversed from the garage. She took a sly and desperate look at her home. Her yard, her jungle. Again, Bishop noticed; this time kept it to himself. He let his attention linger on her wet clothing. How it clung to her every contour.

Why couldn't he make love to his wife the last time? Why couldn't he feel?

The woman in the cemetery I'd hallucinated was my sister, Paulette, my tumor-addled mind throwing more attention on discerning if she was reality than on getting off a lucky shot to shoot the best friend who murdered the best man I'd ever known. But she wasn't Paulette, whom I wouldn't see again. She was Lara, Bishop's unbowed captive, and he held all the cards. My only card was you, Mads, all these years of lies and a baby who isn't mine. I don't care. I'm Jessie's father and she's not mine—biologically. But adoption isn't a lie and biology isn't fatherhood. You said that to me about Tom and our "brotherhood."

Why, God, is it so hard to give Russell Aiken a break? Just one. Once?

19

O N THE SEVENTH FLOOR of the Old Headquarters Building, we keep a single interrogation/observation room unlike all others at Langley. It's used for those rare cases that implicitly involve the director, where the subject is meant to know this to create a sense of importance that can be either encouraged or dashed according to profile plan. It begins with the psychological boost of the elevator ride. Where an elevator down increases reluctance and fear, hope and trust are inherent in ascension. Think Heaven and Hell. Now think Harker watching through one-way glass. He'd been arrested—not Harker (my lame name-game tumor got ahead of me, sorry), *Yuri*. Harker was having Yuri questioned. Yuri the Russian and long-time Muir agent. Sixty-six years old. Sweating. Folding chair, folding table, folded hands jutting a smoldering cigarette over the cheapest-tin disposable ashtray you could ever see.

Tin from Malaysia—isn't that a hoot? But that's where our ashtrays originate. Malaysian tin is ubiquitous. Our lives—everyone's life—infused with Malaysian tin. Can of Spam: Malaysian tin. Can of Del Monte peaches in syrup: Malaysian tin. Penny dropped off the World Trade Center Observation Deck: 5 percent Malaysian tin. Were I to drop that penny, I'd be dropping it from atop hundreds of tons of Malaysian tin. Not just the tin of cans and fasteners and furnishings, and pocket pennies, not only the tin alloy in the 45,000-pound bronze-and-steel Koenig sculpture in front of the Twin Towers, but the guts of the structures themselves: wire coatings, screws and nuts, bearings, and every point of solder in every telephone and computer and calculator and coffee maker, elevator, and device with a circuit.

There's an Agency study entitled *Temporary Furniture Usefulness in Interrogation.* Folding chairs, folding tables, the cheap-tin ashtrays create unease by impermanence. The subject of the interrogation psychologically identifies themselves as temporary as the chair he's seated in. As easily folded and stowed in a closet, permanently and namelessly out of sight. And the chair never knows when, if ever, it will be pulled out again.

The Russians know that too, use it just as well. I know from Vladivostok experience. Like me, Yuri knew about the tin-ashtray, folding-chair trick and he looked down his long, thin nose with Borzoi-aloof valiancy.

"I tell the truth. The code came from Prometheus: to all of us. The entire Achilles 4 network," Yuri declared, stubbing out the butt of a filthy Russian cigarette. "'Paris's arrow flies.'"

Pure Muir. I'm sure Harker has no idea Paris's arrow delivered the mortal wound to Achilles. Harker's a heel anyway. Poor Muir.

Harker's chosen interrogator, a pencil-necked harridan name Hannah Graff—*whom I've always called Savannah Giraffe in my head when I see her, until that other thing grew in my head and made me afraid that if I saw her I'd blurt it and get clobbered*—said, "How? You haven't had contact with Prometheus for ten years."

"Made no difference. Those words we have always known. Have always waited for. All planned and rehearsed. Twenty-five years set procedure."

On Harker's side of the glass, the door opened. Carver walked inside. "We've nailed down a year on the missing journal," he said.

"Great," said Harker. "And?"

"Total agreement from the entire team. Dr. Muir's second year—"

"He's not a doctor. You will not refer to him as that. Am I clear, then?"

"What part of your head you using, sir? PhD, that's a doctor in mine and anyone else's book. My paperwork is going to respect and reflect that reality."

"You're implying?"

"Implications are for guesswork. What I'm saying is Dr. Muir's missing journal is from 1968. His second year as station chief, Vientiane, Laos. I have no idea why or what's important about that, but it's real."

"The year he recruited van Eijk in Malaysia."

"Thought you might say that. Why I'm happy to only be the cop here. Present-day crimes are more than enough for me."

"Be helpful, Bill," said Harker. "Something happened back then. Something thirty-three years later is important enough for Bishop to kill Muir."

"And betray every one of Muir's networks?"

Harker fixed his gaze on Yuri through the glass. "If he or Muir betrayed them at all."

"You want to chase a thirty-three-year-old white whale, have at it." Carver sighed with all the subtly of that whale's spout before adding, "I'm going in, take a whack at our Person of Interest from *this* century."

On the opposite side of the glass, Yuri lit another cigarette. Savannah Giraffe confiscated it. Crushed it out.

Carver lumbered into the room. "Yuri, the only truth I work from is the right-now truth. You were apprehended entering the United States illegally from Kiev with twenty thousand dollars cash. Muir and his games aren't my primary interest here. That's for other more intellectual individuals than me. I'm just doing murder work."

This got the Russian's attention.

"Whose murder?"

"Your one and only 'Prometheus' Muir."

Carver smiled. Panic seized Yuri and the anonymous impermanence of his surroundings began to have their intended effect.

"You caught me at customs! I wasn't in this country!"

"You ex-Sovs are a wily group. You could've contracted it."

"I was against Soviet Union! All of Achilles 4! We honored Prometheus!"

Carver stared from hooded eyes. Yuri's mouth opened to speak, shut, opened again as he fought back the urge to exacerbate his predicament.

Carver indicated Yuri's cigarettes. "Go ahead."

Yuri lit up. Sucked air through tobacco.

"Better?" said Carver.

Smoke through wolfhound nostrils. "Immeasuredly so."

"*Immeasurably.* Good. So where did you get the money and where is the rest of Achilles 4?"

"I will tell you one more time. The money was gift from Prometheus."

"Bullshit."

With his palm, Carver flattened the cigarette into Yuri's face. Didn't mind the burn. Yuri yelped.

Spitting and sputtering, rubbing his lips, and: "The money was from Prometheus. Retirement bonus. End of contract. He made us free." Yuri leaned in close. "Of you, of Soviet Union-Russia-pig-fuck, of all of this. This CIA bullshit."

20

Withdrawn and tense, Lara drove a potholed two-lane road into jungled hills, the rearview mirror never long out of her sight.

Bishop began, "My natural good nature may have grown on you—"

"What?"

"But don't fall for it. If whoever it is you've been pining for since our paths merged… well… you saw what happened at the Batu Caves. That really what you want repeated?"

"Shut up. I had nothing to do with that—them."

"Then come clean and tell me who you do have something to do with."

She looked across at him, annoyed. Worried. "No one. But they found you once."

"Wasn't that the setup?" That twinkle again, playing in his eyes.

"No! And it wasn't a setup. I saw you, and I saw them, and I lost my nerve."

"You're not the lost-nerve type."

She flicked on the radio, turning it up to drown out further conversation. A newscast in Malay.

"What's the lady saying?" Bishop asked.

Lara deadened her gaze to the road ahead.

"It's not a trick question."

"She's saying there's been riots at some of the polling places. The government is blaming it on the PDF opposition party. They're making arrests."

"What else?"

"They're predicting a sweeping victory for Prime Minister Aziz." She looked at Bishop's face. "Mrs. Musa has no chance of winning against him."

"That your opinion 'cause you're voting for him?"

"Everyone's opinion. And I'm not voting for him. I'd planned to vote for her. Instead, I'm with you. They've gone into the weather. Need a translation?"

"Getting it live."

Lara clicked off the radio. "What's your name?"

"What about the group with the green flags and the Ramadan moon? We talked around them last night."

Lara glanced at him. "That's what they're called: Bulan Ramadhan—Ramadan Moon."

"Where do they fit? They support the government or the PDF?"

"Neither. They're fundamentalists. An Islamist extremist faction who broke with the ruling party and joined up—it's rumored—with some Saudis. They spend most of their time organizing militias and calling for a holy war against the ethnic Chinese and Indians. It's where the economics are being fudged."

"Give me more on that."

She looked askance.

"I spend my time hiding the Saudi money to fabricate a narrative that the fundamentalist movement is poverty-driven when the facts prove the religious fervor is highly funded—money used to leverage faith—because some would like to see Malaysia an Islamic dictatorship."

"Like Libya, Iran, Iraq—"

"Closer. We're tracking the same socioeconomic trend coming out of Brunei, Indonesia, the Philippines. The only hope we have is in the faith itself—"

"Who's 'we'?"

"*We:* decent Malaysians who want peace and prosperity without intolerance. Just the same as Christianity, Islam's message is peace. A movement based on intolerance but compelled to embrace a peaceful doctrine is bound to collapse upon itself."

Bishop studied her. "Islam as a love bomb—when's that worked?"

She gripped the steering wheel more tightly. He wished he hadn't said it. He tried to get her back on track.

"You work at the Ministry of State, but you don't sound like this government's biggest fan."

"This government pays my check."

"But you'd run if there was a civil war."

"Race is utmost here. There are the Malay Muslims, the Indians, and the Chinese. But I'm *half-caste*. Nice word this country allows for my racial status. Not allowed by law to call myself Malay, but not able to be considered Anglo European. I'm not Indian. I'm not Chinese. White's the worst—and I'm infected with a lot of it."

"Race as the flu."

"More like AIDS. I have few rights."

"You have a passport?"

"The government keeps it. I handle sensitive economic material."

"Then how do you get out?"

Lara didn't answer. Her gaze tripped to the mirror.

"Lara, what aren't you telling me?"

"Just because you kidnap me doesn't entitle you to every detail of my life."

"Your life is yours. Live it. But I don't want to be part of your death and I'm not so naive to think, out of the blue, Muir sends you orders to pose as your dead father and lure me to those caves. You expected those Special Branch agents to take me into custody. So your real surprise was when I materialized behind you at your house."

"Who wouldn't be?"

"I'll give you that, but like you just said: even independent of you, they found me at the cave so how come they didn't find me at your place? You had Muir's journal—something they'd want. But you didn't share that because you suspected, correctly, they'd be able to decipher it and you'd have no leverage. You're double dealing here—"

"I've told you—"

"You'll embarrass both of us, you lie to me again. The only reason you're cooperating with me is you've stepped on a bear trap and you're watching the steel jaws flying on both sides about to cripple you."

Lara's brow creased. Her face tightened. A sound in her throat that began like mumbling transformed into a moan, soft and constant, building from deep within.

"Listen to me, Lara. This is a world full of bad guys and as far as it goes for you, I'm one of them. And that's okay. That's fair. But I guarantee you: I'm not the worst. I have no desire to hurt you. I want to help you. Get you out of this mess you didn't create and don't want. But I can tell you this. With certainty. You let me walk into a situation I'm not prepared for—"

Lara's moan exploded into a scream. She screamed as loud and as strong as she ever had. Bishop showed more alarm than— even in her out-of-control state—she might have anticipated. She recognized this, stared at him, and increased the volume, the decibels, her impassioned fury, her pent-up fear attacking his very being with sound.

Bishop understood the scream. Understood it because the same scream lived within him for more than thirty years. A scream

kept bottled because it contained the screams of every single individual he'd ever killed for the best, the worst, or for no discernable
reason whatsoever. Once he let it loose, he knew he wouldn't be
able to stop it unless he stopped everything down to the beat of
his own heart and made himself as permanently silent as all who
lived within it.

So he let her scream for both of them. And the scream
continued and Lara beat the cracked steering wheel with her open
hand. When Bishop reached in to calm her, she turned her attack
from the steering wheel, viciously pounding her elbow into him
until he said the only thing he could think.

"It's Tom."

Lara's attack lost it force.

"My name is Tom. Tom Bishop."

Her scream dwindled, dying out as she let the Land Rover
coast until it stalled with a heavy shudder alone on the remote,
rural two-lane road. He could see she was baffled with what to
say next.

"Why isn't it Muir?" she grumbled.

He held her with a gaze of phony indifference. "I lost my
father—who I was told was my father, 'Arthur Bishop'—before
I could remember, if I ever knew him. Man never even existed;
invented by my mother to hide the truth. In the same way
Muir appeared to you in the role of your family attorney, Muir
appeared to me later in my life as a spy. He became my boss and
he made me into a monster many years before I ever learned of
our blood."

He studied her face, her skin still bright red from the exertion
she'd inflicted upon herself. That gleam in her eyes, the tight line of
her mouth, the set of her jaw told him what he thought she knew
already. His words tread close to a truth neither of them wanted.

"He replaced the father I thought I'd lost and, filling all my emptiness, I worshipped Muir before I understood what he was turning me into. Then I hated him for replacing the father I'd believed was mine, the one I longed for, never knowing until it was too late, they were one in the same."

"How do I know you're not lying to me?"

"Not much added advantage in lying for a guy who kills for a living."

"You think that excuses anything you've done to me?"

Bishop gave a single dry laugh. "Start the car before we get wrecked."

Never taking her eyes off him, she switched on the ignition. "I'm not being funny and I'm not driving until you answer."

"The few rare times I give into God and pray, I ask him the same damn thing. His laugh isn't all that funny either."

IT WAS 1943. Dr. Abraham Maslow finished eating an apple, washed it down with a glass of water, and preened with satisfaction as he gazed out the window from his ivory tower at Brooklyn College, minutes earlier having completed his paper "A Theory of Human Motivation." It was set for publication in the next month's issue of the American Psychological Association's *Psychology Today*. His postulation of his *sui generis* theory "The Hierarchy of Needs" would be his greatest contribution to psychology, sociology, and a plethora of upper-management team-training and employee retreats; anyone matriculating past middle school (as I learned was the new name for junior high when touring Jessie's elementary school and asking to meet the sixth-grade teacher. The principal sneered—always your *pal* never a *ple* [pronounced "pill" in my own grammar-school spelling-lesson-crosswords]— until the words emitted from her throat with cigarette-burned disdain: "Your daughter will be sent to middle school for her sixth, seventh, and eighth," to which I responded, "Swell, Jessie's always wanted to visit the Shire," for which I scored another institution that thought of me as an idiot), but… for those who survive the weeding ground of those junior-middle years and burgeon in high school to blossom at college and university, you get Maslow's theory *ad infinitum, ad nauseum,* to the point where you're able to draw it from memory:

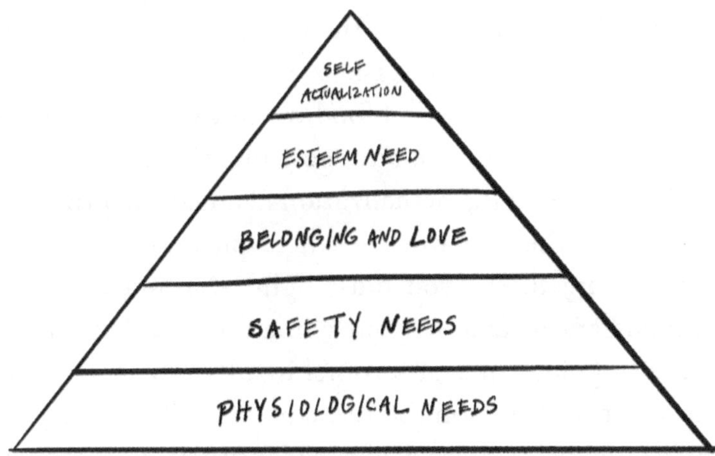

Did I mention cults, gurus, and con artists? They go for it in a big way, pursuing the wallets of those who didn't get Maslow in school by focusing on Maslow's second greatest contribution: the concept of "Identity." Only through self-actualization realized may one achieve true identity.

Maslow tossed his apple into the wastebasket. He took his water glass to the sink. A chill wind rattled the windows and rain pebbled them with droplets. He turned up the thermostat, glad to be inside his office. He looked over his pages before sealing them in a manila envelope addressed to *Psychology Today* magazine and warmed to the pleasantness of "Belonging"—yada-yada-yada, up the ladda.

Like I said, this stuff goes on *ad infinitum, ad nauseum,* now add Bishop. He'd crunched through the ruins and rubble of dozens of blasted ivory towers in bombed and burning AOs (Areas of Operation). That particular apple on that day in particular, when Dr. Abraham Maslow self-actualized into "Identity," had come from the faculty commissary. Bishop had witnessed war orphans eat similar, but for the mold and rot, apple cores—what's that saying about apples? If you're eating one and you reach a worm at the center, was the part of the apple you already enjoyed now bad? They'd eaten the maggots and the ants gladly, apple cores not from wastebaskets but from wastelands. He'd seen refugees fight over rancid food worldwide and it was always the same. The one with the strongest identity and usually least Maslowian naval-gazing actualization claimed the prize. Bishop knew, living in the real world—where physiological and sheltering needs are things you must fight over and don't opt for in a commissary to take to your climate-controlled office suite where the trappings of a professorship allow you the narcissism to gain your true "Self" on the risers of your pile of fancy things, accomplishments, and accolades—identity is not the culmination. The person lacking identity never gets onto Maslow's pyramid. Without identity, there's no will to go after that rotten apple or seared-cat flesh or raw rat that gives you the energy to crawl under the rock to get out of the murderous sun or hypothermic cold. Without true identity (*not* fancy Shire school "Actualization"), there is only the impulse to give up and die. Identity is primacy.

Stripped of identity is stripped of life.

That's how Bishop boiled it all down. How he considered Lara witnessing her subconscious bubbling up to her consciously considering self. She'd had a full, strong identity all her life. It had boosted her step by step up the ladder on the way to Maslow's peak experience fun 'n' games, self-satisfaction without the hangover of smug, and the Esalen Institute supercalifragilistic-actu-al-ity. The phony apple at the top of the ladder precipitous to the greatest slide to the bottom.

Whether Muir had set it off, or other forces Muir was set against—which Lara wouldn't yet reveal—Bishop was the one whom Muir sent in to destroy Lara's false constructs of self. Bishop knew enough about his own identity to understand that once sent in, the situation would be sorted out with violence. Either, like Lara, he'd survive, or Bishop would reunite with Elizabeth. He punished himself by believing he would be happiest with the latter.

LARA HAD RESUMED driving. They entered rolling hills of secondary tropical forest. Secondary due to having been clear cut 150 years ago, but long enough ago that a second growth of trees had repopulated the hardwood forest for present harvest.

"These the trees your house is built from?"

"Most rural houses, but they yield more than lumber. The resins and oils are used in glue, perfume, incense, medicine to cure you, embalming fluid when the cure doesn't take."

She was forcing herself to sound more relaxed to Bishop, but her eyes had resumed their glide, back and forth, windshield to rearview—future to trailing past—like the spider threads her web.

"Oh, God!"

Bishop joined her view. Lights swirled on the dashboard of an undercover State Police car coming up fast behind. The siren whooped. Bishop looked over his shoulder. The State Police car sped behind him, lights flashing. Bishop drew his pistol.

"Please don't."

Two municipal cop cars, blue-and-yellow designs and stripes and nasty lights and *whoop-whoop* sirens joined the undercover car. They accelerated on the Rover: behind and both sides.

"This what you've been watching for?"

"No. I swear it." She couldn't take her eyes off his pistol.

"Eyes on the road."

She corrected her drift. The cops veered in phalanx and swooped past.

Lara didn't reduce speed, kept it easy like you do when cops speed past. Considerate, unhurried, Girl Scouts of Malaysia Activity Safety Standards & Guidelines approved.

A mile later, in the narrowest of valleys between hills, a lumber mill and a cluster of old tin-sided buildings straddled the road. A polling place erected in a loading area. The State Police cars had stopped. Lights still flashed. Lara eased the accelerator.

"Keep cool. Let's see."

Angry workers and their families, gathered at the mill to vote, were pressed back with assault-rifle buttstock and gunpoint. Lara slowed. She stared left. Officers emerged from the polling place with the ballot boxes. Election officials argued. They tried to grab back the ballot boxes. She watched men and women seized, wrestled to the ground. The crowd agitated. A police officer at the side of the road waved Lara to pull over.

"Keep driving," said Bishop, easing into his warm place of warm bullets.

A group of workers broke through the cordon. They rushed the officers loading the ballot boxes into their cars. Bodies thrown. Fists flew. A gunshot rang out.

The officer intent on pulling over Lara did what rural police in "developing" countries designatedly do. He faced the conflict and opened fire indiscriminately as more gunfire blasted.

Two workers fell.

"Floor it."

The gunfire escalated to a non-stop din, workers and civilians slaughtered as the Land Rover sped past. Lara's eyes riveted to her mirrors; Bishop kept a hand on the steering wheel.

"Oh, God, Jesus—they've killed them."

Her body overwhelmed by shock, Lara's foot released pressure and slipped from the gas pedal. Bishop swung his foot over her thighs and onto the accelerator. He grabbed the wheel with one hand, the gearshift with the other, and watched the RPMs. When they dropped beneath 1500, he "burped" the throttle, pressing the gas for a second, then let the pressure off and released the shifter into neutral. As the Rover slowed, he revved the engine over 2600 RPM, gently pushing the gearshift against third gear, releasing the pressure on the gas. When the RPMs fell to 1300, the shifter slipped into place a moment before the engine stalled. In this manner, he managed their speed through the gears climbing the next hill out of the murder valley. There was no pursuit and soon the valley disappeared behind the curves of the road they traveled.

Lara didn't move or speak. She let this go on, Bishop driving across her, the silence between them interrupted only by the occasional grind of the gears. After ten minutes, Lara battered his hands and foot away and took back control of the vehicle.

"Pull over," he said. "I'll drive from here."

Lara ignored him. Kept going. Without looking at him, her voice flat, deadened: "Do you have any humanity?"

Bishop ignored the question. He concentrated on the road. The first road sign they'd seen in miles indicated a crossroad.

"You don't care about a damn thing," she said.

Lara made a turn. Bishop glanced at her. Lara gave him a disappointed look and turned back to the road when he didn't speak.

What did he care about? A father hidden and manipulative, controlling and cruel. Dead where the man should have been years ago. A wife with too big of a heart for her own good who survived the full force of a Chinese prison, worse circumstances before that, only to die from a lump in her breast that hadn't been any larger than an apricot pit when it was already terminal and taking her life.

Bishop's eyes remained alert upon Lara van Eijk. He hated Muir for putting him in this place. This position. This last chess move from beyond the grave.

21

THE TIMBER FORESTS far behind, primary triple-canopy jungle rainforest, dense and deep, pressed from both sides of the road and met overhead. They'd been driving for more than an hour through a permanent twilight when afternoon sunlight filled with smoke appeared like a portal ahead of them.

"Slow down as you enter that, Lara. Real slow."

Bishop checked his gun and held it in his lap. The smoke swirled around them as they rolled into a clear area where a side road fed to a dirt parking lot and the remains of a church, gutted and half-tumbled by fire. The flames were mostly gone. The ruins glowed and smoldered. It had been a strange, small Catholic church. Early nineteenth century, remote, and hidden, constructed in a time of Muslim intolerance that clearly had now returned. But that wasn't the strangest thing about the Church of Saint Agnes. This church prophesied from Muir's notebook, in Lara's memory now the catalog of the falsity of her life, was the strangest church Bishop had seen of any Christian denomination in any country in the world.

The cross on the belfry was a crucifix. A dead Jesus aloft in destroyed architecture against a smoke-blackened sky. Bishop and Lara arrived in time to watch the final portion of roof collapse in showers of sparks. Jesus nailed to the cross plummeted afire.

"*Sancta Maria,*" said Lara.

Bishop instructed Lara where to park. He watched her gather her emotions. After the witnessed murders and after the freakout scream, after last night, after the caves, and all those other past afters invisibly binding them in invisible chains to Muir, they numbly left the car to forge another link to something terrible coming that clung like a smell to the smoke.

Two excited aboriginal boys picked through the rubble, seeking treasures as Bishop and Lara approached. Bishop tossed some coins.

"They're not beggars," Lara said.

"They're hunting things—kids everywhere like to go after pennies. World over, finding coins is good luck, not pittance—hold out your hand to the master—imperialist beggary." He nudged her forward. "Just ask what happened, wouldja?"

Lara spoke to the boys in Malay.

Bishop stalked the debris. He noticed the Ramadan symbol crudely carved into a standing section of blackened wall.

"They're Orang Asli of the local Mai Semai aboriginal natives. A group nationally honored for an absolute adherence to non-violence."

"Never assumed they were responsible."

She snuffed. "They say it was a new militia, recent to the area. Until this morning, they'd been respectful and avoided the mission."

"The Ramadan Moon?"

Lara nodded.

"What else do they know about them?"

Lara asked and translated. "They shot up some farms, burned fields, destroyed grain stores, then came down here just before dawn," she said, depressed.

"What about the priest?"

"They beat him pretty soundly but let him go with a warning."

"That if he and all Christians don't clear out, they'll come back."

"…and kill them all. I thought you didn't speak Malay?"

"These types aren't original."

"The Mai Semai in this district are all Christian. The local chiefs and leading men are meeting over this. It allowed the boys to slip from their village to scavenge here."

Bishop stooped to collect some shell casings. Sniffed them. Lara watched him check their markings while the kids wandered off to explore how fun destruction of familiar things can be. Bishop pocketed the casings. Lara gave him a quizzical look he ignored.

"You wanted an answer, why I wear this?" She pointed at her purple scarf. "Respect. What's happened here is a perversion of my people's faith."

"Didn't you just get through telling me you had no people? Racial AIDs, or something like that? Pick a side, Lara, and ask where we find the priest."

Lara, despising Tom Bishop for his lack of sympathy, did as requested. The boys indicated a well-used path into the jungle that led to the priest's rectory. Too narrow for the Land Rover, Bishop and Lara cut on foot into the jungle.

THE PRIEST'S RECTORY was a lovely, significantly out-of-place Dutch colonial farmhouse lifted aloft on Malaysian pylons and set in the middle of a wide swath of rough crabgrass. Bishop and Lara mounted the steps to the door and Bishop knocked. Footsteps. The door opened a crack. The pale face in the small strip of light, framed in dimness beyond, was beaten. Bruised. It seeped contusional blood. Nose unnaturally canted and black. Swollen eyes appeared as two dark suspicious beads that blinked a fright previously unknown, entirely unwanted. The face belonged to the priest of the Church of Saint Agnes. Lara spoke to him in Malay. He widened the door and motioned them to enter.

He mumbled a welcome in creaky British-accented English. Tall and awkward, the priest carried himself raven-like in posture and stiff-legged gait. His black hair and full-length black habit served only to heighten the avian aspect of his wounded face.

"They cut the phone lines before the attack," he said. "We've sent a boy to the district courthouse for help."

"You won't get any," said Bishop.

Lara's eyes bore in on him. *Don't push.* Bishop ignored her. The priest beheld them without a shred of blessing. They stopped in a corridor outside a closed door.

"We have so little, yet they took so much."

He dipped his chin. An indication to listen through the door. Faint voices. Sobs from within. Bishop opened the door. Crowded inside a drawing room were six Malay families from the raided farms: men, women, children. Elderly. A pet goat. They stared back at Bishop with the wide-eyed shock and immeasurable sadness of sudden exiles. The priest eased the door closed. He gathered Lara's hands in his own. Bishop beat him to words.

"Father, I need to see your baptismal records. Look at me."

The priest did not. He spoke to Lara. "It isn't right for God to do this—to test the innocence of his most peaceful people in such extreme."

"Father, look at me. Are those records here?"

The priest tried to take Bishop's hands too, but Bishop wasn't playing. "I'm sorry. I'm not sure I understand," the priest said.

"Miss van Eijk was baptized here—your church—in February of 1968. It's important. Are those records safe? Are they here?"

Bishop's request confused the man. The priest looked to Lara for clarification. She hesitated. The understanding that revelation would further strip her identity reflected in her face. She embraced Muir's best friend: the life lie.

"It's my godparents, Father. I never knew them. We thought—you see—" She looked Bishop dead in the eye. "I'm an orphan. We wanted to reach out to them if they're still alive."

Bishop studied the woman. Something was happening between them. Shared experience. Shared witness. An after that would beg aftermath. It made him uncomfortable. Not for himself, but for her. It was wrong for Muir to have involved Lara. With such disregard for her life so many years after whatever he'd done—felt guilty about—in changing it the first time. This couldn't but end badly for her.

Lara took her lie to the extreme. "That's all we want from you, all we came here for—from the United States; we had no idea there was trouble and our timing couldn't be worse, but my godparents, Father, they're the only connection to family I have in this world. We're getting married."

As you know, Mads, the desire to know oneself is the greatest urge God gave us. Next to sex. Even if you have to break your promises before Him to get it.

A LARGE LEATHER-BOUND book flung down. Opened. Its pages—superior paper, thick and textured, Muir would like it and probably had, the library smell—*flip-flip-flipped*. Bishop scanned the dates for the one that anchored him, Lara, and Muir to one another's identity… 1948… flipped pages… 1955… 1964. His finger ran down one page, the next. Through the window came the *putt-putt* of a motorbike. A young Malay-Muslim villager approached the rectory.

Bishop's finger stopped. "LARA VAN EIJK." Fountain-pen cursive. Finger-stained. Brown ink. Muir's thumbprint, accidental in appearance, operational in proof, Bishop trained to read it years ago in Germany… for this moment?

"A Rule of Thumb—second, third, and fourth—so listen because it's important, Rusty: A forgery disguises in blue, disappears in black, but is hardest to conceal in brown." Muir had always and only used brown. A thousand documents in brown.

Lara, who had remained with the priest in the drawing room, poured mint tea for the priest and his refugees freshly minted from the morning attack. At the arrival of the Malay boy and his conversation with the priest, she joined Bishop in the priest's office.

"You were right. No one's coming. The courthouse, police station—the local authorities have all been driven out."

"They weren't driven out. They walked off of their own free will."

"Why would they?"

"Lara, the government is supplying the Ramadan Moon their weapons."

"That can't be true. It's the one issue the prime minister and Mrs. Musa's PDF agree on—the violence the extremist militias pose."

Bishop withdrew the shell casing from his pocket. Puzzled, she took it in the palm of her hand.

"Part and parcel with hiding the money behind the movement. Arming your professed enemies makes sense if you're looking for a reason to declare martial law." He tapped the brass. "Government issue."

Their eyes met. Silent acknowledgment that somewhere in the last moments they'd crossed the line from captor and prisoner to a kind of collaboration. Lara dropped her gaze to the baptismal record. There was no godfather listed, but on the space for her godmother, the name and signature read: "Clotho Lachesis."

"That can't be a name—Clotho Lachesis?" she said.

But it was. Two names Bishop didn't want to see. Nathan Muir's neat and tight angular handwriting. Names Bishop had never chosen to know; forced upon him, they were the cast of his fatherless nightmares. His nightmares and all the lies of his childhood—and *maybe* a kid can forget if it's just childhood, right? If it had started that way but sorted itself out—but the nightmare came to life in Vietnam and Berlin, China, and all the rest of the trust of one man to another man who should have said, frank and modest, "I'm your dad" but didn't.

Bishop shut the tome.

"*Is* it a person? A codename for somebody?" Lara said. "I can see that you recognize it."

Bishop gave her a curious look. He headed for the door. Lara followed. How many people entrusted to his care had caring gotten dead by following him? Lara didn't know that. Anyway, she didn't have another choice.

He moved with speed. Lara chased after him, retracing their path back through the jungle, back up the footpath from the rectory to the torched church.

"Whatever that name means, you wouldn't have discovered it without me. Tell me. Help me understand what's happening to me."

"I should've left you with the priest, but even if they clear out, they stand too good a chance of meeting their maker somewhere between here and safety."

Lara's eyes accused. "Why didn't you warn the him?"

Bishop stopped walking.

"What word from me is going to carry more weight than what's already gone down?"

Lara swung a slap for his face. Bishop caught her wrist.

"I'm not here to help them. I've left a big enough footprint already."

Bishop led off again. Lara dogged him close enough to watch drops of sweat run rivulets down his leathery neck.

"Clotho Lachesis was written for two people," he muttered.

"Us?" she said.

Bishop glanced back, his cynical expression exactly his father's.

"Wrong. Me and a guy named Aiken."

"Who's he?"

"My attorney with the Agency. If this goes wrong and they send someone to make an extrajudicial termination of my employment over it, they'll send Aiken."

"Why would they—why him?"

"Because he's my only friend on this whole blood-soaked, careening merry-go-round of a globe."

Bishop pushed some branches aside, held them so they didn't snap back in her face as she followed.

"Someone that close to you—what? Does he just blindly follow orders?"

"No, I left a good provocation in my wake before getting here. Anyway, he knows Clotho and Lachesis. Better than I do, I'd wager. So, one of us will sort this out for the old man."

"They're people?"

"They're witches. Two the three Fates. Clotho spins the thread of life. Lachesis holds the thread and fixes its length."

"Your father's mythology."

"Greeks' first, but yeah. Like your *Sang Sinxay*, I had the picture book of this one, growing up with my mom telling me my dad died somewhere he didn't."

Lara gave him a funny look. "Again, you're asking me to believe Muir knew thirty-three years ago, you, an expert in picture books, would come find his Sunday baptism-*me* baby-book signing? *1968?*"

"And yet, here we are."

They were halfway back to the Land Rover. The cicadas were as loud as the harsh buzz of electrocution. Bishop increased his pace. He heard her stumble behind him. He didn't look back to see if she'd fallen.

An image of her asleep the night before flashed in his mind. He buried it.

He missed Elizabeth. Pledged to for eternity. He silently cursed his impotency those last four hospital nights in Taiwan. He threw his attention on a yellow, black, and white butterfly bouncing through the heavy air across the trail ahead of him. He didn't want to think of either woman, not in that way, and not now. The flutter-by landed on a red hibiscus. It unrolled its spiraled proboscis, pollen collecting as it drained nectar. Was it Bishop diminishing her or Lara using him? Was it borrow or rob? He draining her of identity, she using him to escape the trap of her roots and blossom elsewhere.

"Who was the Third Fate?" came Lara's voice, once again close behind.

They were near the end of the path, the ruins of the church. Smoke still curled and whisked in horsetails behind a screen of short three-palm clusters. The acrid smell of burned-out destruction he'd never gotten used to and never would.

"Atropos. She's the Fate who cuts off life—"

He froze before entering the clear. He thrust his left arm backward, checking Lara's forward progress as his right hand brought up his pistol.

"Ow! What?!"

"Drop," he hissed, and assured his command by sweeping her feet out from under her. Lara collapsed to the bracken. She glared up at him.

Bishop dropped to a single-knee combat-firing posture. Lightly moved a palm frond a few inches. He scanned the Rover and the smoke-blackened, charcoaled rubble through the hole in the leaves. She leaned her head around him. Empty ruins, parking area, Land Rover, lonely road beyond.

Bishop put a finger to his lips. He looked deep into her eyes and moved his finger to his ear. *Listen.*

No birds, no insects. Even the air held its breath. Nature's early warning system.

Lara blinked worry. "They let the priest go with a warning."

"Lara, see that corner of broken wall?"

He indicated it with the black-eyed muzzle of his pistol.

"No."

"Whatdya mean, 'no'? We're not walking out into an ambush."

"There doesn't have to be any killing," Lara said and lunged forward.

Her hand gripped the purple knot of her hijab as she came up against the Land Rover.

She shouted in Arabic. "Assalamualaikum warahmatullahi wabarakatuh!" *May the peace, mercy, and blessings of Allah be with you!*

"Salam sejahtera kepada kamu!" *May peace be upon you!* Returned a shout in Malay from the opposite jungle.

Lara smiled back at Bishop, but he was looking to the right and past her, his gun extending with his vision and firing. She cried out, eyes following the shot to see a young Malay Muslim with an AK-47, aiming, bearing down—

About to kill her?

—crumple.

A machine gun opened fire from the direction the voice had come from.

Lara ducked, loathing for Bishop in her eyes, as he urgently motioned at the piece of broken wall.

"Get behind it! Go! Cover your head!"

He lunged out, shooting, drawing fire. Lara fled. She sprinted for the broken corner of wall. Machine-gun fire spit from the cover of foliage beyond Saint Agnes's Church, carving the dirt a short distance behind her as, comfortably encased in his warm place, Bishop fired twice at the muzzle flash of the machine gun that strafed bullets back toward him, allowing Lara the chance to reach the wall.

She slammed her body hard behind it. Scrunched harder against it. Since she hadn't been shot, even nicked, she was as good as last week.

The machine gun raked back to her. Chewed stone.

Bishop dashed for the Land Rover, firing as he moved. He took position at the front tire and hood of the passenger side of the vehicle behind the protection of the engine block. The machine gun chawed back in his direction. The car windows exploded. Bishop was pinned. A Ramadan Moon rebel spun around the back of the Land Rover, firing, bearing down with focus, but Bishop had already twisted around the front bumper.

Lara, her face half buried in ash, saw it. Saw Bishop drop to his belly, the bullets whiffing over his head, trails of dust and chipped rust vacuumed from the car from bullet velocity pass-by. She saw Bishop pump two rounds into the man's chest without a thought more than tossing a napkin after a boring meal, blood and tissue exploding out his back. The man hit the ground, twitching and dying, and Bishop swiveled onto one knee back toward Lara, fluid, aiming over her head. He fired once more and hit a third rebel who was moving in from the ruins behind her.

Her attacker collapsed behind some fallen timber. He babbled in Malay. Throughout it all, Lara screamed.

Bishop leaned out around the front of the car to draw suppressing fire from the machine gun. He waited. He leaned farther. A fourth rebel was coming toward him from the far right, around the front of the ruined church. His AK drove Bishop back behind the wheel well and engine block with fire and lead. The rebel kept coming. Worked his way around the front of the vehicle. *Bangity-bang-bang-bang.* AK hammer. Second most recognizable sound worldwide after the Nokia ringtone. He made the right headlight and blind fired around the passenger side. He stepped to where he knew Bishop was slain.

No Bishop.

The jihadi crouched, bloodshot eyes darting to the rear of the car. The first rebel's body no longer held a weapon.

Bishop flicked the selector and fired a three-round burst through the rear windows, exploding this third Ramadan Moon rebel's head.

The machine gun located Bishop. Ripped rounds until the *clack* Bishop waited on. He spun away from the Land Rover. Gun leading two-handed—the gun *is you*—he charged the green face of jungle right into the machine gun's smoking barrel protruding through torn branches and smoldering leaves. The machine gunner's hands worked a feed-belt through the breechblock. Bishop kicked him in the jaw, tumbling him back. There was another Ramadan Moon behind the gunner. The jaw-kicked one had been on the gun. He looked in terror as his loader cravenly scrambled off on hands and knees. Bishop executed both. Head-head tap-tap. Never sorrow.

He stepped out of the foliage. He'd let himself into this. He'd led her. His eyes flashed back toward the corner of church wall.

Lara was gone. Gun held high, aiming downward from above his eyeline in combat approach, he shuffle-stepped into the ruins.

"Lara!"

He stopped abruptly, having caught sight of her behind the timbers, cradling the head of her wounded would-be killer in her lap. Tears streaked her face as the killer babbled to her in pain and fright. A young man in his teens. Bishop joined them. Lara squinted at Bishop enraged.

"Lara. Move."

"No. Murderer!"

"I saved your life."

"You started the killing!"

"Don't make this more difficult. Move. Now."

"He's a child, you fucker!"

"No, those two playing here were the children. Ask him what he did with them, the ones I gave the pennies. Ask what he did… Ask him."

Lara's tear-stained eyes went from Bishop to the young man in her lap. She spoke in Malay. The wounded killer understood her and didn't respond. His silence was loud enough for Lara to hear in it the terrible truth. She pushed the dying teen from her lap. Lara staggered to her feet, shaking blood from her hands. Her mad eyes swept the ruin for any sign of the two Mai Semai kids she'd spoken with. She cried out in Malay and she backed away as Bishop aimed his gun at the wounded rebel.

The killer intoned a fervent, "Inna lillahi wa inna ilayhi raji'un!" *We belong to Allah and to Allah we shall return!* Except the *return* never dinged at the end. Bishop rang his bell first, a bullet to his heart. Let's the brain know death a few moments longer.

Bishop looked to Lara. She stared across the ruined church into some thick rubble. The handle of a *parang* machete rose from where the blood-dripped blade had been planted. She went to it. Her body shook.

"Get away from there. Lara."

But she didn't. She didn't hear him at all. Bishop slung his weapon. He joined her. Kept his face turned from what transfixed her. Looking never helped. He took her limp wrist. Gave a gentle pull.

"We have to leave."

Lara wrenched free. "Look!"

"Nope. Let's go."

Tom Bishop tried to take her arm, but this time when she pulled away, she swung back hard, slapping his face with the full force of her open palm.

"God damn you! God damn all of you! You'll kill anyone! Why?!"

Eyes still averted from the gruesome sight within that rubble, Bishop tried to grab Lara by the shoulders, but she fought him with everything she had, pummeling him with her fists, choking on tears and fury. "Tell me why!"

Bishop took it.

Every blow.

Until, in one swift move, he encircled her with his arms and swept her off her feet. And in this way, like a bridegroom with his bride, Bishop carried Lara, hysterical and beating his face, his neck, and his shoulders, away from death and the ruined church where she first met Islamic jihad, understanding it in the form of beheaded children.

<h1 style="text-align:center">22</h1>

THIS IS NOT a western.

Sure, we had our Bishop-Aiken quick-draw face-off. In a Good-Bad-Ugly graveyard replete with golden treasure. Settler woman in his wagon and Injuns on the periphery, sure, but they were the other kind of Indians, and the woman: an unsettled victim of abduction. As Bishop was the only one of us who chose to shoot, let alone shoot to kill, our little hoedown was simply a man-down instead of a showdown. One life lost on boot hill—and let me tellya, pilgrim, you don't get a second. With my diseased mind spinning me west of everything, I went out recalling the last death I'd been witness to in real time: Elizabeth's last night in Taipei.

Muir kissed her brow and whispered, "The supernatural light of the spirit is the only night from which the spirit can emerge alive."

On this night that Elizabeth would slip away from life, I thought the phrase was his and I thought him magical. Three years later, after I had discerned his Prospect Garden French comment to me about cowards, the men of courage, the pell-mell flight was originated by philosopher Jacques Maritain, I would flee into Maritain's waiting mind with the determination to devour it (like the Martian in my head devoured my own) and so to digest his course of thought that when next Muir tried to serve him up, I'd be able to dish some of the old Aquinas lover's duck soup right back at him.

Before Bishop murdered Muir, before I got that chance—the chance to finesse Muir, not to kill him: let's just be clear—but as

I was escorted from the embassy through the rioting backstreets of martial-law KL to my destiny in the city's Christian cemetery, that "supernatural light" remark to Elizabeth sprung to mind and I had to smile to myself, acknowledging Muir had already finessed three years earlier with a Maritain quote in a Taipei cancer ward before I even knew he had the trick up his sleeve.

"La lumière surnaturelle de l'esprit est la seule nuit où l'esprit puisse sortir vivant."

The true ransoming of time that last night in that Taiwan hospital: if it wasn't supernatural itself, it was surreal as a night could get.

That night, Muir revealed to Elizabeth Tom Bishop's core identity as only a father can. Not by revealing Bishop's untold first steps and falls reaching for desires, first words expressing inclinations, first Christmas Santa magic and Jesus wonder, first fight, first perfectly formed independent idea—polestar to the soul—his first kiss, taste, test, love, or lust—those, Muir never knew—but the identity defined through their life of clandestine operations, those deception events anchored in experience of reality that allowed a single identity to emerge from dozens of personas Bishop had been assigned, had chosen, or, by necessity, had been forced to become. To live. To be.

"Compelled to live life through being everything to everyone, Tom learned the greatest lesson a spy can learn: to never lose the thing it was to be himself. Experienced reality," Muir explained, "those vestige lives Tom lived, pretend masks, are the stationary landscape of time while identity is the river rushing from behind us, buoying us in the present, and flowing ahead of us to pull our lives along a course of circumstance."

"Then the past," Elizabeth weakly offered, "the past doesn't determine our future because it was the future once itself. That's the illusion. Who we are is already determined; it awaits us no matter who we think ourselves one day to the next. Does that make sense?" From sunken eye, she gamely embraced us all.

"It's bloodline," Muir said, "and we ride its red river forward; we carry it to where it's already running ahead of us."

Personally, I didn't need Muir's vestigial masks or Elizabeth's Richard Bach brook-babble philosophy to sugarcoat genetic identity. You were there, Mads. You saw. I obediently kept my mouth shut. But you ought to know now that we've come to this place: I've thought a lot about this and consider myself as much an expert as Muir on the matter. Maybe more. Probably more than Muir.

Our codes of behavior, problem-solving, how we balance bliss and sadness, anger and calm, control and chaos, traits, postures, attractions and distractions, the way we laugh out loud and what makes us laugh inside are all ordered and leveled and triggered by our forebears' DNA passed on to us.

Muir's blood river and its landscape of signs and symbols we react to based upon our stream of genetic code.

No genetic test has conclusively proven mental disorders are passed genetically, but it is accepted as actuality and bears out in statistical sampling. Who hasn't heard "She's had her father's temper since the minute she was born." Or "You never knew your grandmother, but she had that same talk-to-anyone-in-the-checkout-line personality." "The boy couldn't help it. Born plain bad, just like Uncle 'Jailyard' Jimmy." "Son, God gave you the exact sense of humor my dad had."

I read a few years back in the New York Times, *"First Gene for Social Behavior Identified in Whiskery Mice—Anxiety and Aggression Gene Discovered," an article I skipped—old news, watch an episode of Tom & Jerry—and went on to the opinion page for a stale-breathed think-piece on the Israeli-Arab Peace Process Question, the* New York Times *and my own company's bread-and-butter business, where the profit in maintaining "The Question" far outweighs—no, better, forgives—keeping peace a process and our bills paid by the answer never found.*

It wasn't until Jessie joined our family, Muir's genetic identity as pre-birth basis of identity concept came clear to me by virtue of your and my gene pool never mixing (although attraction and marriage, it would seem, skinny-dip in the gene pool of compatibility), and the Italian observation I topi non avevano nipoti *(that the mice had no grandchildren) is finally put to rest.*

You and I are altogether absent in Jessie, while traits exhibited by that precious, precocious girl are thoroughly absent in both of us. I'm not talking about her socialized behaviors, the imprints of her Siberian horror-show past, but in her natural instincts and tendencies. She's a rushing Volga to our lazy Potomac. I'm talking about her genetic imprint of heritable behaviors. Half the time I have no idea what she's thinking or how she's thinking it, something one fully senses and takes for granted with bloodline family. How many times have we scratched our heads at Jessie's logic, which works perfectly well for her? I've marveled at her sense of innate compassion—you've pointed out that couldn't have come from me—and your admiration for her unwavering loyalty… I stay silent in pointing out that doesn't come from you.

"The core of our identity," Muir said, "is within us from the moment we develop a heartbeat, because the basis of our identity is immortal in our DNA. So… to tell you about Tom, his how and his why, I must introduce you to my father."

The old spy-cum-professor come down my garden path, chum, wary of the landmines, to my centaur fountain: "Myth as it exists in a savage community is not merely a story told but a reality lived."

"Careful. By your own theory, you'll be revealing yourself," I said.

Muir's attention remained upon fixed Elizabeth. He stroked her cheek.

"Bitsy." Muir called her Bitsy. "Russell knows and I don't deny it: the stories I tell best are the stories that tell best about me."

Bitsy.

"Was your father in the spy game?"

I called her Bitsy once. Her reaction was the pity reserved for society's needy. Special needy. She let Muir call her Bitsy. Reveled in it. And, since she had one of those names with endless nicknames, I figured maybe there was enough for a one-per-customer policy. I picked another to call her.

"Not the spy game Tom and I play," he answered, excluding me.

It's never fair. Nicknames, that is. Most names only get one accepted derivative. Jack for John, Mike for Michael. Jean for Jeannie, Rose for Rosemary. Jack, Mike, Jean, Rose, Evie for Evelyn, Cathy for Catherine, Russ for me (sure, there's Rusty—some use it endearingly; Muir and you, mockingly), and these are all legally accepted signatures—banking documents, contracts; argued successfully even in cases where signature lines have specified "full legal name."

But then comes Elizabeth. Queen of the nicknames. Off the top of my head, I can tender ten legit diminutives for Elizabeth. (That tender top of my head.) Muir's Bitsy. Mads, you call her Beth, and Bishop calls her Lizzie half the time. She lets the one nurse who speaks perfect English call her Birdie.

"My grandfather Linus Muir was the last of the genuine cowboys, while my father—between being a spoiled, indolent-as-a-sultan rich kid and a drunk who died alone in a speculator's shack at the Telegraph Hill oil fields of Los Angeles—broke, tamed, and trained forty-two Spanish horses; drove them—as in 'cattle drive' drove them—to the center of Rome, where they won a chariot race against Pontius Pilate for Christ."

Elizabeth claims there are forty-two valid nicknames for her name. In getting to know her—after the Bitsy debacle—I tried my ten (minus the already reserved Bitsy-Beth-Lizzie-Birdie set) and six more of her forty-two, until she shut me down in exasperation, "Rusty, you're kind of a Dr. Awkward with nicknames. You're a just-Elizabeth with me. Got it?"

I did. Ho! Oh, did I. But she's wrong and I must stand by Wizzy. Wizzy is a legitimate and legitimated nickname for Elizabeth. Rolls right off the tongue: Wizzy.

It's as legit as Mads.

CE N'EST PAS *un western.*

Nor Magritte's pipe.

To boot.

(Which is a shoe, although a shoe is not a boot. Certainly not a cowboy boot.)

Sure, Muir had been called "cowboy" more times than Harker and his Young Turks called him "dinosaur." Bishop too—"cowboy" anytime he wasn't being cursed as "renegade," which does have a Louis L'Amour pinto pony kick to it anyway. All I'm saying is I hope I don't foul this up with too much cowboy kablooey coming right 'round the canyon corner, identity hooves a'pounding. To Muir's way of thinking, Elizabeth's saddle thrown in with him, Bishop was dealt the cards he now played before he was born— before Muir was born, and his father before that, and Muir's grandfather (Bishop's great) one step further back who was the only honest cowboy among 'em—cards dealt from the last of the great bronc busters to his horsing around with a four-in-hand team, Roman bits, and an arena, and a Christ to fight for, whether you knew it or not, in a 1925 celluloid deception operation marked deck. All a matter of semiotics, as they say.

This isn't a spaghetti western, but it's sure something of a picture of one and the appearance of a reality—as Jan van Eyck (no relation) first experimented with on altarpieces, playing (or is it plying?) with the illusion of identity in the house of God; or, as his critic Benedetto Varchi wrote of his work, la pittura fa parere quello che non é *("painting feigns that which it is not")—ought to speak at least a thousand words about identity.*

Early on, Elizabeth's cancer metastasized throughout her skeletal system. Treatment with bisphosphonates effectively slowed the rate of resorption, allowing her bones to rebuild at the same rate as they were breaking down. Effective for seventeen months, the treatment crashed. The rate of resorption increased. Calcium from her breaking-down bones released into her bloodstream and her hypercalcemia became unmanageable. Elizabeth slipped into a coma. The coma signaled her approaching end. There was little optimism she would awaken. Then, three months later, she did.

She had lost her ability to speak and she worked every day to regain it, struggling to make words with whichever of us were with her—people she loved but didn't recognize. Her confusion and frustration were immense. The last DVD she and Tom had watched before she disappeared into the coma was the Rex Harrison musical extravaganza *Dr. Dolittle*. For weeks after she came back to consciousness without context, watching the film was the only thing that could calm her.

I must have watched it twenty times, my own frustration and annoyance excruciatingly kept in check anytime that Ethel Merman schoo of overacting song-and-dance man—what's-his-name sidekick?—The guy who does a chaîné turn better than Harker?—Gave us that stepped-in-gum sticky-cloying "Candy Man"—whatsisname—song?

Whatever. Everyone loved him but me, good for him. Or maybe me.

But we'd sit in that little room and fantasy away to Puddleby on the Marsh while I pointed out, in the 1920s, with the creation of the Soviet Union, one of the first major intelligence coups of the nascent Communist dictatorship was the secret theft of the *Dr. Dolittle* books from the West. Hustled in darkness from London by Russian children's poet-agent-translator Korney Chukovsky, *Dr. Dolittle* was mercilessly transformed into *Dr. Aybolit* (translation: Dr. Ow-it-hurts), a folkloric Soviet veterinarian able to talk to the animals who, with them and the тяни-толкай née (pushme-pullyu), fight capitalistic pirates around the globe.

Among Soviet children required to read and compulsorily love, the intrepid, comical Russian vet and revolutionary Aybolit became an instant success. Like Soviet cosmonaut Yuri Gagarin—first human delivered into orbit on April 12, 1961, an event that launched the all-hands-on-deck Space Race—good ol' Dolittle imposter Aybolit, six years to the day to coincide with Gagarin's triumph, struck another heavy Soviet blow against the West with the Mosfilm release of *Aybolit 66*. A huge international success, *Aybolit 66* played across Europe—well, Eastern Europe— to packed and obedient audiences while, with a feeble Christmas release later that year, and disastrous fifth column reviews, Rex Harrison's *Dolittle* bombed at the American box office, the fallout almost putting 20th Century Fox out of business. Heady Cold War times.

A couple years later we put a flag on the lunar surface, so we have that tick in our win column. Third-floor interrogation room or the moon: ascent just feels better.

We'd watch the movie, and Elizabeth would hold Muir's hand and mistake him for her husband. Vice versa when roles reversed and Bishop was in the room—the father and son still trapped by the yet unfulfilled murder promise between them. Each of those men would, without knowing their behaviors identical, do a dozen "I'm sorry," "No, I'm sorry," "No: I'm sorry" sorries and neither ever accepted the forgiveness she absolved them with: Nathan Muir for betraying her into a Chinese prison; Tom Bishop for devaluing her total forgiveness of his father, thereby deprecating her capacity for love and trivializing her faith in God. Genetic gnostic trait, you see.

I would sit with my dull crooked smile and pretend I didn't hate Tom for not being there every minute with his dying wife and dared him, but only in my mind, to come into the hospital room and hug instead of kill his dad who'd buried the hatchet, or at least had made the Herculean effort to drop it in the sea somewhere between America and China. But my false-brother couldn't put a tin penny of worth on that.

Pennies from heaven.
Penny for your thoughts.
Pennies dropped from on high,
Pennies for a dead girl's eyes.

A DEATHBED REQUEST for a Muir story. I'll try to do it justice now as I remember it—looking back after Muir's death and the things he said preparing me for said same—Muir's father was the son Muir never-did/couldn't-be but wanted to create and wanted all of us to become. Even you. Even Elizabeth, even Jessie and our Nate.

Like spies' masks interchanged until the perfect identity concealed revealed.

It stuck with him, so it sticks with me, and it left precious Elizabeth a final yearning joy, and Tom—because he arrived too late—needs to know what he missed. I think, want to think anyway, that his dad wanted me to brief him on this when the right time came. Dead and gone seems right enough, so here goes; I'll probably get it all wrong, but when your mind says, "What's the point?" I've learned by trial-and-trail and error-upon-errand: that's the point.

The horses.

By the Steeds that run, with panting breath,
And strike sparks of fire,
And push home the charge in the morning,
And raise the dust in clouds the while,
And penetrate forthwith into the midst of the foe en masse;
Truly man is, to his Lord, ungrateful;
And to that fact he bears witness by his deeds.

Linus Muir (this'd be Nathan's grandfather): born and toddled up somewhere East Coast, like Boston, not-Boston, somewhere—

Shit. I can't remember. My fucking mind: because I do remember. The thing inside my head keeps holding things back.

New-fucking-Island—*dammit!*—*Hampshire.*

A horse farm. New Hampshire. Raised horses, broke horses, sold horses—family had for four generations. William Sherman bought a Muir horse way back in the Civil War.

The picture-shows captivated Linus. When he was old enough to leave home, Linus grabbed a wife from a family against that sorta thing and did. He got as far as Nevada, where his money ran out. Cowboyed there for a time and made a rodeo name for himself busting broncs. This'd be—God, what?—1918 or '19 or something like that. Whatever it was, Linus Muir won quite a bit of money. I think I have the *Police Gazette* Belt somewhere he gave me to hold for Tom. Anyway, Linus took his wife and Nevada-born boon baby-boy Bucknell—nickname Bucky—and continued west to Los Angeles.

1920 Los Angeles was the last dangerous shoot-'em up, rootin'-tootin' cowboy town in America; men belted guns on Broadway and checked them when entering bars. They pretended Tombstone was alive and well on Olvera Street and downtown where three years earlier Wyatt Earp shot his way into and out of a crime of international espionage in sprinkler rain on the front lawn of his West Adams bungalow. "The Schulenberg Wobblies," a splashier story than Tombstone (this replete with a gun-toting forty-five-year-old moll posing as a mute teenage boy to hide her German accent), no one without clearance and a members-only card for our Langley Clandestine Services Library will ever know.

Earp sought out the leather trench coat German spies. Linus sought out the moviemakers. Caps and jodhpurs and riding crops and chutzpah and Linus knew his excellence with horses would make him a commodity. He'd deliver their cowboy horses for the cowpoke movies they loved to make, and the people paid a buffalo nickel to view, and it was a suitable place out by the Santa Susana Pass to make a living with horseflesh and friendly people in perpetual sunshine and sage-fresh air, and to raise a family, and all to pretend Tom Mix was real life and they all part of that in the land of bullets that never sting.

So let's get this straight: Nathan Muir's father, Bucky, grew up in an imaginary cowboy world. Linus provided the horses and the stunts for 86 of Tom Mix's 160 cowboy movies. As motion pictures—especially those western two- and three-reelers—became an international phenomenon, Linus's North Hollywood ranch, built along the old Phineas Banning stage line, now known as Riverside Drive, grew larger with stables, lemon and orange groves, and an Olympic-sized swimming pool with a high diving platform for his movie pals.

From the time he could walk and talk, Bucky, Muir said of his father, was well on his way to be a Hollywood brat who spent too many hours at the mercy of his own desires. The only thing connected to reality in Bucky's youth were the hard-knock horses.

"First thing we learn, son, is how to fall off a horse and not break your neck in doin' so. Learn to fall before you learn to ride," said Linus. "Now give 'er a kick. Head her my way. I'll shove you off."

Bucky hated the shoving, fought hard against falling, and his father soon abandoned teaching him to unsaddle off a horse in any manner of skill. Bucky just rode off and rode well enough to never fall.

In pretty much the same way, Bucky approached his youth. He didn't do in high school the lessons necessary to get into college, got easy work on Linus's movie sets he'd walk off of as soon as he got first pay. Got laid, drank, smoked, and turned eighteen like a San Fernando Valley Dionysus. While he didn't get into college by not bothering to apply, he chased the UCLA coeds and broke the heart of a girl who might have been Muir's mother if Bucky had treated her properly.

"Bucky, I cannot date you because you are not real," Doris Reynolds, the Delta Gamma pledge, said one screen-doored Friday. "You're like one of your dad's movies."

"I look like a movie star, but I don't act like a movie star—I'm not a bit selfish or egotistical."

The inability to see himself ran strong in his veins.

"No, you're like a movie-set facade. Your appearance has its own reality, like a flat that looks like a house, or looks like a hotel, but there's nothing behind it… not even a dirty saloon beyond the swinging doors of you. I won't see you anymore."

Linus was already in Rome with Bucky's mother when Bucky went to his father's office at MGM Studios where Louis B. Mayer had the only West Coast access to the new transatlantic telephone line. Spoiled and unfallen, Bucky reached out and touched his mother.

"While you've been wasting your time, your father has built a coliseum. There will be a chariot race. It will be the most spectacular event with horses in modern history and commemorated on film as the all-time motion-picture event. Your father works. What do you do and why are you wasting Mr. Mayer's secretary's money to pay for this call? I know how you wangle things—"

"UCLA is for the birds, Mom."

"You're not attending."

"I've been sitting in on classes."

"You're a Muir: you're a liar. You're chasing girls you should be keeping your hands off of, I am sure."

No one dumped Bucky Muir. "I want a job," he said to spite his memory of cute little Doris.

He could hear the scuttling crabs that clacked claws at the cable that had connected W. S. Gifford, president of the American Telephone & Telegraph Company, and Sir Evelyn P. Murray, secretary of the General Post Office of Great Britain, the first time in history where two people made a call that didn't request, reject, order, alarm, rescind, deny, accuse, cajole, convince, place an order, cancel an order, refute a billing, or a treaty, or an anything, profess love or whisper innuendo, or come right out with the phone sex or the declaration of war; the cable that has allowed people the ability to point at themselves and each other with very likely nothing to say and definitely no substance behind it. Or, that other thing people do on the phone—until we learn to crack burner cellphone transmissions—lie and illegally conspire to commit the simplest petty crime or the greatest terrorist attack they think can't be tracked.

"Happened just that way," Muir said to Elizabeth in her Taipei hospital bed. "Nineteen hundred some odd years in the future, a new Judah Ben-Hur would race white Andalusians for Christ being nailed to the cross."

Bucky's mother said: "Your father needs sixty horses. He will need them broken, and he will need them fifty days from Monday. These horses are not—as had been promised him—in Italy. Italians, ugh. Those people make *you* appear industrious and virtuous. Do this for your father, Bucknell—which, regrettably, I think you cannot—but *if* you do, you may rejoin your family."

The next morning, Bucky sent Linus a Western Union telegram. He was the man for the job.

Linus sent two in response. One to Andalusia, Spain. The other back to Bucky: *Get lazy ass to Madrid. Stop. That's Spain. Stop. Find Miguel-Angel Rodriguez. Stop. Palace Hotel. Stop. Twelve days not paying way. Stop. Not paying anything. Stop. Find your college bank book. Stop. Figure out the rest. Stop.*

BUCKY MUIR wasn't devious, he was clever. He had gotten by in his life on that—on his uncanny ability to find a shortcut around any path that demanded brass-tack work necessary to gain an intellectual, spiritual, emotional life lesson. His life exemplified appearance versus reality. He was lucky because every shortcut he'd taken past learning events had worked. The entanglements real life had intended him to learn living, he'd navigated around with a deadened sensibility of seeming. The trouble he should have gotten into, the trouble that would have taught life lessons of caution and safety and care—of true love—he skippity-doo-dah-ed around. He was too clever by half and then half as clever by too much more for his own good. Never odd or even. Bucky Muir, when he did take an interest in something, could accomplish the major outward results of that thing at such an easy perfection, he never had to learn a basis. For Bucky, seeming was believing.

Nathan Muir was a good-looking man. Handsome a man as you'd ever meet until the day his son shot him dead. He used it to his advantage. He slayed women figuratively with it, and he killed men literally with it (on an equal fast-draw, those looks gave Nathan Muir a fifth-of-a-second more trigger pull; keep your gun tuned and your hair combed: you got a dead enemy), but his father, Bucky, was more than handsome. Bucknell Muir was *delightfully* handsome. I think back now, that disarming smile Nathan used forever to his advantage, was a mockup movie-set facade of his father's smile and blooded to Bucky by his father before him. It's the only way a wasted, wastrelly, waistcoated, ne'er-do-well Nevada-to-LA transplant could do so well and, cheating every corner, could bury love and admiration in every corner of the hearts of everyone he knew, he met, loved, hated, and, ultimately, murdered.

And the one person who saw the heavenly transcendence that swarmed the unwitting man waiting to become from the boy—well, we'll get to him soon enough.

Muir said, "I know, my father sounds like some kind of moralless kid, but I don't think that's the point and I do think—and this is important, so listen: opportunity knocks in more ways than kids are stymied into ignoring. Opportunity is a Second Rule of Thumb—because when it knocks on the door, the thumb is curled back."

When Muir said that sentence, it was the weirdest moment of my life, for I saw tears in his eyes. For the first time, Nathan Muir didn't have an actual Rule of Thumb (which was typically a steadfast tenet built into a paradox). He was reading Elizabeth's vitals on the monitor and knew his promise to his son—Elizabeth's husband—our Bishop, his golden-word centaur-piping promise that Tom could run his mission in Kosovo, service his networks and his drops, and get back to Elizabeth before the end of his world would not hold. Elizabeth did not have the two-week doctor promise. This night was it.

I swatted her cheek to revive and reclaim her attention and, Mads, you slapped my hand to make me stop; and we saw all the line of the Linus and Bucky and Nathan diminished honesty but ever hopeful grin crease Muir's face as Elizabeth's eyes flashed and twinkled her dying light.

Twinkled at happiness unknown but approaching recognition.

"Tell me a little more? I want to fall asleep to the sound of your voice. When I close my eyes and hear it, I hear what Tom will sound like when I'm gone."

She closed her eyes. She breathed, short and shallow. Her heart beat weakly. Her blood pressure fell. We watched and as Muir smoothed out his words and committed to a story he'd known but never told anyone they both lived in words that created Tom alive in the room from dead memories of blood past.

"Your father sounds more unpleasant than you," I sniped, unhappy he hadn't compelled Tom to stay (or included me in his "spy game" comment), and I felt instantly stupid because I always say the wrong thing. Why I write life-and-death contracts.

"Anyway," I said, "what happened to the horses?"

"They were the single, true, pure highlight of that sonuvabitch's life. They're what allowed him my mother and what created me, maybe the best part—I hope—the part that lives in Tom."

BEHAVIORAL GENETICS raises questions about human freedom. If we know genes influence our behaviors, how do we believe we have free will to choose our actions? How did you choose Nate's biological father over me? Is it only an illusion of our ego that we believe we're free to choose the qualities of our temperament? Our capacity for love, honor, faith? Our tendencies to deceive, to cheat, and when we must—which is a must dictated by blood—kill. Identities are born and borne on a river of blood.

23

Nathan Muir's namesake, his great-grandfather Nathanial Muir, traveled with his family to Spain in 1910 to conduct business with Miguel-Angel Rodriguez's father—his name lost to Muir's memory (or, more likely, to mine)—at the Rodriguez family El Rancho Andalusia horse ranch to purchase and export Spanish horses to breed the best qualities of the Rodriguez Andalusian-Arabian mix into the Muir Farms Kentucky thoroughbreds. Great-grandfather Nathanial Muir achieved success with this and for generations produced in one hybrid strain not only race-horses but trace horses and pleasure-ride American saddlebreds. The horse that was everything to everyone, first in the long line of pre-CIA Muir family deception operations.

Just as he'd told it to Bishop, he'd taught it to me.

"First Rule of Thumb, Rusty: When operational, you must be everything to everybody, be their Disneyland [word weight 9]. *But Second Rule of Thumb: Remember to save a piece of who you really are for the trip back to real-world black and white."*

When, that spring of 1925, Nathanial's grandson, Bucky Muir, wobbled into Madrid's Palace Hotel dressed as a Rudolf Valentino-esque Argentine gaucho, suited and sombreroed, discourteously calling out Don Rodriguez's name inside an establishment where Rodriguez's face and family were known—

"Señor Rodriguez! Mr. Rodriguez! Señ-yoor!"

—this predisposed Don Rodriguez against the rude whelp. He would have preferred to have walked out, but personal honor and the honor esteemed to business associates compelled Rodriguez to stay. He smiled—every Madrileño relishing the gleam of the dagger in the stretched lips and sparkling teeth—and he offered his hand to Bucky.

"Did the theater play take place aboard your ship or aboard the train?"

"I look goofy?"

Señor Rodriguez appreciated that. "*Por qué?* Why do you think?"

"Maybe I am goofy?"

"'Maybe' is not giving yourself enough credit."

"I'll say one thing: the women in this country are tip-top. Look nothing like Mexicans."

"They are not for you," said Rodriguez, and then with an appraising eye, "and you are not to look at them because I do not want a single one of them to want you. Take this."

He handed Bucky a telegram.

Bucky glanced at it. It was in Spanish. "I got no idea what this says."

"When you do, we will follow those extra instructions. They are from your father." Rodriguez signaled a waiter for his bill.

"I could use a *cerveza*," Bucky said.

"You couldn't. Here is my bill and the bill for the two nights I have been here waiting for you two days late. You will pay for them."

"What?"

"It is the deal. This is all on you. *Pagarás todo el tiempo.*"

Bucky folded the telegram and tucked it in his pocket.

"Keep the boots, they are correct. Get out of the clown suit. I will wait." Rodriguez indicated the path to the men's lavatory and pinched the right wing of his gray mustache. "A *propósito*, if I uncover you have someone translate *ese telegrama* from your father before you decipher it yourself, our deal is off."

"Señor Rodriguez, I won't lie. That's exactly what I was going to do. I'm more the Sheriff of Nottingham than Robin Hood. I've come to understand that. It's how I'm made. But you seem like a nice guy, a fair-minded gentleman." Bucky wagged the telegram. "I'll do what I can. I want to make this work. And, by the way, I may be dumb, but I'm not an idiot: I've already figured out two of my father's first five words."

"Have you?" said Señor Rodriguez. "*Digame*." And Bucky was already casting his spell with the fire in his eye.

"'Bucky' and 'idiot.'"

Rodriguez laughed. "Puede que no seas un barco hundido después de todo." *You may not be a sunken ship after all.*

"Let me get into some real clothes and you have me, and you getta teach me how to horse around. *Sabe*, as you folks say?"

Señor Rodriguez could see what Linus had warned him he would see. It was given that he would beat the shit out of Bucky over the coming month. Hard. *Duro como la mierda.* Hard as shit. But it was also at that moment, Señor Miguel-Angel Rodriguez opened a tiny corner of his heart to this kid. Why? Because it wasn't only that there was clearly promise grown wild and in need of pruning; there was clearly an angel—a real angel—hanging happily around Bucky Muir's neck. Didn't belong to Bucky, *no propiedad total*, but an angel, and Rodriguez collected angels because, he knew more than any man alive, angels gathered and danced and laughed around the necks of running horses. They gathered behind boys and pushed them into manhood. They gathered around girls and made them wives and mothers, sweet and strong, loving and tender. They gathered around men and made them fight for causes even when those causes were lost. They were pure and they were true, and purity and truth were how Don Rodriguez presented himself to the world.

This boy was bad, but this bad boy would do.

If Don Rodriguez could capture an angel—figuratively or in a dream where he could speak to the holy entity—he would ask why not curl your arms around men, why make us chase running horses? And I don't know enough Spanish in Malaysia to translate to English in heaven, but many thought when the airplanes went crashing through, they heard in the sound of the apocalypse the sound of horseshoes on hoofs on air behind men and igniting fuel.

MUIR'S FATHER did get all holy hell beat out of him and found out later, when he tried to look back in anger, he looked back in blessings and *besos*, because he'd learned to need it—that past. That *detrás de él*, that "behind him" lesson that beat the shit into Bucky. And he learned to hear it. The cherub that Señor Rodriguez had seen upon his neck. Nathan Muir's father learned to give in to it—to give a damn—and it took *his* son (Nathan, just to keep stories straight) until he was at Princeton, at life's twilight, to recognize centaurs are neither horse nor man and, bubbling prettily as they will, will pipe wrens to their death and a final secret would be buried by an American of Korean descent.

Angels are inspiration that enter people. That guard them. That free them. Empower them. Bless them. People see angels as something outside themselves, but they are themselves. It's what Muir had finally understood and done for his networks, allowing them to discover the better angels in themselves after decades grounded in the shadows. Muir gave wings to Achilles 4, to Diana Red, Desert Hydra, and Trojan.

The chains of Cold War slavery had been broken by these networks, Muir's secret knights, but the world was once more in play. New bondage, new chains Hephaestus-forged. A new player Muir couldn't compete with whom he would not be invited back to sport across the board. Muir would not allow his old and underground, noble secret-thieves and guardians of peace be pawn sacrifices in this new war's opening moves.

Muir was a man tortured for thirty hours in Africa and left for dead. Muir was a man who could bury a dead wren by a drowning flute. He could not carry his Cold Warriors out of Jurassic Park into a worldwide web of twenty-first-century terrorism that would kill so many of us. He made them gone. He made them wild horses thundering up the Iberian Peninsula to a circus in Rome. His networks were freed and for all CIA purposes dead—and that was Muir's treason.

TEN MINUTES BEFORE Elizabeth died, she gripped my hand.

"We're the fire—everyone around you—but, Rusty, you're the coal. The true heat. You leave any of us—and you have every right to, every one of us, every day—if you leave any one of us: well, don't. Don't let this family's fire extinguish by taking a coward's way out. For me. Selfish. But for *me*. I'm the one dying here."

Not so far behind you, Wizzy.

I looked her in the eye. Hard. Like a horse and horses don't have any room when they look, no room for later, for what was before, for what might be after. Not endowed with human reason, horses, like other animals, seek out signs as I sought from Elizabeth. A sign: anything that presented the animal with knowledge of something other than itself, my external senses—the powers of sight, smell, taste, touch, and hearing—depended on the action of signs. The imprint of which imprints present meaning upon identity.

For the use of the sign does not necessarily involve inference and comparison. There is thus a certain presence—presence of know-ability—of the signified in the sign; the former is there in alio esse, *in another mode of existence.*

—Jacques Maritain

"—Anthony Newley," I exclaimed. "Dolittle's song-and-dance sidekick."

"Mm-hmm. I'm sorry I made you watch that movie so many times when I came out of my coma. Didn't even know I was doing it. But Dr. Dolittle couldn't have done any of what he did without Matthew Mugg," she said, naming Newley's character.

"The cockney rubbed accent—*accent rubbed*. One-two, not two-one. Rubbed. Me. Wrong."

"Rusty, I don't much care for where this world's going. The news I see. The nightmares I have. I'm almost glad to be getting out of it."

"What nightmares?"

"Foolish things. I dreamed last night I was cured, and Tom and I were flying home. Then a bunch of midgets, dark-faced foreign dwarves: like that Shanghai bootleg *Lord of the Rings* Nathan brought me last week. Long beards. Medieval robes and axes. Took over the plane. Ivy started to grow along the aisles and Tom tried to save us, but it tangled his feet and they lopped off his head and chanted spells in their language until they flew the airliner into the Potomac."

Whatdya say to hallucinations like that? "They spoke Dwarfish?"

"I don't think that was the point," Elizabeth said. "I know what the ivy was, though. My mother hated it in our garden, and she'd make me pull it. Said it bred rats. But it was cool in the summer and instead of pulling it, I'd lie back in its green leafy embrace on a hot afternoon and wait for the evening star. I loved the way it smelled. It always grew back anyway…" Her voice trailed, her breath running out like waves pulled away from land, the final moisture absorbing into sand. "Promise me you'll always be Tom's Matthew Mugg?"

She shut her eyes. She said something like this, and I could hardly hear it: "We're all children. Tell him that. I'm so proud of my Tommy: he found me so many times when I was lost, when I was captured, when I was self-destructive on booze and drugs and running scared, and he, wherever I was in the world, whatever jail, whatever war-zone medical camp, he got me out or brought my refugees medicine, our supplies. How I met him. And he never did kill Nathan. I don't believe he ever will—and tell him he better find someone, because if he holds back that love he has, that volcano inside him dies lonely, I will kill him in heaven."

"Elizabeth?"

Her eyelids fluttered, but she didn't open them.

"I'm sure Tom got my message. He's turning around right now. I'm sure he's already headed back."

"Tom said goodbye the last night and he's sad about it because—and I love him for it—he's real. He's never grown up into fake. Like you did. Like Nathan did. Like I did and Mads. We all struggle with appearance and reality, we match and judge and watch the cards in our hands, our secrets, but for Tom—my Tom— your Tom—appearance *is* reality. The rest of us are just liars."

"Hey, Elizabeth, how 'bout this isn't this conversation?"

"Understand me. You write the plans. For them. For me. For all of us. Maybe for your whole country."

"My plans quintessentially implement false appearance over reality."

"Accepted and lived, a false appearance is reality."

And then I understood the human sign she was showing me. And I saw the way everything she'd said was to tip me off balance. Everything she said was to nail me like a butterfly to a board, three flaps-of-the-wings left before the truth of dead. Before the honeybee backflip.

"How did you know?" I said. "I haven't even told Mads."

"You're not speaking right. You're mixing names, mispronouncing words. You've always said weird things but, Russell, your thoughts are running away from you these days. I'm riddled with tumors. Got them in my head too. I know what they do."

"I can't let anyone open my skull. I'll die."

"I'm dying. So what?"

"Right. And better you than me."

The wrong thing: said it again.

She tried to smile. "Right and better me than you, Rusty."

"The MRI proved it's benign, so why do I care?"

"It keeps growing and it's going to kill you and it will make you insane before it does, and I need you sane. Because I beat you to the finish line, I claim your future. Do you know who won the race? The tortoise and the snail?"

"You need your rest. We'll talk tomorrow."

"Ask my husband. He knows."

What made her the greatest judge of anything?

Sarcasm, like a comma, is all about where you place it. It's in the prosody I weight the question mark. Like her soul, my question mark was lighter than angels dancing on the head of a pin, or as Thomas Aquinas put it in his Summa Theologica:

1. Whether an angel is in a place through [its] operation alone

   … Beep… Beep… Beep…

2. Whether an angel can be moved from one extreme to the other without traversing the middle

   … Beep… Beep…

3. Whether a glorious body can exist with another body in the same place

   … Beep…

4. Whether a glorious body can in any way exist together in the same place with another body
5. Whether God can bring it about that matter exists without form

… beep…

6. Whether God can make the same body exist locally in two places at once
7. Whether God can reduce something to nothing
8. Whether God can restore numerically the same thing that was reduced to nothing

… … beep… …

9. Whether the aforesaid is the creator… Whether God can make infinites actually exist…

… … …b…e…e…p… … …

…Whether God can make contradictories be true together and infinities exist in act together…

… … … … … … Elizabeth's vitals ran flat.

I kissed her. I pushed through the cluster of nurses who'd come to ensure that her final DNR directive was followed. I mumbled an awkward thank you or some other lie. I shuffled past and went to look for Muir.

I FOUND MUIR on the rooftop helipad. He played with the orange windsock, batting it the way it didn't want to go, the way the wind wasn't blowing, batting it as tears covered his face and he didn't know who he was crying for: Elizabeth, whom he had once betrayed to death, rescued, and nurtured life within her for so long; or his son, her husband, who'd lost a wife? Or did Muir weep for his failings? The unborn child he never met, murdered in a fit of passion when he killed his innocent Jewel, the only woman he ever loved in the union of two as one.

Who the fuck was Muir? I thought as I watched him on that rooftop. Had he never learned a thing?

Muir told me, as I collected him in his heartbreak, he wanted his son to know how hard he tried. Every day. To be a father he'd lost the right to ever be, and how every night he prayed for forgiveness for not amounting to much of anything else. He wanted his son to be there. And he beat again at that orange sleeve on the helipad and lamented Elizabeth, whom he'd sold to China for a Russian Flanker—"A Goddamn soulless aircraft!"—and sold out his son and sold out his self and felt useless, bitter. He desired to feel that no one had ever asked him to—

Cross it out: love.

Cross it out: care.

Cross it out: parent.

Cross it out: love thy country—

Love thy wife—what a failure! Love myself?—Imposter!

Cross it out: I protected America.

Cross it out and take me and not her, please, dear Lord-God-Jesus-intervene!

Cross it out.

Nathan Muir had found himself on numerous rooftops before. Nathan Muir had bargained with every devil in the flesh in every war, on every continent, five-star to flophouse hotel, sewer tunnel, basement and rooftop. Nathan Muir had beaten the devil so many times. He'd just never faced his angels. And the angels carry us away, Elizabeth, and each one of us in our time, and he'd seen so many people's time shut off so violently—so many times at his word, by his command through his own son and by my pen stroke ordered—and he'd seen so many children who he always wanted one to look at him, look to him, to know him as family, and he'd never been given that—and when he'd had it, he'd turned his back on it and them because of the murder he committed. Just like his own father, Bucky.

And Nathan stood on the helipad of that Taiwan hospital and kept hitting the orange guidon even as I held him and didn't have any idea—so self-absorbed am I—his son was two floors beneath holding his dead wife and crying and impotent and loving his father not for all he could *not do*, but that his dad had done well, which he'd never let Muir know.

Why do we have to know anything? Learn the secrets that are set in war canoes upon the river to kill us?

IN 1925. Tom Bishop's grandfather, Bucky Muir, faced an Andalusian stallion. Pure black, with beautiful amber eyes—you've never seen a horse like this, certainly Bucky Muir never had—and it spit in his face. Knew what it was doing. Did it on purpose. It spit better than an Arab's camel. Yep, spit in his face.

Bucky Muir had a job ahead of him. He had an inkling it might mean something that he, for once, couldn't cheat but for once could notice important. That kid, and Nathan, Tom, and me—to my own respect—we benefited or lost on a glob of horse spit. It's why we're all here and I'm needing to write you, my unfaithful wife, because Nathan, and Tom, and I gave the best of ourselves to spit in the face of those men who met in conference in Malaysia with such quality room service and turn-down and chocolates on their pillows before they lay their weary heads to rest and fly the friendly skies of violent dreams.

24

Back to Harker's Seventh Floor Conference Room. Back to the deep blue carpet you need snowshoes to cross. Back to the buffet, minutes before Harker would settle on the cold Thai noodles, and soon promote me to Ops, dismissing me to his Citation X and Bishop execution.

Back to the beginning. My οὐροβόρος, from οὐρά (oura), "tail" + βορά (bora), "food," from βιβρώσκω (bibrōskō), "I eat." My ouroboros.

It was Thursday, my last Thursday, and Thursday meant antipasto and Italian subs from the food court Sbarro. Only today, the cold-cut delivery—well, in this room that Harker kept at an artic temperature, just the "cut delivery" to avoid the redundancy of repeating myself by saying things twice as, little did I suspect, I'd done for the last time on Office of General Counsel letterhead— the delivery had not cleared the Dolley Madison Boulevard gate and Harker was faced with spaghetti and garlic bread with antipasto. Harker wanted his sandwiches.

"How do you imagine I'm supposed to make my Italian sub?" Harker shook his plate at the two security-cleared and photo-ID-ed food court veterans, Devisha (by way of Armstrong High School of Richmond, Class of '82), and Fabienne (by way of Gordon, Hurricane of '94).

Fabienne, who'd arrived out of the Haitian frying pan straight into four years over our Burger King deep fryer, didn't have a mind or disposition to take useless criticism.

"Mister Director, sir. We have a saying where I come from, before God saw fit to destroy the place."

We all knew what was coming and, like the hurricane that destroyed her island home, there was no way to defend against Fabienne.

Harker attempted one of Meryl's "Mmm's," to no effect.

"We say, 'All food is fit to eat, but not all words are fit to speak.'"

Harker was in no mood for her Haitian aphoristic approbations. Not today. Meryl Hofmeyr saw this coming and jumped in to save him.

"Ahh. In Australian restaurants and various, mm-hm, subway stations around Tokyo Metropolis—"

For once would she give in and just say 'Tokyo' like the rest of us earthlings?

"—they serve the spaghetti sandwich as a novelty item."

She took a plate, two slabs of garlic bread, a good-sized dollop of spaghetti, and a faint coo of pleasure to prove it to him.

Bill Carver's gruff voice added, "Had one at the Hubert Humphrey Metrodome once watching my Twins."

Fabienne beamed at him. "Only the knife knows the heart of the pineapple."

Meryl offered Harker her plate, lifting the spaghetti sandwich to entice him.

Devisha knew better. "Suh, I can bring them Thai noodles you like jus' in case."

Harker held out two fingers like George Washington in the White House East Room portrait and pronounced, "Go. Go, go please, Miss Devisha," as if he were Dolley Madison instructing young White House slave Paul Jennings to save the work of art from 1812 Redcoat arsonists.

Devisha responded with a beautiful smile that the rest of us read as *Go-go-go to hell.* The two women left.

I wish Bishop hadn't shot me. I wish Bishop had killed him: Harker.

Bill Carver was the next to step up for his lunch.

"Bill, honestly. Meryl can eat what she wants. You don't have to make one of these dreadful sandwiches," Harker said.

"I'm having the spaghetti. As in, spaghetti on my plate."

Harker took Meryl's sandwich from her plate and had a bite.

Ranks right there with coming into someone's home and opening their refrigerator. But worse. Unless they're known to kiss each other. These two aren't.

He left Chiclets tracks in Meryl's bread. Chewed thoughtfully.

"Yes. It's the guessing that's bothering me. Now. Bishop slipped Sedaka first chance he got, and van Eijk is not only in the wind but suddenly missing."

He deposited the bite into a paper napkin and tossed it, missing the wastebasket. He took a little victory lap in soft-shoe place, or at least my tumor allowed me to see that. With fearful bewilderment I noticed the buffet wasn't spaghetti at all. "Is a hot dog a sandwich?" I mumbled, grasping for straws.

Maybe it had been Thai Thursday all along and the spaghetti sandwich incident had been the day before?

All in the weight of a question mark or the wait on the lump in my head.

I gulped back an involuntary gasp, all right, truthfully, a sob. Made it into a phony sneeze. "Excuse me."

No one paid no nevermind. Whatever they'd been discussing, it had been going on awhile. My notes on my legal pad, only a page or two full when I witnessed the Italian part of lunch (or most likely didn't), now filled a dozen pages full. I recovered my composure.

Fabienne has another saying. One she uses a lot, which I figure now applies to me: "Eggs have no business dancing with stones." My brain the scramble, my tumor the rock.

Harker scowled at me. "Aiken, what have you worked with Customs?"

What had I worked with Customs? I casually turned my pages, eyes panicky mice scurrying across my scratch-mark shorthand.

I said, "They'll deal. They've agreed to sign over Yuri and his two agents—picked up La Guardia and Dallas with cash packets, same as Yuri." Found this tidbit: "A third agent on the chain, the Brits have picked up in Gibraltar. We've not responded to their inquiry."

"Let him run. I don't want them to shove the British stink-hand under my nose."

I said, "Customs has submitted for the though dough—*Dough. Though.* The Muir cash."

"Let 'em fuckin' have it! Aiken, what is your problem? We don't need the money, we don't care about the money, the money is the tripwire."

"My thought—legal bearing on all of it—Muir wants you to relinquish it and have to—in other words, 'be forced'—to allow it to be trailed back to him, like a horse to a barn. We make the claim along with the arrests, we keep the money and the betrayal in-house, unable to be examined."

Harker couldn't see that. Harker couldn't understand how that sort of thing trailed back. Meryl did. She understood Muir better.

She bing-banged-child-voiced: "Achilles 4 was an eight-man network. Where are the rest? And what of the other Muir networks?"

Having not been consciously aware of the beginning of this conversation, I blinked. Thankfully she'd not addressed her question exclusively to me.

"Mr. Carver?" She returned to Bill. "Can Yuri produce them?"

"Apparently, Dr. Muir gave them strict orders to sever all ties with us and each other once the code came in. They could be anywhere."

"Each with a twenty-grand bump?" she said.

I grabbed the caboose of the train of thought. "Meryl, you're talking pin money for a man of Muir's wealth."

Carver tag-teamed in. "What's presented itself in the case before all of us is that Tom Bishop murdered Nathan Muir, and you, Director Harker—of good intention, but bad choice—sent him after van Eijk."

"Acting Director," I blurted.

Jackie, the prettiest woman at the CIA and Harker's secretary, cat-walked in, a slinky walk-in like she's in *Cats* and a purr in Harker's ear.

"This just in," Harker translated Cheshire into Cronkite. "Therese Malmud, radio operator for Muir's Trojan network, picked up five first-class, one-way tickets, five identities, out of Cyprus— Paris, Istanbul, Rome, Madrid, Los Angeles. She paid cash."

"We stop her?" said Carver.

Harker shook his head. He thought hard for a moment then, dark and brooding, said, "It's safe to say that we have been had. We should now presume Muir shut down all the networks intentionally."

"He's blinded us in seven regions," Meryl cooed. *Seven regions, emm, eh, ah? Oooh…(sad face).* "Committed treason is what Muir's done. We should take this to Counterintelligence."

"No," said Harker *and I.* He shot me a dirty look. "This is a closed Working Group. I don't want Silas Kingston and his storm troopers anywhere near this."

Underscore, exclamation point. Italicize the italics and embolden the bold. This was unfamiliar territory for me and Harker: the first and only time he and I found ourselves in total and complete agreement.

The bullet-headed and merciless Silas Kingston, heart as black as the inside lining of Darth Vader's cape, is the most feared officer in the entire CIA. A spy who made legendary Langley paranoid James Jesus Angleton—twenty-year chief of CIA Counterintelligence Staff and Kingston's mentor—seem as gentle and benevolent as his middle-named namesake. The chief spy to spy on the spies.

I jumped in. "Legally speaking, Meryl, you're absolutely wrong. Just a fashion of being totally not right, or correct, or true in what you're saying—I get what you're feeling, but you're wrong."

"I think absolutely not."

"And that's why I'm here at spaghetti-sandwich day—" They all looked at me funny. No idea what I was talking about. "You absolutely *are* and that's why the CIA has lawyers—"

"Russell," said Harker. "We don't condescend at CIA."

"We break the law," I said. "And my job is to make that legal. Everything Laa-Laa said—"

"Who?"

Carver laughed. He has grandkids.

"Neither Muir nor Bishop—although his alter ego's crime is exposed—have aided our enemies in any way, no legal statute, no penal code, stubbed-toe-tripped-to-my-loo, and Muir hasn't given away a single secret. He, or—granted—Bishop in murder— just set Muir's agents free. It's not against the law. Especially not in their countries, where the jurisdiction on their espionage lies. Plus, it's tough to prosecute a case against a dead man."

"Fucking good for Muir," Harker grumbled.

I suggested, "What about van Eijk? If the networks weren't blown, then his cry for help is false."

"Makes me more than a little nervous about what Bishop is doing in Malaysia," Carver said. "Especially if we go on the leading hypothesis Bishop waxed Muir and stole the journal."

Meryl: "Maybe Bishop and van Eijk are working this together?"

Cowed silence from the table. Everyone awaiting a sound effect.

Harker sighed, "My God, how I miss the Cold War. You had the good guys and the bad guys. And as much as we hated the bad guys—you know something? They always played by the rules."

The 65 degrees Fahrenheit that Harker typically kept the ice-boxed room felt hot on the back of my neck. "You hated the good guys. Muir and the dinosaurs. Everyone in every one of those networks. Hated them. What they did and how Muir had them do it. From your first step on the first rung of the ladder of daggers you've planted in the backs of your political opponents to get where you are. Sir. Actor Director. You've spent the last dec-dec-decade culling thin-thim-them."

Carver hit me with his knee under the table. I stopped before I went into an unbridled stammer. I shook my head and looked at my lap.

Harker waited until I peeked back up. Met me with his *Delicious! Delightful! Pure candy jacket!* leer.

"I have not culled all of them. Aiken."

Meryl inflated her own smirk on the hiss in his malice.

"People, the only thing I see with any certainty is that all of this was put in motion by Muir to compel me to send Bishop to Malaysia," Harker went on. "The 'why' behind that will come to light when we know the contents of Muir's missing journal."

Harker grabbed Meryl with his eyes. "Pull records. I'll want a summary of every operation Muir was running out of Laos in 1968 in my hands by five a.m. tomorrow. And red-flag anything WMD related."

"Nuke, chemical, biological," she said. "Done."

He piled cold Thai noodles onto his plate from the buffet table and said to my shadow on the wall: "I am not going to let some old, dead triceratops and his Barney Rubble golden boy gone rogue topple my Agency over some useless secret to some forgotten Malaysian conspiracy of thirty-three fucking years ago. Guess what—?"

No more guessing.

Fuck guessing.

I can't believe you'd cheat on me. Again. And this time have another man's child. And have the audacity to make me take it. To make me name it after...

After...?

Panic.

After MUIR, after all the mistakes. After your updated version of your Beardy-Baldy lover of ten years back—and how many more in between?

After we've come so far to get to nowhere.

Go fuck yourself in hell, Madeline.

25

LARA VAN EIJK had seen more than she ever wanted, having witnessed firsthand what 98 percent of humanity never experience: human beings killing human beings in armed combat. Murdered children. Islamist extremists whose perverse version of jihad calls for the murder of the infidel. Al-Qaeda-sponsored Ramadan Moon fighting it out with a guy who looked as inconsequential as a worn-out ballplayer, not the cold-blooded executioner who risked his life for morality and for her. The killers died in a manner they'd chosen to live, and Lara struggled in Bishop's arms, carried out of the incinerated church.

He poured her into the Land Rover. The only thing left her from her father. No picture. No letter. No story or goodbye or excuse why; 1968 would have to mean something to her. Dand van Eijk was the connecting tissue between Lara and her abductor.

Bishop drove through a Chinese community. Lara crunched up into herself beside him. She stared at her hands. If she'd been more brown, or more yellow, or anyone else at all, would life have let her be?

"They would have killed me."

Bishop didn't feel a need to respond.

"Did you know they'd killed the Orang Asli boys? Before you started shooting?"

"Stop staring at your hands. I'm sorry I grabbed you. Like that. Like that at the church."

Lara wouldn't let him dodge. "If they hadn't, God might have made the difference."

"I'm not going to risk God for you."

"That's a terrible thing to say. You're as evil as them."

"God's been terrible to me."

She measured him with a look and judged his mark at zero.

"Let me go. Keep the Rover. I don't care. I don't want it. I just want to be free of all this. Of you."

"Lara, I didn't choose to be here any more than you. I was assigned to meet your father and exfiltrate him back to the US, where I'd have turned him over to people tasked to find out why every network of spies my father ran for decades vanished. I didn't choose, bargain, or want a thing of this."

She scowled. "Muir's death isn't coincidental, is it?"

"No."

Hard as he tried, Bishop couldn't erase all emotion from his single spoken word. Lara glanced at him, attempting to hunt out that trace of what made him human.

"He was killed over this?"

"And I'm the prime suspect."

"Why?" She wasn't surprised.

"Beside the point. The only reason we're sitting here right now is that he expected it, and the reason it happened has everything to do with what transpired here in 1968. And *that's* threatened by what's happening here right now between you and me."

"I just don't understand how he could have known."

"Because you're looking at it from the wrong direction. You're giving meaning to just-in-case contingencies he planted back then precisely because he *couldn't* predict the future. You're making too big a deal out of it."

"No, you're just lying."

"Apparently, an easy club to join in Malaysia."

"Fuck you."

"Like I said, 'join the club.'"

She snapped her head away from him, glaring out the window.

"Because we're not even talking about the biggest lie we both know is staring right at us," Bishop pressed.

"I don't know what you're talking about."

He took a deep breath and said the words he was sure she did. "You can run from it. Easiest thing. Safe. I did when I found out, and up until the day he died." She focused her glare back upon him. "But the truth is, the only person Muir would take a bullet for is family."

"Nathan Muir is not my father. If that's what you're thinking—which *I'm* not—you're out of your mind."

"Your baptism wasn't the only non-CIA event hidden in the journal. The photo he sent you—?"

"Stop this car."

"He also made time to come to my high school graduation."

"You're leaving me here."

Bishop unbuckled the leather belt from around his waist. Twisted left and right to remove it.

"What are you doing?"

"Take it."

"No. Stop the damn car!"

He deposited it onto her lap. "Open the seam along the back."

She stared at it like a snake.

"Pull it apart—the threads are elastic. Works like an envelope."

Curiosity wouldn't deny her. Lara found the seam. Inside was a photograph creased lengthwise and again.

"Unfold it."

She did. The photograph of van Eijk. She gave it a cursory glance.

"Good news: we're not related. That isn't the Nathan Muir I knew."

"CIA claims that's Dand van Eijk. Had it clipped to van Eijk's file record."

She didn't give the photo another look. Didn't need to, didn't want it. She passed it to Bishop. "I'm not related to that person either."

"I know you're not." He tried to be gentle. "The man in that photo is Digby Livingston. Digger. A Welsh friend of our father. For years he ran a newspaper cover operation for British intelligence out of Hong Kong."

Her shoulders sagged.

Stripped of identity, stripped of life.

But he was giving her identity; he felt her sadness and ignored why knowing it, it made him just as sad. Sad for what? Her? For himself? Something forbidden?

Lara squirmed. "Why didn't Muir put in a real photograph of my father?"

"Keep it up. Look: Muir inserted the photo of Digger in the van Eijk dossier to fool my bosses into believing in van Eijk, knowing all along I would recognize that he wasn't. There is no Dand van Eijk."

"Stop saying that. I'd kill myself if I believed I shared DNA with you."

He pretended her words didn't hurt. Sneered at her wounded eyes peering back at him, gauging. The fight-or-flight gleam. She was helpless to his reasoning. They both knew it.

"Muir created van Eijk to deflect from himself."

"But I knew your father my whole life—it was Muir who told me everything I *did* know about Dand van Eijk."

Bishop flashed a sardonic grin.

"Muir's not my father," she said. "He would have told me."

"That's what I said."

Lara withdrew into herself. Her new reality had bent her identity further than she could accept. Bishop eased up on the gas. They were halfway through the Chinese community. A whole different world. Different structures, different rooflines, different desires and needs all built in plastered cinder block and stuccoed posts of plastic lettered signs. Blue-light bug zappers, a seeming necessitation, snap, crackled, and popped at such a high frequency that one would not be faulted to assume insects powered the national grid.

"When did ol' Paw first appear as your estate agent?"

"Is nothing real—nothing sacred—with you?"

"I could ask you, hasn't the unreal easily been just as sacred?"

"The whole life I've lived and believed is false."

"You believed. That makes it absolute reality."

"It was all a lie."

"The lie doesn't matter a bit if you lived it. Anything you live, even a deception, is a reality and as fixed as a truth."

Bishop peered left and right at the Chinese businesses. As other villages before: broken windows, glass swept into piles, plywood-covered holes. Ramadan Moon graffiti. He slowed at an intersection, studied the two gas stations. Rolled on. He struggled for something to say. He remembered an article he'd read. On appearance and ways we see reality. A psychology magazine, the only thing in English, a long time ago in a Pankow hotel room across from an East Berlin church. His first chosen kill, manipulated into it by his father's hidden hand. Regardless of whether Muir had planted the magazine for him to find—to influence—its argument and conclusion had remained, as vivid to him now as the look of surprise on the face of the German ambassador's traitorous wife who had walked into his bullet.

"I want to try something with you, Lara. I want you to think about water. About how you—we, everyone—perceives it."

Annoyance knit her brow. Bishop coaxed her with his eyes.

"It's wet…" he prompted.

"Fine. It's wet. We drink it. Bathe in it. Cook. Swim in it. Drown. Good enough for you? Water's water."

"But it isn't. The molecular, the atomic nature of water—what it *really* is—is blurred to us. It's true nature—we never see. What water truly is doesn't come into play when we perceive it. Interact with it. But saying the true nature of water isn't evident to us isn't saying our experience of water tells us zip about water. Although the experience doesn't tell us a thing about water's structure—all the invisible moving particles of what it really is—our experience tells us certain truths about water. The ones you described."

"You're kidding me with this."

"Just suggesting you can use that water example as a way to look at your blurred life."

He wasn't kidding and she cocked her head at him a look that said, *This better be good*, and he grinned, game for the challenge.

"Our experience of our lives, whether we know how the strings are pulled or what they really are, still tell us certain truths about our personal reality, including the most important thing: the fact that our identity—that's what I'm getting at—*only* exists to us in the ways our experiences appear. Not their essence; not necessarily in truth. But still the legit signs we gather impression from—fundamentally true *or* false—are the essentials and in that become the total truth of our lives. Identities."

Lara looked out the window. A way to attempt to fool herself into rejecting it all.

"Muir told me he wasn't my father. I based my life on that. That wasn't a sign. I'm not the product of a mythology," she said.

"I think all of us are that—exactly. And what you remember of your father, how he looked. Muir told you that too? Mythologized him over and again until you saw him in your memory? Maybe the version of himself he wished to have been."

Lara's resolve crumbled. She stared at her hands, lost to him, to time, to essential memories she was afraid to trust. She ran her thumbs over the prints on her fingertips.

Bishop saw what he'd been looking for. A service station with a mechanic's bay and about a dozen used cars with price stickers on their windshields.

"I'm sure it doesn't help what you're feeling, but the son of a bitch did the same thing to me."

Bishop drove onto the lot. The place was closed. The bulb over the porch was off, but light was visible past the darkened front office window.

"Before I read that thing about water, I was with everyone else, pitting appearance versus reality and hating every time whichever side won out. Appearance *is* reality. Accept that, flow with it, and let the river run through you."

Bishop parked beside the low, sooty building. He honked. Waited. Honked again.

"They won't come out," said Lara.

"They will."

Bishop lowered himself out of the Land Rover.

"Not after today."

He leaned back into the cab and depressed the horn ring. The office remained dark, but two silhouettes shuffled into the room. They peeped out the dirty front windowpane. A Chinese father, his adult son. When they had identified Bishop as Caucasian, the father twisted the door bolts. He opened the door only enough to poke out his skull.

"Sorry. Closed. No business."

Withdrew and attempted to shut the door. Bishop held it open with the heel of his hand along its edge, strength enough to hold the hinges and not to be denied.

"You don't know the business we have for you."

"Gas?" said the son, widening the door.

"The vehicle. Best deal you've ever made."

The door remained ajar as the father and son argued in whispered Hokkien Chinese.

The son stepped outside, closing the door on his father.

"Do you have papers for the Rover?"

"She does."

The son considered Lara with undisguised suspicion. "You have papers for this vehicle, lady?"

She flicked her eyes at both Bishop and the Chinese. "Yes."

He stalked around the Land Rover, his frown elongating with each noticed bullet hole, sneering as he tapped shattered windows dropping glass shards onto seat and footwell. He came back around to Bishop.

"We passed through some election violence." Bishop popped the hood. The Chinese son looked inside for a long moment. Nothing to sneer about in there.

"With the bullet holes, with what is happening, I cannot purchase your car."

"I wouldn't expect you to. I'm giving it to you."

The son showed no enthusiasm. "I will be right back. We will see."

"You have a bottle of water? I'll pay for it."

"I'll give you water. Wait now."

The door closed behind the son.

"What if he calls the police?"

"You'll be done with me when I'm arrested."

"They'll arrest me too."

"He won't call anyone. They'll take the deal. Otherwise, he'd've taken money for the water."

"And that's all I get in return? An Evian?"

"You'll get some answers."

Lara considered this a moment. "You're not here on behalf of your government. Do you have any authority at all?"

"Muir taught me to trust no one."

"Then you're 'rogue,' isn't that the term for it? A lone wolf?"

"'Doesn't play well with others' is how it reads in my file."

She gathered her things. Random papers from the glove box, a sweater from the backseat. Bishop noticed a tremor in her hand, like the first raindrops of a coming metaphysical storm. She tied the sweater like a bandolier from shoulder across her chest to her opposite hip. She found the registration—"I *don't* have the title"— and Bishop told her it wouldn't matter.

He took the registration. Lara held a battered old road map and he took that too.

"I know the way home," she said.

"Home won't be safe for either of us."

"Anywhere I'm with you isn't safe."

"Maybe, but I need you for one more stop."

"If I refuse? Stay here?"

"They won't take you here. You're trouble you don't want to cause them—and I won't let you refuse. People will only get hurt if you try."

TEN MINUTES LATER with the Land Rover disappearing into the mechanic bay, Bishop and Lara downed a large water bottle between them and climbed onto the mid-nineties Yamaha dirt bike—more dirt than bike, the seat held in place with coat hangers—Bishop had traded for. He kickstarted it to guttural, muffler-coughing life as the wife of the older man hustled outside, hands fluttering like startled bats.

Her voice came sharp and strident. Her irate eyes stabbed at the strangers on the bike as she barked at her menfolk. When she finished her harangue, she flung her bat hands at Bishop and Lara, took a threatening step in their direction like Dracula's bride, and resumed her tirade. Her husband pulled her back. He shushed her, leading her unwillingly back to the door, her anger swelling with alarm.

The son translated his mother's outburst. "Prime Minister Aziz has cancelled the election and declared a State of Emergency. He's detained the PDF candidate and her family. Suspended Parliament. State Police are enacting a curfew. Anyone caught on the streets after sundown will be subject to arrest and imprisonment. Leave now. Before my mother reports us all."

He shut himself inside. The locks snapped closed.

"It makes perfect sense," said Lara. "What Prime Minister Aziz is doing."

Bishop looked back at her. He held off from rolling out.

"Why he's armed the Ramadan Moon, why he needs them," she said.

"Sore loser?"

"It's the money. Aziz doesn't simply want to hold on to power, he wants to own the country."

"Thirty billion dollars in international investment."

"And the best way to factor out the international part is to nationalize in response to a fabricated civil insurrection. Create a dictatorship. The banks, industry, energy, foreign assets… We've been running models. None of them made sense. Now they do. But how he plans to hold on to it—? He's almost asking for war with Thailand and Indonesia, and the foreign pressure—your country alone."

"We'd only back off if he had something everyone was afraid of."

"That's not very likely," Lara said.

"Until it is." Bishop kicked into first gear and, throwing gravel, lurched into the street and sped off.

Talking became impossible over the troubled whine of the engine. Bishop racked through the gears and accelerated out of the community. Lara held tight and Bishop felt her grip. Looked down at the elegant shape of her hands, fingers interlaced below his rib cage across the iron of his abdomen. Long, like his. Like their father's. The pressure. And he pictured them making him the dinner he didn't deserve, and she didn't deserve to have had to make at gunpoint. So far from where he wished he could be and so close—imaginarily so—so real and close to all he had lost.

Elizabeth was gone.

Bishop brought the motorcycle to a stop. Behind them a fiery orange sun lowered into jungle green. He was at a crossroads. Signs indicated the road to Kuala Lumpur in one direction. Indicated the road to Ipoh in the other.

"Why are we stopping? KL's that way," she said. "Says so right there."

"We're going to Ipoh. Our father's tin mine."

"We'd never make it back before the curfew. I've never been there anyway. It was just some failed investment of *my* father. Not Muir. And he had plenty of them."

"Or so Muir told you," Bishop said and pulled out the map. "Won't challenge you on that, but I'm guessing you know where to find it. I'm thinking maybe our father told you—showed you once? If not, we cycle around Ipoh until I discover it or get us caught in the curfew." He snapped the map back at her. "Find it."

Lara unfolded the map. Bishop watched her study it.

Elizabeth had always been practical with her fingernails and kept them short. Bishop remembered this as Lara traced lines across the old diagram. Elizabeth's fingernails: short, clear-coat polish, French tipped.

He'd told Lara everything, but she resisted telling him the truth. Muir was not the only one using her. Whoever killed Muir was pressuring her from the other side. She was playing both ends. Lara found the mine's locations and flicked the spot on the map. Bishop couldn't help but picture Lara's crimson polish as blood. His blood, carelessly flicked. He aimed the bike and sped toward Ipoh.

26

BISHOP STOPPED the motorcycle at the end of a jungle road before an old gate centered in rebar-reinforced, crenellated, and galvanized tornado fencing. Lara climbed off first. She walked to the gate. A large sign, like the decal on the Land Rover, depicted the snarling tiger with the Malay words *Tempat Harimau.* A thick layer of rust on both fence and sign, the chain securing the gate, suggested years of abandonment.

"That say what I think?" said Bishop.

"If you think it says 'Place of the Tiger,' it does. It's a warning. Not an 'Open for Business' sign."

Bishop levered the kickstand. He joined her on the weather-beaten access road. Jungle encroached from the sides, most of the asphalt cracked and crumbled, rain-eroded, typhoon-washed gone. There were no recent vehicle tracks. Bishop examined the lock.

"Fine with me as long as this is an abandoned mine and not a game preserve," he said.

"Do tigers make a distinction?"

Bishop grasped the chain. "Do they buy new locks? Stand back."

Bishop shot the lock.

Gravity uncoiled the chain. It rattled to the ground. He gripped the gate but hesitated in opening it. "You ever see one—a tiger? Outside the zoo?" His voice remained casual.

"I've never been foolish enough to go anywhere I was specifically warned they're not in cages."

Bishop was going inside. He didn't have another acceptable option. "Sign's old. There for effect. Distraction."

"Until you smell the tiger's breath."

"Yeah. Until then."

They regarded each other, neither stepping inside.

"I'm not going in there without a better reason than the one you've given me—which is nothing," she said.

Bishop released the gate. He withdrew an item from his pocket. A pewter flask. Embossed with the same tiger head depicted on the sign.

"Found this at your place last night."

"D-V-E are my father's initials." Her voice tightened. "You had no right to take that."

"Nice try. I know where you got it."

He gave Lara a chance to explain herself. No words forthcoming, he said, "Y'know, Lara, as much fun as you are, you're full of crap."

He slapped the flask into her palm. "Muir sent this with the green book. For you to give to me. Not squirrel away as a souvenir. So why didn't you?"

She didn't respond. He could see the debate raging inside her. He was drawing her closer to revelation. He needed it to be revelation; anything forced would be a lie.

"Keep it. It's your dad's anyway," he mocked and flung wide the gate.

BOTH SIDES of the dilapidated haul road, long ago clear-cut as the mine's waste dump, were jumbled with white quartz and calcite boulders blasted from the pit, its berms, and batters. Vines and undergrowth netted the stone while a thick overgrowth of kapok and rubber tree towered over it in triple-canopy rainforest. Once wide enough for two ore haulers abreast, green waves crashed the haul road's boundaries from both sides, tongues of twisting creepers with thick rubbery leaves thrust over its border. The leading edge of nature's tenacious desire to overtake and subsume, to destroy, decay and mulch to bear new overwhelming, self-renewing, ceaseless life.

Bishop and Lara were less than one hundred yards inside the gate when they were presented with another warning.

"*Tempat Harimau*," Lara read from another sign, this one recently hand-drawn on a board and hammered to a tree. "Maybe turn back now?"

Bishop listened to the night sounds. More than insects and birds, there came the chittering howls of monkeys. The grunts of rooting boar.

"Those aren't tigers. Don't sound too afraid to me."

"I'm serious. Let's forget this."

"Muir sent the flask. Means he wanted us here." He caught her eye. "But go back. Wait at the bike if you want. Chain the gate if you're scared. I'll be fine."

"Very funny."

Bishop grinned with his eyes. "Considering tigers, then, what do you think—you safer in front or behind me?"

"Would it matter?"

"Walk behind. Tigers don't paint signs, and men I'd rather meet head on."

Bishop led Lara along the path. His eyes searched the dusk through deepening layers of tangle wafted with the loamy smell of vegetation. Memories of Laos, Vietnam, Cambodia superimposed and primed his senses to where it became as if he'd never left. The farther they hiked the road, the more the foliage pressed from both sides. It brushed their shoulders like stroking fingers to become fervent clutching hands and catching claws. At a point where the road curved left, the foliage from both sides met as curtains. Bishop raised his gun in front of his shoulder. He pushed his way through. Lara kept quick at his heels.

He stopped abruptly, gun arm sweeping back into Lara's chest to check her forward momentum. She staggered back, wind knocked out of her.

"Twice now?" she choked, but her adrenaline was surging, and her sarcasm did little to cover her fright at what she beheld.

The jungle, vanished on their right, giving way to a steep and manmade verge. They teetered on the brink of the van Eijk tin mine. A quarter of a mile long and half that across, it was over sixty feet deep—the level they could see. Two earthen mining benches twenty-feet-thick extended at thirty-foot intervals, but how much deeper the mine pit plunged was an unknown as, flooded, the pit had become a lake. The water: black, beautiful, illusory.

Bishop caught a whiff of smoke. He spun, pushing Lara to her knees with one hand, thrusting his weapon across her back with the other to face the barrel of a WWII-era Tommy gun held by a wizened, whippet-fit native of an indeterminate age between sixty and skies-the-limit—a sky he floated his mind on, a smoldering hash pipe drooping from paper-thin dry lips. He didn't look like anyone Bishop had seen in this country. But as a Marine sniper in Vietnam, Bishop had seen many like him years before.

"Montagnard," said Bishop.

The old man wore a ragged camouflaged bandana tight over his head. His eyes were narrow slits of suspicion and blazed a bloodshot red. He puffed from the long, silver ornamented hash pipe, its chunk of hashish glowing in the dimming light.

"Hmong people," he said, submachine gun unwavering.

"Laos?" Bishop said.

"This not Laos. Here, you trespassing."

"You are, old man. She owns the place. Every bit of it."

He kept the pistol trained on the Laotian tribesman and helped Lara to her feet.

"Why he say that, girl?"

"This is my father's mine."

"Who're you?" the old fellow snapped.

"Lara van Eijk."

On each side of his pipestem, the old man's mouth slid to an ear. He lowered his weapon, swinging it by its strap over his shoulder. He hit on his hashish. Bishop trained his handgun at the fellow's head. The man's grin broadened. He knew Americans like Bishop. Long as he could remember. He spoke to Lara in their shared Malay language to save his life—to give Lara hers—and Lara answered, tentative in response. He offered the pipe. Lara and Bishop declined the hit.

"Lara? What's going on?"

"He remembers me. As a baby."

"Ask about Muir. Use 'Prometheus'—was his codename."

The old man beat her to the answer. "We killed communists. Protected the mine. Later we—"

He was interrupted by a roar. An animal of prey somewhere in the darkness. The man's face lit.

"*Tempat Harimau,*" he said.

"Close?" said Bishop.

Although still fearful, Lara showed a small pleasure at Bishop's discomforted discomfiture.

"Across the lake. They fight each other before the kill. It's playful. Come see. We hurry."

Bishop and Lara followed the hash-smoking Tommy-gunner down another pathway. They arrived at the huge trunk of a shorea tree, a flowering giant with prehistoric hatchet-edged root structures curved and entwining it like ribbon candy ascending its trunk twenty, even thirty, feet. Taller than all the other trees, it soared one hundred and fifty feet, crowning high above the forest.

A rusted but functional bicycle leaned inside the walls of two of the largest root structures. The Montagnard slapped the trunk like the flank of a good strong horse. "Three hundred years old she is."

Boards pounded into the trunk of the tree made a wooden rung ladder to the first saddle of thick branches above the second canopy. A treehouse perched in the branches high above, surrounded by a rope-railed walkway.

"Hurry. Climb."

The wiry fellow mounted the first rung and lunged upward, but his momentum was abruptly checked as Bishop grabbed the stock of the Tommy gun.

"This stays with the bike."

He twisted it off the diminutive tribesman, whose only reaction was a puff of smoke and a fervent "Yes, yes. They feed now. Hurry."

The Montagnard scrabbled rung to rung like the untamed creature the jungle had made him.

Bishop stowed the gun. Indicated Lara climb next.

"This safe?"

"Not the question."

She lifted a dubious eyebrow.

Bishop said, "In my line of work, the guiding question—could say, a First Rule of Thumb:"—surprising himself having allowed it—"Every move we make we base on risk versus gain. You'll know how safe it is when you decide what's it worth."

Lara calculated. "Safe enough."

Bishop followed her close behind. Here, near the edge of the tin mine, they were soon above the first tree line. He could see across the dark lake the evening-blackened face of the opposing jungle. A tiger roared again.

Tempat Harimau.

Their guide passed through the second canopy and mounted the walkway. Slat and cable, it swayed like the suspension bridge it had been fashioned from. Lara reached the top of the ladder. She hesitated.

"Safe, safe," he said, giving a small bounce at each word.

Lara wasn't about to budge but was left no choice as the Montagnard grabbed her wrist. He hoisted as Bishop guided her hips from below.

Lara steadied herself, clutching the rope railing against the slight sway.

"Gangway," Bishop said.

Lara moved tentatively, left shoulder on the treehouse wall, right fingers clutching the rope.

"Risk versus gain?" She weighted the question mark.

Bishop heaved himself from the ladder to join them. "He's the one who'll know if van Eijk and Muir are one in the same."

He examined the exterior of the Montagnard's aerie. Corrugated-steel siding recycled from the mine's perimeter fencing made double-layer walls. Through a loose seam Bishop saw they sleeved a double layer of hardwood boards, vertical over horizontal. Two shuttered casements Lara would call the windows, Bishop recognized as gun ports. The roof was low, gabled, and steep, and while the old man would fit upright along the center beam, Lara would need to stoop. Bishop knew, once inside, there'd be no sense in his rising from a squat if he wanted to keep his head knot-free. Around the front, they found a steel-hinged and reinforced door between two large hatches.

Eyes blazing, the old man opened the door. He gestured Lara and Bishop inside.

Seen from the interior, the treehouse formed a fat, short-legged X. Floor matting was comprised of striped palm and other fronds, while bisected bamboo paneled the walls of the four-chambered arboreal hut. A mounted Browning .30-caliber machine gun on its tripod drooped at one of the gun ports overlooking the board ladder of the trunk. Plenty of belt ammunition.

The Montagnard entered behind them. He made quick work opening battery-powered military lanterns. Other rifles and hand-guns abounded.

"Glad I made you leave your Tommy gun behind."

"I'm faithful to my orders." He offered the pipe once more. "This is my studio. I am this." Once more Bishop declined.

Where Bishop's attention had focused on the weaponry, Lara was busy confirming the studio aspect, which crowded the tree-house hut with pads and canvases, pencils and charcoals, oil and acrylic paints, and all attendant tools and solvents. Two different types of easels—upright and flat lay—situated in front of the two largest windows that cranked open on a repurposed bicycle chain and single-pedal crankset.

Framed, tacked, hung, and leaning and stacked, drawings and paintings, finished works and sketches abounded. All of it devoted to tigers.

Walking. Running.

Restful. Sleeping.

Wrestling. Pouncing.

Killing animals, necks clamped in fanged jaws, swiped paws and tearing claws, spraying fluid eviscerations and raw flesh devoured. Hungry, vicious, sated tigers. The sound of the beasts across the lake offered the art a surreal quality; the room filling with hashish smoke guaranteed it.

Bishop and Lara's host finished cranking open the large hatch in front of the drawing table. He pulled the chamois cover from the costliest item in the fantastic place: a high-power monocular telescope with infrared, gleamed from meticulous care. He lowered his eye behind the eyepiece and aimed it. He waved Lara to his side.

"Look. You must. Your father's true gift."

Lara leaned in. Peered through. She gasped, pulled away.

"He has chained goats," she muttered. "They're…the tigers are eating them."

"Yes. Natural beauty. Purity of purpose." He pulled off his camo head cover, shook and tugged out his lion mane of thick Afro-textured hair. "A tiger doesn't need to know it's a tiger to be itself."

Bishop watched Lara put her eye back to the optics.

He said, "You live up here?"

"No, sir. In the old buildings. Different rooms, different nights. Many, many years."

"Alone?"

"Only me. Always only me. And my tigers." Their host smoked, drifted, dreamed. "One hundred years ago they filled my forest. The miners killed many, drove off the rest. It's taken twenty years to lure them home. But I have time. I'm rich. All this land is mine. Your father gave it to me for a job well done."

"What job?" said Bishop.

The old man hadn't heard or didn't care. He motioned at his art.

"I draw them, paint them. People buy my work in KL. It's best after they feed, so I buy the goats. So? They kill, eat, play, sleep. Make love. I draw. I paint."

"Your name, old man?" Bishop continued.

"They're the heart of this country, yet people of this country managed to kill almost all to the last one. Why they do that, you think?"

He cocked his head at Lara with an owl-like curiosity, his blinking eyes glinting with comprehension of who she was, simply by being. Being here. Being with a name and what that name symbolized to the entire scheme of his entire life. "Your father called me Lucky. Lucky-Boy."

"Tell me about the Three Fates, Lucky-Boy," said Bishop. "You know that story. The one about Clotho, Lachesis, and Atropos."

Paranoia radiated behind his grin. Lara stroked his arm with a gentle hand.

"He's with me, Lucky-Boy. He brought me to you. To hear my father's story."

Lucky-Boy blinked his hazy eyes some more. Noticed his pipe between his lips and puffed it back to life. His other hand burrowed into his hair and gave his head a rowdy scratch over his ear and behind his skull. All three motions seemed independent of the man, more like they belonged to three different puppeteers vying for control over a single marionette. His eyes glazed further as he focused inward. He stared at Lara but spoke to Bishop.

"ATROPOS. No time to plan. We met at the house. Her father and mother. By the river. The chucks in the water. She live there now. The trucks already there long time back and gone." He pointed the mouthpiece of his pipe at Lara. "He make me check on her. Many times when first moved back. Alone in the father's house."

"You were my father's friend. You should have introduced yourself," Lara said.

Lucky-Boy hit the hash pipe. The smoke hung thick around their heads in the still, hot, humid air.

"Orders were never reveal cover. Always operational. Long as forever. Important work for See-ah," Lucky-Boy pronounced our Agency letters. The accompanying frown affected his entire body. "Whole world important to keep secret, Miss Lara."

Bishop leaned in. Placed a hand on Lucky-Boy's bony knee, a control to keep him focused. "Look at me. Did your operational orders come from Lara's father?"

Lucky-Boy blinked at Bishop's face but saw another man.

"In beginning, he was Chief Petty van Eijk to give all orders."

"Chief Petty—van Eijk was US Navy?"

"Anchors away!" He barked. A dwindling laugh.

"Who gave the orders to watch over Lara after she'd grown up?"

"Orders same, only name became different. Your father became Mr. Muir. Make you Miss Lara's sister?"

"Brother," Bishop said.

Lucky-Boy chuckled at his mistake. Pulled the hash pipe from his stained teeth and blinked at the glowing compound in its bowl, making an exaggerated show of pretending he only now understood it made him high. The length of his comedy routine was the same amount of time the horror of his words drove Lara to her feet, whispering the word "No" repeatedly as she lunged outside.

"She gonna jump?"

Bishop could see her swaying on the suspension bridge high above the jungle, where vibrant, pulsing, living, and consuming and voiding primordial life burst new every moment with life and rotted death beneath the canopy. Across the moonlit water, the tigers spoke, but the viciousness of the kill had been satisfied. Lara's shoulders heaved with her lungs. She gripped the rope railing with two firm hands. Her feet were wide, and she was steady. Bishop gave a casual shake of his head.

"My sister can be dramatic."

Lucky-Boy offered the pipe again. This time Bishop took it. The sharing of the pipe, the Montagnard pact; the smoke, the figurative form of shared truth.

"Get to ATROPOS. That was the big one, big op, huh?"

"Two trucks. Big. S'was'night—Miss Lara fresh born." He knew she listened and craned his scrawny brown chicken neck to the doorway. "Like an angel. The Malay blood in her lighter skin made her glow. Pretty-pretty baby."

"The trucks," Bishop pressed. "ATROPOS."

"Drove them here. Big communist trucks. Chief Petty van Eijk and some of the boys from the old squad. Home tribe."

"What were you transporting?"

"He told us no look. We were good boys, good soldiers. Tap-tap on the cap and an extra ration of rum, or a chunk of the hashish. It was one more operation."

Bishop grabbed a sketch pad. He found a charcoal. He was light-headed from Lucky-Boy's oily smoke. He saw his father as a tiger in his mind and wanted to talk about it. He forced his senses sharp.

"Draw the trucks, Lucky-Boy. Do it for Chief Petty."

Lara stepped back inside, emotions buried. She coughed in the smoke, cleared her throat. She took the charcoal and sketch pad from Bishop and thrust them into Lucky-Boy's hands.

"Draw my father."

Lucky-Boy drew. "We drove them into the mine. Deep into the shaft."

"This is a pit mine. What shaft?" said Bishop.

Lucky-Boy scooted over to a metal box. He opened it. He withdrew a golf-ball-sized chunk of ore. It glittered in the light. He handed it to Bishop, who identified it in a glance. He passed it to Lara.

"You found gold," she said.

Lucky-Boy bobbed his head, excited. "Enough for one deep shaft along the vein."

"How was it the government didn't seize the mine?" she said.

"The vein we ran was the only gold ever found. Not worth time or government money. Colonel Muir, after ATROPOS, when he left to the Langley fortress, he gave whatever more gold I could find would take care of me. Before the water."

"Keep drawing," said Bishop.

Lucky-Boy's hand glided with assured black strokes across white paper. Two trucks, small cab long-haulers hauling long, double-axle flatbeds.

Quinter, Kansas. Dad's long-hauler burned next to the yellow smiles and tiger eyes of giant sunflowers pressing the highway from vast fields on both sides. His body, burned beyond recognition, covered his undamaged lockbox of speed and cocaine he'd taken in his futile attempt to escape the inescapable, a sizable amount baggied for distribution undamaged inside.

I never had a chance to say goodbye.

Bishop said, "Goodbye—" inside, you must understand, as I have done, inside where the cancer grows and you can't shape or sharpen life—and he was already moving for his escape hatch when Muir's Malaysian siren's song called him back to Jack and Jill deception's hill.

"First Rule of Thumb: An officer in the field," Muir told me during recruitment before Bishop, before rejecting me from the field and saddling me to a desk. He'd said, "First Rule of Thumb: An officer in the field builds an escape hatch."

Lucky-Boy sketched tarps over a cargo that slanted like ladders atop firetrucks. One on each. Lara's yard, van Eijk's house, materialized behind them in expert strokes. Lucky-Boy populated his drawing with small figures blurred in action.

He gazed at Lara. "Here your mother stood. See, she holding you. I see it perfectly. You in white Christmas dress. You'd had your Christmas-ing service day."

"Christening dress. My baptism."

Lucky-Boy hummed agreement as he continued to draw. Lara flashed moist, impatient eyes at Bishop.

"Lucky-Boy, draw their faces. Larger. Recognizable," said Bishop.

The artist whipped his charcoal to the top-left corner. He sketched an enlargement of two faces side by side. A young Malay woman, worried and stern; a baby with a lopsided pout—the beginning form of the smile Lara had grown into. They appeared magical. About to come to life.

"That's my mother."

Lucky-Boy toked from his hash pipe. He found a knife and emery pad. He sharpened his diminishing charcoal stick. He moved to the next corner. Lucky-Boy drew another face.

"Muir," Bishop said as his father materialized under Lucky-Boy's deft hand.

"Prometheus son."

Bishop's face was impassive.

Lara said, "Why does my mother look angry?"

"She was sad. They fought—she and your father—very disturbed by us."

"What did they fight about?" said Bishop.

Lucky-Boy savored his hashish. Answered some other question he only heard. "Yes. Colonel Muir. Chief Petty van Eijk's Prometheus. His father goose."

Lara grabbed Lucky-Boy's bony shoulder. "Muir *isn't* my father?"

"Colonel Muir kept his wing around him. Always. Chief Petty Danny and your mother. They were the only white men. I was oldest of the scouts Chief Petty Danny brought from

Vietnam—Ho Chi Minh Trail—for the work. Afterward, Colonel Muir gave us the mine to watch. Defend from communists and spies. Buried many in this forest. Fed more to tigers. The old squad stayed until the gold was gone and the waters came. I said goodbye and they returned to our mountain tribe. But I see these waters as what they truly are. Truly mean. Am the only soldier left to understand."

Lucky-Boy moved his hand to the bottom-right corner to draw the last face.

"Chief Petty promised he'd come back. Your mother didn't believe him. Was angry. Sad—I said. But Chief Petty Danny promised. Man of promise. Always kept."

Bishop cheated a glance at Lara. Non-operational. He felt lifted, spun in the air, and set down dizzy, life facing in a different direction. Something smiled inside him, and it scared him.

"They came back for the trucks. Their cargo," Bishop said.

"Yes, sir. Four years later to destroy them with appropriate tools and demolition. Only those were four years of long monsoon. Terrible typhoon three times. And Colonel Muir couldn't get to them, and I and Chief Petty Danny couldn't help."

"They're still in the mine? Underwater?"

"One-hundred-eight meters. I prefer it this way. The lure of water called back my tigers. They have no reason to know what it hides; water means only life and is enough for a cat."

He drew in smoke. Let it fill his lungs. He let it feed his memory and guide life into his hand and out through his charcoal.

"My father. He's drawn him."

With finishing strokes, some shadow beneath the US Navy cap, some shading beneath squinting, sunny eyes, the drawing became complete. A face smiling crookedly from the page. Lucky-Boy handed it to Lara.

Lara touched it, careful not to smudge the lines. She didn't know if she was happy or sad and her expression reflected this. She angled the drawing to Bishop. He did not take it. Although he'd never met van Eijk, he knew this face.

"I told you they would send a man—my best friend in the world?"

Lara narrowed her eyes.

"I'm not your brother, Lara. The man they'll send to kill me is."

Lara turned away from Bishop. Held the picture but didn't look at it again.

Stripped of identity is stripped of life; appearance: only reality.

"If I'm to meet my only family…"

"Means I'm to meet my maker. Y'know, I liked you a little less optimistic."

She didn't seem to hear. Bishop knew he was high and knew she was as well. Anyway, now was not the time to rush things. He watched her and she pulled her hair back high and smooth, a big knot at the back, and looked away from him out the window at the stars. She reminded Bishop not of someone he knew, not of Russell Aiken—although he could see my deep resemblance, why Lara had reminded me of Paulette in the first place—but in that treehouse, Lara reminded Bishop of someone he'd read of somewhere, someone the same as she, a young woman lost of identity.

Lucky-Boy appreciated what he observed between them; he'd gotten them to the place he'd intended since he'd watched the gate eight days and nights in a row after last orders from Prometheus to await their arrival. He smiled to himself, drifting at the sound of the tigers woofing and moaning to their cubs in the haunting way tigers express signs of love. He put his hash pipe away and crept to his monocular to observe the cats and to continue the unfinished drawing on his drawing board easel with curves of orange and stripes of black pastel.

BISHOP FLOATED on the vocalizations of the big cats. An image of Italy came to mind. At first, he imagined horses stampeding the Spanish Steps of Rome under falling stars at dawn and had no idea why as he'd never seen such a thing in his life, but he allowed his imagination to wander around another Italian corner. A corner by the sea. By a war monument glistening in the rain and a woman in a window. He'd never been here either. It was only a story he recalled. A story by Hemingway he'd read once and never more than half listened to, hearing it later, but to read it even once was to absorb it and he knew the story almost by heart from many readings by the Muslim wife of his Kosovar agent.

She read out loud from a book she studied to learn English. She used the book of stories to bolster her dream of being anywhere but Pristina. The Muslim wife of his Kosovar agent held a dream that after the war, after helping the American, Bishop in turn would help her family. She had wanted to change into someone else. How many times had she expressed to Bishop her desire to be an American woman in an American Muslim community? She read it out loud to mask the voices of her husband and Bishop making whispered plans. Out loud so no one would hear them through the thin walls in the Pristina apartment.

And there was the night Bishop now envisioned when his Kosovar agent's Muslim wife finished the story in laughter because her daughter entered sleepily from the family bedroom carrying a large yellow cat spilling from her small arms.

"Ai e bën shtratin shumë të nxehtë," the child rubbed eyes and complained. *He's making the bed too hot.*

"Erblina," Bishop said when the mother returned from putting her daughter back to bed. "You have more than the American woman in the story. You have both a cat and a kitten."

"The story come to life," she said and curtsied.

Erblina was raped and dead.

Her daughter, raped, dead.

Bishop's agent: executed.

Elizabeth.

Dead.

Only the story had persisted. Returned to life with Lara and with tigers.

It renewed itself inside this treehouse and inside of Bishop. A thing inside himself he believed, until this minute, he had mercilessly killed when cancer had taken Elizabeth. It had lain, a dead seed he'd sewn in weakness in the rocks and boulders of the waste dump of his soul. Its lifeless shell now cracked by emerging life with the power to rend a mountain.

Bishop noticed Lucky-Boy's drawing had slipped to the floor, Lara's hands open and empty in her lap. Fingerprints. Her unique identity.

Bishop flashed to a frightened Korean girl—not a story— another cat, black and struggling in her arms. Blood smeared across the philtrum split of the cat's black upper lip between wet, red-dipped whiskers.

He knew what he wanted to place in Lara's hands and give without restraint to her, but the only cats he'd brought her to were devouring beasts in the hot May night.

PART THREE

ELUSIONS

"No man ever steps in the same river twice, for it's
not the same river and he's not the same man."

— Heraclitus (circa 535–475 BC)

27

Early in 2000, Harker and his Young Turks scored a heady victory for the Agency over all our obvious enemies past, present, and future. Except the Chinese—word returning that China as an enemy would be a non-starter across the board. Still, old Soviets, New Russians; New Germans, old Stasi East Germans, secret-cell re-emergent Nazis run by septuagenarian Hitler Youth; terrorists, terrorists, terrorists: every race, creed, and color; eco-warriors who would dare destroy humankind to save the ecology, others who would wound the environment to perish humankind; foreign government-sponsored criminals from Russian *mafya* to South, Central, North American narco-armies supporting South Central crack gangstas. Arms traffickers. Human slavers. The Vatican. The New World Order. Old-time Illuminati. Rogue American military and law enforcement, and a dash of former in-house, homegrown, disgruntled, Agency-contract nutjobs.

Harker's Operation BIGSHOW, as he referred to this task force, was embedded within and run out of the CIA OPA, the Office of Public Affairs. To be fair—and Harker readily admitted this—all branches of the military, and the FBI, and the DEA, were already running parallel programs against their own particular enemies to high success ratings. This is how, temporarily seconded to this fledgling BIGSHOW in August 2000, I found myself in Los Angeles, California, able to bookend Company business with a second-opinion consultation and follow-up with the neurologist-neurosurgical team of Dr. Susan Levy-Waxman and Dr. Rashmi Patel at the Cedars-Sinai Medical Center's Maxine Dunitz Neurosurgical Institute.

Our first operation out—CIA, not medical—our Los Angeles asset received intelligence that the FBI was pushing his network for jurisdictional control. As this was our bold move into this AO, Harker convinced the outgoing DCI (Director Central Intelligence) that maximum efforts be made to maintain jurisdiction with an in-person in-field meet. Show our seriousness to the asset and his network with an officer from the Office of General Counsel, yours truly, to negotiate and lock down commitments and guarantees in writing.

The face-to-face with the asset—set for 4 p.m., Wednesday, August 23, 2000—allowed me a three-hour window for my first appointment at Cedars at 11:30 a.m. with a results review two days later, Friday at 10 a.m. Drs. Levy-Waxman and Patel came highly recommended by both my University of Maryland Medical Center's Brain Tumor Treatment Center neurologist, Dr. Carlson, and Elizabeth's oncologist, Dr.-can't-for-the-life-a-me remember his name—that guy—the doctor Muir arranged for back in '95 or '96—whichever—before the Taiwan option became available. And *Dr-whatshisname*, with Muir's help and his China apology tour, scooted Elizabeth overseas for what he claimed and would turn out to be the best life-extending treatment Elizabeth could receive.

My first recollection of symptoms, barely noticed, go back to '98. Touch of dizziness on stairs—not every climb but sometimes. Morning headaches. Vision issues. All, I was confident, were stress-related and or due to the approach of aging—natural and as slow and destined as a river in Russia. Oh, occasional memory lapses, botched pronunciations of common words, blanking names, and having to double, even triple trip to the grocery store.

Stress. Age. No worries.

Until one Monday morning, stress and aging had nothing to do with it. I failed at the *New York Times* crossword. Not the

Saturday—oh, mentioned Monday already (see the crap I'm dealing with? Or not dealing with, as is the case). Saturday puzzles are deliberately the most difficult puzzles of the week. By the same token, Monday's puzzle is always the easiest. To note:

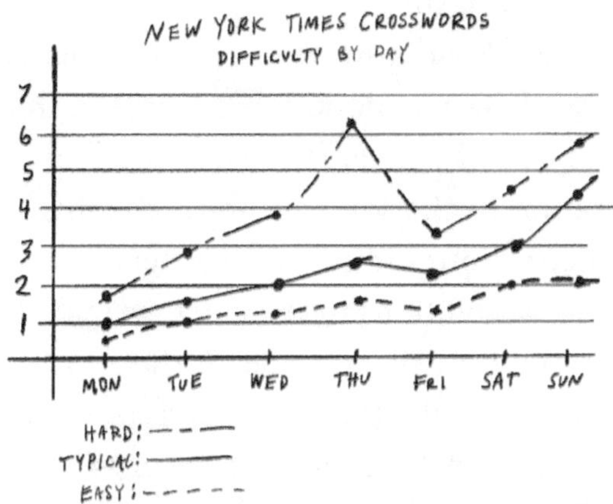

The difficultly curve began with the Old Gray Lady's first puzzle editor, Margaret Farrar. Madeline, you know my love of words and wordplay, my addiction to crosswords I will never rehab or cold turkey from, but as all memoirs are only useful if they're confessional, I admit this without shame. In my early throes of puberty, I awoke at night from a too-realistic, sex-based, and home-runned dream involving Ms. Farrar. Didn't even know what she looked like, but will say for the record, my Margaret had the beauty and the body across and down to match her lovemaking skills.

There you go. My admission. No nocturnal shame. No need for more emiss—*omission*.

Farrar chose to craft her crosswords progressively more diffi-cult as the week progressed. She figured, as many people didn't have to work on Saturday, they'd have more time to solve hers. She referred to her Saturday *Times* crossword as a "two cups of coffee" puzzle. When Will Shortz became editor in 1993, he decided to steepen the difficulty slope: "The Monday puzzles I edit," he answered an interviewer, "[they're] probably easier than they've ever been before, and the Friday/Saturday puzzles tend to be harder." Shortz's Monday crossword was dubbed "the puzzle anyone in America can solve."

My failure that Monday in question is not that I didn't solve it. Seated at my headquarters desk, I finished it in five minutes flat. Before any first cup of coffee. It wasn't until I was straightening my workspace prior to checking out for home that I noticed some of the word intersections didn't match letters. Some of the words, while valid/possible solutions to the clues, weren't the *correct* solutions and I'd simply misspelled one of the words at the across/down intersection to make them fit. Seven of them. Fear gripped me. What had I done? What could I have possibly been thinking? Since when—I mean, *really* when—did I ever torment *myself*?

In growing panic at home that evening, the misorder of my mind fueling a disorder inside my home, I ransacked bedroom, study, the TV room: dug out every old drugstore-to-stocking-stuffer puzzle book I could find. My crossword history audit took seven hours. It led me to dawn and the dawning realization that for the past six months, matching with the onset of the dizziness and the headaches, the blurred vision that came on instantaneously and went away just as fast, I'd been—I scolded myself to bolster my denial—CHEATING.

But I knew I wasn't. I cheat for a living. Cheat on a grand international and professional scale. I write the rule books to cheating. I don't bring my work home with me. I don't cheat for pleasure.

Not like some.

This was a betrayal—Langley has me sugarcoat those too, just ask Jack and Jill about their well—not only of myself or Mr. Shortz, or Mrs. Farrar (yes, I'd discovered, A: she was happily married and I'd never have another chance with her; B: she was not much of a looker, and anyhow I'd already moved onto Jayne Mansfield, Raquel Welch, and Bond girl Ursula Andress fantasy four-ways), *but* my betrayal tracked ocean-liner all the way down and across the sea and time to England.

Mr. Arthur Wynne. Liverpool. Inventor of the modern crossword. Boundless reverence for this man I'd betrayed with my sloppy Monday mash-up. My great admiration proven ipso facto bound within this black-box memoir is Wynne's first puzzle that started it all. Every clue and all Wynne's answers hidden within these pages to ferret out. My penance—not inside me or Bishop, as I'd said—lurks inside my writing with arrow-tipped accuracy.

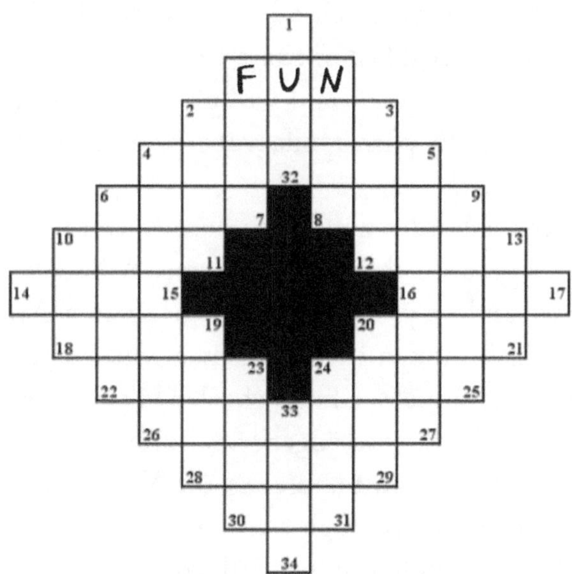

It's in my blood. I can't live without crosswords; but *It* is also in my blood, and I cannot live as long as that remains.

I FLEW the 7 a.m. American Airlines Flight 77, Dulles to LAX, putting me into Los Angeles a little after 9 a.m. local time. I'd travelled with the officer in charge of this task force Jix, (non-legit nickname for Jackson) Haisley, whom I ditched with the phony excuse that I'd be staying in La Crescenta at the family home with sisters, Paulette—who'd "neva-evah" move out—and Jeannie, the oldest of the three of us, who'd moved back when her husband passed. I made this family reunion sound so boring, uptight, cigarette-smoke-filled, bad cooking, memory-lane, house-robed and threadbare-slippered of a good time that Jix had no intention to accept my invite to sack out at the ol' homestead in order to pocket his hotel per diem (as, government pay what it is, all of us try to do). In fact, Jix didn't even want to grab breakfast or share a cab—neither of which my true schedule allowed for—and we split outside baggage claim, confirming our 3:30 p.m. rendezvous prior to our meet with the asset.

I'd reserved a Ford rental sedan and drove off the lot in the Geo Metro supermini they forced on me. A Suzuki motorcycle engine turned sideways with a Geo (or is it a Metro?) body popped on top. Although it couldn't do a wheelie, the experience was otherwise the same as a four-wheeled bike with a third of the visibility blocked by the passenger seat. I drove into Beverly Hills, a dodging insect, between Suburbans and Yukons, Hummers and Escalades, their music as much a danger as their insect-crushing tires, pounding bass buffeting me with constant cannonade recoil. My trepidation was even greater at what to expect once I'd met with Drs. Susan and Rashmi. Dr. Susan—she insisted I use the professional to put me in awe, and the familiar to put me at ease—had done two of the three telephone interviews solo, while Dr. Rashmi had been on for the third. It never occurred to me

Dr. Rashmi Patel might not be a woman. But, night before, it occurred to me Dr. Rashmi might be a man.

Their literature accessible on the World Wide Web, along with a copy of the brochure already mailed to me, contained both doctors' photographs. But while Dr. Susan was clearly female, Dr. Rashmi wore a Peter Pan haircut—the kind that says "lost *boy*" but is always worn by women playing the fellow on stage. Dr. Rashmi's darker complexion glowed naturally with only eyeliner for makeup. Tip-off? No. Problem is, a large percentage of the men of India wear Surma. Technically not eyeliner, Surma is used to (other than to make men look ridiculous):

1. Keep eyes protected from dust and pollution.
2. Keep eyes cool because of its soothing effects.
3. Provide relief to stressed eyes.
4. Provide moisture to dry eyes.

Those technicalities, however, were lost on me. Surma equals Maybelline Define-A-Line any way you blink. Unless you're calling it guyliner and star in a boy band or a movie or live your life on the West Side below the Sunset Strip.

Like Dr. Rashmi, I was the lost boy now.

I reread their webpage and their brochures. In a perfect ten performance of compositional gymnastics, nowhere in either place did the inscrutable doctors refer to themselves with gender-specific third person. Good God, I already had a brain tumor. No room left in my skull for a mind-fuck.

And then the miracle happened. Dulles check-in. The pre-boarding flight attendant—smiling, attentive, and Subcontinent South Asian American *female* all the way—she assuaged my confusion with pleasant relief.

"And I thought *I* was happy today," the flight attendant said, complimenting my dopey whole-faced grin.

I pointed at her nametag: "Blessed God. Blessed Allah. Blessed Jehovah. You're a 'Rashmi'!"

She laughed to hide her worry for me and chided, "Also a Hindu."

"Yes, you are. Indeed, indeedy, and in…"

"Indian, sir?"

"Indescribable good fortune, you *miraculum.* You gotta tell me—"

Jix lay a hand on my shoulder. "You okay, Rusty?"

"Russell, and yes." I didn't take my wide eyes off of the new Rashmi but dialed my enthusiasm down a notch—I hadn't meant it to get so out of whack—and finished my question with a less deranged face. "Where did you get you name, *your*—ma'am—Ms. Flight *ah*-name—Rashmi?"

"Thank you for all that. I'm named after my father. Rashmi." Flat. Done with me. "Ticket and ID, sir, and will you be checking any bags with us today?"

I ARRIVED AT Cedars Sinai Hospital and checked in at my second-opinion doctors' offices. Filled in the standard clipboard of blanks, of which I had to check too many "yes," and was instructed to make my cash payment (I was hiding from my insurance) to the cashier.

I was escorted back. Both doctors waited for me inside their consultation room, hands folded in front of them, which released as if on springs for handshakes before I'd crossed the threshold.

I opened my mouth and said, "Tits."

Dr. Rashmi's rising hand in handshake had jostled Victoria's secret.

"I beg your pardon," said Dr. Susan.

"—iiiit'Ssso nice to meet both of you."

"Welcome, Mr. Aiken—you're all right with Russell, though, I believe you told us?" said Dr. Rashmi.

Deep-voiced like a man.

Dr. Carlson had forwarded my files—neurological exam results, blood work, MRIs, his conclusions, and treatment plan. We discussed the latter two subjects first. I had a low-grade astrocytoma glioma tumor, Stage II, growing from the brain tissue of the occipital lobe, pushing into the Wernicke's area between the parietal and temporal lobes, the pressure on the three regions creating the various symptoms I experienced and suffered. While the MRIs left little doubt my tumor was benign, Drs. Susan and Rashmi agreed wholeheartedly with Carlson's recommendation— eight weeks ago, they'd scolded me—I proceed with a biopsy.

"We drill a slim burr hole into your skull and insert a hollow needle on a stereotactic frame connected to a computer and guided by MRI scanning. The stereotactic needle allows a thin biting instrument inserted through it to remove bits of tumor for our pathologists," said Dr. Rashmi, making horrid biting pantomimes with her fingers.

Dr. Susan tag-teamed in. "Our pathologist, Dr. Ed Choi— great guy, you'll want to meet him—will analyze the sample under a microscope to determine if it's cancerous or benign."

"I've already been advised it's one hundred percent benign. This sounds like a step backward."

"99.999: yes," said Dr. Susan.

"But drilling a hole into my brain—"

"Your *skull*—" Dr. Susan.

"Tumor—" Dr. Rashmi.

"—helps put you at ease those point three zeros and a one back."

"A biopsy is the only way to definitively diagnose a brain tumor and give a prognosis to guide your treatment decisions," said Dr. Susan. "Dr. Eddie will also provide a molecular diagnosis of the physical appearance and growth rate of your biopsy sample. It's indispensable for what we have ahead of us."

"This information"—tag, you're it, Rashmi—"helps to govern our decision-making about our entire treatment plan."

I wondered if my cancer was a contagious type that had spread to both of them that they now included themselves in my disease.

"I've put aside time in the OR for Friday morning. Just the two of us," Rashmi intimated, as if inviting me to her box for the opera.

For the first time I could remember, needing something like I needed a hole in my head sounded necessary and beneficial.

We went on with less invasive tests from there. Fresh neurological exams to check mental status and memory, cranial nerve function (sight, hearing, smell, tongue, and facial movement), muscle strength, coordination, reflexes, and response to pain, followed by a new set of MRI brain protocols to gauge tumor growth. I told them I'd see them Friday for my results and when asked if I would be joining Dr. Rashmi for my biopsy, I flunked the hearing test and hurried to the elevators and my waiting Richard Scarry-style scary Suzuki motorcycled car.

I MET JIX at Il Fornaio Cucina Italiana, on Beverly Drive in the heart of Beverly Hills. He'd spent all five meals' worth of his meal per diem on his lunch, which alarmed me to the point of admonishing that money doesn't fall out of the sky, to which he rapturously declared it didn't matter as the meal was worth every penny spent. I had an uncontrollable instinct to fill him in on my "pennies from heaven" dumb bomb—not stupid dumb, but "non-smart bomb" penny dump—but held my tongue, fearing a field officer like Jix might be too dimwitted on the subject to appreciate it. Or think me dumb. Anyway, he had a plan of his own as I bolted my espresso and he paid the check, saying, "This bill we claim as the meet with our principle, get it reimbursed as an expense, and then where we're headed now, we *both* claim as our per diem out-of-pocket lunch. You'll be a pal and work out the paperwork?"

I swallowed perceptibly. *Guy's a total pill.*

From the seductive aromas of Italian cuisine, of roasting garlic, tomatoes, baking bread, hot oil, veal and beef simmering braised and seared, of coffee mingled with the piquant scent of fresh chopped herbs, rosemary sublime…to the pickles, sauerkraut, pastrami, and scorched coffee of Canter's deli on Fairfax only long enough for our asset to tell us we were meeting his network at 4:20, but "Don't sweat it, the network's right down the street if you want to nosh a minute or two with your coffee."

I hadn't eaten, so I noshed—picking a pickled tomato— before we made our way to CBS Television City. Designed in the International Style as a testament to the electronic age at the dawn of television, a factory building of black and white and glass panels, all meeting at sharp edges—not unlike the meeting we were headed into—as space-age as our Old Headquarters building, which also wasn't once the real space age hit. We elevatored to the third floor, where three all-knowing female executives arranged by size, hair color, and breadth of smile represented the network. All vice presidents of various levels of the network vice presidenciary offi-ciouscy—two fabricated words for fabricated VP differentiations.

Our asset—I'll call him David to spare him any embarrassing blowback—was not what Hollywood calls "good in a room." He was pitching a CIA show—"Think *CSI* meets CIA in an interna-tional procedural. Twenty-five foreign cities in twenty-five weeks.

All LA shot. All centering on a reinvigorated Agency launching a full-on, balls to the wall—writer's calling it, wait for it… *War on Terror.*"

I wanted to ask Jix, who'd read the pilot, if *terror* meant there'd be a horror aspect to this series. I didn't presume even Harker would go for that, but the VP trio placated the producer that the writer's vision for *terror* was a sexier word than *terrorism*, which didn't test well at all (David going for word weight 10 all the way) and *War on Terror* was as good as etched in celluloid stone. I wondered why the writer wasn't with us in the room to hear the good news until it dawned on me the VPs and Executive Producer David were third-personing the writer right in front of his face. His face being David's booze-blotchy countenance. Took to our work pretty well: a double identity of writer *and* producer hidden in one 1970s shag-haired talent. If they didn't see a conflict of interest and David knew what to do—Run, run with it; who am I to stand in the way of genius?

"This is only one of my shows. I'm running an empire here," he unblushingly said to me later.

"We see it the same way on that, David. Question is, with a procedural—especially establishing series signature sets—have your agents eyeballed the polish and are they willing to allow full production access?" said Black VP.

"And at what level? This doesn't work if we're not getting exclusive eye candy to pop from," Brown VP.

"The agents can jump in, knowing, of course, Les would definitely need an Operations Center with the big boards all around. FBI has already promised one, Bruckheimer-Bay quality. And gadgetry. Stuff we haven't seen. Q stuff but cooler. Picture this: Z level… if your agents have the same levels the Brits do. But—and this is the big but—I also have some content concerns,

David, we've gone back and forth on—" Goldilocks big on the *but*, not big on the *back and forth*, I could tell. "I'd also like the agents to address these. Primarily, we want to keep the show homegrown. Couldn't the CIA—instead of operating out of foreign embassies—operate out of our American Embassies here?"

I knew enough Hollywood lingo to know "agents" meant David's negotiating reps, the folks who do all the real work and pull all the strings. I didn't lift my gaze as I drafted a list of "on location" Langley access we were willing to offer that I thought would sink whatever the FBI had pitched to steal ours and the show's jurisdiction.

Jix waited, his expression equal parts tough and mysterious, hands together over his knee.

Black VP chimed in, "Agents, your cue."

I glanced up from my legal pad, assuming David's agents had arrived. They hadn't. Jix grabbed the ball and ran with it.

"We recruit agents, ma'am." He flipped open his CIA credential ten times cooler than the Texas Ranger character postered on the wall.

"We recruit agents to spy for us and betray their countries for the United States. We're not agents, we're CIA officers. Oh, and we put embassies in foreign countries because that's where we spy. America sort of works as a single, fifty-state, five-territory embassy for Americans all on its own. Haven't yet found a need for our own embassy in our own country, if you see what I mean."

Their three heads leaned in to gaze at his credential as if his credential were a holy relic.

"No rule against me letting you hold it." Jix offered it into Goldilocks's fingers. He swelled. "That's no prop, Miss."

He let a little Texas twang get the better of him. I jumped in with my offer.

1. *Langley exteriors. Existing, already approved stock footage.*
2. *Old Headquarters exterior. CBS filmed. Parking, bus depot—similar space age design, main doors for active filming with actors and real CIA personnel (strictly extras).*
3. *Old Headquarters lobby to be used in filming dramatic scenes with actors.*
    3.1. *CIA Official Seal.*
    3.2. *CIA Memorial Wall.*
    3.3. *Bill Donovan (OSS Founder) statue.*
    3.4. *CIA Motto.*
    3.5. *Security gates and front interior hallway.*
4. *Production Designer/Photographers access to (for CBS soundstage reproduction):*
    4.1. *Baffled soundproof corridors.*
    4.2. *Open Source Intelligence Monitor Center (Bruckheimer-Bay Big Boards—which are just TVs hung like in airports. But lots).*
    4.3. *Director of CIA, Acting Director Harker's Suite:*
        4.3.1. *Outer Office/Secretarial.*
        4.3.2. *DCI Conference Room (and "Acting" Buffet).*
        4.3.3. *DCI (Acting) Director Harker's personal office.*

Jix shot me concerned eyes, but, hey, this was Harker's big show...

5. *New Headquarters Building*
    5.1. *Atrium. Ground level and Second Floor for active filming with actors.*
    5.2. *Escalators. Same.*

> *5.3.   Food Court. Same.*
> *5.4.   Art Gallery. Same.*
> *6.   Former Office of Technical Services Bungalow, now forgery*
> *and photo museum, for active filming with actors—*
> *Already staged at Langley to look real deal. And finally:*
> *7.   Anything seen/photographed will be deemed declassi-*
> *fied and carry full reproduction production license.*

"All of these items—except for item one, stock footage—have never before been filmed and used in any public informational or entertainment mediums."

Here I gave a dramatic pause to let them savor and delight over all we were giving them (and, if anyone at HQ had deigned to listen to me when this idiocy began, giving all our enemies, who, while not liking the American way, way-like American TV), but poor salesman David jumped right on top of the moment.

"So just what are these new notes? I don't recall back-and-forthing with you, Angela?"

He bore his impolite eyes into Goldilocks. She ignored him and focused on Jix. I could swear she was pouting.

"Officer Jix. You've read the pilot?"

"It's excellent. Absolutely excellent. Genius writing. Meets all our approvals. Let us give you the real McCoy. We're ready to go CIA all the way, which would be the Agency—not the Bureau—who'd fight this 'new' War on Terrorism."

"*War On Terror*," David piped up. "I'm not budging."

"We've not budged you," snapped Black VP with a rubber-band smile.

"Agency's behind *that* all the way. Super title," Jix said.

"Thank you," said Goldilocks. "And thank you, guys, from my team, and Les"—Off our stupefaction—"Mr. Les Moonves, our

'Director of Intelligence' as you'd say," and she got obedient laughs from Black and Brown.

Halt. Don't want to come off racial here by unintended means. To be clear, these are three white girls. Just distinguishing by hair color when mentioning them. CBS hiring goes deeper than hair and skin, proving it's always what's beneath: colorblind brains of gray live matter.

Why the hell did I fucking blurt out "Tits"? God, it's this gray thing inside my *matter of fact matters. Brain.*

"One tiny thing. This bad guy David has created," said Goldilocks.

He rolled his eyes. I didn't much like David. It didn't take a Hardy boy to deduce that he was his own worst enemy.

"This bin-Layden, bin-laddin-Aladdin," she stretched the last part out for effect. "See what I mean? Too Walt Disney. And this al-qweeda-qwayada, potato-patata. Don't you have something— someone dramatic-mysterious-*sexy*—our audiences can better get a grip on? Better relate to—love-to-hate villains are what we're all about here."

Yep, Jix took this little wordplay all the way back to Harker for his continued and Acting amusement.

David lunged to his feet. "How many times I gotta say: Osama bin Laden is *real!* Al-Qaeda is *real!* They're a big deal! They're *scary* bad guys."

Jix was about to agree with David to the suicide bombing of David's project, but Brown Hair chimed in: "David, point is, we have a highly respected newsroom right down the hall. If your characters were real, *we'd* have heard about them."

"Officers?" David pleaded as though we were cops at his car accident.

Jix spoke in a voice all winks and elbows. "Bin Laden? Sure: real guy, bad actor. But not the worst. Not by a long shot. Small potato-potatas, if that's what you want, David. But we'd be happiest, and you would too, with someone audiences will get— and newsrooms. Not PLO, the Israeli question is a minefield for Les and you guys, but how about we go with Islamic Jihad?" He drew me in with a glance. "Russell, you could get David here some heretofore—lookit, I'm talking like Rusty now, *heretofore*—operations never revealed to the public, declassified for our network partners."

David got his green light.

We opened all doors to CBS for their pilot with the promise from the Young Turks of a Hollywood red-carpet star-studded premiere to take place in our Langley-located Dome theater sometime in September before the new television season.

THURSDAY NIGHT, David, Jix, and I celebrated his green light over Chinese food. David's choice, which Jix and I cheerfully assumed would allow us to divvy up the rest of the food per diem until we walked into the most gourmet Chinese restaurant we'd ever been to and ate the best un-Chinese food I've ever eaten. A Mr. Chow in Beverly Hills that cost in un-Chinese food fashion not only my entire dining allowance, but also both our hotel allowances. I got back to my Motel 6 (wasn't about to deal with my sisters that trip), to a presumptuous message from Dr. Rashmi's office confirming my biopsy surgery appointment for the morning.

7:57 a.m., three minutes before they opened their office, I called to let both Dr. Rashmi and Dr. Susan know I was "passing" (TV term, I'd just learned) on the procedure. They could forward my new MRIs and tests to Dr. Carlson and thank you very much it was a real pleasure—

Wasn't, and a total humiliation with my tits comment—

—and I was sorry I wouldn't be seeing them again.

I was packing when my phone rang a few minutes later. I figured it was Jix confirming our meet for breakfast and answered, "Heading to your hotel."

"I'm not at a hotel, Mr. Aiken." Dr. Rashmi, cold as the blade of an ice skate carving a circle in the thin ice around me.

More like a bone saw whirring a circle around and through my skull.

"I'm sorry, Doctor—"

"Yes, and you will apologize to me in person at our scheduled time, or I will bill all lab work and test analysis since your last appointment and now—including this telephone consultation—to your insurance, which Dr. Carlson was only too happy to provide me just now."

"IT'S THE AH-COMMENT—first comment, I made—"

"The 'tits'?"

I was in her office, her serious office with her serious desk between us, my MRIs in their sleeve, my test results in a binder: prisoners to negotiate between us.

"A good place for us to start, Mr. Aiken."

What happened to Russell?"

"Yes," she said. "We will be finding that out."

If ever a woman looked ready to kill me, it was right now. I didn't have to take that. Wasn't going to. Put both hands on her desk and pushed to my feet. She covered both my hands with hers. Soft. Warm. Tender.

This took me so completely by surprise, I plopped back into my seat, careful to leave my hands beneath hers, where for the first time in months I felt safe. Tears burned my eyes.

"Tissue?"

"No. Don't move your hands."

"Okay." She soothed me with her sympathetic tone. "You must do the biopsy, Russell. I'm going to demand it and you will do it, but your MRIs did add another couple point-nines to your tumor not being malignant."

"That's good news."

"It is. The bad news is, it is growing much faster than any of us—including Dr. Carlson, who viewed them early this morning on the East Coast—would ever have anticipated."

"This isn't about my comment."

"No, my tits are exactly what this is about. Exactly related to this rapid growth. Dr. Susan and I both know you didn't mean to say that. Out loud, anyway. Am I right? It's something you would never say to anyone upon first meeting."

I shook my head no. I slipped my hands free. I took the offered tissue and dabbed my eyes.

"I'm proud of my breasts. My partner is too. She likes them more than I."

"Dr. Waxman-Lev—Levy-Waxman—?"

"No. My partner-partner. I like to please her with my looks, which she prefers look like"—she spread her hands and chuckled—"look like…me. The reason you said it, couldn't help saying it, and why you got Dr. Susan's name incorrect right now is entirely symptomatic of increasing pressure on the Wernicke's area and on the lateral sulcus, which is the part of your brain where the parietal and temporal lobes meet. This is causing your difficulties with names, your blurting of private thoughts—an aggressive behavioral side effect—and where the tumor is pressing on your occipital lobe, which is giving you your vision problems. As your tumor grows and these pressures increase, these symptoms will likewise increase in occurrence and severity. You are likely to begin having visual hallucinations. Have you experienced anything like that?"

"No." *Yes.*

I have them with more regularity than I've already admitted. In fact, I better admit now: Harker probably didn't say *Frankenstein* instead of *frankincense.* As in gold, frankincense, and Muir. And—as much of a Neanderthal as he is—he's probably never called out Barney or Betty by their Rubble surname. Like I said, there were no spaghetti sandwiches that day. *However,* cults have roped in greater men than Harker, and the Arthur Murray mania is alive *in* well (ding-dong-dell) in that footloose fool.

"The name thing isn't so bad," I said.

She disproved that with my tests. It was the crossword puzzles all over again. My list of "seven items you find in a kitchen" I had only itemized four. Refrigerator—one, but didn't come up with toaster, didn't have oven, didn't have silverware drawer. The other three I listed: bed, mirror, and car.

She continued to the next report.

"Your writing sample and free-spoken language recordings exhibit hypergraphia and paraphasia. The first is characterized by the intense desire to write or draw. Forms of hypergraphia can vary in writing style and content, sometimes forcing a need to combine words with drawings and diagrams. Stream of conscious. Free association of incompatible concepts. Topic distraction. Inappropriate humor—"

"Writing distractions is my job description. I'm good at the now-you-see-it, now-you-don't construction."

She humored me. "Hypergraphia is abnormal, but it's not automatically bad. The condition isn't necessarily a debilitation or even a handicap. Both Lewis Carroll and Dostoevsky had hypergraphia. Van Gogh. Stephen King. Joyce Carol Oates. So by itself and to degrees it is not a negative. Unless it's being caused by a foreign growth."

I write OPLANS about curtailing foreign growth!

"I've read Van King—Neverland-mind—oops, boom, stepped on one there," I said, trying to turn my slip into a verbal pratfall behind enemy lines.

"As for the paraphasia, this accounts for your increased idea generation characterized by the production of unintended syllables, words and word associations, or phrases—like you just displayed. Pattern repetitions. Rhymes, backward writing, and palindromes during both writing and the effort to speak. Are you drawn to crossword puzzles?"

In French: mots croisés. The Italian: il cruciverba. Your Russian кроссворд, Garbo Ninotchka pronounced crossvord. Me? A cruciverbalist—? Latin for "cross", crux, crucis, as in crucifixion or the crux of the matter, and verbalist, "one who stresses words above substance or reality."?

"Nope. Never. Don't see the point. I mean, one time. On an airplane. And it was more than half-finished before I even opened the you-know-airline flip-pages thing. So the other guy—or woman, person, other (no judgement)—was worse off with it than I. No, I've never really been drawn to them. Or drawn them."

She lightly and absently rubbed her left earring, watching me.

"Due to your tumor, the umbrella term for your condition is Wernicke's aphasia."

She let that sink in a moment.

There's one I left out of the kitchen a moment ago.

She asked me, "You are employed by the government, correct?"

"Yes."

"Do you work with sensitive, classified material?"

I didn't answer.

"Well, I believe you do, and your silence confirms it. It also confirms that you don't want to lie to me, which I'm grateful for."

"I assure you. My work isn't frontline. It's contracts I double- and triple-check and have checked for me. Nothing is slipping past me."

"I'm going to have to trust you as the best judge of if-and-or-when you'd judge yourself unfit for your duties."

"Thank you, Dr. Rashmi, I understand."

She relaxed a bit. Reflected, deciding I could tell, whether to share something with me. "What the hell. You made the past two days a laugh riot at our house."

"You told your partner?"

Dr. Rashmi flashed a smile at my returned embarrassment. "Thanks to you, Roxanne now calls me Tits-Patel."

Their treatment was opposite of Dr. Carlson's recommendation. He'd wanted to go straight in and cut the tumor out. That's why I'd come for a second opinion. Drs. Rashmi and Susan believed the time for that was past, due to the tumor's size. They would begin with a course of powerful stereotactic radiosurgery (SRS) to immediately shrink and slow future growth with one high dose of intensity-modulated radiation therapy (IMRT). This would be followed by an awake craniotomy, where I would be locally anesthetized but kept in a semiconscious sedated state in order for me to be awoken from time to time to have me speak or make movements so Dr. Rashmi would be best able to navigate the most delicate parts of my brain.

I signed some paperwork. Dr. Rashmi filled with gladness. She'd only been wrong about one thing. I lie all the time. And I never went back to see her.

28

Bill Carver slid open the telescopic legs of an aluminum presentation easel. This was the Old Headquarters Building secure reading room, accessed from the Clandestine Service File Center. Carver's team of investigators was surrounded with stacks of files on the old Muir networks. Agent dossiers. Polygraphs. Station reports. CONPLANS and OPLANS. Debriefings. Sigint. Intercepts. Surveillance reports. Finances (Agency and personal), telephone records (operational and personal). Reading, studying, making notes. Every network a mythological name—and aren't all spy games when they work mythologies? Tricks and deceptions? Zeus dressed as a swan to screw a maiden?

Why did the girl reject sex with her deity, but then goes for it when a swan seduces her? What the heck was her name? Dela—? Adel—? Leda. Yep. Why did Mads have a baby with another guy who's not me? She wasn't afraid I'd kill her (Leda's excuse). I specifically made a point of not killing Madeline's first lover (I caught). Or her. Didn't kill myself. For the guy with the gun, I'm the biggest didn't-kill-'em guy out there.

She said she loved me from the minute she saw me, and I know she did. Guess she has the same problem I do mixing words—from and for—and the appearance of love and how I received it was my short-lived reality of love.

They were attempting to find the penultimate Muir myth that connected all the networks to his final swansong call that vanished them. Those networks designed to be compartmentized [not a mind-slip; our official word has no *mental* in it] broke form and acted in concert to orders from Muir, long retired-slash-long replaced by new case officers, new protocols and procedures, missions, and orders. What Carver was discovering revealed a pattern of interconnectivity between Muir's networks independent of any CIA compartmented security or regulation.

Carver placed a foam-board-mounted enlargement of Nathan Muir's crime scene photo onto the easel. Gunshot, head splat, death grimace bloody, it loomed over his team, who, Carver noted with quiet satisfaction, automatically referred to the image every time they lifted eyes from their reading and notes to ponder.

In the face of death photos like this one, Carver had cut his teeth. Saigon. 8th MPs at Long Binh. A shaved-head shavetail MP lieutenant investigating suicides and murders. Carver's major always displayed the pictures. Ghastly photos. Ever see a dead eighteen-, nineteen-, twenty-something kid who's starter-pistoled a gun in his mouth, temple-drilled, throat-slit, gut-stabbed, or fragged himself? Awful. And unnecessary.

There was something unnecessary in all of this. Carver couldn't put his finger on it. The size of it, its impact around the globe. It packed a wallop for the Agency, but the agents themselves, their only crime was that Muir had long ago roped them into committing treason against their own countries. In any honest business, all these folks were doing now was taking their retirement from a crime well done. The panic surrounding it came from the CIA's direction, not the networks. Harker was behaving like a drug dealer upset when all his best clients get clean. Stop using. Stop buying. Stop breaking the law. It's much more the CIA's system to keep them on our junk until they're tapped out or skull-tapped. Van Eijk, with his cry for help from the inferno at the center of Malaysia's gloomy circle, his secret knowledge of sinister fates befallen the lost networks, wasn't real. Muir simply had van Eijk operating on a separate set of instructions from his other networks. They weren't the catastrophe. They were the bait to panic and confuse Harker to such an extent he'd do anything and use anyone to get to van Eijk. Even Tom Bishop.

So why the fuck did Bishop kill Muir but go after van Eijk when Muir's intention was for Bishop to go after van Eijk in the first place? Tom Bishop isn't getting anything out of this… and that's a problem when you're working a murder case.

Carver looked at Muir's death photo. He'd liked Muir all the way back to 'Nam. Bishop too. Fucking unnecessary. He sat at the broad reading table he was using for a desk. His lead investigator, Christy Garcia, approached with a file. Her eyes sparkled with excitement.

"Whatever you got, fun as you may think it, I don't want any— if it's gonna destroy the little of my case I *think* I understand."

"'Fraid so, sir. But I'm going to come off looking genius, so I'm liking my odds."

"We'll see about that."

Carver held out his hand. She pulled a page from her folder. A summary of Nathan Muir's marriages. Updated at the time of Muir's retirement, it listed his first marriage. While a Marine Corps asset of Charlie March not yet within CIA ranks, Muir's wife, a South Korean national, Kim Jin, died by suicide, 1950.

His second wife, Sandra March (sister of Charlie March), married 1951, one week after Muir's induction into the Agency. Divorced: 1952.

Third wife: Veronique Segraves, married 1968, divorced 1984.

Fourth wife was Tracy Hutton, 1988 to 1990.

"Your point?"

Pinkie extended, with an exaggerated regal bow, Garcia handed him a binder-clipped report. Various colored page markers protruded throughout.

"Genius and a thespian."

"What are you talking? I'm straight as whiskey."

"Means 'actor.'"

"Oh." Garcia grinned. "Yeah. Well, I hear they're filming a TV show here coming up. Just getting ready for my big break."

"I'll bet." Carver examined the top sheet. "Bishop's recruitment interview and polygraph follow-up. Summarize."

"During recruitment and processing, Tom Bishop provided his mother's name as Sandy Bishop."

"Two Sandra's. Common name. I assume there's more…"

"Maiden name Gibbs. This fluttered true on all three of his polygraph tests. Agency also interviewed her at her home in Los Angeles, her neighbors, job, the usual."

Carver flipped pages, verified by her markers.

"All checked out," he offered.

"Down to Tom Bishop's birth certificate."

"And Bishop Sr.?"

"Arthur John Bishop, USMC, killed in action Korean Peninsula, Battle of Bunker Hill, August 11, 1952—seem to have one of them everywhere we fight. Anyway, Sandy Bishop is recorded with the Department of Defense as having received dependency and indemnity compensation for two years before her own income disqualified her."

"Okay. Seeing all this…" He gave her a shrewd look. "So far this isn't your best 'Agatha,' Christy."

"Yeah-yeah, sir, hold your horses. This is definitely my very best. I dug around with the mother's birth date on Bishop's birth certificate. Sandy Bishop née Gibbs blows out candles same day as Sandra Muir née March."

Carver placed the report on his table. He leaned back, folded hands across his belly. "You have captured the flag on the

Bunker Hill of all my attention. Any idea how come no one ever caught this?"

"Charlie March—remember, Sandy's own brother—backstopped and approved all Nathan Muir's reports and background investigations on Bishop. Pair of them buried the trail. Buried it well for the 1970s when Muir handpicked Bishop. So well, in fact, there is no indication Bishop ever found out the truth of his bloodline. It's never popped on any of Bishop's annual polygraphs. He's never dug around for it on his own. If this were still the twentieth century, I wouldn't have been able to get onto it myself."

Christy Garcia slapped a final document on Carver's table. A court decree stamped and signed July 16, 1952. From the Superior Court, Van Nuys, California, it granted a name change petition by one Sandra M. Muir to legally become Sandy G. Bishop. "A separate order—same judge, same date—conferred the same name change to Ms. Bishop's sole custodial infant son, Thomas."

"What happened to the real Bishop's war widow?"

"No widow due to the fact there was no Arthur John Bishop. I'm afraid, sir, Nathan Muir and Charles March committed fraud against the Marine Corps and Pentagon with that. While they're dead and can't be prosecuted, Sandy Bishop, party to said fraud, would still face federal felony charges."

Carver pushed to his feet. "I draw the line at moms and widows. Excise that entire thread and put together your report. Just the kind of thing Harker and Laa-Laa Hofmeyr would go after."

"Laa-Laa? Like the Teletubby?"

Shaking his head as he went for the door, Carver said, "Aiken coined it. Pretty good, huh? Though more and more, I think he's losing his mind." He grinned at her from the door. "And stay away from those Hollywood weirdos when they come 'round. I'm in no mood to go looking for a new resident genius."

CARVER ENTERED the DCI's private office as Acting Director Harker locked three Top Secret briefing books into a briefcase with a wire leash. He handed it to an armed plainclothes body-guard who secured it to his sleeve cable.

"Wait for me in my outer office," Harker directed the man, who, with an acknowledging glance at Carver, left the room.

CNN, Fox, MSNBC, and some other news networks played closed-captioned on wall monitors in easy view. Images of Malaysian rioting, bloody students out in the curfew fighting Royal State Police, tanks rolling from bases. BBC flashed "Taped Earlier" in the corner of their screen as they displayed video depicting a village in flames at sunset, Ramadan Moon funda-mentalists with submachine guns and machetes and the happiest grins you could see in HIPC. A scatter of dead litter the dirt lane behind them.

Harker held two memos flat in his open palms like a set of scales. "This one from our Southeast Asia Intelligence boys: in no uncertain terms it claims the Malaysian election is proceeding smoothly; the chance for civil war nonexistent. This other: President Bush directs I put the embassy on alert for evacuation, worried this is Iran '79 all over again."

He took his seat. The massive hulk of his new desk inspired the exact opposite of the confidence Harker had meant to achieve with it when he'd spent the taxpayers' money to gift it to his ego.

"I've only got a few minutes before I head over to Pennsylvania Avenue. Turn up something definitive on the Bishop-Muir of it all?"

Carver didn't like the airy happiness he was getting from his boss. He saw him, tilting back in his chair, hands locked behind his head, the perfect illustration of an overindulged child on a bring-your-kid-to-work day smirking behind daddy's desk.

We have that, the "bring your kid" thing, and I suppose I should've brought you, Jessie, although I'll be damned if I know how the clearances work.

"We have turned up something," Carver said.

"Well?"

"Bishop still off the grid?"

Harker affirmed it with a dip of his chin.

"Van Eijk—any sign of him?"

"No. Nothing."

"Where's Aiken?" Carver said.

"Just under three hours out from Muharraq Airfield, Bahrain, where a chopper is fueled, warmed, and ready to take him to the carrier *Stennis*, where he'll grab an F/A-18 to COPE TIGER joint-exercise Korat Royal Thai Air Force Base. I have an NOC, runs some interference out of Bangkok, Nick Albro, standing by to handhold Aiken into Kuala Lumpur."

Carver had no knowledge of Nick Albro, but knew what men like Albro were for.

"If you have Albro, why send Aiken at all?"

"Aiken is the only person who can draw Bishop into the open. Albro will give Aiken something untraceable. Solves a whole set of problems."

Carver frowned. "We got a lost agent key to our lost networks inside a foreign nation in flames, and you're playing a game of killing two birds who squawk at you wrong with a Nick Albro stone? Pardon me, while I'm not surprised."

Harker scowled. "No orders given and nothing to do with that. It's in their hands, but counting Muir, this whole clusterfuck will rid my Bush of three peckers."

Harker grinned white candy teeth at what he believed a clever presidential pun.

Carver gave Harker a skeptical look. "Honestly, I'm gonna let your bush be your own business." He launched into Garcia's Muir-Bishop discovery.

I'd never heard of Nick Albro either. His NOC status, however, I knew only too well. Bishop has always operated as NOC. Means Black Bag/Black Ops covert actions are undertaken without the protection of the US government, and without the political safety-net, that officers under Official Cover (as I traveled) are extended. A NOC caught denies, and is denied, recognition by the United States and most often, if not executed outright, never sees the torch of freedom, light of day, or Mom's macaroni and cheese ever again.

Why I'd been sent and not Nick Albro right off the bat is one of the hard-luck mysteries of my terminal life. Even a wee bit of help in the cemetery would have been appreciated, but by then, tough guy Albro was nowhere to be seen in the Malaysian civil unrest. "Not my problem. I'm just your delivery boy," he'd said, dropping me off at the cemetery to meet with Bishop alone.

To be honest, I disliked the muscled-out, urine-yellow Oakley sunglasses hooked to the back of the collar (what kind of tool finds that a convenience?) douchebag from the moment I met him, and my first thought as my mind wandered away from him was a fantasy of Albro off the mac-'n'-cheese list sooner rather than later.

Harker said, "His fucking son? Charlie March's nephew? Puts high gloss on the word *clusterfuck.* Verifiable?"

"Hundred percent, sir. Now on one hand, typical murder investigation, you always look to family first."

"Son kills father. So this confirms Bishop killed him." Harker savored the words.

"To get to van Eijk?" said Carver.

"That's right. Bishop and van Eijk are working together on this."

"Then why did Muir have van Eijk send us Bishop's invitation?" Carver shook his head. "Fact that Muir and Bishop spent their whole lives hiding their shared blood from us, united-by and together-in that deception through thick 'n' thin—and there's been uncommon, I might say 'mythological,' thicker and thinner with those two—speaks to something else entirely going on between those two, *other* than patricide."

"Time of death puts Bishop in the room."

"Without a direct eyewitness, TOD is only an approximation."

"Bishop is the witness!"

"Not helpful, Director Harker. All we can say for sure is Bishop was in the room within the window we've established. Now, we've been able to do the math on the temperature fluctuations caused by Muir's automatic thermostat settings warming and cooling the corpse core temperature, but that only narrowed the window from six hours to one and a half and that's as good as we're going to get. In my experience, an hour an' a half can allow for a lot of coming and going."

Harker rose on shaky shoes, a lot less dance in his feet. "I'll head out with you." He opened the door, allowing Carver to pass through before him.

In the empty room they left behind, the curfew in Malaysia continued on TV, Ramadan Moon rioters continued their mayhem in wild abandon, and most people on the planet continued not to care. They didn't much care in Thailand or in Singapore. Didn't care at the Port Authority, NYC. Didn't care at the Boeing 737 simulator at Pan Am International Flight Academy in Mesa, Arizona, where instructors had recently graduated the worst candidate to ever pass through their school. They'd complained to the Federal Aviation Administration about candidate Hanjour's piloting skills and they questioned whether his pilot's license was genuine. The FAA didn't much care about that either.

IN FALLS CHURCH, Virginia, Saudi pilot Hani Hanjour watched his television for the same Malaysia reports with eager attention. He cared explicitly.

29

BISHOP CARED. Had cared since Lebanon 1982, ticking down to tonight. To tomorrow. To sometime soon he had to pinpoint. And Lara cared for reasons she desperately needed to escape. Reasons of opposite intention and necessary outcome speeding to collision between the two of them. The dirt bike's headlight now disconnected, they cruised in darkness into Ipoh proper, capital city of the Malaysian state of Perak.

A city nestled in the embrace of towering jagged white limestone cliffs capped with thick jungle that spilled down stony faces pocked with temple caves. This nineteenth-century East-meets-West tin mining boomtown was a collision of cultures and epochs. Modern high-rise apartments shared walls with rickety night kitchens; dark glass and steel skyscrapers of the New Town are a turn of a corner to the colonial railway station, Victorian municipal buildings, Edwardian Tin Miners' Club, and the Dickensian shophouses of the cobbled Old Town. Bishop crossed the Kinta River onto Ipoh's main thoroughfare, the Sultan Idris Road, now devoid of traffic.

"Where would we find the highest concentration of tourists?" said Bishop.

"Is that how you see us?"

"Don't want to be seen. Most deserted and least patrolled by military. These situations don't turn on foreigners until they've built enough steam against the prevailing rule of law. Also—"

The knocking of a nearby vehicle's badly tuned engine cut Bishop off. He hit the throttle, and launched the bike over the curb to slide in behind a large concrete planter overflowing with date palms and exotic flowers. A military jeep bearing four assault-rifle-toting State Police cruised the main road and passed without seeing them.

Unconcerned, Bishop continued: "Also, if we're going to tuck in for the night, we'll get a little more leniency with those who cater to the outsider."

"The Empire Hotel is the former British governor's converted mansion. Big five-star tourist trap. And keep your tucking to yourself. You've gotten all the leniency from me you'll ever get."

Bishop juiced the gas, and this time popped the clutch causing the bike to lurch forcefully into the main road. Lara crushed into him and held on tight so as not to whipsaw off the back. She dug her fingernails into his chest, hoping it hurt, and Bishop didn't mind at all.

TWO MILES and two more dodged patrols later, Bishop cruised into the forecourt crumbling-plantation grandeur of the Empire Hotel. Much of the crumbling was due to recent violence. Anything that could be smashed had been. Wooden adornments showed signs of attempted arson. Spray-painted Ramadan Moon symbols and Arabic writing covered walls. Everything dripped water and firefighting foam.

Bishop stashed the bike. He and Lara hurried to the front entrance. Bishop pounded. The door opened partway. A liveried Indian bellman in his twenties, "Vicky" embossed on his Empire Hotel nametag, regarded them with apprehension.

"Sir, missus, what are you about in the night outside?"

"We need a room," Bishop said.

"Good sir, there is a curfew. There is nothing I am legally in the ability to do."

"We'll get caught if you don't," said Lara. She carefully pulled back her hijab, laying it across her shoulders as if it were nothing more than a scarf worn for a motorcycle ride.

Bishop glanced over his shoulder at the growl of another patrol. Vicky's worried eyes tracked with his. Headlights swung their way. Vicky widened the door. "Please, sir, missus, inside, please."

The main door shut behind them and the patrol rolled past.

Vicky escorted them through the empty lobby, the empty dining room, and upstairs to the guest room Bishop rented. Night paid plus extra that Vicky tucked into the pocket of his tunic.

"Tonight we have an excellent Japanese Wagyu tenderloin. Sixty-five days aged."

"I'm sure something simpler—" Bishop said.

"Served with a Malaysian herb and spice compound butter, roasted potatoes, and a side of *acar awak.*"

Bishop eyed Lara.

"Traditional pickled vegetables," she said.

"Sounds great. Care to share one?"

She nodded.

"I'll bring two. We had full reservations for election night dinner. Plentiful steak, few to serve." He smiled awkwardly, uncomfortable with Lara's troubled demeanor, his eyes continuously bouncing off the purple scarf. "Now that you're out of the night, missus, nothing left to fear?" He drew a suspicious line with his eyes to Bishop.

Their disheveled hair, hard-worn condition of their clothing, sweat-streaked grime on their faces from the day's violent encounters… Bishop exhibited no reaction; a few simple words from Lara and she would be free of him.

"We came to visit for our anniversary," she said. "Didn't plan for a curfew, let alone getting trapped in it. My parents live two miles away, if you can believe it."

Vicky couldn't, but he bowed, backing away, with a, "Welcome to the Empire Hotel. Please enjoy your stay."

"Medium rare. For both," said Bishop.

Vicky bowed again and was gone. Bishop faced Lara in the narrow entryway into their room.

"Why with the hijab? I was getting used to it."

Her eyes searched him for sarcasm she couldn't find.

"He wouldn't have let us inside." She pulled off the scarf. Bunched it between her hands. "You shouldn't be too surprised if I'm not feeling all it means after today."

The misery in her voice tinged with exhaustion touched Bishop unexpectedly.

"It compliments everything about you." Softening to his own fatigue, allowing his emotional discipline to slip, he added, "I never thought I'd meet someone as brave as you ever again. I wouldn't have hurt him if you'd said something."

"I know."

She looked into his eyes, and he recognized in hers, beyond her exhaustion, surrender. The concentrated fight that had burned torch hot since he'd first caught their flash had sputtered to a dying flicker suffocated by the last vestiges of self, the pressing emotions of her shattered identity.

"This isn't the worst, Lara. You'll survive this."

"How can you say that? Of all people? Muir did the same thing to you and look what you've become."

Bishop couldn't find a worthy answer for that. Lara excused herself past him. He followed her into the room. He found a bottle of sparkling water.

"Did you kill Muir? Kill your father?"

He opened the bottle. Offered it to her. She shook her head and declined.

"Ten years ago, I promised if I ever saw him again, I would. I've spent the past decade avoiding him so I wouldn't have to go back on my word."

"Did you go back on it? Did you kill him over all this?"

"No."

He held the water without drinking. Tired, nerves frayed, strangers who in the span of twenty-four hours had experienced together more than most companions experience their entire lives. Despite this, or perhaps to spite it, neither knew what to say next. They were extremely aware of the other's presence. Lara shook her head and billowed her dark hair. It smelled of smoke, of road, of jungle.

"You want the first shower?" Bishop asked.

"It's all yours. The water spins down the drain backward from where you're from. At least that's the appearance of it when it's wet."

"Aren't you and the world full of surprises?" He almost touched her with a comforting hand. "Look, don't beat yourself up over what's happening. This lone wolf always gets home."

He was giving her a sign. Giving permission. He walked into the bathroom and closed the door with a loud click.

After a moment, the sound of running water broke the stillness. Lara watched the bathroom door and didn't blink, waiting for more than a minute. She swiveled her legs onto the bed but not to recline. She lowered them over the other side. She planted her feet on the floor in front of the nightstand. Her body deflated as her spirit left her. Bishop had been right about her from the beginning. Other forces were at play. No right and wrong left to decide upon. She lifted the receiver and dialed the number she'd been forced to memorize.

The lone wolf always dies alone.

UPON ENTERING the bathroom, Bishop closed the door, making sure the latch click was audible. He turned on the shower. He laid his pistol on the counter. You never press bad luck, so he removed the clip and stowed it under the facial tissue box cover. He waited a minute before he silently opened the door. Just a sliver enough to watch Lara swing across the bed over to the bedside telephone and place her call.

Bishop didn't move. This had to happen. This is how she would survive. This is how Muir planned it and Bishop didn't know at the time and wouldn't believe it until it occurred—but Muir, who played every move in his head before committing to the game, must have known—that before the passage of twenty-four hours, Bishop would choose my sister over me and gun me down. Bishop let Lara complete her call without interruption, listening to her reveal their location and, yes, that she would make sure he didn't leave—

Lara whispered, "Yes. I told you I'd do anything. Even if it's that."

A knock on the door.

"Room service," called Vicky.

Lara replaced the receiver and Bishop closed the bathroom. He removed his clothes. He got himself under the Savoy showerhead that mimicked the downpour of the previous night, feeling the weight of the water. The weight of everything. Trying to remember how it felt before he'd met Lara.

Met? Threatened at gunpoint and abducted. Terrorized.

He shut his eyes and took the water in his face. She'd now set his enemies upon him—her enemies too, he wouldn't believe otherwise—and he'd let her do it. He visualized Lara asleep the night before behind the mosquito netting, identifying her when he'd found her writing paper and learned her name. Sleeping and beautiful. And he pictured Lara as he'd seen her that morning, so long ago, half naked and peaceful, and how he'd covered her in the robe that reminded him of his father's story of Jewel. Her wedding dress and the horrible what-if he'd not murdered his wife, not married Bishop's mother, and we'd have all been safe because Tom wouldn't be among us.

He amused himself at having dodged a psychological bullet—his lust and Lara not being his sister—but didn't allow the memory to arouse him. Or the feeling of her in his arms as he'd carried her out of the church rubble, how she'd fought and beaten him.

Or the joy in her eyes at the drawing of her mother.

The smile in her voice when she'd teased him about the tigers.

Her beautiful hands.

He braced both his hands against wet tiles. He stared at the water twisting backward around the drain. He liked Lara's gallows humor—so long as it would only be his hanging.

He'd not felt this way since Elizabeth.

He shut off the water. Grabbed a thick towel.

AFTER THE STEAKS, after a glass of wine, after the potatoes and the pickled *acar awak* eaten in silence; after the jug of coffee, staring at everything but each other, pretending they were at a quiet dinner and not in a secret war Lara had no idea Bishop had already surrendered to; after a bite of a lychee cookie with candied ginger, Bishop remarked, "You grew up in an orphanage?"

"A boarding school. I was the only orphan."

"And the money used to pay for it came out of what you were led to believe was an inheritance?"

Unsure, she spoke deliberately. "Twice every year, sometimes more, your father posing as the estate attorney would deliver the checks. I told you all this."

"Before I was interrogating for information. I'm asking now so I can know you."

Lara dabbed her lips with her napkin. "Don't."

"Later you used the money to pay for college. Did you like it?"

She deliberately folded the napkin onto the tabletop beside her finished meal. "We aren't friends. We won't become friends. We will never have anything more between us than empty space between the two shells we live inside that you want to pretend are lives, identities, but I know are not."

Bishop pushed away from the table. "You know? Maybe I'll let you be. Take a walk around the lobby. See if they have a bar."

"Wait."

He pretended not to see the flush of guilt flood her cheeks. He fought back the urge to speak. He needed to know he hadn't misjudged her, and he needed to hear it from her without influence.

"Go," she said. "Take the motorcycle. I know you enough to know you'll make it."

"What?"

She was so close to giving him the truth. It wouldn't make a single difference to the mission choice he'd already made, but in a personal place inside himself, Bishop wanted to hear it because her truth had grown to mean something to him. Maybe everything.

"Leave. I'm telling you, right now. Go back to America and leave me—leave my country and *my* people to our misery."

He carried out her order by resuming his seat. He said, "Your father died on a highway in Kansas, for all I know, crippled before that by drug addiction. My father was murdered last week because I arrived a day too late. Whatever we're fighting about isn't why or what or how we're supposed to be doing it."

"Stop it. Jesus, you and your myths. Water chemistry lessons. Family guilt for people I'll never know. You gonna give me Lucky's tigers and kittycats now?"

What was it I'd said to Bishop: You cut through the politics and you're everything to them—brother, lover, confidant, friend?

I'd stolen the idea from Elizabeth, who'd made the observation about her husband over a Thanksgiving dinner in Manhattan where the four of us had contrived to meet. She'd said Bishop handled his assets and held on to them less by tradecraft than by caring, and through caring, by healing.

"Lara, I was sent here to find your father. I was told he could help solve the disappearance of a number of our agents. I've found him. But he wasn't Dutch, and he wasn't named van Eijk. His name was Daniel Aiken. Everything we've been running around after, all your lies, all of mine, are all bait for the real reason my father, Nathan Muir, wanted me here."

"To find those trucks Lucky-Boy hid, and our two fathers stashed in the mine."

"No. If that was most important to all this, he would've spelled it out for me. My mission was to find you. Brave, complicated, backed-into-a-corner, amazing you. He set this whole thing in motion to get me here to take your hand and to help you. I'm sure of it."

"Dammit! Don't you get what's happening?"

"It's all going to be okay. You. Me. Tonight."

Lara lunged, grabbing his biceps and pulling him, saying, "You were wrong. You don't know the worst of it. I warned you: my goal is to survive. I've never had any way out of this, and I've done a terrible thing."

She tugged at him, trying to lift him from his seat.

"I know, Lara."

"You don't! You don't know, or you wouldn't be here!"

"I'm where I'm meant to be."

"Why couldn't you have been smarter? Why would you have ever trusted me alone for even five minutes? I've betrayed you."

Her truth. All he'd wanted. Freely given.

"I watched you on the phone. I'd have made you do it anyway." He spoke as gently as he'd ever spoken to his wife, or to Jesus when he thought God was listening in.

Lara recoiled. Horror isn't staring into a black lake of betrayal; it's the thing below the surface staring back with eyes that know all that crawls through the sludge, black on the bottom; in its unblinking watchfulness it promises never to let those things rise to eat you. And that thing was Tom Bishop. She shuddered, disbelieving.

"Why didn't you stop me?"

"Why did you try to get me to leave just now? The worst thing you could possibly do for your survival after that call. Every move you make, I got to tell you: you impress me."

"Fuck you! Is all this just a game to you? My life? Your own?"

"Muir said it was. Said so from the beginning. Before I knew anything."

Bishop watched her pace in small circles, overwhelmed with confusion, anger, and gripping herself in doubt.

"Hate him or love him, he's all I know and all I got. And I'll tell you another thing—just like he told me: it *is* a game and it's not one we want to lose. It doesn't get any easier. I'd have forced you to make that call with a gun at your head because in my line of work I have to—I *must*—see all the moves to get ahead of what's next. Your move. The next move. It's always been the only way to get you out."

She planted her feet. Leaned toward him as if defying a physical force in his words. "They're going to kill you." She clenched her fists. "To save me, I gave them you. That's the only game in town."

"None of that bothers me. We build escape hatches."

"That doesn't mean anything! Stop being reasonable with me!"

"Can't help it. I owe it to your brother."

"The one you say's coming to kill you?" She laughed at him, shaking her head. "The only escape hatch you have is called the door. Go before it's too late."

She grabbed him again, teeth grit, pulled with all her might. Bishop took her by the wrists.

"You think I'm talking about me. I'm talking about your father. What my father, Muir, needed me to tell you about him so you could, I don't know, find some peace from all of this."

He pressed her wrists together and imprisoned both her hands with his. He sensed the warmth inside him, which he'd lost with Elizabeth and given over to killing, return to him as living emotion. She went still in his grip, and Bishop, holding her hands, for the very first time realized how fragile Lara was, fragile because she was alive and she was precious. She calmed a bit in the warmth of his grip. The complex emotions in her face simplified to resolution.

"I don't know him. Not really and I don't care. You saw me make the call. That's *my* escape hatch. From all of you. Muir included. Please… Tom?"

The sound of his name passing her lips carried a current. An electrical connection joined and running between them.

"Why are you so fucking stubborn?" she said.

"Dand van Eijk-Dan Aiken built his escape hatch out of you. An identity. A life he created that when things became too much for him in this brutal business of ours, he could disappear into it—your life with your mother—never to be seen again."

"Not so kind to your friend."

"Your father's initial reasons, his needs—they belonged to him. I can't pretend to know them and I'm not going to guess. Russell, your brother, didn't end up with him anyway. But he never expected ATROPOS. His loyalty to Muir, to the safety of the world—as they saw it at the time—and he gave it all up. What I'm saying is—and I think Muir's dedication to you all these years proves it—he didn't abandon you. He simply didn't survive to open your trapdoor."

Emotion filled her eyes. He heard vehicles faintly through the windows.

"Did you know him?" she said, not wanting to speak at all.

"No. I met your brother long after the accident that took your father."

"You say it, but I don't have a brother. I can't. I've had no one my whole life and now, to save *that*, I've betrayed the one person connected to all the real people I'll never know."

Bishop released her hands. He stood and pulled her into his embrace—so long since he'd held anyone—and though she didn't make a move to hold him back, arms like deadweight at her side, she tipped her forehead into his chest. He stroked her hair and waited as if they had all the time in the world.

"Those drawings Lucky-Boy made?" she asked. "They identify something extremely dangerous—or you wouldn't be here."

"They're Russian missile launchers. Nuclear warhead capable, and Muir never let a capability go to waste."

She pulled away. She stood there, shaking her head at him, trying to deny it all. Bishop gave her a shrug and a gentle closed smile, as if to say *That's all I got, so here we are.*

She walked away from him. To the door. She grasped the handle. "If you care anything about me—"

Bishop removed her hand. He could hear tiny sounds beyond the door. The shuffle of fabric. The scrape of a gloved hand withdrawing from pocket or pouch.

He swung her around the entryway corner between the bed and the bathroom wall, whispering, "This isn't my escape hatch, and it isn't yours, so play your part and trust me."

The door burst open, and Bishop hurled Lara face down onto the floor. A flashbang grenade scuttered into the room to explode with blinding light. Three battle-dressed Special Actions Unit (UTK) commandos stormed in, submachine guns aimed as Bishop put his heel on the small of Lara's back to ensure she didn't move and get shot as he locked his hands behind his head.

Sedaka came into the standoff. "Hello, Bishop. Guess you didn't expect to see me again. Don't get sloppy here in front of your girlie-friend. You know where this airplane is flying, and you know you don't get off it until the champagne's gone and the hangar is dark."

The UTK commandos beat Bishop to the floor and cuffed him.

Sedaka ordered: "On your feet, Miss van Eijk."

"I've given you what you wanted." Lara pulled herself up against the wall. "You got him now. Give me my passport and work papers. We're finished."

Sedaka grabbed her by the arm and propelled her through the doorway. "You'll wait in the hall."

She grabbed the doorjamb and craned back at Bishop. "I hope they kill you." Lara spit in his face. "Rapist, fucking pig."

30

3 A.M., ROME, the morning of July 23, 1925. From the train to the set, Bucky Muir had to cross a portion of the city to make rehearsals with horses and chariots by noon.

"Dad," he spoke into the telephone at the freight yard.

"Talk to me. You're a day late."

"The horses are broken."

"All of them?"

"I learned to fall."

If pride had a sound, it would have been the moment's silence at his father's end.

"Glad to hear that. But, son, none of them are here so they might as well be magical Pegasus-ies," said Linus before giving into personal frustration. "These damned Eye-talian wranglers—I've lost more'n a hundred local horses."

"How?"

"First time one so much as limps, they shoot it. Sonsabitches. Bucky, you don't know how much your horses are going to mean here. 'Specially if they are broke like you say."

"They're broke." Bucky Muir paused. "How much trouble could I get into if I take them through town?"

"Where through town?"

"From the freight yard to your set. Rodriguez was supposed to arrange the trucks. They're not here. I'm pretty sure I'm in the center of Rome."

"Are you drunk?"

"No, sir."

"Are you with prostitutes?"

"Not since yesterday."

"Do you have any guns?"

Bucky hesitated.

"Still there?" his father asked.

"Had one. It's gone."

"Fine. What does Don Rodriguez advise?"

"He's no longer with us."

"'With us' as in with you and your wranglers, or the other 'with us?'"

"Don Rodriguez limped."

BUCKY'S ANDALUSIAN horse drive through Rome started out orderly enough, quiet as could be hoped for, but along with the loss of Rodriguez, Bucky had lost to desertion all but four of the dozen wranglers who'd set out with him. And, when at five minutes before four, Bucky lost control of the herd, the horses stampeded the Spanish Steps, and the last four Spanish hands fled as well, and Bucky met the dawn from behind the barred windows of a Roman jail.

A photographer captured the horses thundering up the storied public staircase. It is one of the famous Italian photographs from those early days of moviemaking. The photo made Bucky famous. Italian Futurist and metaphysical artist Carlo Carrà did a cubist painting of the event—a wild arpeggio on his earlier 1917 *Il cavaliere dello spirito occidentale (Western Horseman)* canvas—Bucky bent back, head pitched forward, face and body, horses' heads tossing, ears pinned back, legs pumping, shoes throwing sparks and the flash of spurs… from seventeen angles at once while in flight over, among, and hanging on to manes and tails a company of angels swarmed.

The horses? As Muir told it that night in Elizabeth's hospital room, the MGM publicity department got into the mix to keep the Italian slaughter of one hundred of their own horses out of the international press, while Louis B. Meyer provided the *bustarella* payoff to ensure Bucky's Andalusians arrived at the stables on set and were ready for rehearsal the following day.

Bucky Muir was—as we say it in our business—persona-non-grata-ed from Italy. Linus Muir hustled his son from the jail straight to the train that would take him to Paris and from France, a boat to England, which got him onto the Cunard Line's R.M.S. *Mauretania* to America.

Two nights out, aboard a massive ship in a tiny hole in the sea, under the stars the moment after Nathan Muir's unplanned conception, Bucky Muir's mind drifted to the hole in the sea where he had hidden the corpse of Miguel-Angel Rodriguez, and the hole he'd put in that Spaniard's head, and that still felt as good as what he was doing with the beautiful girl he'd bared his soul to for the two days he had known her, and she had listened to the truth of who he was and rather than take pity on him, or disdain him for his shallow past, she'd taken him into her embrace and made him whole. Crazy, but on that ship she'd learned to fall, and that falling in love with Bucky Muir—the kind of love to last a lifetime—created life on the shuffleboard deck of the ocean liner cutting space through water as it appeared to take the three of them home.

THE UTK COMMANDOS took turns beating Bishop with their fists and continued with their boots when he fell. Bishop took it without a sound, his eyes holding on to the dark almond eyes of Lara van Eijk-slash-Aiken outside the door staring in, terrorized but fighting for him, and waiting on Sedaka, her betrayal and Tom's unequivocal embrace of it linking them in the moment appearing and experienced in starkly different terms—shame, necessity, the event and its truths, secrets, lies each of them put to it, manipulated and falsified, that defined themselves and identified each with the other.

The Malaysians tired from their exertion. Bishop's bloody head flopped to face Sedaka: "Before this is finished, you're going to beg me to spare your life."

"No," said Sedaka. "Before this is finished, you'll tell me where my nukes are."

Lara shouted, "I want my passport. My working papers. I want my life back!"

Sedaka smiled blandly. "Patience, Miss van Eijk. You've been a brave girl and I know you can stand it all a wee bit more. You'll wait here for me inside your room. Take a shower. You'd like to get his sauce outta your snatch, right-oh?"

He signaled his men to haul Bishop away.

THE CLOSE OF A DAY unlike any other in specifics, like too many others in theme to Bishop's world where evil, a sin, is alive. There was the magnetostriction of fluorescent-tube ballasts. That nasty murmur worse than the Malaysian-jungle Hemingway cicadas—no relation—which knows no nation, no politics, no saints or sinners, no God: an equal-opportunity annoying hum. His head lolled back, Bishop stared into the tubes as he regained consciousness. Wrists and ankles plasticuffed to a hard and heavy wooden chair dragged from the hotel lobby. Both his sleeves were pushed above his elbows, his left arm sporting a blood pressure cuff. Arrayed in front of him: Sedaka and the two plainclothes Special Branch agents from the yellow Honda. One held a collapsible baton and beat it in his open palm with force much less than he'd used in getting Bishop to the chair.

"Nice to see you back with us," Sedaka said. "Ready to get started?"

Bishop's pain wrenched at his anger, pulled at his hatred. He knew what was coming. He gathered his strength, focused his will. He pushed back those raw desires counterproductive to his needs with all that was cold and dead within him, quelling all living emotion recently returned.

"Ready for whatever you got, bitch."

Sedaka produced a hypodermic and a pharmaceutical box. Block letters on the box read: "TRAPANAL." This was the manufacturer's trademark name for the rapid-onset, short-acting barbiturate sodium thiopental, commonly known by its more successful competitor, Abbott Laboratories, as Sodium Pentothal.

"Sure you know what you're doing, Sedaka? Thirty-four states use that junk on death row."

"Don't fight it and we won't have to go there."

He filled the hypo with 50ml. "Test dose for you. Assess tolerance, unusual sensitivity, blood pressure—you know the drill."

He plunged it into the antecubital space—layman's terms: elbow pit—of Bishop's right arm. Over the course of his service with the Agency, Bishop had "dry run" every truth agent used in interrogation. Sedatives and hypnotics that alter higher cognitive function, including LSD, 3-quinuclidinyl benzilate, ethanol, scopolamine (big one with the Gestapo back in the day); the potent intermediate-acting hypnotic benzodiazepines: midazolam, flunitrazepam; and the short-/ultra-short-acting barbiturates, including amobarbital and today's serum of choice: thiopental.

"Anytime you're ready, Tommy-boy, you can tell me where the nukes are... Fourth of July rockets' red glare, ol' buddy, ol' pal. This was the sticking point during my little chat with Muir last week at Princeton. But, then again, we did that one drug free."

"You'll be choking on that man's name as I watch you die."

"Yes, yes, you and your little bird one-note song," Sedaka said. "No appreciation for the lengths I went to flush Muir out. Discovering ATROPOS, the girl, and the monthly payoff he'd suckered Headquarters into all these years."

Within one minute, thiopental attains peak concentration of about sixty percent of total dose in the brain, causing unconsciousness. In about five minutes, the drug distributes to the rest of the body, hypnotic semiconsciousness returns, full consciousness ten minutes later. Once Sedaka established his baseline, depending on how good he was, he'd continue injections to maintain Bishop as long as possible on the edge of unconsciousness in the hypnotic state.

This knife edge between full sleep and hypnotic-suggestive dream-state is where Bishop would be vulnerable, his answers unsupervised by his will. Why dry-run training is crucial. As Bishop went under, he laser-focused on the information he wanted Sedaka to know on the slight percentage advantage this would give him as his mind stumbled headlong into the fantastic light where he would not know what was asked and, inside out, neither would he know what part of his hallucinations he verbalized.

"Old Nathan wanted to play games, sending the journal, drawing you in. Involving his old agent's girl. I merely want the weapons, Bishop. It's important. I know what you're feeling, so when I say, 'It's important,' you are going to agree with me."

He took Bishop's blood pressure as Bishop fell into the black void of senselessness.

BISHOP HEARD his heartbeat. It thrummed in his ears, soft at first, each beat uncomfortably slow, each beat increasing volume and his presence. He heard a voice echo, faint from above, as one might submerged in a pool of water. *Here he comes…* Then present and clear:

"So where are they? Ready to give it some attention…? It's 1968… Muir and van Eijk doing a little dirty work. Scoot in Scud launchers, a couple nukes disguised as Soviet, a reason to take out Hanoi. You know, your first war. C'mon, give it to me, baby. Sedaka, your old pal."

Bishop blinked open his eyes in time to watch Sedaka prepare and administer another dose and Bishop was seeing Laos. 1960s. Green Berets and Montagnards he'd supported as a sniper. He heard: *"Stealing some nukes dressed to look like a Soviet delivery to Hanoi… Where are they, Bishop?"* and Bishop saw Muir's fireplace at Princeton and the young Asian girl he'd caught; the young red-flower-dress Korean. Muir's jewel? Jewel alive?

Bishop fought his mind back to one last clutch of free will: *interrogate them,* and he was gone.

Right 80. Left 22. Pass 0, left again to 16, than pass 0 again for 33.

Not Jewel. The Persian cat with the bloodstained lips. Bloodstained paws. She watches the journals burn in Muir's fireplace. Yellow flame. Green jackets. White pages become black pages, leaves of ash and Bishop is there:

"Who are you?"

"Amy Kim."

"You work for the outfit?"

"He was recruiting me. I guess." She jerked her head to Muir's desk across the study behind her but wouldn't look at Muir's bloody, broken corpse.

"Why are you here?"

"I take him to church on Sundays."

Baptism. Clotho Lachesis. ATROPOS.

"Yes, Bishop," says Sedaka. *"Go on…"*

"Why are you burning these?"

"He told me that if anything happened to him, to take them from the shelf and burn them." She looked at Bishop with sad and frightened eyes. "They were all over the floor when I came in."

Everything on the floor. Everything ruined. The safe: open and empty. Amy saying, "Right 80. Left 22. Pass 0, left again to 16, then pass 0 again for 33. He told me to tell you. But it was already open when I got here. I'm sorry."

"How do you know who I am?"

"Dr. Muir said to verify you by the photo."

Lara hands him her own photocopy. Her fingernails blood red like Muir's desk. High-school graduation. His father's cat laps blood.

The cat. The sentiment. Muir's blood. Amy weeps. "I was too late."

"The cat was trying to make herself so compact that she would not be dripped on." Pristina. Erblina.

IDs scattered on the forest floor, skeletons of the raped and the dead.

"Any earlier, you'd have ended the same as him. Trust me. A man like Muir: nothing important was inside that safe."

"Why did he tell me to give you the combination?"

"So I'd trust you. To let me know there's something else here he wants me to have. He give you any other instructions?"

"Nothing."

"Anything unusual the last time you saw him?"

"He had me bury a bird. A dead wren."

She tells him about it and Bishop gives Amy the cat. "Take it. It's yours now. He'd want that."

He ushers the girl and the cat to the door.

Bishop returned to half-consciousness hearing himself quoting Erblina, quoting Hemingway: "Did you get the cat?' he asked, putting the book down."

"Yes! The green book. The coded book. Holds the answer. What's the cat?" said Sedaka.

"'It was gone.' She's gone. Raped. Mass grave. Flooded pit. I don't want to tell you, you fucker."

"I know… I know. You stuck it in Miss van Eijk—can't say I blame you. But you will tell the rest, can't help yourself. The missiles. The launchers. Muir and van Eijk… You know all this."

Bishop grinned; Sedaka didn't know what he was talking about, but Bishop floated to Lucky-Boy's drawing. The Scud launchers.

Charcoal drawings becoming real. Muir and Lara's mother, a baby in her arms; an argument with Danny Aiken, CW05, Chief Petty Officer United States Navy. Swirling charcoal animation.

"Take On Me!"

"We're all friends here, Tomcat. Relax. Talk a load off your mind."

Willard Hotel. The Stephen King book arcing across the room in a softball pitch to Aiken. *"The world is a worst case scenario and I'm afraid that all you sense is true."*

Harker leaning in. Obscenely close. "Nice piece of work this last bit in Kosovo," and him not there and knowing he's not to talk and knowing his brain is taking all the back alleys to talking not-there: there.

Elizabeth becomes. Lara becomes. Erblina and her daughter and every one of those Muslim women raped dead in the Djakovica Woods become—

Sedaka's pasty, looming face: "Come now, you can do better. They're not in Kosovo. Where are Muir's missiles? Who's Lucky-Boy? What's the cat? Tell me. It's important." Bishop focusing, the drugs wearing off; Sedaka juices him again.

THE SIGN ON her car. The sign at the mine. Sign a'the times. The tiger emblem. Chuffing—animated—snarling.

"We're same team here. C-I-A. Nothing wrong with filling in your pal Sedaka."

Camp Bondsteel airfield. Evening. A hangar telephone. Calling his father. Calling Muir.

"I could have used a little support," he is saying, wishing even at that moment he'd articulated the enormity of what he felt with something better.

"You could have shown up for your wife's funeral. Tom, I'm not worthy of you at my grave, but she was."

"Shut up. I meant here. Kosovo. You could have been here for me, Nathan."

He hears the crinkle of a wrapper. Coffee Nips in a bowl of his father's blood.

"The mistake you make is thinking I haven't. What's coming is bigger than Kosovo. I need you back. You need to see me."

"What about my promise?"

"To see you one last time. I should have welcomed you and your promise long ago. I'm afraid as things are what they are, you'll be too late to deliver my deserved justice."

Bishop clenched his chest, muscles tight to cage his heart. "I don't understand."

Sedaka says, "Something's happening with his blood pressure."

"You will, Tom. And you'll make it okay. I'm counting on you, son," says Muir.

And ohhh, does Sedaka laugh in the rain.

The other Sedaka. No relation.

"Focus on the weapons. Where are they? A mine? A tin mine? *It's important."*

Walking hand in hand with Lara…

Bishop garbled Lara's words. "An old tin man my father owned outside of Ipoh."

"A man. Outside Ipoh. What's that? An old tin *mine?*"

Saliva dribbled from Bishop's mouth. "Yesterday. Lucky-Boy Yoda Ewok treehouse, 'Three hundred years old she is.'" Bishop chuckled. Choked on spit.

His back stiffened. Chest pain. Noticed his breath coming short. Noticed his heartbeat hardly coming at all. Hypotension heart failure. His glassy eyes focused on Sedaka, who frantically worked the blood pressure cuff.

What was the point? He'd lost his heart…

He'd found a new heart.

Bishop forced a whisper: "Going to make an angel out of you, baby."

Bishop couldn't hear his heart anymore and wouldn't be able to Neil to Sedaka.

"CHRIST! I'M LOSING him. Jack him up. Hurry." Sedaka beat his chest as Bishop's vision dimmed on one of the Special Branch agents filling a different syringe. Better be Dexedrine—

LUCKY'S TIGERS. Tunnel vision. Goat blood lubricating large cat teeth tearing fur and hide and flesh and, and falling. Falling in, falling into jungle, through an escape hatch, into a pit of waiting tigers.

Sedaka narrated, a Marlin Perkins Merlin—"Here's Jim in a tree"—Wizard of Bill Burrud Animal World of Wild Kingdom of Oz yellow brick flash of light—*Tin Man*—behind his eyes—

"Come on back, Bishop, there you are… You see a tin man— Tin *mine*, right? Help me out. Which one do you see? There's hundreds in these parts. Name it. *It's important.*"

Bishop saw a tiger lunging at him, claws bared and snarling teeth dripping goat entrails.

His heart hammered like a Detroit V12.

Brain too.

Courage too—eyes open and wild and not in the interrogation room at all. Jungle. Pit. Tigers. Goat-goo: "Tiger! Tiger mine! Ipoh!"

Sedaka leaned in. "The tiger mine?" Swivel of his head to his comrades. "Ipon Tiger Mine make sense to you boys?"

They don't know. One leaves to check it out.

"So what happens to me?" Bishop was there. Lara said that too. But he's saying it now. He can't stop the ride.

"Nothing very good, I'm afraid," Sedaka answers.

He turns as the Special Branch agent re-enters. He gives Sedaka a nod.

Sedaka knows his work. He touches Bishop's cheek. He says, "So you're sure of it, Bishop: the Tiger Mine, Ipoh. Tell me what's in your heart. The bombs are in…?"

A prisoner to the drugs, Bishop: "…he hid the bombs. Intended for Vietnam. Muir sidetracked. Save the world. Deep shaft. Underwater. Gold."

"Tempat Harimau…" says Lara. "'The place of the tiger…'"

"With the launchers, Tommy?"

Bishop stared at Sedaka with unseeing eyes. "Soviet Maz 534s, mobile Scud missile launchers. Lucky knows. Lucky-Boy—"

"He's 'tin man'? Guards the mine?"

Bishop sees the telescope chamois hide the Browning .50-caliber machine gun.

"Guards the mine. Yes. Operation ATROPOS, Third Fate. Cuts off life at will."

THE EMPIRE HOTEL in Ipoh catches first light as the sun glances off the Kinta River. Lara huddled in a corner, knees clutched to her chest. After Bishop had been hauled off for interrogation, Sedaka had shoved her back into the room and told her he'd return momentarily with her work papers and her passport—the proof of her basic identity, which was all she had left—and she would be free to go, free to rejoin life as it was. But Lara would never be free to regain anything she'd known. The hours passed in silence. Lara knew Sedaka wouldn't show, and her psyche collapsed her into the corner amid broken shards of her betrayal and shame. The final pieces of a lifelong false identity.

How would she see herself now? Who would she present? They are choices that proceed from inner life, are shaped by experience, which informs inner life, which steers experience in an ever-evolving cycle of personal growth. The only experiences that create, grow, and complete identity are experiences judged real. Truths you apply to your self.

As light crept into the hotel room, Lara saw her reflection forlorn and staring from the back of the door. Everything a mirror reflects is both inert physical truth and active truth—event as phenomena. Everything reflected in a mirror except one thing. Yourself. An individual looks in a mirror and sees not only their physical representation (as Lara saw), but when looking at one's own reflection, our self appears alive, real to us unlike anything else inside the rest of that reflected world. But we are not apart from that world. Conscious mental states are identical to how they subjectively appear or present themselves to us in our experience of them. Conscious mental states (the unknown lie of the life Lara had been living) are, whether true or false, indistinguishable from the way they feel. There is no such thing as unfelt pain. The experience of pain makes it clear: pain when it is not felt ceases to be.

Once perception of that mental state changes (painkiller administered to pain, light administered to darkness, truth given to lie), reality becomes something else and the earlier cannot be returned to. Better, it can be left behind because the mirror image where self observes self does not vanish, does not collapse, it will continue reflecting "living" truth whichever way one chooses to spark life's light.

Life, like water, is not experienced true by experiencing its component parts but by the experience of how it presents itself for observation and utility. Lara observed this as the reflection of the river's water flickering brighter than the rest of the sunlight in the room, dancing across the wall and onto the glass surface where night dissolved into morning. She'd survived. No matter the deceptions that had brought her here, she was still herself. A forehead dot—not Hindu, but Gallup—long ago painted by others, now vanished. Psychically rubbed clean. Her feelings were still real and part of her existence, which made all of her part of the world's existence and she understood the secret. Life lived inside her. Life lives beyond her imprint of conscious mental states. The fires of emotions and feelings and thoughts and imaginings, truthful experiences and false illusions are dependent on life to exist, but life is never dependent on their presentation.

She had not slept. As unfit as Tom Bishop, although she had not been injected with drugs. She'd been injected with life. And history. Secrets solved. Others revealed to be...revealed.

Her reflection smiled at her as tearful hope rolled down her cheeks. Life is pure beyond self. Purity we name God. God needs nothing more than a constant experience of faith to continue within you. The Shahadah her workmates prayed five times daily. The first of the Five Pillars of Islam explained to her but never understood until this moment: the declaration of faith. Was this

Allah, the official god of her state? Or Buddha, the half of her genetic imprint belonging to her through her mother's blood? Was this Matthew's door opened by Jesus that she'd grown up knocking? Vishnu? Yahweh? Nathan Muir's Zeus? Is religion a thing of the blood, the unseen property of water? Is the meaning of identity the blur itself, the flow of a river?

She noticed her purple scarf tailing from beneath the bed. She pulled it to her, taking comfort from its gossamer folds, wiping her tears, and bundling it to her heart.

The destruction and reconstruction of her life by Tom Bishop right to the moment she betrayed him had led Lara nowhere else but to Lara. She wrapped her hijab around her head and tied it at her throat. This had been Muir's purpose from the beginning.

31

THE PRESIDENT of the United States, George Bush II, sat behind the Resolute desk in the Oval Office.

At least my third eye of a tumor insists he could have. Insists, looking around a corner I've never stood on, I should add, in vivid hallucinatory il-relief.

"The lost networks: you're now saying they're all a ruse, Director?"

"Correct, Mr. President," said Harker.

Harker sat upright like an expectant cotillion dancer on one of the two mahogany armchairs angled beside the president's desk. Vice President Dick Cheney, in a suit black as a preacher's, his face blank as a stone, slumped forward, elbows on knees, a CIA Top Secret briefing book held by its edge with both hands and dangling toward the floor as if insignificant. An identical binder lay centered on the desk before the president.

Bush said, "Boy, that's disappointing. What about this Bishop fella of yours?"

"He's still rogue in Malaysia. We now believe at Muir's bidding."

And so, if this happened at all, it might have happened like this:

Bush shot Cheney a sidelong glance. Cheney kept eyes bored in on Harker but encouraged his president with the arch of an eyebrow.

"How's that fit with you sitting right here five days ago convincing me he murdered Muir?" said Bush.

"I admit, Mr. President, that the evidentiary trail, as it's been uncovered, has led our investigation in a direction divergent from that original hypothesis."

Bush flashed Cheney a quick *What the heck?*

"Thank you, Acting Director, for clarifying that," Cheney murmured, sarcasm turning the gravel of his voice. He waggled the CIA Top Secret folder between his legs. "Your having left this out of the President's Daily Brief suggests a level of unaccountability desired by your specific office. Is that correct, Harker?"

"When you understand the magnitude of Operation ATROPOS—"

"I understand the magnitude," Cheney said. "What I'm trying to establish is the circumference of exposure you have here."

Bush scrunched his lips judiciously.

"A small, compartmented task force. Besides the three of us, only my deputy director—"

"Ms. Hofmeyr," Cheney interjected.

"And Bill Carver, my deputy director of Forensic Investigation, Office of Security. Nathan Muir—"

"I'm sorry. He's still dead, isn't he?" Bush said.

"My apologies. I'm trying to be thorough."

"Take your time." Bush smirked.

"And Operations Officer Tom Bishop. Oh, and Russell Aiken of the Office of General Counsel. Total membership of our closed circumference."

Cheney added, "If Bishop didn't kill Mr. Muir, it's safe to say whoever did is another boundary point on our not-so-tight little circle. Also add this missing Dutch-Malay agent, van Eijk. And that's all 'tight' to your way of thinking?"

Cheney cleared his throat. This was a signal for his president to open the briefing book before him.

"All right, Director Harker, run it up the flagpole for me."

"By all means, Mr. President. Operation ATROPOS. Formalized third of September '67, scrapped sixth of February '68. This operation developed from an Oval Office request by President Johnson—"

"Always trust a Texan, even if he's the other team, what I say," said Bush.

Harker continued, "This was a request of the CIA for a swift and decisive way to end the Vietnam conflict. Cable traffic I've included, between the White House and CIA Director Helms, charts the progress of these discussions. Various scenarios were presented and considered. I've included all of these in Appendix A, although only one proposal concerns us today."

"Page eighteen, George," Vice President Cheney advised the president.

"As a decisive option to end the Vietnam War," Harker said, "your predecessors believed that a tactical strike on Hanoi with a low-yield nuclear weapon would not provoke a retaliatory strike from Moscow."

Simultaneous: "Not a bad pitch," said Bush. "Fucking idiots," said Cheney.

"Idiots," repeated George II and Harker went on.

"Johnson, however, refused to use a nuclear weapon unless similarly provoked. Thus, Operation ATROPOS. The scenario had a pair of American nukes slipped into Laos on stolen Russian Scud launchers and made to look for our satellites *and*—more importantly—everyone else's as if North Vietnam was positioning Soviet weapons against Saigon. Nathan Muir's job, as station chief, Vientiane, was to coordinate this deception."

"With or without presidential oversight—backfiled and archived?" said Cheney.

"Without, sir. Sirs. ATROPOS was a Black Op all the way."

Cheney cracked the corner of his mouth, quarter-grin, quarter-sneer, other half hidden. Harker was encouraged.

"The nuclear weapons were a twenty-kiloton pair we'd stashed among the four, call it five hundred warheads deployed in the

Philippines. The Scud launchers were captured Egyptian traded to us by the Israelis after their Six Day War. The operation was a 'go,' and on twenty-eighth January '68, implementation was tasked to Nathan Muir."

Bush glanced at Cheney. "Dad always liked that guy when Pops ran the outfit. Sorry he got plinked. Really am."

Cheney adjusted in his seat, stretching the tightening in his chest. "Goddamn it, what were we thinking?"

"The analysis in support of the 'go' decision you'll find in Appendix B. It is quite compelling."

Cheney still hadn't opened his briefing book, but Bush found the appropriate page. And then, because Bush did listen and wasn't half as dim as he pretended: "World War Three is always compelling to you hammerheads."

"What we now believe happened is Nathan Muir, using the Tet Offensive as a diversion, and with the help of his agent Dand van Eijk in Kuala Lumpur, secretly redirected both launchers and warheads to Malaysia, where the two men most likely hid them. The final communication on this operation is his cable of fourth February 1968—you'll find on—"

"I got it," said Bush. "Page twenty-four. Get a load of this, Dick."

Cheney summarized from memory: "Muir reported product lost during ocean transit and unrecoverable due to search and recovery depth limitations of the time."

"Muir dumped two nukes in China's swimmin' hole? Didn't ever go back for them?"

"They weren't there, Mr. President," Harker helped him along.

"According to you"—Bush slapped the briefing book—"we didn't know that. Sort of thing *I'd* go back for."

Cheney finally sat up. Confident and relaxed. "George, we lost two nuke submarines: USS *Scorpion* sank that year, '68; the

Thresher back in '63. We didn't have the ability to recover their warheads and reactor plutonium until 1985."

"When my dad was in your post," Bush remarked to Harker.

"That's right," said Cheney.

"Dad never told me."

"No one's been told," Harker pitched in. "We hid that operation under the cover of the *Titanic* discovery. The Agency prides itself on making these things invisible."

"Okay. But those nukes were legitimately lost, Muir's nukes weren't. So how the hell did he get away with it?" the president said. "Who ran the investigation?"

"Nathan Muir and he buried it. Vietnam escalated. Nixon came in and the focus changed. Two unrecoverable, lost weapons from a Black Op that never took place were less important than a body count growing larger every day in front of TV-tray TV-dinner families before *Wonderful World of Disney* came on."

"Don't give me flipping Disney." Bush was getting riled by word weight.

Cheney said, "So we have two hot nukes *not* at the bottom of the South China Sea, ready to surface in a country about to flash into civil war—"

Bush: "A paper trail a mile long and none of you shitkickers with any idea they were there until now!"

"Congress gets ahold of this—" Cheney shook his head slowly like the bull he resembled. "They've been looking for a way to take the Party apart since Iran-Contra."

Bush pursed his lips. "What do these Muslims even want? We could turn their deserts to glass if they push any harder at this. I'm about that fed up."

Harker said, "A full-blown civil war in Malaysia is not a foregone conclusion."

The president said, "Which of the three disabled monkeys aren't you? That prime minister is setting himself as a dictator, with a pair of our nukes you folks lost to back him up. He's going to seize billions of dollars in US and foreign investment, and he's going to get away with it because he knows we can't let this out. This is a dirty secret, Harker. Our worst nightmare—American nukes in the hands of a Third World dictator—what the hell are you going to do about this?"

Vice President Cheney completed his smile and aimed it, without humor, at Harker.

Harker opened his leather folder and passed another document across the coffee table. "For your signature, Mr. President."

Cheney leaned in and gave it a quick look.

"That what I think it is?" said Bush.

"A Presidential Finding for an Executive Action against Tom Bishop and Dand van Eijk."

Bush gave Cheney his full attention. Cheney offered a confident tilt of his head. No one spoke until after George Bush II signed the Finding and slipped it back. Jeremy Harker tucked it into his folder.

"Okay. So what does that buy me? Dick?"

"Director Harker," said the vice president. "Explain to the president your idea for those nukes."

HARKER PRACTICED his 5-iron empty-handed swing in his office when, "Well, well, well," Meryl Hofmeyr trilled, coming through the door, Bill Carver following behind.

"We're a go," said Harker. "Cheney and the president agreed to let us use the two stray nukes exactly the way they were intended."

Carver was far removed from the White House—he hadn't liked the last one messing with that chubby girl, and he didn't like this one any better, but he hadn't liked the opponent either; in fact, he exercised his citizen's right not to vote knowing the whole race for the White House was a Harlem Globetrotters show most of the time anyway.

Carver deadpanned: "I'm not sure bombing Hanoi's gonna solve my Muir murder."

"Don't be glib," said Harker. "Who's to say these nukes aren't the Russian strays they appear, smuggled into Malaysia by insurgents? Insurgents sneak them in to use in their civil war, but we catch them in the act."

"Mmm," went Meryl. "Puts their prime minister on notice and, more importantly, strengthens our position with Thailand and Singapore. You suggested this, Jeremy, hhmm?"

"Mine all the way and they loved it."

They gazed at one another like dancers in a pas de deux. Carver cut in.

"Your plan requires we let the Muslim insurgents first acquire the WMDs?"

"Ramadan Moon is a fanboy splinter of—as Jeremy so aptly put it—the al-Qaeda JV team." Meryl tutted.

"Bill," Harker soothed, "this is Malaysia, not the Middle East, and certainly not America. We got this wired."

Carver rolled eyes, wide and contemptuous, across the pair of them. "How dumb do you two have to be to want to do the same dumb ideas we're trying to get out of with these Arab-Muslim-goat-fuckers twice as rough as the Vietcong with twice the facility of capability? When you go home, Acting Director, sir, does your wife greet you *every* night with 'And how inept was your day?'"

Harker and Meryl Hofmeyr stared and blinked. Shaking his head, Carver made for the door.

32

I NSIDE THE IPOH Empire Hotel basement storage room, where the Malaysian Special Branch had rigged their interrogation cell, Sedaka relaxed in a chair similar to the one in which Bishop slumped unconscious. Sedaka smoked a cigarette. He ashed and turned at the sound of the door.

"Colonel Ibrahim has arrived to see you," said one of the Yellow Honda Special Branch.

Sedaka burned Bishop with his cigarette. Bishop jolted awake, disoriented.

"Welcome back."

Tobacco is not an aromatic plant to begin with; Sedaka took a drag from his cigarette only to spit at the new Bishop flavor. He threw the butt on the floor. Bishop grimaced pleasantly at him. Sedaka rose. The Yellow Honda agent replaced him in the chair.

"Careful with this one, Ahmed. He's nastier than a rat in heat and twice as mean," Sedaka muttered and left.

The agent considered Bishop. He didn't look mean. He looked near dead.

Bishop jerked his chin at the floor. The smoldering butt. "Lemme finish the smoke?"

The agent spotted Sedaka's cast-off tobacco, stepped in and crushed it. Bishop shut his eyes in misery. The agent stooped for the butt and flicked it into Bishop's face, allowing Bishop to nail the bridge of the man's nose with his head. The agent reeled backward. Bishop planted both feet on the floor and hurled his body head first—chair and all—into the man, driving him into the wall. The agent's hand went for his gun, but Bishop, doubled over in the chair, torqued his back, twisting hard, pounding the chair repeatedly into the agent before the man could clear leather with his Walther P99. Bishop beat the man until the chair broke apart. His hands came free. He grabbed the syringe from the table where Sedaka left it and stabbed it into the man's chest. Just a needle, nothing left inside it, but it was all Bishop needed to get his opponent's hands clutching for it, allowing Bishop to deliver full-strength cupped-hand double blows to his eardrums. Instant concussion, eardrums ruptured, Ahmed dropped, insensible.

SEDAKA MET COLONEL IBRAHIM and his bodyguard at the hotel's front entrance. He briefed him on his success with Tom Bishop.

"You best be right, Mr. Sedaka. Three hours ago, the military broke with the Special Branch and Prime Minister Aziz." They rounded a corner. Ibrahim continued, "They've surrounded the Royal Palace and are demanding the prime minister surrender. If we're to put a lid on this and get Ramadan Moon and our special friends' continued backing, we need those weapons now."

They stopped outside the basement storeroom door.

"Allow me to introduce you to Tom Bishop, CIA."

He pulled the door wide. The dead body of the agent slumped at their feet. The syringe protruded from his chest, a broken chair leg from deep within his eye socket.

Bishop was gone.

"Goddamn it, Colonel! I can't leave your men alone with Bishop a hot minute!"

The crack of repeated gunfire drew both Ibrahim and Sedaka to a casement window. Eye level to the room made it ground level outside and good enough to witness the body of Ibrahim's driver dropping in front of their faces. Less than five seconds after that, Bishop took off on the dirt bike. He weaved between the corpses of the three Special Actions Unit commandos who'd stormed his room the night before.

Colonel Ibrahim said, "You better pray you've gotten this right."

"I don't pray. I do."

Colonel Ibrahim ignored the comment. "The woman?"

"I've been holding her in case we needed her for something else."

"She's served her purpose. Kill her."

He issued orders in Malay to his bodyguard. The younger man drew his handgun, seated a bullet in the chamber, and left the room.

SOMETIMES DOING NOTHING is the best something to be doing because it leaves you open to something else. I'm behind my desk in my New Headquarters Building office finishing the book Bishop had tossed me at the Willard, doing diddly-squat one hour before Thai noodles and my unexpected promotion, three before I board Harker's Citation X. At this earlier point, I'm expertly sitting idly by, door open against my chronic claustrophobia. I'm trying to remember the contents of the sack lunch I made and packed this morning. A little exercise I've had since returning from Los Angeles—memory games trumping radiation and the saw—and my mind blanking on sandwich contents. The goop with the chopped pickles, the apple chunks, the celery. Paprika. The one that's not egg salad. I've spread it on bread for thirty years. But before I got to the meat of the question, my brain switched on an easier memory of a more difficult sack's content: Muir's face disappearing beneath the zipper of the body bag.

Something else flashed across my conscious to collide with my brain tuna [sic/sick], I mean tumor-not-tuna: a dead bird sinking to the bottom of a fountain. There was something to that, not

the TUNA SANDWICH (see? I got this.), but the whatever—
something to elude with the wade-wait-weight of water—was
wrenched-wrung from my mind with the ring of my secure phone.

"Aiken."

It's the green telephone. Secure and untraceable.

*Why green? Which usually means "go," "open," "free." Shouldn't the
secure phone be "red?" Who inside Langley do we want to fool—besides
everyone all the time?*

We all have the green phone on our desk beside the
normal-connection black phone. Primarily used in-house or, in
this case, that rare occasion with the field in-operation when it
becomes easier to adjust my paper plan than make a readjustment
in reality. I was prepared for the gravity of the call, though not
the caller.

"Hey," came Bishop's familiar voice.

Sᴜʟᴜɴɢ Mᴇɢᴀᴛ and his wife, Puspawati, provide a working
payphone outside the door of their 7-Eleven Snack Pit Stop off
the E1 Expressway in Taman Tambun on the outskirts of Ipoh.
Mounted to a wall of white-painted bricks covered with posters
for the local Lost World theme park: friendly tigers, waterslide
abandon, fire-breathing demon dancers, Barbie and Hot Wheels
Island, caves, camping, and Jurassic Dino-Park. A ferocious
brontosaurus, neck bent, jaws wide, loomed above the telephone
as if to devour the caller's head like a cabbage. I shouldn't quibble
as to the Malaysian depiction of the gentle vegan as a carnivore
because the brontosaurus isn't even extinct.

Can't be.

Never existed.

No Dino for Wilma and Pebbles, no bronto burgers for Fred
and Barney, and certainly this factual proof the ethical reason

the other Barney show never *ever* depicted a brontosaurus as one of Jessie's favorite purple T-Rex's friends. To stop Jessie from watching the show, I pointed out that, as a T-Rex, Barney would necessarily feed on one of the hapless children he lured and lulled with song after each episode ended. I'd wanted to scare her out of watching. This backfired into a five-days-a-week, year-long morning battle cry, "Daddy, let's pick the kid Barney eats!"

The brontosaurus was in fact the apatosaurus, its false identity a deception purposefully played on science by the cutthroat paleontologist who, in a professional war to claim naming rights to the newest dinosaurs his fossil-hunting hooligans dug in 1885, plopped on another creature's skull and created the brontosaurus. Seems the problems of false identity stretch back millions of years, its ripples destroying reputations and conceptions of reality like a nard-aimed kick, textbooks, and the most basic building blocks of self—fight or flight, feeding, fear, and fornication. We all have experiential truths that form identity derived from our brain's limbic cortex, otherwise known as the "lizard brain."

None of this was on Bishop's mind as he buzzed through the clot of locals—those living in the apartments above the 7-Eleven and the Chinese restaurant on one side, the Merican [not a red, white, and blue Anglo-slang sales pitch, but an Indian-Muslim surname: Merican] Fabric Shop & Handmade Suit—Dress, Sewing, Repair, Laundry on the other—loading their cars to flee; others from the countryside with cars and carts swarming the 7-Eleven to stockpile water and soda, large propane gas tanks, anything butane, snacks, candles, batteries, and toilet paper: rolls and napkins (packaged for sale or off the hot-dog counter) or bundles of blue bathroom paper towels at 10 ringgits a pop/poop. Too consumed by the panic of martial law and the threat of civil war, no one paid Bishop more than a fleeting glance as he dropped coins into the phone without noticing the Thunder Lizard threatening from above.

Last thing on the dinosaur, I swear. Second to last. First: all dinosaurs are a fad. Granted, a fad mostly with children, or childlike adults, but why start youngsters out with the debilitating distraction of faddism? I hate the obsession. The obsession is why I've never obsessed on anything. And second: that whole Aeroflot flight from Narita, Japan, to Vladivostok I shared with other prospective adoptive parents—all from the evangelical service we adopted through. The walrus next to me got in my face because I wouldn't agree with him that dinosaurs were on Noah's Ark approximately 4,350 years ago.

I pointed out that if the raptors could take out as technologically sophisticated an operation as Jurassic Park, they would have wreaked havoc and wrecked the boat. He laughed at my use of fiction to support my argument and directed me to Job 40:15–24:

> *Look at Behemoth,*
> *which I made along with you*
> *and which feeds on grass like an ox.*
> *What strength it has in its loins,*
> *what power in the muscles of its belly!*
> *Its tail sways like a cedar;*
> *the sinews of its thighs are close-knit.*
> *Its bones are tubes of bronze,*
> *its limbs like rods of iron.*
> *It ranks first among the works of God.*

To my great luck, the Bible clutched in his fist was annotated and illustrated:

It was his entire life-view. How he saw himself, how he would have the world see him. How the fat man and his wife would mold the inner and outer lives of the six Russian brothers and sisters they'd agreed to keep together in adoption as a family.

I presented myself as persuaded. "Marvelous. I hadn't understood that passage until today. It absolutely identifies the behemoth, ipso facto, as a, a,"

"Brontosaurus," he claimed with authority.

Mm-hmm. It sure did.

"I DIDN'T TELL THEM," I told Bishop, knowing he'd know I meant what he'd done to Muir. "I didn't have to. They have video covering your entire trip to Princeton and onto his street. They have DNA."

"I expected Harker and his Young Turks to get it wrong," said Tom. "I didn't expect it of you."

"You're telling me now, from a Malaysia on-the-brink, what you chose to evade in person. Why call me?"

"You're my lawyer. I need Harker. Means I need you on the call."

I patched him through.

"Director Harker here."

"Tom, I've got the"—couldn't help myself—"*acting* director on the line."

"Line security, Bishop?" Harker asked.

"Not much left secure anywhere in these parts. But it's a payphone. It'll be good for a few minutes before the international exchange gets run back and Malay enforcement bumps against your firewall."

"All right. What do you have for me?" said Harker.

"Operation ATROPOS, 1968."

I can't verify it because I wasn't on the Seventh Floor, but I'm fairly certain by this point Carver was actively listening.

Harker said, "I'm recently read in."

"Deep background me, Harker," Bishop said. "I have to know why."

"Muir was meant to slip them into Laos on Soviet launchers so we could get GEOINT satellite imagery on them, claim imminent nuclear threat to Saigon, then use it as an excuse to vaporize Hanoi."

"But Muir decided to save the world instead," said Bishop.

"He and van Eijk stole two nuclear weapons," said Harker, and call it a symptom of my brain tumor, but I laughed. Figures Muir did.

"Aiken, the sound of your breathing on the line has already been a nuisance, but that bleating is going to cost."

Operational and heightened, tortured and angry, Bishop barreled over it. "Explains a lot. Why he kept me at a distance, pushed me away. He didn't want me tainted. He was protecting us."

"Well, fucking good for you. Do you know where they are now?"

"Sedaka's doubled."

"Sedaka?" I interjected—was it possible I'd been fooled by the flub? "Meaning?"

Bishop said, "Meaning he killed Muir, Russell, and he's selling the Malaysians the weapons."

"Don't talk to Aiken. Talk to me: I'm the man in charge," Harker ordered. "Does Sedaka know where the weapons are?"

"They do, and I do. There's still time to destroy them before the Malaysians take possession."

"I can get a SEAL team on station in less than two hours. You have coordinates?"

"I need a few things first."

"Aiken, take this down. Bishop, talk."

I clicked my ballpoint. The sound reminded me nothing so much as the catch of the trap I knew would now—and has—ensnared me.

"Ten thousand dollars mixed denominations, US; ten 10-gram gold bars, PAMP Suisse, or Vacambi."

"I presume for van Eijk?"

"Like I told you when you showed me that photo, there is no van Eijk. Just bait to lure me here to find the Broken Arrows for Muir," he said using the codeword for lost nuclear weapons.

"Ridiculous. Bishop, if there is only you, you don't need to exfiltrate on your own. Get to the embassy. A helicopter from our Thai base will airlift you out."

"Harker, that won't work."

*Neif—ugh—*And. If. *And if there is only you. I believe I sensed it. I did, did I? The otherness? The something more than him in his voice. Someone working off the plural of is.*

"You've done your job. We'll take care of it from here."

"I'll give you fifteen hours to get what I need to the embassy. I'll contact with a rendezvous."

"Make it easy on yourself, Bishop. If it was Sedaka and not you with Muir, what's the harm of turning yourself in at the embassy? Either way, I'm the only one with the power of forgiveness."

"No. There's something else I have to do."

"What?" said Harker.

"Do we have a deal?"

"I can arrange the kit. The money and the gold." Ever helpful me.

"I'll deal. Give me the coordinates for the nukes."

And that's how I got my forever wish: lethal promotion from my headquarters desk to the headstones of my field of bad dreams.

33

IN PRESIDENT EISENHOWER's farewell address, January 17, 1961, he famously warned against the immense military-industrial complex and its "total influence [over the] economic, political, even spiritual" life of America. Upon hearing this, his predecessor in office—the thirty-third president of the United States, Harry S. Truman, who created the CIA on July 26, 1947, when he signed the National Security Act into law—added to this, commenting, "I never would have agreed to the formulation of the Central Intelligence Agency back in '47 if I had known it would become the American Gestapo." Caused a lot of hurt feelings at headquarters and anger in America that he would use such a word as *Gestapo* to describe one of our institutions of security and freedom. He chose to elaborate on his comments with an op-ed three years later in the *Washington Post* published December 22, 1963.

"For some time," Harry wrote, "I have been disturbed by the way the CIA has been diverted from its original assignment.... [T]his quiet intelligence arm of the President has been so removed from its intended role that it is being interpreted as a symbol of sinister and mysterious foreign intrigue—and a subject for cold war enemy propaganda." He said he would like to see "its operational duties be terminated."

The former haberdasher felt our Agency was becoming criminal. He'd never intended the agency he'd created to get involved in "strange activities." It wasn't hard to decipher what strange activities the ex-president was referring to, as this was exactly one month to the day John F. Kennedy fell to assassin Lee Harvey—

Shit, blanking—Lee Harvey, Harvey—not the invisible rabbit, not the cartoon creator of Casper—Lee Harvey—why do assassins always have to go by three—Lee Harvey-what?!—names?

Goddamn me. I boarded Harker's Citation X with verbal instructions from Deputy Director Meryl Hofmeyr to accept but not to sign for the packet I would receive upon arrival in Bahrain and another in Thailand.

"The ransom cash? The gold?"

Although she was younger than me, she smiled with a motherly fondness that, on the tumor-driven free wheel of my mind, superimposed thespian Jessie Royce Landis as Cary Grant's mother in *North by Northwest*, the exact eight years age difference between all of us. Both. Them. Me. Her. Younger woman playing older man's mother. She shuffled off my mortal confusion with:

"Resolve the Bishop–van Eijk problem with sole discretion, Russell."

But I heard "Roger," as in Grant's Thornhill character admonished by his younger mother, and declared, "Oswald" in interruption and, trailed by her: "Mmm, Mr. eh-*Aiken*," followed by some upward-inflected diphthong I waved away and goodbyed as if batting bees buzzing my ears.

That's how wrecked my brain was as I left for Malaysia.

My pilot didn't introduce himself but did show me how to work the monitor and DVD player, directing me to Harker's current collection of movies. *Dirty Dancing, American Psycho, 12 Angry Men, Meet the Parents, Bosom Buddies: The Complete Boxed Set* (Seasons 1 & 2), *North by Northwest, Singin' in the Rain,* and *It's a Wonderful Life.*

I chose not to wonder if the *North by Northwest* coincidence existed prior to my discovery of the disc or imagined of my conversation after takeoff. Instead, I chose to enjoy, for the umpteenth time, the Jimmy Stewart, fuzzy jammies, Christmas tearjerker while wondering about "umpteenth."

Umpty, the root word, means "of an indefinite number." Right out of the gate, *umpteenth* is sliding away from its purported meaning as soon as it slips your lips or slips my mind. And if *umpteenth* is intended to mean a HUGE number, why diminish it by affixing a suffix that only gets us thirteen through nineteen times by limiting the indefinite number to "teen?" An oxymoron matched only by the slow as an ox *y* moron who picked the films.

Somewhere over the Atlantic, I engaged with the movie. As the familiar story unfolded, a sinking sensation filled me with dread. Insidious things are at play in this beloved sacred cow. I'm not talking about the bah-humbug FBI investigation J. Edgarnezer Scroo-ver tried to cultivate against the film as "a weapon of communist propaganda and infiltration." George Bailey's no commie, he's the greatest flim-flam man in Hollywood history. Professor Harold Hill pales in comparison.

1. *The president of the Bailey Brothers Building & Loan ("George Bailey") knows his uncle is a useless drunk. He also knows the dangers of alcoholism through first-hand experience with the Pharmacist ("Mr. Gower"), who through criminal negligence brought on by intox-ication almost poisons a customer. Bailey betrays his fiduciary responsibility to his depositor/shareholders by:*

    1.1. *Allowing known alcoholic ("Uncle Billy") to drink on the job.*

    1.2. *Allowing "Uncle Billy" to handle despositor's/ shareholders' money without a BBB (Bankers' Blanket Bond)*

2. *George Bailey creates a Ponzi scheme by which Bailey secures and awards real estate loans that fail to meet banking standards and practices, then kites the property values to secure additional loans, repeating the process in a neverending cycle of Securities Fraud. By his own admission when accused by a depositor, Bailey states, "I don't have your money. It's in Tom's house… and Fred's house."*

3. *After Uncle Billy, under the influence of alcohol, loses all of George Bailey's depositors' cash deposits [Note: Bailey uses a legitimate financial institution, the Bank of Bedford Falls, for his own banking], he compounds his problems with misdemeanor Criminal Mischief when he refuses a legitimate bailout offer by the majority Stockholder in the Bailey Brothers Building & Loan ("Mr. Potter," to whom George Bailey has a fiduciary responsibility to run the business at a maximum profit, something George Bailey admits at the Meeting of the Board he has no intention of doing), this bailout by Potter would:*

   3.1. *Cover his depositors' losses, pay debts, and protect his depositors' liability from default and foreclosure;*

   3.2. *Protect George Bailey from arrest and prosecution;*

   3.3. *Be an offer George Bailey has a legal requirement to present to his depositors/shareholders.*

4. *Instead, George Bailey acts to commit Insurance Fraud with his life insurance policy by disguising his own suicide as an accidental drowning, conspiring to:*

   1.1. *Avoid fiduciary responsibility to the depositors/shareholders he has defrauded.*

   1.2. *Transfer responsibility for his debts to his widow ("Mary Hatch Bailey").*

> 1.3.   *Make Mary Hatch Bailey unknowing co-conspirer/criminal participant in:*
> 1.3.1.   *Insurance Fraud.*
> 1.3.2.   *Receipt of Stolen Property.*

5. *The Reckless Conduct and moral crime of abandoning his children.*

6. *Using the questionable claim, he was saved from drowning by a Heavenly Angel ("Clarence Odbody") no one knows, no one sees, and no one can identify, George Bailey (whose assets should have been turned over to better management in bankruptcy court) commits Fraud against the very same people he's defrauded the entire movie by taking from them a literal barrel of money bailout as a "no strings" gift.*

7. *Finally, George Bailey commits Fraud in the Inducement of a state official, when he cons the Bank Examiner sent to arrest him and seize his assets into giving him money in collusion with the continuation of Bailey's subprime-loan Ponzi scheme.*

After a refueling stop in Paris, I went on to *North by Northwest* with its much more believable plot of CIA mistaken identity and Eastern Bloc spies fighting over art-artifact-smuggled microfilm on George Washington's nostrils.

IN HIS OWN WAY, Bishop was having as hard of a time as I. After the 7-Eleven, after the phone call, after I couldn't face the fact that the Cary Grant mother-son thing was a post-takeoff illusion of my conversation with Deputy Director Hofmeyr and I took my irascibility out on Christmas, Bishop steadily worked his way down Asian Highway 2 back toward KL. Refugees streamed in confusion toward the hoped-for protection of the capital city and Bishop was thankful for the dirt bike that allowed him swift navigation through the slow mash of traffic and inevitable breakdowns, nimbly avoiding or slicing through occasional masses of demonstrators and columns of police and military. Soldiers in the open transports Bishop passed clutched their assault rifles. Faces blank of expression but eyes distrustful of the Caucasian, they were like soldiers everywhere who, not yet ordered to combat and committed to violence, are willing to avoid conflict.

This lasted for the next few hours, but with one wrong turn—right for where he was headed, wrong for what transpired—Bishop met conflict firsthand, running into four State Police swinging bodies of dead rioters alley-oop into the back of a dump truck.

They shouted for Bishop to stop. Climb off the motorcycle. To raise his hands, and they raised their Heckler & Koch submachine guns, and Bishop shot all four of them: the last the most surprised, as he was the only one whose brain got the full two seconds it took to be aware of what took place.

Bishop grabbed one of the HKs and all the ammo for it he could find. He pulled the magazines from the dead men's handguns they wouldn't need but he would. Didn't want to run low at our cemetery rendezvous. He took five minutes to siphon gas for his bike.

He rolled on.

BACK AT LANGLEY, back at the Ops Center, Harker was at the eye of the storm, on the line with the National Reconnaissance Office.

"No. You listen to me: we have a civil war on our hands and personnel in the field, so if I request a neutron-sniffing Bloodhound-7 over that country, you NRO eggheads don't ask me for authorizations with a 'we'll get back to you in the morning.' You task that bird this instant, and you hope to God your wasting time with this internecine bullshit hasn't cost American lives! Am I being fairly clear…? Yes? Good." He slammed the receiver.

Harker faced Meryl Hofmeyr, who held out a set of TOP SECRET documents.

"The order packet for SEAL Team Four insertion into Malaysia to interdict against our lost WMDs, Acting Director, sir."

Harker gave her a funny look at her lack of mmm's, tsk's, and vocal whirs. If he'd taken his thoughts a step further, he'd have recalled her speaking was the kind of careful talk they train us at The Farm to use when wearing a wire.

"They're closest?"

"Aboard the *Iwo Jima*—an assault ship in the Nimitz Battle Group. They're closest to acquire the lost Weapons of Mass Destruction," she articulated with care.

Harker signed the authorization. "This gets finished and it gets erased."

LARA VAN EIJK swung her gaze to the opened louvered wall panels of her home at the sound of the dirt bike. Expectant, knowing. Bishop alive. Returned. She left her single suitcase on her bed, some personal belongs and clothing beside it she'd been unable to pack. She walked for the door, resigned to whatever fate he'd brought her.

Bishop stopped halfway up the front stairs as she stepped onto the veranda. The submachine gun was strapped across his chest. He held it with both hands. Not aimed, but ready. Guilt tracked tarantula footsteps across her face.

"All I'd wanted to do was escape before you returned. I opened my suitcase, gathered some things. I couldn't fill it. I sent the cab away two hours ago. I've just been standing there."

"You alone?" Bishop said without a hint of emotion.

"I am."

"Sedaka keep his end of your bargain?"

She shook her head. "I'm not the woman in those papers anyway. I'm purely me now."

"You're okay with that?"

"Circumstances being worse than the worst nightmare I could ever invent; I'm surprised to tell you."

"Tell me what?"

"Tom, I've never felt whole my entire life. Until now."

The way she said it to Bishop, for Bishop, it meant more than identity. He didn't speak. Neither of them moved. The emperor cicadas, insects the length and twice the width of a child's forearm, crackled mercilessly with volume more than equal to their size.

Every fear she'd ever felt from him now reflected back as vulnerabilities in his eyes.

"I was afraid I'd lost you," he said.

"And yet, here we are."

She offered her hand. The first time she ever reached out for him. He took it but made no other move.

He said, "I'm going to get you safely out of here, but you'll have to trust me completely."

"I've wanted that since I first saw you. Why do you think I dropped my dress?"

"You didn't know I was there, Chalk Girl."

She smiled, soft and warm. "I hadn't seen you. But I can't think back to it now without believing I knew, and I wanted you to see me the way no one who ever really cared about the me-of-me ever really has."

Bishop didn't bother deciphering her, her meaning, the impact of her present safety more than enough for him. He simply squeezed her hand.

"I'm tired, Lara. For what I have to do, I'm going to need some rest."

"Won't they come here looking?"

"At some point they'll follow up, but right now I pose a greater threat to Sedaka elsewhere."

She tugged his hand and he stepped toward her and let her lead him inside.

NIGHT HAD FALLEN when Bishop awoke to the sound of his name softly called in the darkness. He let himself rise slowly from his sleep, led by the sound of Lara's voice. He remembered coming inside, undressing, unselfconsciously handing her his clothing to wash, lying down on his side and wrapping himself in her sheets and tumbling into sleep. He felt her atop the covers beside him and opened his eyes to her tender face framed by her falling hair. She wore her father's Navy robe.

"Feeling better?" she said.

"Gone from being run over by a train and buried by an avalanche… to just the avalanche."

"Rocks or snow?"

He cocked half a grin at her. "Soft snow, now."

The river doors were open. He heard the burble of the water and the birds finding their night-voice, and he stared into Lara's eyes and saw a vibrant soul glowing forth. He'd denied himself that for four years.

"What's he like, my half-brother?"

I swear to God, I am tempted to stop right here. Jump past. But, as I'm the only one who's seen around every corner in this travesty-met-tragedy, Bishop might as well own it.

"Russell?"

"What's he like?"

"An upright-walking, non-stop-talking, tail-wagging dog."

Where's he get off yanking my chain?

"That says more about you than him."

Rubbed her fur the wrong way too. Good.

"Doesn't that depend on if I'm talking Cujo or a Labrador retriever? The man's my best friend. The older brother I never had."

"I'd say you're more wolf than dog."

"You're no Little Red Riding Hood. Or maybe if you want to get Freudian…"

"I *want* to know about Russell."

"Faithful by nature, loyal in practice. He's a stickler. Likes to interrupt."

I definitely do not interrupt.

"But…"

Always a but.

"Russell can't help but chase any stick he's thrown. He's obsessive, tending toward the neurotic, but ask him to dig up something, he'll dig with abandon until, whatdya know, he's found where all the bones are buried. Some you didn't even ask for." He paused, then added, "He stood for me at my wife's funeral. He buried her for me."

"Where were you?"

"Not where I should have been."

"I'm sorry. For everything taken from you."

He tried to smile so she wouldn't have to claim any of his pain. She released his hand. She rolled onto her shoulder, halfway above Bishop, and slid his head into her breast, placing his ear over her heart.

"Loss can't find you if you lose yourself," he said.

"Are you still lost?"

The front door burst open. A grenade clattered across the floor. Another grenade arced through the air. Bishop rolled their bodies off the far side of the bed as the two fragmentation grenades exploded, the first shredding the room from the floor, the second from the air. Suppressed automatic gunfire cut through the middle. Bishop wrapped Lara in his arms and hurled his body through the balcony doors. They hit the rail and he levered over it, lead chasing them as they fell to the river below.

They plunged into the water, their backs hitting the stony riverbed, the current tearing the robe from Lara and stealing it, swirling away as the heavy current pulled their naked bodies apart. Lara lurched in the direction of the far shore, but Bishop, wrapping an arm around a stilt as though part of a ship, grabbed her, wrenched her around, shoving her to the bank where her house stood. He scrambled through the mud behind her. Bishop propelled her against the base of the house, turned to the stilts at a scratch of movement, above and inside, that carefully approached the balcony.

She saw what he intended. "You literally have nothing," she whispered.

"Not much different than walking out of Eden."

Bishop scaled the piling with the agility of a lizard. He bunched into a ball against the hatched wooden balustrade, toes curled on the balcony edge, hands below the top rail. A UTK commando rushed the rail, submachine gun leading. The man leaned out, scanning the dense foliage across the river through night-vision. Bishop sprung upward, fully extended, his hands seizing the gun barrel suppressor, tearing it from the startled commando, whose instinctive reaction to recoil from falling gave the weapon to Bishop, whose hands shuffled the weapon around as he fell once more to the water.

Barking into his radio, handgun out, and back at the railing, the commando was only able to get off a single shot, shockingly loud against the muffled submachine gun burst from Bishop jackknifing out of the water that drilled through the commando's face shield and out the back of his head with scalp, bone, and brain matter.

Lara rushed to join Bishop, but he drove her back with him against the wall.

"Hold my knee," he said, slapping her hand there. He indicated that she watch one corner of the house while he watched the other. His approach clear, he felt the change of pressure in her fingers. He crushed her body beneath him, firing behind his back as bullets ripped from the corner Lara watched, splintering the wood inches above them. Bishop's head swung around, following his gun already firing, his eyes in time to see the second commando crumple.

Bishop hoisted Lara onto her feet, guiding her naked body behind him.

"Keep your palm on my back. Head centered below my shoulder blades. No matter how low I get, I want you lower. I'm your wall."

They duck-walked in tandem to the opposite corner from the dead commando. Bishop peered around it. Clear. He rose into a crouch and dashed to the front corner of the structure. Lara's hand stuck to his strong back the whole distance.

A Mercedes-Benz Unimog, light-armored utility 4X4, its short bed rigged for troop transport, blocked the driveway at the jungle's edge. A driver, similarly armed, stood wary guard beside his vehicle door. Bishop dropped him with a single, silenced shot.

Bishop ran to the mini-truck, Lara moving with him as one. They spun around the back of the vehicle.

"Clothing?" said Lara, catching her breath.

"Working on it."

Bishop instructed Lara to stay put and rushed to the house. He stopped at the base of the wide, heavy stairs. He squinted into the darkness of the broken door, the steel battering ram used to open it abandoned on the veranda. No sound. No sign of movement. Bishop burst forward, flat against the left side of the doorjamb. A slicing motion with his hand signaled Lara.

WHAM! WHAM! WHAM! She pounded the back gate of the Unimog. Bishop saw the suppressor-encased circle of an HK submachine gun emerge, aimed at the mini-truck. Bishop pressed his gun barrel into the wood and fired a five-round burst.

A body collapsed within.

Naked, Bishop stalked inside.

BISHOP DROVE, Lara beside him. She'd dressed for hard travel: mesh hiking shoes, jeans, and layered tank top, blouse, light-weight black raincoat. Bishop, his own clothing beyond useful-ness, wore black battledress uniform utility pants, an Under Armour compression T-shirt, and a tactical vest all acquired from the largest of the UTK commandos—all of it too small. Between the two front seats, a large yoga bag held a change of clothes for Lara, covering a second submachine gun, four grenades, and all the ammo he'd been able to gather. They each wore a tactical Kevlar helmet not particularly for safety but, as Bishop explained, to offer a moment's edge of misidentification if they were unfor-tunate enough to be stopped. Bishop updated her on his call with Langley. Lara asked why he hadn't tipped me off to the truth of the situation, why he hadn't revealed her to me, especially if her half-brother was being sent on false information to kill him.

"Couldn't risk them overhearing and sending someone else."

He emerged from her driveway lane onto the bus route road. Aimed the mini-truck toward KL.

34

Aboard the amphibious assault ship USS *Iwo Jima*, an SH-60 Seahawk helicopter lifted from the deck. Ten Navy SEALs in full combat/demolition gear rushed beneath it. They snapped carabineers to the Special Patrol Insertion/Extraction cable unspooling from the helicopter's belly. As the Seahawk rose, the SEALs lifted into the air fast-roped in two-man pairs, each above the next on the SPIE rigging line. Free swinging in the air beneath the bird, the Seahawk rotored around to fly them to the Malaysian coast.

I awoke with a start as the Citation X touched down in Bahrain. I fought back a terror I'd experienced for the past month. Can you recall from childhood an overnight spent at grandparents' or a friend's home when you awaken in panic not knowing where you are? That would provide a glimpse at the overwhelming fear I experience now whenever I open my eyes from sleep. Not recognizing my surroundings is nothing compared to my inability to recognize myself. This can last anywhere from thirty seconds to two minutes: I am helpless, without concept of my own identity. I have no memory of my name, no notion of what I do, why I am where I am, where I have been, where I am going, who I am with. I am a blank slate, helpless and alone. Some mornings, I am able to tell my empty self to calm. But most mornings I cannot find an inner voice to soothe me, and I submit to hopeless tears.

Two minutes after the pilot opened the hatch, I wiped my face, grabbed my laptop case, and climbed into the darkness, where I was escorted at a jog to my waiting UH-60 Black Hawk. As I reached the hatch, a ground crewman brushed past me to brush-pass the canvas grip of a small but heavy satchel into my free hand.

JUNADA ANSWERED his apartment door. A Malay Singaporean descended from five generations of British uniform services railway workers, he was an engineer with MTrans Monorail Malaysia, constructing the KL straddle-beam system that, after years of setbacks, was nearing completion.

"Salaam alaikum," said Lara, Peace be upon you, and extended both her hands.

"Wa 'alaikum salaam," he said. And upon you be Peace. He briefly embraced both her hands in both of his before laying his right hand open upon his heart. He called over his shoulder in a British public-school accent: "Fendy! Come! See who it is!"

Lara forced a smile to her troubled face. Preceded by the slap of bare feet on the parquet floor, a long-limbed and athletic woman near in age to Lara, over six feet tall and wearing workout sweats and a cut-off T-shirt wet with perspiration, came into the hallway behind her husband, tying a vibrant, sassy-patterned Malay-Muslim *tudung* over her head as a scarf.

"Oh, you don't need that, it's—"

Fendy pushed past her husband, her arms wide for enthusiastic embrace, squealing, "Manjalara! Junada, look at my beautiful spar! It can't be so bad outside if she's able to come here. Manjalara-loli-lu! We haven't dared step one foot outside in two days! We—"

She cut herself off as Bishop stepped into view from the side. Fendy stepped behind her husband, tying her headscarf.

"Lara? Is everything okay?" Junada said.

"He's with me."

"Are you in trouble?" he pressed.

"His name's Tom."

"But are you in trouble?"

Lara tried to maintain her happy face—"Yes"—but it crumbled away. "We are."

Junada didn't know what to say next. What to do. Fendy pushed her way in front of him, her face filled with awe.

"Is he…?"

Lara mirrored her gaping wonderment with a twinkle in her eyes.

"From your *pelindung ksatria*? Did you know?"

"What's a *penguin-dung*, one of those?" said Bishop.

"'Knight Protector,'" said Junada. "Fendy? Lara? Who is this man?"

Fendy raised an eyebrow and cocked a strange grin in Bishop's direction. "You look a bit like him, but the *pelindung ksatria* was much more handsome. You're not a lawyer, are you?"

"You knew my father."

"You knew his—this man's *father*?" Junada spluttered. "Fendy?"

"I had no idea," Lara said.

Fendy grabbed Lara's hand and pulled her past Junada and inside. Bishop remained in the hallway. Junada stared at him, seriously confused, entirely mistrustful.

"Why do your clothes not fit?"

"He lost his clothes," Lara shot over her shoulder.

Junada was appalled.

Fendy laughed. "Juju, let him inside. She said they were in trouble." She squeezed Lara's shoulders, fastened her in a serious look. They spoke in hushed Malay.

Junada pointed. "What's in the yoga bag?"

"Yoga," said Bishop.

Junada considered his wife and Lara, listened to them a moment, gestured Bishop inside. He shut and locked the door.

BISHOP FOUND FENDY's smile the most engaging he'd ever seen. Where most people smile to reflect happiness, friendliness, non-threatening engagement, Fendy's smile projected instead of reflected: when Fendy smiled, she created happiness. Fendy beamed through dinner. The four of them ate prawn *sambal* with *nasi keruba* blue rice in straight-backed chairs around a kitchen table of heavy hand-carved wood.

"The blue color comes from the butterfly-pea flower we use in the cooking," said Fendy. "The scientific name for it—"

"Fendy," said Lara.

"—is *clitoria*. Tom, would you like to guess why?"

Lara blushed. Fendy laughed.

"How did you know my father?"

"Manjalara and I work together, and before that, we attended school together. I didn't board same as she, but we've been best friends since grammar school." The woman spoke a mile a minute. "*All* the girls had eyes for your father. Everyone jealous of Lara's *sateria penyelamat*. Even my Lara-loli-lu was jealous."

Bishop looked at Lara for translation. She averted her gaze.

"'Knight in Shining Armor,'" said Junada with undisguised distaste.

"We believed—wanted to believe, I guess, all of us girls," said Fendy, "the Mother Superior and he had a thing going. Manjalara burned over that. Oh, so angry. Such a heart-crush. Always believed Mr. Bucknell Esquire would one day throw her over his saddle and ride off with her." She batted her eyes at

Bishop, challenging him not to admit this desire had transferred and transformed.

"Catholic school. But you're Muslim," said Bishop.

"Yes. We are," Junada said as an unsubtle reminder for his wife.

Fendy squeezed his hand. "An infidel converted for love."

Junada focused on Bishop. Without breaking his gaze, he said, "How long will you be with us, Lara?"

"The rest of the night. We'll be gone in the morning."

"Has this man involved you in something criminal?"

"He just chose the wrong time to visit. Really, Junada, there's no need to worry."

"My father died recently," said Bishop. "There were some unexpected things that needed to be settled."

"And why are you dressed in—what I would call police-type uniform?"

"My luggage was lost. My suit became unwearable."

"Why?" Junada probed. "You are in my home. I have a right to know."

"We were caught in some rioting," Lara said. "The police broke it up and helped us out. They donated it to Tom. You should have seen it. Very rough."

"Last question: why are you not in your hotel, Mr. Bishop, and you, Manjalara, at home?"

Bishop made a sudden show of eating a mouthful of rice.

"Tastes sweet—I get that part—but why isn't it pink?"

Fendy and Lara burst out laughing. Junada rose. Lay aside his napkin. He kissed his wife's lips, Lara's forehead. Bishop rose and offered his hand. Junada faced him. Fendy cleared her throat. He reluctantly gave a handshake and a cool goodnight.

"This should fit," Fendy said, giving Bishop a black suit—one stitch and a set of silk-covered buttons shy of a tuxedo—a shirt and a tie. "My father also died. This spring. I've not gotten around to donating his things. Now I know why. Praise God and trust Allah in all things."

Tom thanked her. Fendy let them know where they could sleep: Lara in the guest room, Tom on the sofa; what might be the preferred arrangement would be going too far with her husband. Bishop asked if she had a detailed city map. She did. She suggested whatever he had to do the next day, maybe it would be better if Lara remained with her.

"Thank you, Fendy, but I'm going with Tom."

"You *are* in trouble."

Lara's eyes pleaded Fendy for understanding. She touched Lara's cheek.

"I love this woman, Tom. You take care of my Loli-lu."

"She'll be safe with me."

"I will," Lara assured her.

Fendy retrieved fresh towels and showed them the bathroom. They exchanged goodnights. Lara went after her friend. She stopped Fendy with a gentle hand. They spoke again in their language.

When Fendy had left, Lara said, "I'm going to pray with her in the morning."

"I'm glad."

Lara moved into the guest room. Bishop remained in the hallway.

Eyes luminous, Lara said, "You won't let me wake up to find you gone?"

Bishop shook his head. She waited. He didn't move. She shut herself inside. He waited until the light extinguished beneath her door.

BLACKED OUT and invisible in the final hours of darkness, the *Iwo Jima* Seahawk hovered over the jungle canopy two miles from the Tiger Mine. The SEALs on the SPIE rigging dangled like spiders. On the squad leader's radio call, the cable unspooled, lowering the Special Ops team into the otherwise impenetrable green. Released from their cable, the American warriors primed weapons and moved out, vectoring in on the rumble of vehicles. The echoing rip of heavy machine-gun fire across the lake brought the SEALs to an abrupt halt.

LUCKY-BOY RAKED his Browning .30-caliber machine gun from behind a vine-tangled berm of stone castoff, taking out the cab of a troop transport and three of a squad of UTK commandos bailing from the back to take cover on the haul road. They answered the wizened Montagnard with concentrated small-arms fire. A second squad deployed behind them into the rainforest on the opposite side of the road. Lucky-Boy cut apart four of them. A British-era 1960s Ferret armored scout car rolled forward, its light machine gun chewing apart Lucky-Boy's cover. The old man rolled and scrambled. He took cover and returned fire with his Tommy gun, wounding another man, who went down howling.

"Jesus Christ!" Sedaka said as he and Colonel Ibrahim ditched their jeep.

They ducked behind it as more UTK commandos moved into the foliage on Lucky-Boy's side and leapfrogged—cover-fire, move, cover-fire—after him.

Lucky-Boy sprinted again only to stop short as the squad, having deployed through the jungle on the other side of the haul road, flanked him.

The Ferret rolled forward. Stopped. Fired two smoke grenades from the launcher fitted to its hull.

Gunfire silenced. Smoke billowed into Lucky-Boy's position. The sound of movement came from ahead and behind and from on the road. He unloaded the Tommy gun, firing into the cloud and striking flesh. He tossed the Tommy gun and swung a shotgun harnessed across his back. He turned to fall deeper into the jungle behind him, only to be met by the *clink-clink-clink* of spoons popping from three hand grenades. Two clattered against the stones around him. One thumped into the mud at his feet.

The seals heard the distant triple crump of the grenades.

Silence.

A trio of shotgun blasts, shrieks of surprise, then a finishing burst of gunfire and excited shouts in Malay.

The SEALs moved forward.

Colonel Ibrahim's lead elements gave the all-clear. Sedaka clambered after the colonel back into their jeep. Ibrahim shouted orders in Malay. The convoy, which included two large flatbeds and a truckload of military engineers, rolled.

Bishop was awake when Lara joined him on the living-room sofa. He didn't know how to say it. How could he tell Lara that Elizabeth had welcomed Lara inside of his heart? And then she knew, and then he kissed her.

And then she held her hands to his face as if it were the most natural thing to do, to leave her fingerprints on the skin of someone she could cherish.

This time. This place. This man.

And then her hands: gliding up the iron of his chest, fingers weaving the coarse, curls of hair that filled the hard valley at the center of his breastbone. Her hands, one after the other over his heart, feeling its hammer and recoil, returning them to his face. And then wrapping his neck, and then up the side of his skull and then around the back and then pulling his face to her heart. And then, and then, and then: his full inflexible passion and her gentle power. The ready ease with which they joined and together knew exactly who they were and why they'd come together, and that birth and rebirth come in many, many forms, all of which bear us into the supernatural light, beyond the sun, beyond fire, beyond the electric into one with the spirit. They made love, glorious bodies forgetting everything, even time itself, being only present for the other.

PERFECTLY TIRED, slick with each other's sweat, beads gleaming in the faint cast of first light like scattered white diamonds, they lay on their backs, side by side, fingers interlaced between them. They faced each other and emerged alive.

In whispers, Bishop opened his heart. They spoke the simple phrases of their attractions, the simple, secret catalogs of all the qualities they admired and desired in the other, unspoken as they'd fenced and fought and shared their life-altering odyssey of the past two days, and Bishop chose to do now what he'd been unable to do with Elizabeth.

Unable to do with his father.

He knew today that he and Lara would necessarily part. More than anything, he yearned he would return to her, but Bishop squarely faced the part inside of himself where fear told him he would not. Fear was healthy. His whole life he relied on its early warning system in calculating all things operational. He never relied upon his heart. Lying beside Lara, he chose to lay it bare.

"I came here—Malaysia—to die. I've been on that road a long time, since I lost my wife, and I came here believing I would right my father's wrongs and go out in some befitting blaze of glory. Or slumped in a puddle. Wouldn't really matter."

"I'm glad you've changed your mind. You have, haven't you?"

He rubbed his index finger across her lips. "Shh."

Lara knew it was a final goodbye. She was grateful it came in the form of a goodbye given privately to her, and while maybe that was selfish, she cared strongly and deeply enough for my friend that she recognized his real goodbye was to himself, a man whose soul he'd unfairly shut in a hospital room in Taiwan and left behind as he went to hunt death.

"When Muir's greatest wrong turned out to be you, well, that called for some of what we call 'inter-operational improvisation.' My re-centered mission goal became bringing you to safety and giving to you a thing unfairly denied you. Me too—our whole lives—a proper family. The primary objective of my mission is you. If you cherish anything about me in times to come, cherish that. I'm confident I've achieved that and it's good."

He stroked her face, smiling at her. He kissed her lips and forehead, smiled again, and then continued:

"My father, who knows me better than he ever allowed me to know myself, understood if he sent me objectively for you—sent me with the truth—I would not have come. If he'd clued you in, you'd not have met me. We would have rejected each other and all of him, and the size of that mistake would have been catastrophic. Not only to us but to the world."

"Tom, I don't want to separate you from finding peace with your father, but our pasts were entirely corrupted by that man. I'm having trouble with any kind of esteem for what he did to you. And me."

"I know. In our case—especially you—it all stems from the corruption of ATROPOS."

"Muir was Atropos. You have to see that."

Bishop denied her with a wag of his head. "Nathan Muir was Prometheus and like his codename namesake, he stole fire. Nuclear fire he hid from the CIA in treason and from humankind in faith."

He gazed at her face and stroked her cheek. "My work has put me alone most of my life. Sometimes days and weeks on end. Inching into a position; sitting in a hide somewhere. I never had the chance of college. Like you. Like Russell. But my mother taught me early on to 'always bring something to read.' I've gained a lot. More than most, as I'll read anything I find—just needs to be in English. My course of study conveyed in other people's fingerprints. Sometimes, though—when I don't have anything but my thoughts—I try to translate what I've read into understanding the past. What the past—distinct from present and future—is; mine, everyone's, inability to touch its experience."

He'd spoken his way into the deepest roots of his soul's guiding principle; thoughts that had always escaped clear formulation suddenly and purposefully coming clear to him. He propped up on his elbow, the vigilance leaving his eyes, replaced by wonder, like pushing through a jungle screen into a bright sunlit clearing.

"In my world, and Russell's, and yours—though you didn't choose it—what carries forward from the past is, from our own participation, inconvenient. All we ever find are the masks we shape to it to suit our current needs. You strip those off, but they're just covering more masks and more masks and we can't turn them over fast enough to find our one true face."

He felt he was on to it now, and in that, something stronger worked, rushing against him as though riding a wave of thought into its own riptide.

"Or, we sense it already building into itself *in the present*, try to stop the past before it happens, and events irrefutably make their mark—but whether it's a successful airstrike or walking into an enemy ambush: they only can happen because all events of the known and agreed-upon past have led those of us who perceived a different future beyond the moment of the airstrike, the moment of the ambush—than what must come to be. And happenings are already the past: gone and unreal."

"I don't—Tom, I'm not understanding."

His wonder dissolved into frustration—and maybe we're not supposed to pinpoint these things, any of us—and Bishop collapsed backward onto a pillow. Lara nestled alongside his body into the circle of his arm and pressed her cheek against his face, and Tom Bishop kissed her hair fallen over her ear. He whispered, "I'm not either. I've lost it."

A toilet flushed somewhere within.

But he hadn't, and he thought, *You freed me. I'm freeing you. That's what I mean when I tell you, truthfully, I love you,* but he said, "You know what my favorite smell in the world is? The smell of jungle in the rain. In it are my terrors, my excitements and anticipations, my victories, my losses, and the smell of your breath, your hair, and your skin. The place I want to come home to."

Lara kissed him and hurried away. Bishop quickly dressed in a dead man's black suit. He straightened the pillows. But for the blanket he folded, he left no sign that anything to do with his life had happened there at all.

35

Nick Albro met me two moments after my F/A-18 landed in Thailand and I came down the ladder rushed by the ground crew.

"Mr. Aiken—Nick Albro. You ready for this?"

"For what?"

I accepted the chick-gun one moment and leapt onto a great big UH-60 chopper the next, dawn coming over the jungle, and I must say: it's beautiful, that part of the world, as the globe rolls like a blue and green marble into the sunrise. The pink in the sky flows into orange and the promising indigo of day, and the Black Hawk I was aboard with my new pal Nick Albro, who kept grinning at me, soon lifted into its glory. We went through the whole Rule of Thumb/Stare Decisis on the gun, and I let *the chop-chop-whomp-whomp* rotor crush of noise drown the rest of him out. I watched the palms and other trees flapping, swaying, bending in one hundred variations of green at our departure. The rainforest canopy, lifting on the updraft, revealed a mosaic of purple and red, coral, and yellow. I shut my eyes to rest.

I'd read Bishop's King book about the lost girl. The baseball game. The closer with the helluva last pitch. You don't have to get farther than the first line to apply King's words to both of us: "The world has teeth and it can bite you with them anytime it wants."

Some people survive the bear in their path—like his character Trisha—only to be devoured by the tiger behind them and, unlike King's Trisha, our world has taken out the "can" and the "anytime it wants," leaving: "The world has teeth and it bites you with them." Period.

We're not children. We don't have the innocence or the time left to watch whether the ball breaks left to the outside or to the right, over the plate. We've made all our choices and we swing hard at every pitch until the teeth tear out our throats and our world takes the only thing it ever wanted, that which it was always going to savage: the constructs we believe hold our life together.

BISHOP SPREAD the city map that Fendy had provided him and studied it for the location we would rendezvous. He could hear the Takbir from the back of the apartment.

"Allahu Akbar," God is Greatest, and the recitation of the first Subhanaka, led by Junada. He listened to Lara pronouncing the Arabic she did not speak, followed by Fendy repeating the prayers in English.

"Audhu billahi min-ash-shaytanir-rajeem Bismillah-ir-Rahman-ir-raheem." I seek refuge in Allah from the Devil. In the name of Allah. The Beneficial. The Merciful.

Bishop drew a measure of peace from her willingness to join in their devotion, prayers he'd heard hundreds of times among allies and assets in the Middle East, Central and Southern Europe. His knowledge of Arabic—rudimentary "good morning," "good evening," here-to-there, "how 'bout a coffee?" Get through a tricky day in Lebanon, bolstered to mission-defined, asset brief/debrief conversational tools at the Defense Language Institute in Monterey, California, incrementally expanded to traded thoughts and feelings among agents and, as was the case with Erblina and her daughter, their families in Kosovo—surprised him with how much he understood the prayers before translation.

"Subhana Rabbiyal Adhim... Subhana Rabbiyal Adhim... Subhana Rabbiyal Adhim."

How Perfect is my Lord, the Supreme...

"Sami'Allahu liman hamidah"
Allah hears those who praise Him.
Bishop listened to Lara and drew his measure of peace from the prayers praising God and elaborating the faith.

> *In the name of God, the infinitely Compassionate and*
>   *Merciful.*
>   *Praise be to God, Lord of all the worlds.*
>   *The Compassionate, the Merciful. Ruler on the Day of*
>   *Reckoning.*
>   *You alone do we worship, and You alone do we ask for*
>   *help.*
>   *Guide us on the straight path,*
>   *the path of those who have received your grace;*
>   *not the path of those who have brought down wrath,*
>   *nor of those who wander astray.*
>   *Amen.*

With ears to hear, all we need is to listen, and understanding will follow: it is never the message of the God, but the corruption of God's message by men. Bishop found in the Quran the same message of peace, morality, and salvation he found in the Bible, and in the Buddhist Sutras, the Torah, and the Hindi Veda scriptures. They existed in both opposing scales that his father held in balance to his world view he drew equally from: philosophy and mythology.

Why am I here? What is my purpose?

In the prayers of the faithful, the same commitments to a higher power that taught love and forgiveness, family and community. The meeting of the spiritual with flesh and bone. The moral code, its standards, principles, behaviors, conscience, values, and rules of conduct; beliefs concerned with good and evil and right and wrong.

"Assalaamu Alaikum Wa Rahmatullah."

"May Peace and Mercy of Allah be upon You."

To Bishop, what he'd so far witnessed in Malaysia with the violence of the Ramadan Moon seemed a betrayal of the faith practiced by Fendy and Junada with Lara, and by most Muslims in this country and upon this globe.

On the map, he located the Christian Cemetery hilltop near the city center. He decided it would work well for our meeting point.

The corruption of religion by men had withstood the test of time. It had and continued to infect every religion in human-kind's soulless desire for power, wealth, and domination. The devil, Bishop considered, operates at his evil best against God and humanity in the disguise of promoting the faith and the faithful he wants most to destroy. Lara and Fendy emerged in their hijabs. Armored against Satan, Bishop thought, and if religions, their scriptures, their liturgy, and their worship could be viewed as a code necessary to open the path to God, the devil is a deception operation meant to deceive the world with a false-flag key that unlocks a bottomless well to a pool of fire.

"I'm blessed by what I heard," he said.

Fendy thanked him, charming both he and Lara with her explosive smile. She inquired if he'd located what he needed on the map. Bishop indicated he had and asked if he could make a telephone call to the US Embassy.

"Of course," she said. "Afterward, though, my husband has repeated his request that you leave directly. He also desires, Lara, you remain with us in safety."

Lara rejected the offer with an easy shake of her head and a clutch of her friend's hands.

Fendy pursued the subject with her in Malay and as they talked it out, Bishop went to the telephone. He made the call that would direct me to the cemetery and seal my fate with his lead.

Nick Albro and I flew in over the heart of the city. I watched fires burning in rural pockets. Military troops, armored vehicles, tanks protecting state buildings. State Police tore down barricades erected and defended by mobs of demonstrators they bludgeoned. People wounded and killed. The election, the results the people wanted, the woman of strength, of beauty-shining-through commonness and upraised by true courage: suppressed. We swung over the Central Market, where an anti-aircraft 20mm tracked us from a spot where days before Popular Democratic Front candidate Nurul Mawar Musa had marched hopeful toward legitimate victory only to be met with state-sponsored violence pummeled toward illegitimate defeat. Our "Friend or Foe" radio beacon signaled "friend" and protected our passage.

"Fuckin' Third World bullshit," said Nick Albro.

We aimed for the US Embassy, where we'd been cleared to land, and I half expected to see a Saigon-lite rooftop paper doll overloaded helo extraction.

"Just get me on that roof."

A pair of Boeing Model 234UT Chinook, twin-rotor heavy-lift helicopters—the civilian version of the Marine Corps bird in uninterrupted service since the Vietnam War—wearing the markings of Malaysia's largest timber company, hovered over the black lake that filled Muir and Danny Aiken's Tiger Mine, indenting the water's surface and throwing waves in pairs of congruent circles of rotor downdraft. Thick winch lines dangled. A group of divers rose from beneath the surface.

Colonel Ibrahim and Sedaka watched from their jeep beside waiting military flatbed transports, the Ferret scout car, and the addition of an Alvis Stormer combat vehicle. The divers signaled the helicopters. Ibrahim listened in over the radio.

"Both warheads and launchers have been located intact," he said.

"Finally, your men get something right," said Sedaka.

No one noticed—or if they had, they didn't care—that they were in the tigers' feeding area, the goat tether posts and chains sticky with blood. It was a clearing and Ibrahim and his crew of engineers were glad to have it for their pair of military flatbed transports.

THE SEAL TEAM watched the activity from their nine o'clock position to Colonel Ibrahim's twelve, concealed within the overgrowth that grew all the way to the mine's lake edge.

The team leader spoke into his throat mic: "Grey Goose to Belvedere. Do you copy? Over."

AT LANGLEY, Acting DCI Harker and Deputy Director Meryl Hofmeyr in the ATROPOS Ops Center heard the call over headsets.

"We copy, Grey Goose. Over," Harker responded.

"We are on-site with visual of the mine. Hostiles in the water, on shore, and overhead, preparing heavy lift of presumed warheads from below surface. Over."

"Stand firm, Grey Goose. Waiting for sat-confirm. Repeat: do not engage. Over."

"Grey Goose standing firm on your order, over."

Harker swiveled in his chair. He faced a console behind him where a technician monitored the NRO Bloodhound-7 satellite telemetry tracking and command system.

"Bloodhound-7 in range, coming on target."

"Visual," said Harker.

Harker's technical team swung into action, transferring the real-time feed, infrared, black-and-white, and neutron imaging on consoles and separate overhead monitors. Ibrahim's troops and vehicles clearly visible, the civilian helicopters hovering, their lift lines buried in the water.

One of Harker's two senior analysts, his Malay boys out of the Southeast Asian Section for the Directorate of Intelligence, overseeing another console directed the capture and enlargement of imagery clearly showing the Malaysian designations on vehicles and personnel as his partner identified the units. Facial biometrics worked on hi-res enlargements.

"Colonel Josef Ibrahim, Malaysian Special Branch: confirmed. And… Paul Sedaka, CIA chief resident—sorry, sir—also confirmed."

Meryl Hofmeyr gave a low hum. Flashed suspicious eyes at Harker.

"Anything in his clothing to give him away?" Harker said.

"No, sir."

"Good. Mr. Sedaka is on special assignment SCI Top Secret classification. He cannot figure into this in any manner or association. See to it Sedaka's image is scrubbed. Where it can't be scrubbed, altered unidentifiable."

"Yes, Director."

Chatter grew between the various stations:

"Five minutes remaining overhead on target on my mark…Mark."

"Code inserted. Sedaka's facial structure obscuring."

"Reading neutron trace signatures forming beneath the water's surface."

And Harker said, "Give them a minute… Come on… Come on…"

Weapons ready, the SEALs monitored the activity as, once more, the divers surfaced along the winch lines. Signals relayed. The lines grew taut beneath one and then the other Chinook. They began spooling.

The first Scud missile broke the surface in a shower of brackish water. Identifying Soviet markings added for Muir's 1968 ATROPOS deception were visible where the divers had rubbed away years of silt.

"This is excellent." Harker did a pizzazzy little échappé of excitement. "Make sure to capture plenty of those markings, then."

The first Chinook moved toward the shore and Ibrahim's waiting flatbeds. Less than a minute, the second missile broke surface.

Sedaka extended his hand to the Malaysian colonel. "Let me be the first to welcome you and Prime Minister Aziz to the family of nuclear armed powers."

"Grey Goose to Belvedere: we have eyes on two Soviet-marked Scud missiles, warhead-tipped. Request permission to commence action. Over."

Inside the ops center, Harker watched three visual confirmations of the SEAL Teams words: infrared, black and white, and, most importantly, the nuclear devices' neutron signatures incandescent green below the helicopters.

"Grey Goose, waiting on your orders." Meryl gave Harker a verbal elbow.

"Tell them to stand firm," he snapped as he leaned in over the satellite tech. "Looks good. Print hard copies, each system."

T HE SEAL TEAM , waiting on orders, watched the Scuds lowered to engineers and waiting flatbeds when a burst of machine-gun fire opened on them from behind. The firefight was instant and savage as Ramadan Moon rebels set upon them with overwhelming force in a maelstrom of fire and lead.

The 20mm cannon atop the Alvis Stormer vectored on the SEALs' position.

O BLIVIOUS TO the extent of which his SEALs were under fire, Harker barked into his headset: "Belvedere to Grey Goose: you are cleared to engage. Over."

His eyes drifted to the overhead that with the orbital movement of the NSA satellite now included the SEALs in its feed.

"Belvedere to Grey Goose… Come in, Grey Goose."

The gunfire flashed. Bodies fell. The 20mm cannon fired once, twice.

Radio silence of dead air. The Ramadan Moon rebels moved toward the SEAL Team's position as the Bloodhound-7 feed flickered.

"What's happening? Where are my men?" Harker shouted.

"We're moving out of range, sir."

"Forget the SEALs! Put me back onto the warheads!"

But the feed was lost. Only static. Harker's face filled with gut-punched horror.

"I HAVE NO IDEA where Russell's mind is at," Bishop said as he drove the stolen police vehicle, Lara beside him.

"You won't kill him. Promise me."

"I have no intention of killing anyone. Ever. Doesn't mean it doesn't become necessary when my feelings get hurt."

Lara's eyes flashed disappointment. "You wouldn't kill my brother. Not after everything."

They wended their way through prime KL real estate. Lush green, quiet, large, and modern wealth-built and-reflecting homes, Western in living space but all of them built on Malay-styled fortress blocks of quarried stone foundations. No indication of the civil unrest escalating on all sides and throughout the nation on these streets. Bishop had nothing against the rich over the poor, or the haves over the have-nots, but he always wondered why, before they started looting and burning, why they didn't leave their own neighborhoods for the neighborhoods like this. Aside from some armed but lazing gate guards, there was no one to be seen.

Bishop stopped at the cemetery gates. That the Sikhs in the guardhouse didn't blink at the American driving a Malaysian police vehicle indicated more eloquently than words that Bishop's call to the embassy had greased the wheels for us. The gears in the boom barrier box turned and engaged the gate arm to lift the bar and allow them inside. Bishop drove the tree-covered hill on a winding jungle lane to emerge on the level crown, a green lawn chessboard of gravestones and monuments—the last remains of remaining colonial rulers. Bishop pulled to a crumbling mausoleum surrounded by a bar of wood or iron.

He removed the clip from his handgun. He checked its action, replaced the ammo. He seated a round, hot in the chamber.

"My only objective here is to collect what Russell's brought me. Without your passport, it's the only way I can get you out of this country to safety."

"But if he's here to kill you, he won't have brought anything."

"Not how we play it. He has to bring it to draw me out and gain my trust. To find and sink me later if I get away with it and try to bank it or sell it."

"Isn't that what you plan to do with it?"

"Like I said, the only plan I have for it is to get you out of here to safety. Sad to say it, but I value that over Russell, and I can promise you this: if our position were reversed, he'd put your safety over me without a second's thought."

Lara crossed her arms, resigned to whatever the Three Fates dictated would happen.

To her.

To Bishop.

To me.

And—*snip*—to the thread of life.

"His father cheated on his mother to produce me. His escape hatch, you called it. What if your Russell only sees me as a bastard?"

"He's more opinionated about more things with enough pet peeves to fill a zoo than anyone I've ever met. Where family's concerned, though: I've never met another human being with more natural generosity of spirit than your brother."

"Him?"

Lara pointed past Bishop to me walking from the bottom of the hill where Albro had left me. I carried the satchel of money and gold.

And they waited, and while Bishop might've been right in principle, Jessie—even your mom would have to agree on this—minutes later and lying in the grass between gravestones with a hole through me, blood pouring out, as I am here in my last moments of consciousness, the top of my head gone: your dad just kinda wishes my generosity of spirit had rubbed off a smidge on him.

ON THE SHORE of the Tiger Mine pit lake, Sedaka watched the Ramadan Moon rebels parade. They dragged the corpses of the

Navy SEALs among them. Hollered. Chanted. Fired weapons into the air and into the bodies when they were finished with them. They went back into the jungle with their machetes for heads.

"That was close," Sedaka said.

"Like everything with you."

"With *America*. Tough adversary, but we beat 'em," Sedaka said from behind an uneasy simper.

Colonel Ibrahim gave orders in Malay to his engineers. They finished chaining the missiles to the flatbeds. Strapped tarpaulins over them.

Sedaka said, "I suppose all that's left is the small matter of my final payment. I have here"—he pulled a note from his jacket pocket—"an account where my fee can be wired."

He handed it to Ibrahim, who looked at, folded, and scratched his thin moustache with its edge. "Get out of my jeep."

"Pardon me?"

"Out."

Sedaka did as requested. Interlaced his hands behind his back to hide their shaking. His uneasiness read in lips stretched taut across *teh tarik*-stained teeth, saliva seething through the spaces between.

"By the way, Colonel, you ever find yourself on the Cote d'Azur..." Sedaka winked; his confidence waned.

Colonel Ibrahim pulled his handgun from his hip holster.

Sedaka looked between it and Ibrahim. If yellow teeth could drain white, they would have matched his pallor.

"Colonel, I—I don't understand. Not in the least."

"Our business is complete."

"Yes, a job well done by all, I must say."

The colonel thumbed off the pistol's safety.

"...Oh..." Sedaka muttered, mouth mimicking the circle of the gun barrel aimed his way.

Colonel Ibrahim shouted more orders to his men.

"This isn't necessa—"

Ibrahim disagreed before Sedaka finished, shooting the American Orientalist, CIA self-proclaimed Vietnam Expert, Nathan Muir's killer, Lara's blackmailer, in his ample falling-striver's gut.

Sedaka thumped to his ass with, "FUCK!"

His eyes pleaded. His breath increased in rapidity while diminishing in capacity. Sweat welled from his brow and rivered his cheeks.

"I—I'm going to leave you now. Leave you alone. Just, just let me stand… Here… Right."

In the seat behind Ibrahim, his bodyguard lifted his submachine gun, but the Malaysian Special Branch colonel casually pushed it away.

"Going… now… We're. G-g-gh-gh-hood."

Impassive to Sedaka's struggle as he straightened along the fender rail, their faces coming obscenely close, Ibrahim watched Sedaka shove off, turn away, and, clutching his seeping wound, stumble into the jungle.

36

*L*ET ME RETURN *to March, two weeks—Jessie—after the birth of your brother. You remember: my trip to your "Grandpa" Nathan's to wish him happy birthday and to tell him we were giving Nate his name. If you've read this far, you're grown and know what your mother knew and like she, I am gone.*

Madeline and Nate certain to be ever-remembered, me to be forgotten, except, I pray, by you.

If you've gotten this far in this brain-ragged memoir, I'm less sure now than I've ever been with what happened when, to whom, and to how. I'm a Saturday New York Times *Crossword Puzzle Answers diagram with my numbers and my lines bereft of clues. Bereft of whys and lost of wisdom; drab as a fool, detached as a bard—*

No that's not right—"Detached."

Doesn't fit the boxes in my mind.

I'm missing the word that circles back the tail-eating snake of my soul, like the saw that cuts to the root of all problems.

I'm not there. Won't accept the grind of the craniotome. I owe it to me. I'm here: *Friday, March 23, 2001. Muir and I bundled against the returning chill of a Princeton afternoon. The spot for a twilight spy or time killing two two killing time, Muir's bullet—*

Dammit! No! Bishop's bullet *to kill me—or is it my other twin (growing hard like a sprout from a tree Muir will recommend I become more like) inside me?*

Jack and Jill: twins, wells, cemetery hills, and the towers came tumbling afffter.

A penny for your thoughts.

I'm sorry if I'm scaring you. I'm scaring me, Jessie, sweet girl.

There was clover in the cemetery grass. There was clover beneath Muir's feet—or just foot when one is—appearance real—false proph-et-ic prosthetic? And mine firmly planted.

"On a clover, if alive, erupts a vast, pure evil; a fire volcano."

Ahh. There. I've looped and loaded back. My ouroboros aloof—never detached.

It's what artists learn to do. So I paint my mind a picture for your imagination.

From the jungle of Malaysia to the garden of my mind, to the Class of 1946 Garden on the west side of Maclean House at Princeton. A natural bench, our feet in spring clover. The place quiet and hidden and choked in its approaches to tell you, daughter, this:

"Nathan," I said. "Your father—his story, of horses and biblical chariots, Jazz Age movie fantasy the one hand, memory: reality on the other."

"Who's to say memory isn't all fantasy?"

"Because it's shared experience."

"Shared fantasy?" He popped a Coffee Nip and leered at me.

"Fine, Muir. Say it is. I don't care. That's not my point. I'm here, you're here, and I know you left something out when you told Elizabeth about-about, about your." Mind-slip. "Father."

"Nothing slips past you, Rusty."

"Thank you."

"I mean it. In everything—and you're never going to fail me at that, now are ya?"

His leer was fake, his probing eyes as real as his soul. I didn't dare answer, knowing spoken words are the first footsteps toward a lie. I simply met his look and that was enough for him.

"You want to know how Bucky fixed Rodriguez's Italian limp."

"Yes. Did your father kill his father's friend?"

"Yep. Sure did. So?"

"Did. As in *murder* him?"

"You're a twice-around-the-block guy. Like to have been a place before you walk up the first time. That extra look-see at a thing that—if I taught you anything, I taught you that—so you know it's all murder."

His every compliment made me feel small.

Is this how he spoke to my father? Is that how Muir made Chief Petty Danny Aiken feel and did my feelings, responding to Muir, respond from the part that was my father? Did my career measure up to the hopes he'd placed in my father replaced in me?

That knowledge still ahead of me, all I could do was miss the empty space of it.

Muir launched back into the story as if he'd been telling it all along. "They'd made the harbor at Barcelona mid-morning. Drove the horses into the waterfront cattle pens and Bucky and Don Rodriguez were finished by mid-afternoon. After forty-five days herding and breaking horses from the rugged Sierra Madres of Granada, across the olive-, almond-, and cork-treed tawny plains of La Mancha, along the rugged coast through Valencia, and into Catalonia.

"You have to remember, the Barcelona you know after they spruced it up for the Olympics—"

"Why do you do that? You know I've never been to Spain. My desk keeps me bound from anywhere."

"Rusty, how would I possibly know where you haven't bounded off to?"

"You keep tabs. I know you do—Vladivostok—so just get on with the story."

"When my dad, Bucky, got there, Barcelona was a hotbed of rebellion. Workers' riots, military strongmen, political assassinations, anti-church demonstrations, anarchist bombings. My bloodline gravitates to that, I guess, but anyway, the harbor was a dirty and polluted, thieves and prostitutes, what-do-you-do-with-a-drunken-sailor gateway to Dante's Second Circle. Perfect place for Bucky, where, by all accounts, he indulged in the Green Fairy."

"I'm sorry? Your dad was gay—or, I guess, bi?"

"Stop guessing, you idiot. It's what they call absinthe."

"Ahh. The hallucinogenic alcohol."

"You know something? You interrupt most when you're wrong. No, it's not hallucinogenic—that would be your LSD drug of choice."

"Not fair. That was one time and you set me up," I said, and I pictured Nina as not a day gone by since that New York City trip in 1978 when we made love, and the twenty-four hours we spent in Cuba, 1991, the night Muir rescued Bishop from China, where on the moonlit sands on the beach at Caiberién—having evaded the Cuban spymaster Trigorin—I held her in my arms again, more love offered me than I'd ever known.

Nina is a love I had only a moment in this life and a moment later in Havana. A truer, more faithful, more honest, more pure lover alive in memory than anything I've watched slip through my fingers like miniature hydrogen and oxygen marbles since: Nina.

"Bucky came back late, two-oh-five in the morning, hammered and spent out, to the *pensión* dormitory room Don Rodriguez had acquired for them and their wranglers. He'd thrown himself onto his cot, but the sex and the absinthe had left him energized. He knew he had to get some sleep, the transfer of the horses—they had forty-nine of the original sixty they'd set out with, eleven lost to banditry along the journey—the loading of them onto the ferry they'd booked to take them across the Mediterranean was going to be hard work and exhausting. But Bucky also noticed four of their eight vaqueros weren't in their beds, and when he knocked on Don Rodriguez's door at two-ten, he discovered his father's trusted friend also away.

"Bucky figured they were at the corral. Figured they were preparing for the work ahead, figured he'd wander down to help.

"Men and horses were moving in the light of three trucks. His wranglers working with some campesinos and some laborers who were attempting to load a dozen of his father's horses onto the trucks, Miguel-Angel Rodriguez taking a payment equal to ten thousand US dollars from the leader of this group, one Pedro Lamarca."

"You certainly have all the details."

"I don't tell you what isn't important," said Muir and found his pocket flask.

He drank and offered it to me. "Your favorite. Macallan 25."

"You know I don't."

"I know, so"—Muir screwed shut the captive top of the flask, flashed it at me, and pocketed it—"Rodriguez and the others were all a little surprised.

"'What's going on?' my father called and stumbled over.

"'You shouldn't be here, *Angel*,' which is what Rodriguez had taken to calling my father. 'Get back to the rooms. I will explain later. This does not concern you.'

"'They're stealing Dad's horses.'

"'They're buying them. Go. Now.'

"Rodriguez was angry. Lamarca angrier, and he showed that by showing a pistol in his belt. He didn't draw it. Yet. Lamarca and Rodriguez argued. Bucky didn't move. Didn't know what to do. Rodriguez went over to him, put a fatherly arm around him, brushing off the angel. He told Bucky that Lamarca and the others were Los Solidarios."

"Ah! Soldiers," I said.

"Good Spanish guessing, Rusty. No. It means solidarity. Furthest thing from soldiers. They were anarchists. And they'd paid for the horses—though they were desperately poor. They needed them for their movement to fight the communists and the new ultra-right fascism—and they weren't going to leave without 'em, so he might as well get used to it. 'Besides,' Rodriguez said, 'the Jew Louis Meyer can afford it.'

"Bucky didn't like the Jew comment; he insisted they were stealing from his father. They were ruining his name and his reputation. Rodriguez suggested, while Bucky had broken the horses—nothing could take that away from him—he hadn't done much in protecting that name with a trail littered by empty booze bottles and cast-off prostitutes whose reputation Bucky hadn't cared for a whit. In the end, Don Rodriguez counseled, Bucky's father wouldn't be blamed. Nor would Bucky. Rodriguez would see to it. Sometimes a noble but desperate cause that presents itself, taking a risk to assist in it, is the very thing that *makes* a reputation. 'My horses. Your reputation, *Señor Muir.*'

"Between Rodriguez and Lamarca and some more booze, they almost convinced Bucky to let the horses go—the movement, the times, the passion of rebellion, all those romantic things a kid like Bucky might draw toward and more than halfway did—but they made a mistake. Bucky *was* the Sheriff of Nottingham. The good guy. Law and order. Honest pay for honest work."

"Not sure that's how Robin Hood goes."

Muir laughed. "Get real. Robin Hood was an opportunistic thief and a communist."

"Anyway, Bucky was backing off—going to look the other way—when he saw one of the campesinos leading Bucky's own pure black Andalusian stallion, with the amber eyes, the one that spit in his face but that he'd formed a bond with on the trail like no human Bucky had yet known."

"Your mother."

"Dammit, Rusty. You going to tell it or am I?"

He stared me down a beat.

"Lamarca reassured him, 'No, no, Señor Muir. *Este no es para el carne de perro o por pegamento'*—This one's not for the dog food or glue Rodriguez was selling them for—*'su esplada es para mí montar.'* This horse's back was for Lamarca to ride.

"Bucky didn't know the word for *glue*, but *dog food* was easy, and he flew at Lamarca. The gun came out and Lamarca got off a shot that missed Bucky before Bucky got the gun. Lamarca's men were armed, but all of them were wanted and the gunshot spooked them more than it spooked the horses. They got away with seven of them and half the wranglers joining their cause.

"Bucky's stallion they left behind. Hit in the right front cannon—bone shattered—it stood, shaking and ruined. The stallion knew he was done for, he had no purpose, no identity left him. My dad stroked its muzzle, put the barrel of the pistol against the black stallion's skull, and pulled the trigger.

"Don Rodriguez tried to say some comforting words, a kind of half-assed apology. He didn't finish as my father's next bullet was for him. Bucky found an old barrel and shoved the body inside. He weighted it with some heavy tackle, sealed it, and rolled it off a derelict pier.

"At five a.m., Bucky and his remaining wranglers loaded the remaining horses onto the ferry, and two days later offloaded them from the train that took them from Civitavecchia to Rome. The rest of the story you've heard."

I gave him an up-from-under look, unnamed suspicion fingering its way along the back of my neck. "You've said you didn't have a good relationship with your dad—you or your mother. Did he tell you this or did your mom?"

"I never met Bucky," said Muir.

Suspicion's fingers clenched. Hard.

"I clearly remember you saying he made his fortune speculating oil in LA."

Muir drank again.

"That was my stepfather. My biological father made love to my mother two days out, and I was conceived, and my dad spent the next three days and nights committed to spending the rest of his life with her. She the same for him. But when they landed in New York Harbor, the police were waiting. Before leaving the ship, Bucky charmed the captain into marrying them. He kissed my mother goodbye coming down the gangway man and wife, he was arrested for murder, clapped into irons… Returned to Spain."

I stared at Muir, uncomprehending. "Your father spent his life in a Spanish prison? MGM couldn't get him out?"

"It would've been different if it had been self-defense, and his lawyers tried for that, and yes, my grandfather used all his connections. Problem was: my father had taken the ten thousand dollars. They found it hidden, sewn in his saddle, and that got him murder in the first.

"Six years in, though… about the time a kid—kid being me—gets past asking why he doesn't have a dad to why this new one, my stepfather, had to come into the picture, my mother received the first of what would be many letters she shared with me."

"From Bucky?"

"From the Great Pumpkin—who do you think? The return address was Marseille. A dictator had come and gone in Spain and with the new republic, prison reform was undertaken. Bucky and a few others escaped in a transfer. The others with him were all hunted down and executed, but Bucky made it to France and to the Port of Marseille, where, captured by French police, he was given the choice to return to Spain for another trial and certain execution."

Muir popped another Coffee Nip.

"Or?"

"Or what?"

"Execution 'or'?" That, or?"

"Become a mercenary for France."

"You're trying to tell me he joined the French Foreign Legion?"

Muir was serious. "That's absolutely my life. I swear on my mother's soul that she received every one of his letters and read them to me. I have them. They're in the house—you'll give them to Tom after I'm gone."

"You're not going anywhere," but even as I said it, that's when I began to fear he was—he knew he was—he was telling me without telling me.

"He became a hero. A record of derring-do unsurpassed in combat in Africa and Europe and Asia. My antics, Charlie March's: hell, they pale by comparison. Bucky Muir made me the man I am—choose the life I chose.

"Of course, I knew by the time I was fifteen my mother, in cahoots with Bucky's sister—"

"Your Aunt Linda—"

He dipped his head, his gaze warmed; faraway, peaceful, and pleased. "The old witch on the mountain." He caught my eye. "She'll live past a hundred if the Fates have their way. I'll trust you to keep an eye on her. The two of them wrote all the letters."

I refused to acknowledge his gloom. "Fifteen seems a little old to figure out you've been played."

"Some of us don't have your acuity. Just ask Hercules and Oedipus."

"I'll take it up with Jesus."

Muir looked at me without mocking. A pride and tenderness that came without a sting. "Dumbo's mom never told him who he got his ears from."

He'd moved on to secretly tell me to seek my own father, to walk him back from the dust of a Kansas highway to a wet and bloody jungle border between Malaysia and Thailand, but I was dull of hearing and, without mockery, I'm even more uncomfortable with the Muir I failed to understand.

"Some cover stories are better left unexposed," he said. "My stepfather made us wealthy, but he made my mother miserable. Not only with words, the drinking, and the women, but with hands and fists and hard oilfield workboots. I was lucky he didn't pay attention to me, but I understood the letters were as much for my mother as they were for me.

"The last we heard from Caporal Chef—would be senior corporal in our Army—Caporal Chef Bucky Muir, who at one point had made it all the way to sergeant major during the darkest behind-the-lines battles of the big WW-Two against some heinous Nazis; got bumped back down for rescuing some Jewish children, AWOL against orders—God, Mom and I would stay up nights with those letters; that gal had one heck of an imagination. But anyway, the last we heard from Bucky was an unfinished letter from his commanding officer that arrived from Paris a week before I joined the Marine Corps. The Foreign Legion was fighting the First Indochina War—"

"Vietnam," I said. "One day you'd end there—"

Abandoning me to headquarters deskwork while you laid claim to your own blood son.

"Korea was first, but you know all that. Bucky Muir was killed in an ambush. We put a cross in our garden."

How foggy my head—foggy and dizzy in that garden, tongue itching to feel the threads on the neck of the opening to his pewter captive-top flask—

The tiger! The tiger—yes!—I knew I'd seen it. Why he offered the flask to me in the first place that afternoon. The son-of-a-bitch KNEW I wouldn't drink. He wanted me to see my father's coded initials! His tiger!

"Muir: it was all fabricated. Also, you were born in 1929—*Ben Hur*, you even said so, was released in 1925. So how do you get conceived on a boat in '25, but not born until '29?"

"You know, try never to believe anything I say. 1929 is the year my mother married my stepfather. He adopted me—I didn't have a choice—and all other paperwork on my life till then was conveniently lost to erase the existence of my real father and, as that other man liked to say, my bastard birth."

I was angry with the old spook. "You've based your life on a fairy tale. The choices you made, your relationship with your own son—followed a pattern that was the furthest thing from predestined. You didn't have to be that father you never had, living up to yours and your, your, your—

Jessie, this was the first time I consciously admitted (and promptly hid from) the fact that not remembering the word/concept/idea of Muir's mother wasn't some funny memory fart. This was the first time the tumor opened its blood-red eye at me and leered.

"My mother," Muir prompted, eyebrow tilted with slight concern.

"Your mother's hero fantasy myth."

"Would it have been better to admire a spoiled Hollywood rich kid, not even twenty yet, who loved a horse so much he committed murder and was chained to a wooden seat, the iron strap of a garrote vil cranked tighter and tighter by handlebar from behind in the hands of the executioner until his throat crushed and he strangled to death inside a Barcelona prison the day his trial ended? I've fought my whole life to be the fantasy my mother gave us because my other option was real life, and that was a drunk and a cheat and a wife-beater and, sadly, hard as I pushed that away: I inherited too much of all those and they've cost me. Cost me plenty."

"Is everything a lie?"

"Didn't you learn anything in college?" He smirked.

"I'm not talking about that—I'm talking about *everything*."

"It's the fundamental question 'everything' takes identity from. Plato tried to tell you. Aristotle, Kant, the other Russell. Me. Try this on for size: 'We do not need a truth to serve us, we need a truth that we can serve.' Even when that truth is a lie. No," he corrected himself angrily. "*Especially* when that truth is a lie."

"Is What Truth A Lie, Russell? Are you with me?" Dr. Rashmi said, her voice a loud whisper out of the fog. "Good. Move your fingers. Okay. Now move one. Very good—"

PART FOUR

DISILLUSION

"We need to know The Tiger is a dangerous animal.
We need not know that all tigers are not. Identifying
the personalities of individual tigers does not serve
our need to survive. Granted, it might make us more
enlightened individuals and friends with some tigers,
and I am all for that. I applaud that, but one must
recognize that there is a tribal instinct in humans
and it is at its base an instinct for survival."

— CHARLIE KAUFMANN, *Antkind*

37

"A RE YOU WITH ME, Russell? Say my name?"

Recognition—this wasn't Dr. Rashmi—but the name wasn't fastened anywhere hard to my memory. "Nathan," I said.

"Very funny. Wrap you up, you'll be fine," said Bishop.

I lay on my back in the cemetery clover. Hell, I was rolling in it—except I wasn't rolling, just coming conscious, but I was alive and that's always good if you want to keep pace with time.

"You shot me."

"Only way to save you."

Bishop helped me into a sitting position.

"What?" I said. "Was I in the path of some airborne Ebola?"

"You were in the path of your pal's bullet." Bishop jerked his chin.

I swiveled and regretted it, pain burning along my right arm and radiating into my shoulder.

Nick Albro was fresh out of time. Flies—the original first responders—already gathering.

Bishop pulled a pocket handkerchief from the suit he wore. It was thirty years outdated, making it Doug Henning magician big, soft, and silky. He tore my sleeve, wiped the wound, both sides, the white silk gleaming bright red, the only miracle in the transformation being the erythrocytes, leukocytes, and platelets—three determining fates of my existence; now not me at all but living blood nonetheless—imbuing the silk with their life.

"Clean through. Good thing you work those triceps. Gave me something to miss the bone with."

"I'm not believing that."

"There's a lot coming you're not going to believe." Bishop set to tying off the wound. He gave me a direct look. "You didn't think they'd use you as bait? Didn't you kind of suspect something other than a hospitality host? Phony Tahitian 'Tane the Peace God' runes on his steroids, the douchebag shades, dance club tiger stripe parachute pants—"

He let his guard down in the flash of a private smile. The one that made you feel special because it *was* special, and you were special to him. I was hurting. Only lead I'm used to as a lawyer is in a pencil, and I don't hammer pencils through the bottom side of my left upper arm. But that smile: I hadn't seen it since before Elizabeth got sick. Over four years ago.

All of this airplaned around the globe of my tumor as I jumped into the path of his Albro sentence: "And the alt-rock billygoat scruff. When we were kids, that's the kinda jerk used to sell *Grit* newspaper for prizes."

Bishop gripped my right hand and hauled me to my feet. I teetered. He steadied me. "Back of *Boys' Life* magazine—you remember that?" His voice tightened at my non sequitur. "And why?"

"If you sold enough subscriptions, you'd earn a target pistol. Or a bow and arrow." By way of explanation: "I was a big fort builder as a kid."

He walked me toward the police vehicle. Lara, whom I was about to meet, was out of the Unimog. She gaped at us, incredulity, fear, anxiety all mixed in one, like an Asian version of my sister—exactly like—which I was about to find out.

"*Grit: America's Greatest Family Newspaper,*" I said.

"What were you doing reading that? You weren't a Boy Scout."

"Uniforms were a little too queer for me."

Bishop made a fist. "Under other circumstances, I'd give you a pop in the arm."

"One's enough. Thanks."

I was nervous about the woman. I was nervous about why he had her and what our plan was. I wanted anything else but to talk about reality. I chuckled a bit. "'Course that kid probably grew up reading the ads in *Soldier of Fortune*. Probably wants to dig through the back issues when he gets home, see how he got the job wrong."

Bishop puzzled my words. He stopped. I stopped.

"Russell, none of us are Boy Scouts and he's no kid. He's dead."

I lifted a one-hand surrender. "Uh, I know."

I noticed Lara carrying something over.

"We were both his targets," Bishop went on. "He planned to drop me first. Needed to and he knew it. Only problem was I made sure to keep you between me and everything behind you. Once he made his move, I moved you with the first shot. His shot missed, my second did not. Whatever ID he has, we both want to hope someone can trace it back to someone who cares. Okay?"

I kneaded my forehead and stammered. "Wh-whatdya want me to say? I, uh—fffhh—We were both joking."

It wasn't the joking part he'd reacted to. I'd lost track that Albro was deceased.

"I found this in the truck," Lara said, now staring, now trying not to look at me.

She handed Bishop a first-aid kit. Only then did she meet my stare head on. "Hi, Russell. I'm your sister, Lara van Eijk."

You ever see Casablanca, *Jessie? DVD, or whatever they have by the time you got around to watching it, whatever year you're now reading this?*

He'd told her about the stakes we faced with ATROPOS—about Sedaka and Ibrahim's plan for the warheads. He'd given her his two little people in this crazy world climbing the hill of beans speech. There was a pail of water to fetch, and Bishop was going to fetch it and if he was to fall, Lara wasn't going to be anywhere near the tumbling after.

We'd had some time, Lara and I—not enough before the bloody incident at the Thai border—and I would have liked to have learned about her, heard about what she might've remembered of my father. Your grandfather. Her past or I could share mine—which belongs to you, Jessie, as well, for what it's worth—and maybe we'd have found someplace we met, a world apart and without knowing it. Maybe we'd liked the same pop song at the same time, or the same book, or felt the same about something as big as God or as simple as a dog or as faithfully loving as both. Maybe we both spread mustard on graham crackers or wished on the same star to fall in love and maybe laughed at the same joke in the same movie at the same time and had it between us to discover.

But all Lara wanted was to talk about Bishop. How he'd broken into her life and stolen her heart and how she'd known from the way he'd made love to her he was saying goodbye. She remembered it all, but she was emotional, and our drive wasn't easy—I'll get to that in a minute. And Tom, knowing better than most, that most people miss their chance at last conversations, had some big things he wanted her to hear.

I didn't get to transcribing it until later when Lara was already gone. I couldn't check it with her, and whatever she'd shared with me of her responses to his words, any protestations, argument, she either kept private or the beast of my diseased brain has gnawed them from my memory.

The world is a forest of dripping fangs and life is its tiger.

Bishop tied it up for her. "You're going with Russell and I'm staying here. My job is to erase my father's past and prevent the future it was meant to create he couldn't stop."

And Lara argued halfheartedly because she knew she wouldn't dissuade him. This was moments before she saw me shot; when he put the money and the gold in the Unimog: "We have a past now. It's worth a future."

"For that to work out, ATROPOS needs to be finished. I must finish it. Erase the past once and for all and you mustn't be a part of that, or whatever future I make of it will be lost. When you go, you go for both us."

Lara knew then, that moment, their whole experience of each other, all their moments, was all a long goodbye. Their future would only exist if she went on without him from the cemetery.

BISHOP OPENED THE first-aid kit. He got rid of the bloody hankie, flushed the wound with disinfectant, dried then super-glued the entry and exit wounds, gauzed and wrapped my arm. Lara and I spoke throughout.

"You're Dand van Eijk's daughter?"

"Yes. That's who I knew as my father."

"He wasn't my father," I said. "My last name—my father's—is Aiken." But already the words were jumbling in my afflicted brain. "Dand Aiken. Aijk-Eiken. Van Dan."

Bishop glanced from where he worked on my wound. "You're officially scaring me, Russell."

"No—wa-wait, wait! I see it. Dand van Eijk. There's a D, there's an A, there's an N. Dan. There's a second A, there's an I, a K, an E, and an N."

"Aiken," said Lara.

"And his middle initial, J."

We stared at each other as if only now were we real.

"Dand van Eijk is my father's name. In an anagrammatical form."

True to his nature, Bishop took a monumental revelation to the construction of my past as much a part of the day as the white clouds exchanging places with the gathering rainclouds overhead.

"Russell, I'm going to count on you to take Lara across the border into Thailand."

I spoke to Lara. I said the only thing to enter my mind I could form into conscious thought. "Two sisters. Did Tom tell you? One's nice, one's not so much—I almost mistook you for that one."

"Two more than I ever believed I'd have."

She gave Bishop a worried glance.

"I know you're overwhelmed, Russell—"

"You shot me."

"I'm hoping that's all this is," he went on while I disguised on my face the fact it wasn't. "But listen, Lara has no passport. No paperwork. You're going to have to get her through on your diplomatic ID."

"If that's not enough?"

"This better be."

He opened the driver's door of the Unimog and retrieved the satchel. He transferred a pair of handguns and two extra clips from the yoga bag, added them to the satchel as well. "Take the embassy car. Give me forty-eight hours to get to you or contact you through the embassy."

"After that—I take her back to the States?"

Bishop met my open look with inevitable eyes. All he said was, "Nathan and I spoke before I left Kosovo." A flash of mischief for me, he said, "I told him, in light of current situations, I'd let him off with a warning on my whole death-promise thing."

Aﬅer ᴛʜᴀᴛ, after he and Lara embraced long and hard, exchanged promises and a final kiss, after he and I shared some parting words, Lara smiled tenderly at both of us, pretending everything was all right and would end that way. I walked her past Albro's corpse. I didn't stoop to search for the car keys. I was happy to find them tucked between the headliner and driver's sun visor.

In the end, I have not given justice to Tom and Lara's farewell. Bishop knew the cruel truth of his situation and the forces that pushed from the river in his veins that ran unbroken and made real the present. The past, not fantasy, but red and alive inside him. Blood impulses unbroken from his primogenitor, who, lost on the hunt, recognized the bear—not in the forest, but as a heavenly constellation in the night sky he remembered from outside his smoky cave—and fought his return to those he loved by remembering and guiding on its bright sign.

I am not good at farewells. Jessie, you know better than anyone alive as I have never given justice to your mother's parting. Her screaming:

"I'm telling you, Rusty! Get it through your thick head. It's too late. The constant confusion, the stumbling and stuttering, the hallucinations! We were only playing house since I found a man I could have children with. Since Nate's arrival—we've been playing madhouse! Looney bin!"

"I-I-I'm going flying to Malaysia! It's work!"

"'Going flying.' Sounds great. I sure hope they've put you in charge of something," Madeline mocked. "Nate, Jessie, and I are leaving you. We are moving in with Nate's father as soon as his new house is finished. I sincerely hope you didn't let this go too long. That you don't die. But I am going to marry that man. Divorcing you. I'm—"

You didn't let her finish. You shoved her in the stomach, knocking the wind out of her and you, Jessie, the supple, healthy branch out of the stump of my tragedy, screamed in Russian: "Убирайся, сука! Убирайся из нашего дома!"

Get out of here, you bitch! Get out of our house!

Madeline barked that she didn't want you anyway. And even though you screamed, that made you happy, I'm sorry your mother said it. I'd always wanted you and did my utmost as a father. With promises to you I would return to Cedars Hospital once home, I booked the familiar Flight 77, Dulles to Los Angeles.

38

Paul Sedaka, little precious life left in him, pushed Lucky-Boy's bicycle, a kind of wheeled crutch, along the haul road leading out of the Tiger Mine. The road curved. He came around it to find the Mercedes-Benz Unimog blocking his further passage. Bishop, a submachine gun slung low on his hip, a handgun in his fist, stepped out of the foliage at the former CIA officer's agonized approach.

"…Bishop…" Sedaka puffed and stopped.

He gasped for air, each exhale a moan. Bishop made no move to assist him.

"Talk."

Tears streaked Sedaka's bloody, dirt-smeared face.

"They have 'em… They took 'em…"

"Where?"

"Help me, Bishop. I'm begging you. I *am* begging you. Please."

"Where are the warheads?" Sedaka reached out to Bishop. The bicycle fell. Bishop aimed his pistol.

"Five—"

"A ruin. Don't let me die."

He stumbled one… two steps and collapsed to his hands and knees.

"Four."

"A hydro power plant. Never finished… Fifteen miles… Mercy, for the love of God."

"Keep talking."

"Talking…" And Sedaka rocked back, whimpering, sitting on his fat, blooded bottom. "Talking… yes. There's a rail line. Tell you everything… You'll help me, right?"

"Three."

"Wait! The plan was to remove the warheads. Okay? I'm helping you… Transfer one to a new rocket…"

"The other?"

"Selling to Ramadan Moon. Some Saudi sheik has provided a train. Hush-very-hush. Those crazy bastards plan to… detonate it. I dunno how, I swear."

"Where?"

"ENOUGH! LOOK AT *ME*!" Sedaka covered his face with his blood-soaked palms. He fought to remain conscious, struggled with each gulp of air. He was the color of paper, and the rocky dirt around him shone red with his blood.

"Two."

Sedaka whimpered. "…Don't know… I'm dying, Bishop."

"Where do I find this plant?"

"…just… up the road. Only one road. You can put me in the back of your car? Right?"

Bishop said nothing. Felt nothing.

He screwed his eyes shut and screamed, "Muir was the better man!"

Bishop leaned in, considering, accepting it as Sedaka's all. He lowered his gun.

"You're a saint. You're…"

"One." Bishop turned his back on Sedaka. He mounted into the Unimog.

"I have money, Bishop! Two million dollars, half of what they were going to pay me. You can have it all…"

Bishop engaged the engine. He worked the 4X4 around. Sedaka scuttled to the bicycle. Tried to climb onto it. He fell.

"Bishop! You fuck! Don't leave me!"

Sedaka struggled to right the bike. He climbed onto it again. He wobbled forward and fell again.

"Bishop!" But Bishop was gone.

This didn't mean Sedaka was alone.

ALL THAT WAS left at the scene of the firefight were the bodies of the dead Americans, the dead Malaysian Ramadan Moon rebels, and some of their number critically wounded, too far gone to have been treated or taken. These were the men the mother tiger and her cubs came for first. Among this streak of big cats was a male of two years with inquisitive wide eyes and large ears its face had yet to grow into. Had it not been born with a lame paw, it might have already ventured on its own from the streak; as it were, he kept somewhat apart from the others. He felt the natural pull of the solitary hunt in his heart-beaten river of blood. The inevitable breakup of the family bond. The tiger sniffed at blood dripping from the monstrous red-orange and spongy petals of a swath of the parasitic corpse flowers growing from the tangled roots of chestnut vines. He sniffed, licked his nose, and got his first taste of Paul Sedaka. The tiger swished his tail, acquired the traitor's living scent. He loped off alone.

KUALA LUMPUR COWERED silent and frightened at midday the day after the election riots. Suspension of civil rights with the martial-law curfew. The implementation of a Malaysian State of National Emergency. Schools, businesses, banks, and storefronts: closed and shuttered. Transit and city maintenance suspended. Trash blew along abandoned streets and thoroughfares as I drove Lara from the cemetery hill through the city, heading for the North-South Expressway. Royal Police manned checkpoints and barriers. Military presence in daylight was minimal, even slightly bored, but where it made itself known, the firepower backing it was lethal and deep. Special Branch darted in their vans and unmarked cars, making searches and arrests of those on lists long ago written in hopeful anticipation of a day like today; allow the searches, detainments, and the arrests of those who, for whatever reason true or false, petty and yearned for, were deemed politically or socially undesirable.

Absent of all civilian traffic, vehicular and foot, the capital city shocked Lara with its vast emptiness and she remarked on it. How, when alive with constant humanity, she'd never seen it as it was: imposing and prideful. Hollow aspiration without soul. A monument to money-trading and its supremacy. She told me about the Batu Caves and the chalk line she'd drawn to lure Bishop into the trap conceived by Sedaka for the enemies of her country pushing from within to consolidate their power. She told me how he followed her and scared her into the truth of her life. How her revulsion and rejection, her horror at his violence, had grown into something everything she valued told her was irrational, and she asked me, "How can everything you learn about falling in love, you plan for, you search for, polish with rag dreams until it's radiant inside you and that you believe—because it's how the stories all go—that around a warm sunny corner, on a shaded parkland path, the movie line or a sweaty dance floor you find it reflected by the one you were meant for: how can all that be wrong to what's become of me?"

I slowed for a police checkpoint. My diplomatic plates and the American Embassy Consular Officer flag, with its blue field and thirteen white stars in a circle around a white capital-letter C like a college rah-rah pennant mounted on the hood of my vehicle, allowed us to pass through. A sullen, though respectful, look and the brusque wave of a white-gloved hand.

"I've made a mess of love over and over and over again," was all I gave back.

She looked hopeless in her distress. I heaved a sigh. No idea how to answer her any better. She was my new sister. I wanted to make a good impression. I didn't want to talk about Tom because, while wishful, I didn't believe we would see him in Thailand. Yet, without bolstering her hope, I knew I wouldn't be able to get her to leave the place of her birth, her life, her home without connecting it all to a future with him.

"I don't know if Bishop—uh, Tom—told you, but I'm a lawyer."

"I didn't believe it when he said so, but now that we've met… Spies use lawyers."

"You'd be surprised how often. That's how I met him, but that's a whole 'nother story I'll let him tell when he meets up with us. Your question—about love—it reminds me of our highest court. Our Supreme Court Justice Mr. Potter—ugh—that's not, that's the movie"—my brain was spiraling—"it's, pot-pot-pot of stewwww—Jimmy Stewer—" I pounded the wheel until my head cleared: "No! Stewart-fucking-Potter!"

I blinked to diffuse the tears welling from my embarrassment.

Lara took a steadying breath. She spoke with cautious tenderness. "Russell, there is something wrong with you, isn't there?"

I didn't answer. Police at the entrance to the Expressway stopped me. I unrolled my window and held open my diplomatic passport. The officer commanding the roadblock barked back the cops approaching us. His eyes lingered on Lara in her purple hijab. They exchanged customary Muslim greetings and once again we were let through. The highway was empty. From its height we could see smoke plumes surrounding the city rising to gathering storm clouds from the burning and terrorized towns and villages of the countryside. I accelerated.

"I have a brain tumor. I don't want to talk about it so don't you. All I was trying to say is there was this Supreme Court case. It was about this French film. Called *The Lovers.*"

"I've seen that movie."

"People were trying to say it was obscene so they could ban it. It's funny how my condition is, is, is muddling my reasoning while connecting things on links I never saw. I watched *It's a Wonderful Life*—"

"Another good one."

"Oh, don't get me started: it's a horror film—but Mr. Potter, the good guy—"

"Bad guy—"

"Reminded me of Potter Stewart, the Supreme Court Justice— but you also got Mr. Potter and Jimmy Stewart—and the case about that movie about love and lovers and how Potter Stewart famously ruled that the Constitution protects all obscenity except hardcore pornography. He said, 'I shall not today attempt further to define the kinds of material I understand to be embraced within that shorthand description; and perhaps I could never succeed in intelligibly doing so. But 'I know it when I see it.'"

"Is this your tumor again or am I to follow all the up-and-down and back-and-forth directions of all that? Because it sounds like you just degraded what Tom and I have and called it porn."

"No! I meant, I can't tell you why love appears between two unexpected people in unexpected places, but 'I know it when I see it.'"

Lara brightened and I saw my father in her glow.

"You're seeing a doctor?"

"I did. I will."

"You'll be okay. God wouldn't have brought us together, only to tear us apart."

I felt my fondness growing. I pushed my puzzlement aside and said, "Years ago I wrote a contract with God. He's doing his part. We just have to make sure we keep doing ours."

THREE HOURS LATER, stalled in refugee traffic headed for the Thai border—most of it streaming away in the opposite direction after having been turned around at the Malaysian military checkpoint we approached—Lara was tense and silent as my vehicle's diplomatic status was recognized. I was pulled out of the traffic jam and ordered to wait at the side of the highway.

For ten minutes we watched every vehicle, with and without Thai license plates, turned back from the heavily guarded checkpoint. A tank allowed for zero argument.

A Malaysian Army major, palm on the butt of his holstered pistol, two combat-armed enlisted men in tow, approached my window.

"They're not going to let me through," Lara said.

"They're going to let us both through."

I whirred down the glass.

"Good day, sir. Passports please. Her papers as well."

I showed the major my diplomatic passport, remembering not to hand it over. He snatched it away.

"I'm on a diplomatic mission to our embassy in Bangkok."

He kept my passport. "Her papers. Now."

I stuck a hand into my breast pocket. He tightened his grip on his pistol, his finger looping through the trigger guard.

"Take it easy. This paper should take care of things."

"Slowly."

His eyes met mine. I could tell he already anticipated the color the paper would be as he stepped away from the doorframe where he'd shielded his body and now blocked the window view of the two soldiers behind him. I saw them share a look. They shared his same suspicion. I withdrew two bundles of US Federal Reserve Notes. Cash: $2,000 of it.

"Are you offering me a bribe?"

"No. But I'm sure there is a tax to cross the frontier. I trust you to pay it for me."

The major shoved the bills into his tunic.

"There's been terrorist activity between here and the border. Our station has been closed. Much safer for you to wait in Bukit Kayu Hitam until we clear the area tomorrow."

"We don't have that kind of time, Major."

He leaned in, questioned Lara in Malay. Whatever they discussed, he was satisfied. He tapped my other breast. Felt the second bundle I'd shoved there in case. He crooked a finger, and I gave him another thousand dollars. That's when he noticed the satchel that contained the rest of the cash, the gold, the handguns.

He motioned for it. "Give it to me."

"That's sensitive diplomatic material protected under international treaty. You'll have to kill me to take it from me."

He narrowed his eyes. He aimed his pistol. "Give it to me."

I swallowed. Lara spoke again in Malay, cold and disdainful without looking at him. The major's lips sealed, corners of his mouth twitching. I could swear his eyes turned red. He shoved his pistol back into its holster, returned my passport, stepped away, and signaled us to proceed.

We passed the tank. The highway beyond, jungled on both sides, threatened with its stillness.

"What did you tell him?"

"That what was in the diplomatic bag wasn't his biggest worry. That killing you, could be explained."

"Thanks, I guess. What changed his mind?"

"I advised him, when they identified my body after killing me, they'd uncover why this paperless Malay-Muslim woman was being secretly driven out of the country by a US diplomat. Colonel Ibrahim would personally see to it he was hanged."

"You lied."

"There's a lot of that going around."

39

THE HYDROELECTRIC POWER plant on the Kinta River was erected to never see the light of day to illuminate the dark of night. It was the purest example of how $30 billion international investment is used in boondoggle schemes by profiteers to siphon money from the public trust to private pockets while the World Bank lenders disguise their profiteering as public value. Only the rail spur Bishop had come alongside four miles back was functional, confirmed by the military freight engine and flatbed that now rushed past. Bishop identified the rail line on Fendy's map. It connected to the main civilian and military infrastructure, where, at the end farthest from where Bishop headed, the train would make its return trip to the international transport hubs of harbors and airports.

His mini-truck's light bar strobing, he approached the high barbed-wire gates protected by a hastily erected machine-gun nest. Four UTK commandos guarded entry to the installation. One stepped out, arm extended, palm outward in the universal sign for stop.

Bishop depressed the accelerator to the floorboard. Fifty yards out, the commandos opened fire. Bishop dropped sideways, one hand gripping a submachine gun while the other held the steering wheel steady under the hail of lead. The windshield blew out first, then the armor gave way. The puncture-proof tires withstood the gunfire longer than Bishop had hoped. They shredded as the Unimog plowed into the gun emplacement. It took out the machine gun and its operator as the three other Malaysians dove from its path. Bishop rolled out into the tangle of sandbags and heavy automatic weapons, blind-firing his submachine gun until he'd emptied the clip into his remaining three targets.

Bishop tossed his spent magazine in exchange for two more he stripped from the bodies of the dead. He snatched a radio from one of the troops. He loaded grenades, handgun, and the rest of his ammo from his duffel. He let himself through the gates on foot. The road ran a fair distance through jungle, then crested a rise. Bishop activated the radio.

"Calling, calling: CVN-65, CVN-65. Come in. Over."

The sky had darkened with storm clouds pregnant with impending rain. The pungent zing of ozone smelled like a backyard summer pool and thickened the air. Bishop took to the edge of the road, a quick dive into thicket if he needed it, and moved along the asphalt. He changed channels. He put out the call a second time, continued moving, waiting for response. Called again, waited, moved, switched channels:

"CVN-65, are you scanning these channels? Do you copy? Over."

Shy of the crest in the road, Bishop veered into the heavy green bracken, shadowed black without daylight. Crouched, he crept toward the vantage point. If they had a second emplacement, or were sending reinforcements after his attack, they would wait to hit him as he came over the top.

"Repeat, repeat: CVN-65, CVN-65, do you copy? Over."

Aboard the USS *Nimitz* primed for action, ready and hoping for vengeance after losing contact with their battle group's SEAL team during the firefight that wiped them out, a second-class petty officer scanned radio frequencies in the aircraft carrier's communications center. He perked up. Bishop's voice crackled over his headset.

"This is a US Agency asset on the ground calling CVN-65. Do you copy? Over."

The petty officer flipped a switch, enabling his and Bishop's voice to broadcast over his workstation speakers.

"This is CVN-65 *Nimitz*. Identify yourself. Over."

The communication division officer walked over and stood behind him as he locked in Bishop's frequency.

A Malaysian voice cracked through: "Who is this? This is a Malaysian military channel. Get off this channel!"

Bishop ignored. "Repeat: This is an Agency asset on the ground in Malaysia. Codename TITAN," came Bishop's response, using the van Eijk codename. "That's Tango-India-Tango-Alpha-November, attached under Chief Resident Sedaka, Kuala Lumpur Embassy." He took a breath, knowing he was pushing it. "Since 1968. Over."

The radio operator glanced skeptically at his lieutenant. Skepticism was a luxury of opinion. She nodded he continue.

"Go ahead, Titan. Over."

BISHOP PARTED A CURTAIN of foliage in front of his face, revealing the half-finished hydro power plant spread across a small, cleared valley before him.

"I have an IMMILFOR B. Authentication designation: Romeo-five-seven-seven-X-ray. Over."

His eyes scanned the concrete frames of incomplete buildings; reservoirs and turbines; massive and rusting transformers; concrete abutments of a dam that would never be finished; and a quarter-mile beyond: the two nuclear missiles on the flatbeds, on which Colonel Ibrahim's engineers were in the process of changing out the warheads. The first was in mid-transfer to a gleaming SS-23 Spider short-range tactical missile on its mobile launcher. The second warhead was being prepared for transfer onto the waiting electro-diesel locomotive. Where Ibrahim commanded his soldiers, these irregulars were taking orders from a pair of Middle Eastern men in business suits beside an armored pearlescent white Hummer.

"I have visual on two hostile Scud missiles, nuclear-tipped, twenty to thirty enemy personnel, and a light tank. I am requesting immediate military assistance. Over."

Of the enemy personnel Bishop observed, ten of them were Ramadan Moon working with the civilians.

Aboard the *Nimitz*, a code officer processed Bishop's given identity and IMMILFOR designation.

"Be advised, Titan, we are confirming. Over."

The Malaysian voice returned. "I repeat: You must get off this frequency!"

Keeping to the jungle, Bishop scrambled to the facility.

From the *Nimitz*: "Titan, why isn't this transmission encrypted and on the proper channel? Over."

A group of UTK commandos in a jeep, backed by a light-armored personnel carrier, rolled out from the main group, heading up the road toward Bishop's position.

"Things are a little tight right here, *Nimitz*. Hold on a sec."

From the aircraft carrier, skyward to the Ultra High Frequency Follow-On (UFO) satellite system, back to earth at Point Magu, California, and routed Top Secret Secure to the CIA, Bishop's ECHELON-triggered communication was simultaneously reaching Harker from NSA, Fort Meade, established and backstopped. Two separate verifications, Harker's Oval Office promise of Black all the way, had slipped his grip.

"Confirm TITAN and IMMILFOR B designation," Harker ordered Meryl Hofmeyr, "but do not engage or assist."

BISHOP WAITED until the jeep drew parallel to his position. He opened fire. The commandos scattered to cover. The quad-machine guns on the APC swiveled to Bishop's position and chewed it apart, but Bishop was already gone, scrambling behind a ten-foot-thick concrete wall of the abandoned dam construction.

ABOARD THE *NIMITZ*, the code officer swiveled his seat to the division officer. "We have CIA confirmation, ma'am."

"Asset and IMMILFOR designation?"

"Affirmative, ma'am."

The lieutenant donned her own headset. "Titan, this is Lieutenant Jackson, USS *Nimitz*. Can you go active-secure on HAVE QUICK, over?"

"Negative. I cannot…change channels. Can you…buzzer our friends? Over." His voice came breathless, gunfire in the gaps between words.

"Can do," Lieutenant Jackson replied. "In the meantime, what are the target coordinates? Over."

HALF THE DISTANCE to the launchers, among the structures and engineering works of the complex, Bishop braced his back against a massive nest of turbine piping and caught his breath. Two grenades hit steel above his head. One dropped and detonated harmlessly between the heavy piping. Bishop hurled his body through the doorway of a control bunker as the second grenade bounced behind him. Shrapnel from its explosion tore into the backs of both his legs. He cried out in pain. He twisted back through the doorway, threw suppressing fire, and dodged deeper into the facility. Legs giving out, he stumbled and crawled.

Two infantrymen stormed his position. Aiming high, they missed. Bishop shot them down. Dragged himself behind a transformer. He read his GPS.

"Four-tick-twenty East Long, by one hundred—" Another pair crashed toward him. He dropped them one after the other. Reloaded and finished with: "By one hundred-tick-thirteen North Lat. Over."

In the open downhill area beyond the structures, the warhead transfer almost complete, with a grind of treads, the tank moved position. Its cannon rotated toward Bishop's location as more troops advanced. The tank fired. Undershot, the round blasted apart transformers. A steel-lattice transmission tower crashed to the ground; powerlines whipped through the air.

Bishop hauled himself to his feet. Stomached the intense pain in his legs and lurched from the cover of the pump turbines down along the penstocks piping. A second tank shell obliterated the position he vacated. He was close enough now to hear Colonel Ibrahim shouting orders to his men who bolted the first warhead into the new launcher.

A crane lifted the second warhead. Swung it toward the waiting flatcar.

"That's your own position, Titan. Confirm. Over."

Bullets tracked toward Bishop from Malays converging from all sides.

"Affirmative, *Nimitz*. Danger Close Range on my position. And we're running out of time here, Lieutenant. Over."

"Hold tight, titan," said Lieutenant Jackson.

"He's called in his own position—is that correct, Lieutenant Jackson?" came the voice of her executive officer behind her.

"Yes, XO, correct as stated and confirmed." Into her headset: "Titan, we are launching a strike force now."

TWO BOMB-LADEN F/A-18 Super Hornets catapulted from the deck. They hit afterburners, ripping into the storm clouds and out of sight.

PAUL SEDAKA WAS not going to die from his bullet wound. A combination of luck, bad aim, lousy diet, and lack of exercise had seen Ibrahim's bullet punch into his belly fat and angle through a thick roll out his side, missing any vital organs with its path. Having staunched the bleeding after getting over his crying jag when Bishop abandoned him, he'd stuffed the toe of a sock into the wound and wrapped it with the torn-out lining of his wash-and-wear suit jacket—$89 out of Hong Kong fucking wasted—he'd righted the bicycle and tottered Bumi-barefoot forth. He was almost to the entry gate and allowed himself an acerbic smile. Oh, all the mistakes and misfortunes life heaped upon him, but Paul Sedaka always came out on top. Always had, always would. Western man rising from Asian morass. And half the dough safely stashed in Zurich. Stupid ass Bishop.

A blur in the foliage drew Sedaka's jaded eye. He stopped. Saw nothing in the rainforest shadows. He pushed onward. Another flash. Maybe orange, or was it black? Something there. Sedaka tried once more to swing a leg over the bike frame. He winced as the sock plug popped and his wound tore open, but his foot found the far pedal. He pushed onto it, choking back his pain, shaking his lightheadedness as blood resumed its flow. With a cry, he threw his weight forward, pushing off the ground, striving for the left pedal, finding the left pedal, striving for balance: finding balance. With massive effort and horrible ache, he pedaled wobbly to the middle of the road, aiming for the gate. He gathered speed.

A young tiger can leap thirty feet through the air. The kinetic force of the bullet was nothing compared with that of the tiger that hit him like an airplane, claws embracing Sedaka from behind, one pinning his arms while the lame paw raked his chest. The tiger sunk the lances of its teeth deep into the back of Sedaka's neck, clamping, crushing—mouth filling with delicious blood—as momentum took both of them down.

Sedaka twisted, twitched, shook, and was hammer-shook back.

The tiger's jaws tightened with every second of life draining from the man.

Sedaka was dead and the hungry May tiger fed.

40

GOD'S CONTRACT.
The one I wrote the night after I secured Muir's secret confession to Charlie March's murder and his own retirement ten years ago on Captiva Island.

God [the promisor] signed over to humankind [the promisee] free will and I signed on the dotted line for faith: a spiritual choice to blaze a path toward grace with strength and compassion, our best morality, our humblest forgiveness, our purest love, and truth.

Years later, Jessie, when I'd gone to Vladivostok to bring you home, I finally got my chance to meet our promisor. It involves you, my feelings for you upon your adoption. I've never told you this—never told anyone, in fact—until I told Lara as we left Bukit Kayu Hitam for the border and the unknowable threat of terrorists we'd been warned were operating in the free zone before Thailand.

Trying to assuage Lara's fears and keep her positive—her mind off of Bishop behind us onto what might lay ahead—I'd been describing you to her. I'd gone through my Bullwinkle versus Boris Baddy/Baddy Boris and Natasha at Vladivostok airport and she'd asked, "How did you come to the decision you were best-suited to take on Jessie's life, to erase her past, take her from her homeland, to completely change her identity?"

"Life in a Siberian orphanage isn't a catwalk—"

"Like modelling? What do you—?"

"No! Cake-cat—er, cakewalk." I deflated. "Which was a slavery thing so that is what Siberia was. Forget it, I—"

"I meant you: How did you know you were right?"

Jessie, I didn't. I didn't think I was right, and I was frantic to reject you.

The night before I was to appear in Russian court, I'd been billeted in a barracks dormitory once part of the Soviet Army base eight hours north of the city, where your village had existed for over three hundred years. A base abandoned since the fall of communism, most of the former soldiers—their government unable to transport them home—were off in the wilderness, woodcutters employed by the oligarch-controlled timber industry, and by "employed" I mean enslaved. I couldn't sleep. I doubted myself and my mission. I doubted you and the vast damage from the abuse inflicted on you: your person, your soul, your psyche since your birth. I looked at my marriage, the nature of my work, all my fears for who I was, who I wasn't, my track record of personal failures.

Cockroaches crawled over my face as I tossed atop the cot. Fully dressed—including my heavy coat, boots, and the fur hat I'd bought off a drunken sailor in the Vladivostok flea market pulled over my face— I pushed off the cot, out the thin plywood swinging doors into the subzero (Celsius, not Fahrenheit) air.

Across the rutted dirt road was a birch grove. Narrow trees tightly packed, trunks with stark white bands of bark glowing in the metallic sheen particular to birch, broken by horizontal tiger stripes of depthless black lenticels. There was no discernable path between the trees. I wandered among them, meandering crookedly through those spaces wide enough to accommodate my shoulder width, raging out loud at my fears, my inadequacies, and my sudden certainty I would be incapable of fatherhood.

A heavy hand grabbed my shoulder from behind. There was more power in it than I'd ever felt in my life. It checked my emotions and held me immobile. I knew not to turn. I heard a voice louder and more familiar to me than my own. I knew, although only I had heard it, it did not come from me or from any human. It came from the world and the universe beyond, and I heard it like a radio call through the speaker of my soul.

God spoke.

RAIN SQUALLS HIT as I slowed our approach to the Malaysian border crossing. True to the army major's warning, the white-painted brick station was abandoned; its surface, pockmarked red, showing through as if bleeding from scores of bullet strikes. Smoke churned through broken windows. Office equipment cluttered walkways and littered the road. Strewn paperwork whipped by the wind, danced, and turned to soggy pulp across manicured lawns that bordered the highway to where it hung in the fauna of the surrounding forest or landed to sink in mud. Behind the building, the hulks of two civilian cars and a government truck burned, snapping and stubborn.

Farther on, arson-destroyed customs sheds smoldered.

Fences and gates lay cut-through, torn, trampled.

The pass-through kiosks lining the frontier were demolished. Windows smashed, doors hanging by hinges or ripped free and strewn.

Not a soul in sight. Whoever had done this had met no resistance.

"We haven't seen anyone in a long time," Lara said in a hollow voice.

I glanced at her, but she stared at her open hands as if looking for a bird that had flown or the Host unreceived.

We cruised through into the buffer-zone no man's land between Malaysia and Thailand. I swished my eyes between the road ahead, my mirrors, and Lara.

"You never told me what God said to you."

I smiled, remembering.

"Your smile's crooked," she said.

"Is that a fact?"

I hoped I sounded light.

She gave me the same crooked leer right back. "Mine too."

"It wasn't words. At least not as we know them, but I understood. He said, 'Trust life.'"

Two plumes of black smoke billowed ahead. As we neared, a family van and a Volvo SUV revealed themselves flaming in a ditch at the side of the road. The husks of bodies—two families' worth—engulfed in fire were clearly visible inside. In front of these, a Mercedes-Benz sedan and a BMW sports car idled in our lane, doors flung open and empty. I slowed as little as possible to avoid the suitcases and boxes, the strewn clothing, pieces of furniture, toys, and other possessions that littered the blacktop. All four vehicles had Thai license plates. Hijacked before making the safety of their home.

"Give me both guns, one at a time," I said.

I'd made it through the detritus when two young Malays—one with a dripping *parang* machete, a .45 in his waistband; the other carrying a military assault rifle—stepped from the drainage ditch at the side of the highway. Both wore headbands with Arabic characters and the Ramadan Moon symbol finger-painted in blood.

I hit the gas and shot forward as the assault rifle barked semi-auto in our wake.

Lara handed me the first pistol. I primed it. Unlocked the safety. Handed it back.

"Put this back in the satchel. It's yours. Safety off. Like a camera, point and shoot."

The second gun I primed and shoved behind my belt. In the rearview mirror, I caught sight of the two killers, along with a third, pile into the BMW. Two others were visible wrestling a terrorized teenage Thai girl—clothes shredded and hanging in rags from her muddy naked body—back into the forest.

"Now, give me one of the gold bars."

I was pushing the Ford to its limits, but the BMW was swift and gaining. I closed the gold bar inside my left fist.

"When do I use the gun?" Her voice was steady with forced calm.

"Guess it's like pornography—" I was scared shitless. "You'll know it when you see it. Now, hide the bag behind your feet under your seat. Gun's live, so keep the bag from moving around."

"Gun's snug."

The BMW pulled parallel to my window. The killer with the assault rifle brandished it in a signal for me to pull over. I wasn't about to, but they accelerated until, halfway past my front end, they side-slammed us. Lara gave an involuntary cry. I fought to keep control of the wheel as they slammed into us again, cranking their wheel into our Ford. I braked.

"Ahead!" Lara pointed through the windshield.

The Thai border crossing loomed out of the rain three hundred yards away. Fully manned and backed by soldiers. At 80 mph, the distance closed rapidly.

The BMW braked, beginning a turn in the opposite direction—driver assumed I planned to flip a bitch—preparing to cut my parabola. Instead, I hit the gas and shot past them.

100 yards. The border gate raised.

The BMW driver threw his car into reverse and executed a perfect bootlegger turn, his front coming around and hacking across my quarter panel, throwing me into a 180-degree spin that I completed in a stall.

I pulled my pistol, ordering her: "Leave your gun where it is. Wait on my obscenity."

Lara looked at me like I was crazy. She powered open her window, leaned out and backward-screamed at the Thai soldiers all stares and motionless. "Help us! They're going to murder us! Help!"

The Thais did nothing. There was nothing they could do—any first shot across the border an act of war.

"Get back in. Let them pull you out."

"Are you insane?!"

Yes. Completely fucking out of my mind.

"We'll get ourselves out of this."

The three Ramadan Moon killers surrounded us.

"What? Tell me what we're going to do. Russell!"

"You'll have to feel me. Feel it when I do."

"I don't know you!"

"It's in our blood."

"Now's not a good time to test that," Lara said, fighting back trembles.

The leader tapped the squared-off end of the *parang* against my window. Motioned me to get out with a sharp gesture of his free hand. His partner, muddy toes wiggling in sandals, covered me with an old AK-47.

I raised my hands. In one I had my US Diplomatic Passport. The other, I lifted my gun into view by the trigger guard and upside down.

"Throw out gun! Throw out gun!"

I kept the gun in sight. Activated the window. Lara squeezed her eyes shut and crouched into herself. I dropped the gun. It clattered on the asphalt. I raised my passport. The killer grabbed it and hurled it to the ground.

"Out! Out! Out! Out!" He brandished the sword.

The Thai soldiers at the border watched. They did nothing.

I opened my door, whispering back over my shoulder at Lara: "Give me as much time as you can before you open the door."

"I'll never open this door!"

"We have to control this. You'll get out, but struggle. You have to stay within reach of the bag."

I stepped out. The thug outside Lara's window pounded and shouted. She watched my feet knocked out from under me.

"On your knees, infidel dog!"

I pushed to my knees. My executioner prayed out loud. He lay the blade of his bloody *parang* against the back of my neck.

Lara threw open her door, watching me in baffled horror as her hopeful rapist yanked her out of the Ford. He shoved the rifle's barrel between Lara's breasts, his eyes like a snake regards a birdling first-flight-fluttered to the ground.

She screamed at him in Malay, although this time she didn't invoke Allah as she knew He couldn't reach them.

The Malay rapist ripped her hijab from her head and with it a handful of trailing hair. She yelped in pain, he threw the purple scarf into the mud and tugged at her, but she held fiercely to the doorframe and twisted her feet until they mired in the mud.

I opened my left hand and dropped the brilliant yellow bar of gold—

CLINK.

Time froze. My executioner snatched it up.

"Where you get this?!"

He came around in front of me and swung his *parang*, slapping my face with the blood-sticky flat of the blade.

"There's more! Shit! Lara, fucking give it to them!"

The obscenity struck Lara as intended. She snapped at her captor in Malay, pleading with him. He looked to his leader—all three men's eyes danced greedily—and his leader gave a jerk of his head. The young thug released Lara. She grabbed the satchel, her hand dropping inside of it, and pushing it into her captor's chest pulled the trigger, blowing his heart through his back.

I drove the top of my head between my executioner's legs. He swung the *parang* but with little power and less aim. I felt it slice across my shoulder as I rolled for my gun. Seized it, thumbed the safety, and fired. Lara's gun barked from behind the Ford, drawing the third terrorist's instinctive full auto AK-47 return fire back at her.

The *parang* clanged as it hit the pavement and my executioner whipped out his pistol. We both fired. My training was better than his. As he staggered and fell backward following the trajectory of his physical thoughts, I was already drawing down on our final target, who raked rounds along the Ford away from Lara for me, finger never slackening his trigger.

I triggered two rounds into him as his last five rounds ripped the air at twice the speed of sound past my skull. I heard four of the five rounds hit the Ford. The fifth hit the pavement. Whining off, it bounced into my skull.

41

CAUGHT BETWEEN the unfinished substructure and superstructure of the hydro power house, Bishop made an assessment. His leg wounds were weakening him from pain and blood loss. A gash across the side of his head, more dramatic than dangerous, poured blood across his face, his left ear, and down his jaw and neck. He was dizzy; lethargy competed with adrenaline. His ammo was low. He had two grenades left, a full-clip handgun with two clips in his waistband. He slapped his last magazine into his submachine gun. Malaysians hunted him on all sides but had yet to find his location. He'd allowed himself to be pushed back, away from the train and the Spider missile, but he knew: for the airstrike to destroy the WMDs while they were inert and unable to be armed, he needed to be closer.

Bishop gathered every ounce of strength left him. He allowed himself a single, clear memory of Lara. Her face with its mix of bravery and earned trust when he'd kissed her goodbye. He pulled the pin from one of his grenades and lunged forward.

He hit the corner of the substructure building and tossed the grenade. Shouts greeted it before it blew hello and Bishop lurched into the rain of dirt, gravel, and debris, selecting targets and firing as he ran through their midst. He was at the base of the quarter-built dam, the smoldering transformer housing construction ahead to his left, the concrete lip of the tailrace: a massive, angled sluiceway that normally would extend over released river flow. Here it extended over an area like that found on the seashore. Gravel and mineral deposits, rich with silt and overtaken by yellowing weeds, ochre vines, and rubbery green vegetation spread below in place of running water.

Fifty yards ahead were the two warheads.

Also, a second tank. There was nothing Bishop could do about it. Its turret swung his way.

Bishop threw his last grenade behind him, stalling his pursuit as the tank cannon erupted with fire. The shell screamed in, overshot into the five-hundred-foot-high dam wall. The blast concussion hurled Bishop over a wooden rail along the lip of the tailrace wall and into the riverbed.

Colonel Ibrahim met the two al-Qaeda representatives with *Salam Alaikum* and *Wa-Alaikum-Salaams* and accepted a large aluminum case opened against the elder terrorist's chest to reveal it filled with US dollars. Two more similar cases were taken from the Humvee and carried to Ibrahim's jeep.

Bishop couldn't move or think. The chlorine-like scent of ozone was thick and pressing. Thunder cracked and rumbled in the heavens. Raindrops came hard and heavy. Reviving. Bishop shook his head as faces turtled over the concrete lip. He rolled to his belly and they saw him.

He crawled for the safety of the overhang as they rained fire.

"The railway is cleared to the harbor," Ibrahim said. "The ship provided is cleared for passage to New York City for agreed-upon arrival on—"

The approaching roar of jet aircraft drowned out his words as all eyes lifted skyward.

Bishop pulled himself out of the range of the gunfire. He knew he'd been hit again. Didn't know exactly where. He didn't care all that much, cared more that he was able to smile at the all-American scream of the Hornets as they whipped overhead, hitting thruster, and gone.

He whispered to himself the last thing I'd told him, my own form of a blessing in my own code—the best I knew—passed on before I'd walked with Lara for the Ford.

Bishop whispered, "War reviled, deliver raw," and, screaming down the sky, the pair of two-thousand-pound GBU-10 laser-guided bombs took out the train and the Spider missile launcher, disintegrating both Muir and Chief Petty Aiken's ATROPOS warheads as a full complement of anti-personnel dumb bombs wiped out all life in the power plant above him.

THE THAI BORDER GUARDS stared in amazement at and with deep admiration for Lara, who dragged my body from the site of our gun battle to their border pass-through.

The chief border officer spoke to her in Malay. "I cannot allow you to bring his body across. I'm sorry."

"He isn't dead," she said in English and slapped down my passport. "This is a US diplomat with international transit privileges."

She invented that last part. If I'd have heard it, I'd have kissed her.

The Thai officer signaled a military medic from among the gathered crowd. He validated her words and shouted orders to his team, who rushed forward as my body was pulled across.

The border officer held out his open hand. "Your passport?"

Lara pointed at the site of our gunfight. "I'm not going back." And she plunked down the single bar of gold. The border officer examined it. Considered it.

The passage of two US Navy jets hitting their afterburners overhead encouraged his decision.

He placed the gold bar back into Lara's hand. She placed it into the satchel. He held out his hand once more.

"Oh," Lara said and relinquished her pistol.

"You'll accompany your companion in the ambulance. Refugee status granted."

The border officer pushed the button that unlocked the pedestrian baffle gate. As Lara ran to the ambulance, every man she passed performed the traditional *wai*. Palms together at the level of their chest, they bowed.

I WOULD HAVE liked this to have gone a different way. The lies, the wishful thinking I've given you in these pages... All the excuses I've made about my tumor's pressure on the Wernicke's area and on the lateral sulcus: "which is the part of your brain where the parietal and temporal lobes meet beyond," so sayeth Dr. Rashmi.

Difficulty with names and places, times, hallucinations.

"Убирайся, сука! Убирайся из нашего дома!" Get out of here, you bitch! Get out of our house!

Not a lie. Not some kind of temporal, visual illusion. That all happened. You were there, Jessie, and she got out.

Madeline left us.

She took your brother and she left us for good, and though I said I'd booked Flight 77 to Dr. Rashmi, I did not use that ticket. I did not see Dr. Rashmi next in Los Angeles but in Malaysia.

Needless to say, the making love to your mom was the pail dropped in the well of lies, and her pulling me back to fuck me once more, hard "for good measure," her destruction of our family. A fucking of my life, yours, and Nate's. Like one of my crosswords, I'd finished all my "Across" clues and answers but run out of room at the end to start over now at "Down." Or do I have that backward? Name now one man who would have tried harder than I and suffered more for it.

Maybe the sandaled fella whose slug slam-dunked my head got his passel of virgins (in paradise, are they use-once-and-that's-it—one shot, one thrill, no exceptions for eternity?), but my sex life hadn't been good—as in had been nonexistent—for three years and wasn't made any better after that scene in the kitchen two days before I wound up here.

Bangkok.

And thanks, Jessie, as if you didn't know; thank you forever for defending me. I know I was not physically fit to take this mission, and I deceived everyone to have it. To get to the field as an ops officer as Nathan had once promised me. The only excuse I can offer is my only consideration at the time: to be with Bishop once more before the tumor slayed me. And nothing could replace meeting Lara, saving my own sister.

I mentioned wishful thinking and here is my idea on that. Lead is known to cause cancer; can a bullet cure it?

EMBASSY OFFICIALS directed my ambulance to Bumrungrad International Hospital Neuroscience Center. Lara stayed at my side, holding my hand all the way to the surgery, where the doors slammed in her face. She stood there, staring, all emotion crushed out of her, until a nurse steered her to a waiting area, where she was met by CIA Officer Danielle Getz, operating undercover as a commercial officer liaison to the US-ASEAN Business Council. Late twenties and in her first overseas posting, Danielle became Lara's temporary best friend and bird dog at the order of her Agency mentor, Deputy Director Meryl Hofmeyr.

Of the 238 brain-penetrating gunshot wounds from my own state of Maryland last year, 208 were fatal. In the United States, overall, 20,000 people die every year from gunshot wounds to the head. With 53 percent of them from suicide, I'd say that rigs the survival rate a bit in my favor. Really, depending on the angle you look at that, there is a bit of active achievement boosting the 95 percent fatality rate since suicides are aiming for success. Those of us with the desire for fatality failure—8,000 of the 20k (there's a 7 percent group of gunshot-to-the-head fatalities considered "cleaning" accidents, although it strikes me a little odd because, what is it the NRA likes to say: "Guns don't kill, people do"?) out of the 285 million Americans—we'll look for every bullet-hole loophole to increase the 5 percent survival rating, even if only 3 percent of us come away from it with any kind of quality of life. What I'm trying to say—for the record— suicide hurts everyone.

Bullets cause damage two ways:

1. The crush of the bullet.
    1.1.   Where it goes in—
    1.2.   And what it cuts through.
You can keep it in mind this way, Jess. Like real estate, it's location, location, location.
2. The shock waves of the bullet. The tissue surrounding the bullet path is stretched and deformed by a temporary vacuum as much as forty times as large as the bullet itself. The risk of damage/size of vacuum is determined by:
    2.1.   High velocity/large caliber.
    2.2.   Low velocity/small caliber.

As I ever endeavor to be difficult, I went under the knife with that one mixed up—a low-velocity, large-caliber wound. Couldn't have been a better deal for me. The ricochet cut the velocity from 2,300 feet per second, fatal shock-wave terri- tory there—to about 900 fps, less than a .22 rimfire. Closer to a high-end pellet gun. Small-caliber bullets with low velocity are typically soft lead and less aerodynamic. Tend to flatten and fragment for maximum bullet crush and tissue damage. The large-caliber rounds—like the one that punched into me, was a full metal jacket: aerodynamic with zero fragmenting. These usually double their damage by lengthier trajectory, cutting their way in and cutting on out.

My bullet entered the right frontal lobe tip toward the forehead, well above the base of my skull, passing through no vital brain tissue or vascular structures as it ran into the hard mass of my "beautifully dense and enlarged" (that's what Dr. Rashmi said) glial tumor.

"The bullet did half my work for me." She smiled at me when I'd regained consciousness after my second operation she'd flown in to perform, and had—"move your fingers… Good"—talked me through.

But she'd never have needed to come had it not been for my Thai neurosurgeon, who'd not have had a gunshot wound operation to perform had it not been for the emergency room surgeon, who upon my CT scan performed the emergency craniectomy to decrease pressure inside my skull, who'd not have proceeded had not the EMT inside the ambulance who'd administered the Glasgow Coma Scale, accurately scoring my level of consciousness and gauging the severity of my trauma based on my EVM (Eyes, Verbal, Motor) responses and calling them in to the hospital, who'd not have had a test to administer had not the combat medic administered first aid and stopped the flow of blood from the wound and hooked me to a plasma bag, had it not been for Lara, who took my wallet before dragging me, found the number for Madeline, who contacted Dr. Carlson, who telephoned my neurosurgical team of Dr. Susan Levy-Waxman and Dr. Rashmi Patel at the Cedars-Sinai Medical Center's Maxine Dunitz Neurosurgical Institute.

Had it not been for Muir recruiting my father from the US Navy and had not my father cheated on my mother in Malaysia, I would not have had Lara to drag me over the line and I would be dead.

"Soumountha could tell that Koumphan was exhausted and near his end," comes Lara's voice. *"She begged him to return to the palace and find someone to heal his wounds. He told her that he could never return to his kingdom without her. Even though he might die, he would never abandon her and live separately from her. It was impossible."*

In the middle of the night two days after my second surgery, I awakened from my medically induced coma to Lara at my bedside reading to me from what appeared to be a children's book of foreign fairy tales.

"'I will never give up Soumountha. Never!' With those words, Koumphan abruptly transformed himself into hundreds of thousands of chickens flying into the sky. One of the chickens swooped down, grabbing Soumountha, and then flew back into the sky…"

She smiled to see my eyes. I noticed she held my hand. From the combined and equal warmth of our connected palms, our fingers interlaced, it became clear she'd been holding on for a long time. A combination of the surgery and the no host bar's no holds barred worth of drugs left me—for once in my life—speechless. Not so much without words—I had words carooming up, down, sideways, and roundabout the cavity in my skull forty times larger than my thoughts, only I couldn't transmit them to my voice box. I squeezed her hands three times. "I love you," like I do with you, Jessie, since you were little, and Lara squeezed back three times, plus one. Maybe she knew the game, returning an "I love you too," or maybe she just wanted to one up me. Maybe she stuttered.

All she said was, "They expect you'll have a full recovery. The doctor went over your EEG and PET scans with me. Your brain activity is better than they'd dared hope."

I squeezed again. She stroked my face, leaned in, and kissed my cheek. She stood, squeezed my hand once more, and released it.

"I'm leaving now. You'll see me again."

I wanted to ask if she'd heard from Bishop, if anyone had, if God be praised, he'd appeared. The fact she didn't mention him at all told me all I needed to know. I gazed hopefully after her, but she didn't look back to see hope lie.

The leaving part had been certain. The seeing her again, however, had not meant in the hospital, or, as it turned out once I'd been discharged, an encounter in Thailand. Lara was gone. Vanished.

Dior droid Danielle Getz explained that Lara had been granted citizenship under my father's name that went uncontested but allowed that she'd kept her van Eijk surname. Per Meryl Hofmeyr's orders, the Agency reclaimed the remaining cash. All the gold: missing. I signed an affidavit swearing to the veracity of my statement. The gold had never left my possession our entire escape to the Malaysian/Thailand border, and I had used the gold and cash that was missing to bribe our safe passage. Whether believed or not was inconsequential.

Where had Lara gone? Danielle had no idea. As her passport had not logged in any system, it was likely she was either still in Thailand or had—and this was Danielle's opinion—slipped back into her home country of Malaysia.

"We talked a lot. We became BFFs, Russell. Lara couldn't get over bailing on her life. She's one of those *Moslems*, you know. You shouldn't have expected otherwise."

I smiled my crooked smile, my heart breaking for my sister. I finished the rest of my paperwork with the hospital, my insurance—ultimately, I was trapped into using it—and the Agency. I was given a four-month paid leave, after which I would return to duty "on assignment" back with the Office of General Counsel from the Directorate of Operations until such a time as my health review on fitness for duty, and my operational and conduct review for Malaysia and for the loss of private citizen, contract agent Nick Albro, and CIA Officer Tom Bishop, could be adjudicated.

I ARRIVED HOME June 1, 2001, to the 1938 brick-built Tenleytown, American Traditional townhouse Madeline fell in love with the first week after we started dating. Madeline had not yet taken Nate and left us for her entertainment attorney-lover/baby-daddy—"Construction on our Malibu beach house won't be completed for at least three months. Jessie, we're building you a room. I don't know what's wrong with you: our backyard is the beach!"

"Шлюха. Сука," you said. *Shlyukha. Suka.* Cryptic Cyrillic crossword clue: Op. of Purity's princess. [English answer: Whore. Bitch.]

"Stop with the foreign talk. You know you won't be living here because this house—*my house*—"

I'd bought and gifted Madeline the house as a wedding present the day of our marriage. Legally it was hers.

"—I'm selling it with the divorce. Good luck with whatever dump rat-trap your father finds for you."

42

THE CLOSED HEARING on CIA activities in Malaysia took place June 4, 2001, by the Senate Select Committee on Intelligence, Hearing Room SD-106, Dirksen Senate Offices. Fifteen members, eight of a majority and minority membership from each of the Appropriations, Armed Services, Foreign Relations, and Judiciary committees, with the remaining seven composed of four members of the majority, and three members of the minority, backed by aides, clerks, and lawyers, faced Acting Director of Central Intelligence Jeremy Harker III, his two attorneys—one devil for each shoulder—and Deputy Director Meryl Hofmeyr. Questions and answers had volleyed back and forth like a ball between a pair of country club tennis teens for two hours, sounding the *Plop-ploop-plip* of hollow air, and the session was winding down to a love-love finish with as much gravitas as the keepers of a porcupine petting zoo might muster in acknowledging they have no intention of addressing why they'd opened the gate for guests to have entered in the first place.

Blah, blah, blah "…the appreciation and gratitude, not only of this committee, but of the entire free world for your alertness and diligence in preventing a would-be dictator from seizing power in an emerging and friendly Asian state, and for stopping the proliferation of rogue nuclear weapons to Third World groups who would use these to settle their differences."

For emphasis, the Committee chair, Senator Anthony DiBacco of New Jersey, projected onto a monitor the satellite photo enlargements of the warheads at the Ipoh Tiger Mine, Ibrahim's helicopters lowering them to their flatbeds.

"Before closing this session, Director Harker, do you or the deputy director have anything else to add to these proceedings?"

Harker leaned forward to his microphone. "Thank you, Mr. Chairman. We've spoken to the bravery and sacrifice of our Navy SEALs, and of the heroism and success of our Navy aviators, I would like to add two names to the record who have not been mentioned today. Individuals who also made the greatest sacrifice a man can make, an officer and his agent who together tracked those rogue Soviet weapons from Eastern Europe to Kuala Lumpur and died so that the people of Malaysia might be spared the horrors of nuclear enslavement and annihilation. I would like entered into the record the names of Thomas Bishop and Dand van Eijk."

"I believe a moment of silence would be appropriate here," said Senator DiBacco.

Everyone in the chamber bowed their head. The moment passed.

DiBacco grasped his mic. "If that is everything—"

"One more thing, if I may, Mr. Chairman." The Minority Chair Senator Margot Silverman, spoke in a voice louder than her diminutive size might suggest.

"The chair recognizes the Honorable Senator from Indiana."

"Thank you, Senator DiBacco."

The very blandness of Harker's expression broadcast how unexpected this interruption struck him. It went from bland to blanched as Senator Silverman produced a letter, the same letter being distributed in copies to each committee member by two of the senator's aides. Harker glanced at Meryl Hofmeyr. If she noticed, she did not let on.

"I am holding a letter that has come into my possession from a Ms. Lara van Eijk. You might know her, Acting Director Harker, as she is the daughter of your mentioned fallen officer Dand van Eijk and the goddaughter of former CIA officer Dr. Nathan Muir, late of Princeton University, who recently and tragically was murdered."

DiBacco cracked his gavel. "We have heard testimony today to the effect that Dr. Muir's death was a suicide."

"I assure you this letter will clear all of that up soon enough."

Harker, fury blossoming red from neck to forehead, covered his mic and leaned across his left-side lawyer to Meryl.

"Do you know anything about this?"

Meryl accepted a copy of the letter at the same time Harker and his attorneys received theirs. While the two attorneys sped-read, Meryl Hofmeyr laid hers in front of her and smoothed it like a doily on a tea table.

"Mmm, huhn," she offered and turned her most professional smile to Senator Silverman.

"As you'll notice," said the senator from Indiana, "Ms. van Eijk's letter is notarized and includes a sworn statement taken and signed under Federal Court witness, that all contained herein is the truth as she knows and witnessed it. Sir, her letter references a certain Operation ATROPOS. Now, this is something from way back, oh, in 1968."

"It would please the chair if the Honorable Senator from Indiana would explain the relevance of this ancient operation to today's proceedings."

"I'm getting there. Mr. Harker, would you like to explain, or shall I?"

Harker consulted with his attorneys. He took his hand off his microphone.

"I am aware of the operation, Senator. As it remains at the highest Top Secret classification and thirty-three years in the past, I would need more time to organize a briefing on this subject matter."

Meryl Hofmeyr leaned into her microphone. "I am fully briefed as of May 9 of this year to all details of Operation ATROPOS and would be happy to speak to it."

"Madam Deputy Director, is this in support of Acting Director Harker's sworn testimony of today?"

"No. It is in opposition," said the CIA proto-Teletubby, nowhere near as frivolous now as she had always seemed.

The wheels on the bus go round and round

Round and round

Round and round…

"I am also aware of the contents of this letter, since events in Malaysia and Thailand brought Ms. van Eijk into my personal care and protection."

"Meryl," Harker snapped.

But they don't teach tap dancing at Arthur Murray. She ignored the man.

"As we would not like, any of us, left—ahh—and right, to see this blow up another Iran-Contra in our faces, I would also, at this time, call in our deputy director of Counterintelligence, who has led the investigation into Acting Director Harker's… mmm… *handling* of our Malaysian operations," and here made the tiniest of bird noises, a *tsst–ts–tst* kissing of her tongue.

The chamber erupted. The gavel pounded, but it was the entrance of Silas Kingston, chief of CIA Counterintelligence, that quieted the room. The overhead lights gleamed off his helmet of brown hair tightly curled against his skull; a modern-day Quintus Arrius returned to Rome. His disdain cut like an alligator's smile, half as friendly and twice as deadly.

Sing along with Teletubby Laa-Laa:

The wheels on the bus go round and round…

Crushing Harker into the ground.

Kingston was sworn in and, as these things often—strike that, usually—go, his opening statements peeled back what from the outside looked like the untouchable prickly shell of a Malaysian rambutan that was our Operation ATROPOS and revealed it nothing more than a pliant cover for a soft, sweet fruit beneath.

"The greatest danger to our national security as it pertains to Malaysia isn't their terrorism sideshow but the Chinese twenty-three percent stranglehold on the Malaysian population; their seven-million number is one of the largest concentrations of overseas Chinese in any country. In World War Two, Imperial Japan failed at the creation of a Greater East Asia Co-Prosperity Sphere. They failed due to their implementation of this policy by warfare and subjugation. China has taken over their quest for this Asian holiest-of-holies—Asian dominance presages Chinese world dominance—through economic warfare and control of regional energy production and distribution."

Here, his eyes met mine as if pinpointing me his future Judah Ben-Hur for some purpose I did not yet comprehend.

"Malaysia is one of the three main terminuses—Taiwan and Hong Kong the others—whereby China infiltrates the West, and the US infiltrates the East. Acting Director Harker's Mickey Mouse hide-the-nuclear salami operation threatened to upset decades of the most sensitive anti-China work in this country, where…"

The wipers followed the wheels, horn followed wipers, doors, driver, babies, mommies… all around the spinning globe.

Harker's conference room buffet ended that day, giving him all the time in the world to dance around the golf course, and I hoped I would never see him again until with a final putt he dropped into a hole in the ground. But getting rid of Harker didn't bring Muir or Bishop back to life nor Lara back into my life and our family. June warmed into a sticky-seersucker-shirt-back, hot-sidewalk July in Maryland. Meryl Hofmeyr retained her position as President George II pushed through his new director and, if you can count this as a Harker legacy, cameras rolled with our CBS partners.

Busy with my fitness hearing and exculpation for my involvement in the "Mishaps of Malaysia," as Meryl Hofmeyr dubbed them for the infantile, I paid little attention to who Harker's permanent replacement was and so, true to form, allowed him to get off on the wrong foot with me when I was introduced one Saturday in a random corridor after delivering a set of CONPLANS to Lynn Kingston in Ops Planning.

I won't bother you with her story here but to say: the apple that fell from the Silas Kingston tree sits withered and rotting at its base. This young, sad, and haunted beauty, closet drunk if ever I could sniff one out, whom I'd grown fond of in the past months since returning, saw me to the door of her office, releasing me right into the path of a boy-of-a-short-ruddy-fellow in jeans, tennis shoes, and a leather bomber jacket.

"Russell, meet George," Lynn Kingston said.

He looked over, innocent and congenial as can be—way too friendly to be anything but physical plant staff. "Good to meet you, Russell," George said. "Keep up the good work."

"Yeah, you too." I grinned back.

I swear, he looked like a janitor from Queens. It didn't help that he told me he was on his way to the CBS filming taking place that morning in the Old Headquarters lobby. He was hoping to get a part as an extra. To make things worse, I clapped him on the back and wished him a "Break-a-leg, Georgie."

That afternoon, Director George Tenet walked off set and returned me to the Office of General Counsel at permanent status.

The television production was the talk of the Agency—which was also now the name of the series, *War on Terror* deemed by CBS Legal as "triggering" to international markets—and everyone was excited for the Hollywood red-carpet premiere in our largest auditorium fondly known as the Dome (after its Sunset and Vine twin). The invitation should have provided a clue that our focus was a bit off:

THE DIRECTOR OF CENTRAL INTELLIGENCE
and the CBS TELEVISION NETWORK

CBS

cordially invite you and a guest to attend
the Premiere Screening of the new CBS series
THE
AGENCY

7:30 p.m.
Tuesday, September 18, 2001
CIA Auditorium, George Bush Center for Intelligence
McLean, Virginia

Reception to follow
CIA Original Headquarters Building
Main Lobby
Business Attire

Guests please R.S.V.P.
no later than September 11, 2001
(with social security numbers)

Please bring your invitation along with photo identification – allow time for security access.
(THIS INVITATION IS NON-TRANSFERABLE.)

In case you missed it, look closer, Jessie. The R.S.V.P.
Meryl Hofmeyr refused all my requests to contact Lara. She informed me in no uncertain terms that Lara wanted nothing to do with any of us. Especially me.

"She's my sister!"

"Too little, too"—*tsk-tsk*—"late, I'd say," said Meryl.

She said that Lara wanted only to be left alone. That Bishop and I and both our fathers had ruined her life. "And if you do somehow find her—which I assure you, mmm, you won't, had better not—she has been instructed to contact my office directly. And you, hnn? You will be dealt with to the"—tongue-click—"very best of my capabilities."

I could give a shit.

I hired private investigators in DC, New York, Los Angeles. They discovered zilch. Convinced that Meryl and her Teletubbies were hiding Lara from me, I chose to remain hopeful. Bide my time. Still, why didn't Lara reach out?

Word came back from my investigator in KL. A series of photos. Lara and her friend Fendy out shopping. Lara wore a high-fashion Hermès headscarf. She was smiling. I paid my investigator and told him to leave her alone. At least she'd found some shred of happiness.

MADELINE put the house *I'd bought and paid for* on the market and opened it for showing the weekend of July Fourth. Did it all patriotic with flags and bunting and pinwheels in flowerpots for showings with Liberty Bell cookies baked and on a platter. I asked if she'd like me to dress as Uncle Sam and pass out lemonade.

THE LAST WEEK of August, I was still deep in my physical and speech therapy and had not put any effort into finding a new home. Around the time Madeline was gleefully calling the West Coast, discussing her and Nate's new life-to-be in Malibu, I received a welcome but unexpected call from Muir's secretary Gladys Jlassi.

"I've found it, Mr. Aiken."

"Found what exactly, Gladys?"

"Nathan's will. I was boxing books as I'd promised myself I'd do for months now. It was tucked into the pages of one of them. If it hadn't fallen out, I wouldn't have found it at all," she said and laughed.

The upshot was Nathan Muir had left me his Princeton brownstone. We discussed lawyers, New Jersey probate, Madeline's sale of *my* house, and we scheduled the second Saturday of September for Jessie and me to come up. Permanently. Then, having said our goodbyes and about to disconnect, I shouted into the receiver: "Gladys!"

"Yes, Russell? You okay?"

"The book, what book did you find it in?"

"I'll go get it. We'll have a look."

She described the book as having a plain red-leather cover entitled *Prometheus Vinctus* by Aeschylus. Translation: Prometheus Defeated.

Content unsurprising, I asked her the edition and translation. While not a valuable book per se, it was an edition from Macmillan's Classical Series of 1898, and Gladys chuckled and went on to tell me, according to the bookplate, Muir either borrowed or lifted the book from Harvard's Widener Library and never bothered to return it. The translation, she told me, was by E. E. Sikes and St. J. B. Wynne Willson—

Coincidentally or not—this being Muir—cousin to crossword puzzler Wynne.

—both of them scholars and lecturers of St. John's College, Cambridge.

I asked if she could find the pages it had been tucked between.

"I can do you one better. Nathan must have accidentally left the open book in the sunlight. The old paper faded a rectangle in the shape of the envelope."

I didn't speak. Silence returned from the other end of the call.

"Do you say it, Gladys, or do I?"

"Dr. Muir never did anything accidentally," she said. "The top part of the fade mark is perfectly in line with the print. It's created an underlining effect. Shall I read that line?"

"Please."

"It's most of a sentence. Shall I read the three words that begin the sentence on the line above, and the last half of the hyphenated word that ends the sentence below?"

"Please. Yes." I wanted to reach through the phone and grab the book out of her hands.

"'In Europe, the *wren* is described by Norman peasants as the fire-bringer.'"

My heart clenched.

"Is the first word of the underline *wren*?"

"Why, yes, Mr. Aiken. Does wren mean something to you?"

"Read me the first line of the page."

"'If fire has to be stolen from heaven, the most suitable thief is most naturally a bird.'"

I pressed Gladys. Had she noticed any other fade marks in the book, any notations?

"This fade mark here was definitely where I discovered the will. It's Roman numeral page nine. I know it was at the front of the book and the envelope shadow matches perfectly."

"I don't doubt you, Gladys. Just look through. Every page. It's important."

"It always is." She chuckled. "It's times like this I can feel him smile down upon me. You too, Russell. I will call you back."

We hung up.

The wren, the bird. The bird, the wren. I feared it something Dr. Rashmi had cut from my memory.

Muir's codename was Prometheus.

Prometheus stole fire = Muir stole nukes.

What was his quote? His last lecture about the Vietnam War, the Montagnards (ah, Lucky-Boy); Muir had been speaking to me through his student—what was her name?

I'd not been having problems with names since my surgery, although the radiation therapy had jumbled things. The Asian student. The American girl of Korean descent. Jewel? No. That was his first wife…

What had his student—the girl who called me—what had she said? It was Aeschylus too…

"Of my own will I shot the arrow that fell short of my own will."

Prometheus's arrow = the nuclear Broken Arrows.

And something to do with a tie clip. Broken. Arrow-shaped.

"Nothing do I deny. I helped men and found trouble for myself."

Helping men = abandoning Lyndon Johnson's and Director Helms's horrifyingly inept Operation ATROPOS. Ditching the nukes. Claiming them lost.

Found trouble for himself = Sedaka; Muir's murder.

There had to be something else in the book.

GLADYS CALLED ME back two hours later.

"Two other places. The first, still in the introduction, Roman numeral page fourteen. The word *Lastly* is circled."

"In ink? Pencil?"

"I'm sorry, I mean traced. Like he used a pen without ink. An indentation around the word."

"Lastly," I said.

"That's correct."

"Okay, we'll follow his advice and read it last. What's the other?"

"It's a glass stain from a drink." Her voice warmed with fondness. "The stain is whiskey. His Macallan 25. I know the glass. It was his favorite. Cut crystal. His only one. He'd lost the others. Told me a thousand times his wives broke them throwing them at him."

I could hear the old man saying that.

"It's cut with a bunch of angles. The pattern looks like a gold starburst sticker they glue on awards and such. That's on page one hundred and twelve. Kind of a half-circle at the bottom, it perfectly frames a bit of dialogue, like from a play, that goes on to the next page, where the whiskey frames the rest of it."

"Read it to me."

Gladys cleared her throat. "Here goes. I'm not an actress, though."

"You're great. I'm ready to write it down."

"It's an exchange between 'P.' and 'Ch.'?"

"That would be Prometheus and Chorus."

Gladys cleared her throat again. "P. Prometheus: 'Necessity can break my bonds.' Ch. Chorus: 'Who then controls the action of necessity?' P:"—and I whispered it along with her—"'The three Fates and the Furies.' Ch: 'What! Not Zeus? Is he subordinate to these?' and Prometheus says, 'Yes, he cannot escape Fate.' Chorus says, 'Why? What has Zeus to do with Fate, except that his supremacy is *fated*—author emphasis, not mine—'to last forever?' And Prometheus answers: 'This I will not tell.' And that's it for that one."

"Except *our* Prometheus does tell. Go to *Lastly*, please."

"'Lastly,'" she read, "'if we assume that Prometheus was the fire-drill, the most salient characteristic of the myth—the stealing of fire—cannot be explained, or only by very forced interpretations, as a'—set in quotes—'*disease of language*; whereas, on the supposition that Prometheus was a superhuman being—"

Gladys laughed out loud.

"I'm sorry, Mr. Aiken, but that sounds *just* like our Nathan, doesn't it? But it's written that way in 1898. I promise you."

My mind was elsewhere…

The Class of 1946 Garden is on the west side of Maclean House.

"You certainly still have the disease of language. Rusty, you've never needed an oracle. Common sense, yes. Oracle, no. Want my advice?"

"Therapist hasn't done me much good," I said.

"Never will. They're in business to stay in business. I'll solve it all for you right now. Won't charge you a penny. Russell: be more tree-like."

He rubbed his hands. He studied me a moment. He gave me a smile that brought back all his youth and none of his tragedy. Along with all the perceived betrayals he'd never done me, hard as I'd complained, and he'd insisted were for my own good. I smiled too. No crook in it—at least I tried my best. I'd never seen it before, this mood in him. Happy resignation? Knowing sadness with a grin? Teasing as always. And my puzzlement increased as my better-new smirk expanded.

Muir tapped me once, twice on the shoulder and pushed to his feet. I gave him an up-from-under look that expressed my disappointment with his advice. He fixed me in a direct stare, not needing me to speak to articulate my inner dialogue.

"You'll get it," Muir said. "I have zero doubt in you anymore. No more the tromped-on tiger-striped cat, you. But here's one that's easier. You want it in English or the French?"

I'd learned the English. Maritain's Range of Reason. *"A coward flees backward, away from new things. A man of courage flees forward, in the midst of new things."*

Gladys had continued: "'—a superhuman being—anthropomorphic from the beginning—his theft of fire is illustrated by similar stories told of numerous birds and beasts and heroes, none of whom had anything to do with a fire-drill.'

"That's the whole of the sentence. The paragraph as well. There is more on the page."

Birds, beasts, heroes...

Wren, Tigers, Bishop, and Lara?

I'd gone quiet when Gladys spoke again, "Are you still there, Mr. Aiken?"

"Yes. Thank you. You've been amazing."

We said goodbye and I promised I'd see her soon with Jessie.

I WAS SLEEPING in the spare bedroom, where I'd been since returning home. *My* home. For Sale by Madeline. My wife. Divorcing me and taking my son to live with his disinterested Hollywood father in Malibu, where Nate could scamper out and dig sand on the shore until he was old enough to jump waves, then old enough to surf. Would I know him? Would Jessie and I get to see him? Have him visit? Ever again hold him or feed him or tuck him in and sing "Day is done"?

I stared at the tiger-stripe pattern of shadows thrown by my Chinese elm tree *I'd* planted the first year we'd lived here, and I spoke to the gathered darkness:

"Amy Kim."

I got out of bed. At the back of my mind, I noticed a sound, out of place at—as the travel clock I was using for my alarm showed in glowing radium—3:28 a.m. I grabbed a scrap of paper. Couldn't find a pen. Switched on the light. The sound, an idling engine, increased in sudden volume as a car raced off. Squinted through the shutters at its receding taillights, sound and distance computing in my head, I knew it had been idling in front of *my* mailbox. I didn't recognize the car from any of the neighbors. A prospective buyer? I hoped not; they'd give Madeline more than she was asking for *my house*. On that, I vowed not to tell her. I clicked a pen. I wrote:

Wren = Grave.

Why the bird? Why the grave? The wren is Prometheus... The grave = Muir's Grave?

My deliberations returned to words he said to me ten years earlier at his place on Captiva Island:

"This job kills everyone it takes. Some bang-to-the-back-a'the-head quick. Others cut by cut, one piece carved at a time. The knives: that much sharper as the years grow long and leathery tough. Once we realize that and admit it—admitting it, Russell, that's the important thing—we work to minimize the collateral damage among those on the outside as we defend against all the ways it stalks us. Until we force it to take our unnatural lives by natural causes in the last and tightest corner we've backed ourselves and lured it into."

I wrote:

Grave = Spy's Last Huddled Corner.

But Muir didn't die of "natural causes." The bird might've. Not Muir, and he knew Sedaka had Lara under his thumb and was coming for him. For ATROPOS.

"First Rule of Thumb: An officer in the field builds an escape hatch."

I wrote:

Spy's last corner = ESCAPE HATCH.

IT WAS AFTER FOUR by the time I'd finished, and I lay back in *my* guest bed—

Why is it me who's using the travel clock, when it's your mom who's splitting?

—listening for the return of the car. Wondering not who—this would have to be Meryl Hofmeyr's work, as she'd found her new calling with Silas Kingston and his Counterintel janissaries—but why? What else had our Malaysia operation, me the last living heir, kicked up?

Why had Silas Kingston stared at me so?

But the car did not return. I listened to the birds outside beginning to wake and twitter and to call. I fell back asleep and dreamed about the dozens of birds in my yard alone, the hundreds of thousands that cohabitate our human cities. Swarms of birds fill the air. Like us, like Muir's wren, like Lara's *nyak* demon transformed into a thousand chickens: all of them die.

43

"I saw a seagull fall out of the sky once," I commented over my shoulder.

Jessie rode in the backseat among a few of her boxes that hadn't fit with our suitcases in the trunk but contained things so important to her she wouldn't allow them into the movers' truck last week to Princeton. "Dead. Seagull just dropped out of the sky."

"Where? Malibu?" She smirked.

"Ha-ha. It was a beach. But in Cuba. A place called Caiberién."

"Maybe someone shot it."

"I didn't hear anything."

But I had. Nina on the shore of a lake she'd lived as a young girl. She'd pulled my cheek against her chest.

"Hear my heartbeat. Listen to how real I am."

The sound of love made to the tempo of warm water, rolling, falling, pulling back to roll again, and afterwards a seagull's cry yanked our attention to the sky in time to watch a seagull die in mid-flight and plummet to the ground.

I checked my rearview. The gold Chevy Impala lurked five or six car lengths back as it had since we'd picked it up on Connecticut Avenue, onto MD-185 North and the Interstate 495. When I slowed, it slowed. It followed onto the US-50 and then the US-301. The driver was alone—protocol if they weren't planning an intercept and/or had forward surveillance ahead.

"Heart attack, maybe."

"Or a brain tumor," Jessie purred.

"Thanks a lot, birdbrain."

I was trying to talk about anything else but closing the book on Madeline—wife and mother. This larger-than-a-single-wren-dead-birds conundrum had puzzled my mind for days.

"I got a birdbrain boss," I said. "Talks like she's a Teletubby."

Jessie giggled.

"You know? Has all the little noises and bird twitters."

"Anything that tweets is a birdbrain. How long till we get there?"

"We're past halfway. I'd say hour and a half, about."

Halfway. We'd entered Delaware and were on the DE-1 toll road. Here the follow car should drop back and peel off the highway as the lead car drops down and resumes the tail behind. I kept my eyes forward, waiting to pick them out. Nonchalant about it.

"You looking for someone, Dad?"

"What I'm thinking—this dead bird thing—you never see any. Not really. I mean, where are all of 'em?"

"I saw a dead crow by the swings once," Jessie said and suddenly burst out laughing.

"What's so funny?"

"Turn up the radio! Turn up the radio!"

I did.

"да иди ты!" Jessie's go-to: "Are you kidding me! Shut up!"

"What?" I didn't recognize until it reached the chorus. Nelly flippin'-a-frittata Furtado: *I'm Like a Bird.*

"You're so weird, with things like that always happening to you, Dad."

I'm serious about this bird thing.

"For the number of birds—all around us, all the time—you'd think you'd see more dead ones. Birds don't have a care-removal-disposal industry for their dead like we do. It's not all cats and snakes climbing into trees. We should constantly be seeing dead birds under our feet. *Constantly.* And they don't live that long."

"I saw a dead man once. In the river where they'd let us play behind the orphanage."

I glanced at her in the rearview. Sour face. Siberia. Bad memories.

And the gold Impala five or so cars behind us.

"Just think about the flocks of pigeons in the city, the sparrows—thousands of 'em. Clouds of blackbirds along the highway. The crows that pass over our neighborhood in endless squadrons. What about all the birds that live in our trees? I never find any dead birds anywhere in the yard—year after year. Where do they go to die? Must be thousands all over the place, all dying all the time."

I glanced back. She was bored. Russian memories had dampened her spirit. She stared out the window.

"I wonder what Mom's doing."

I didn't care. I was on to something and I'd been studying. I had the intel on the matter. "Jessie, the bird population in this country is in the billions. Compare that to the, say, 300 million people. That makes us only *3 percent* in numbers. I mean, compared to birds. Now, stick with me, we're doing a math problem here. There are approximately 870 human deaths per 100,000 populations annually. So per 1 million that'd be 8,700, times 300 equals 2,610,000 dead people each year, which is only—remember— 3 percent of the amount of dying birds. And we have a sophisticated system to keep our dead out of sight, but birds, what do they got? I'll tell you what they got—they got nothing."

"The birds outside won't live as long as me. And Nate for instants."

Ha! She got the word wrong, but she was listening. Compelling stuff. I hit the steering wheel.

"My point exactly! Every time we step outside, it should be raining dead birds."

I took a deep breath.

"My question: corpus delicti, meaning 'show me the corpse,' even though it doesn't, but corpus delicti: the trees must be filled with nests filled with bird skeletons," I said.

"At the new house, I could climb a tree. You think there'll be a good climbing tree? I've never found a nest."

We entered New Jersey. The gold Impala remained on my tail.

As we neared the Municipality of Princeton, I crept over to the far lane. I cut my speed, closing the gap between us, then at the last moment whipped across four lanes barely making it onto the New Brunswick Pike. The gold Impala didn't even attempt it.

We'd shaken the one tail and I drove around circuitously—"You lost, Dad? There's a boy over there you could ask directions"—until I was certain there was no one else behind us.

GLADYS, watching for us through the window, rushed out the front door. A big hug for me. An attempted one for Jessie, who didn't like hugs—three attempts on her defenses until, liking or not, my little girl got one.

"That's more like it," Gladys said.

She grabbed Jessie's small hand. Left me behind as they marched inside. Gladys's voice trailed behind. "Come see how I did your room. If you hate it—and I'm hoping you will—we'll get right away to setting it right. I love arranging rooms. Don't you, Jessie?"

Jessie raised her shoulders but gave the smile that mimicked mine. And Lara's. With the little crook as she'd practiced it. Like a new leafy branch off my old tree. I watched them enter. Endings and beginnings. A twinge of fear. I let my aibohphobia get the better of me. Are we not drawn onward to new era? Are we not drawn onward, *we few*, drawn onward to new era?

Rallying, I followed the pair inside.

I sat in Nathan's chair. The chair he'd been murdered in. I'm glad Gladys kept it and Muir's bloodstains embraced me at Muir's desk. I'm glad I was there. I allowed the warmth of memory buoy me over the weight of sadness.

Jessie had asked as we'd turned past the corner postal box and onto Muir's street: "Grandpa Nathan who gave us the house. Was he killed here?"

"I told you he was, yes."

"You think he's a ghost?"

"You believe in ghosts?"

She nodded.

"Then I bet he'll be around for you, sweetie."

Gladys had left the *Aeschylus* for me on the desk. The blood-red pebbled-leather cover stared at me. Or was it Muir's ghost staring over my shoulder? I planned to go through every word of the book, but first—before Meryl could get Silas Kingston to throw a tap on me—I pulled Amy Kim's number off my cellphone and dialed it from Muir's land line.

She must have recognized the number on her caller ID because she answered, "Yes?" and said nothing else.

"Do you recognize my voice?"

"Yes."

I had no idea what Muir might have explained to her about signs and countersigns, setting agent meets, or his use of figurative shorthand.

"I'm calling you of my own free will."

She said, "I shot the arrow."

Great, Amy!

I said, "Tie clip."

Amy disconnected. Since I gave her no day or time, she would meet me day and time at the last place she heard Muir say those words. The place he'd lost his tie clip. His final Monday 9 a.m. lecture in the Prospect Garden under Dimitri Hadzi's pipe-playing centaur.

THE NEXT DAY, Sunday, I took Jessie to the Episcopal Church at Princeton in the University Chapel. It appealed more to the students than the formal high church worship practiced at the massive, gothic Trinity Church of Princeton. As it appealed more to the students, so too had it appealed more to Muir. Jessie and I walked in the warming sunshine of the September morning. Gladys had stayed the night on her offer of spending the first few weeks with us as we acclimated to our new home.

"It's no problem at all, Mr. Aiken. My boys are grown, my Albert is gone. It will be purely a pleasure for me."

Jessie commented, "I invited Gladys—she said I could call her that—to come with us, but did you know she doesn't go to church?"

"She's Muslim."

"She goes to a mask," she said.

"Mosque. Yeah, I know…" I trailed off. The gold Impala followed behind us, keeping its distance.

We entered the church. I sat in the back where I could watch the door, but I had no way of knowing if my tail came inside. Amy Kim did. Come inside, that is. We didn't see each other perfectly.

When we left, the gold Impala was gone.

MONDAY MORNING, I left Muir's brownstone before Jessie and Gladys were awake. Two hours before Amy Kim and I were set to meet—no sign of the gold Impala—I walked toward the Prospect Garden, blending in with the mass of students and professors rushing about with registration, orientation, and all the other excitement of the day before the first day of classes. I bought a coffee from a lad with a cart. I waited at a bus stop on Washington Road. Watched cars and pedestrians. I recognized no one. Identified no threats. An hour and a half later, at 9:15 a.m., I ambled down the Streiker Walk pedestrian lane and entered the garden.

Amy Kim rose from the edge of the fountain.

"Hi," she said shyly. "You're Rusty."

I didn't correct her.

Thanks a lot, Muir.

"The wren," I said. "It was a wren, right?"

She bobbed her head yes.

"We need to find it."

She pointed. "I buried it there—"

Her mouth clamped shut. A funny look on her face. Someone approached us from behind me. I spun, shielding her with my body as if that would do any good in any kind of long run. No outrunning bullets.

Striding toward me—jeans, tennis shoes, baseball cap—

"Lara."

She stopped. She didn't say a thing. Her expression showed a kind of distrustful optimism.

"Why did you come back?" I said.

"How do you know where I've been?"

"From Malaysia. Why did you come back? You were there last month."

"I've never gone back."

"I saw photos."

"They weren't me. I stole the gold, Russell. I had to escape. I said goodbye to you—I don't know if you heard."

I raised my voice. "I assumed you meant goodbye till tomorrow. Not months and months without word. What were you thinking?"

"I'm sorry for that." She flashed her eyes to Amy Kim. "She was at the church yesterday. Who is she?"

I said, "Ms. Kim. Muir's last recruit."

"Well, his student. I'm Amy. One of you want to tell me who she is? Why all the hugger-mugger?"

Hugger-mugger, one of Muir's favorites.

"She's my sister. Half-sister. *Sister.*" I redirected to Lara: "Meryl Hofmeyr told me you wanted nothing to do with me. You've certainly acted as if that were the truth."

"Mrs. Hofmeyr is a bitch."

"Mrs., huh? Her mister ought to be somethin' t'see." I grinned.

"You don't understand. She threatened me with a dozen different crimes if I *did* contact you. She came to Bangkok. Had me write a letter. A whole confession of everything. Everything-everything. She said I'd be erased—not just my identity. Me. I've been hiding out. Selling the gold. Moving so they can't track me. Living by cash."

Eyes wide, Amy planted herself on the fountain's edge. "Aren't you two gonna hug or something?"

I took the first step forward. Lara rushed into my arms like an arrow from a bow, pushing her head against mine, holding me and saying in my ear: "He's gone, he's dead, he's gone, I can't forget him. I can't get over it. Any of it." And I held my sister in the garden like a flower fragile and wilted with all the petals, love me, love me not, yanked and tossed.

We exhumed the wren. As I expected, it was unchanged from when Amy buried it. Once having been an actual wren, alert and fastidious, merrily at its unending tasks aching to be rewarded, this particular bird had been taxidermied into a concealment device. Inside we found a key. Taped to it a name and address. The name read, *Lara van Eijk Aiken.*

"You have your passport on you?" I asked.

"I'm afraid to use it."

"We're not putting it through the system. It's only to prove your identity. Ms. Kim, can you find this address?"

"I could drive you. Would that be okay?"

"Nathan would insist."

The address belonged to the local PNC bank. The key belonged to a safe deposit box. The safe-deposit box was co-owned for ten years by Nathan Muir and Lara van Eijk. She remembered signing the signature card on her graduation from the University of Nottingham Malaysia Campus accounting program. They would only let Lara into the vault alone.

"What do you think is in it?" she said at the door to the vault area.

"Your escape hatch."

And it was. Lara's and Nathan's. Lara came out of the strong-room with two envelopes. One was a letter written to her from Muir. The envelope was thick. He'd had much to say. She has never told me what words he left her, and I have never asked. The other envelope contained a set of keys and the deed to Muir's Captiva Island home signed over to her name two days before his murder.

"Do you know where this is?" Lara asked.

"I've been there."

"I want to go," she said.

"We can go in the morning."

"No. Now."

After introductions between Lara, Gladys, and Jessie, who loved the idea of a mysterious, exotic aunt, Jessie said, "You're a stranger. Like me. I have two other aunts in California. One's mean. One's okay. But I already like you best."

After lunch and a quick explanation where we were going, we took Lara's gold Impala to Newark Liberty International. We booked the last seats on the last flight of the night, taking off at 9 p.m., one stop in Charlotte, and arriving in Miami a little before five in the morning.

I rented a car at the airport and drove the three hours to the island. I recalled the last time I'd made this drive, headed the other direction. Drunk out of my mind and ready to drink more. Nathan Muir's Sig-Sauer I'd stolen, prepared to kill myself for my lost love of Madeline. Two-weeks-and-change short of ten years ago.

I thought about her, Jessie, right then, about Mom and baby Nate leaving that morning for their new life in Los Angeles on my unused American Airlines ticket.

I hadn't bothered to call. Nate wasn't speaking yet, so what was the point? I hoped, though, Madeline had been good enough to call her daughter and say goodbye.

We caught a thunderstorm for the last third of the drive. The temperature was already in the eighties by 8 a.m.

THE SUN had returned. Steam rose from the blacktop as I made the turn from the road and drove down the clay-and-seashell driveway. Muir's house materialized through the dripping palm jungle. The broad wraparound porch. I pictured Muir standing there holding his tumbler of twenty-five-year-old Macallan— whiskey the same age as Madeline had been at the time.

How 'bout a drink? Got everything, long as it's scotch and rainwater.

"You ready?" I said.

"He feels more like my father than *our* father." She didn't need to say his name.

"Kinda feels that way to me. Don't fight it. Trust me, you'll lose."

"Thank you for bringing me. You never saw it, but this resembles so much my—*our*—father's house in KL. Up on pilings and everything. The water—it's behind it, right?"

"Yeah."

We climbed the porch stairs. Walked over to the sliding-glass doors beside the rattan sofa, matching chairs, and the coffee table. The ashtray and the ceramic match holder stolen from the Vientiane bistro were where I remembered them. Ten years and it might have been yesterday.

"There's a story about that sofa I'll tell you some time."

Lara unlocked the door. I followed her inside. I stopped in my tracks. The partially burnt American flag displayed in Muir's office for years had found its way here, hung in a place of honor. Muir's flag from his Korean War; Tom's from his war with his father. Muir must have always held out hope there would be reunion. I smiled again thinking it would make for a swell conversation starter in heaven when they met.

44

IT WAS 8:50 A.M., Tuesday, September 11, 2001. I stood in Muir's—now Lara's—living room and I could smell the old man. I could feel him. I told Lara about the flag and that it had meant everything to both men: what brought them together and what tore them apart. I let Lara look around the kitchen, the downstairs—the guest bathroom, the library den, the back bedroom with the funny old sea captain's bed. On the living-room windowsill, Muir had a collection of beachcomber relics: interesting seashells, some beach glass, a piece of driftwood that looked remarkably like an aircraft carrier, and, funny, a marble worn by waves and sand to rough and faded seafoam green. I put it in my pocket. It would join the jar of green marbles residing on my dresser in our Princeton brownstone. It was the first one I'd found since Nate's birth.

Some dumbbells were on the floor. I lifted one. Good for Muir. Heavier than I'd expect. I could hear Lara moving around above, inside Muir's master bedroom, which included his work desk and his master bathroom, across from a third bedroom to make the floor plan.

I noticed something strange: a walker. Since when did Muir use a walker? Age had made him more infirm than any of us had guessed.

A louder dash of feet upstairs. Lara screamed.

"Lara?!"

"Russell!" She screamed my name this time.

I hit the stairs as she came barreling toward me.

"Oh my God, oh God-oh-God-oh-God!"

She charged past me and out the door. I followed her as she plunged down the steps. She spun, panicked, faced me: "Where-do-I-go- to-gettothewater?!"

"What's going on? What did you see?" I showed her the head of the trail that leads through the tropical woods to the back bay.

"I'm afraid it won't be true if I tell you."

But I knew. It was in my sister's face. My cellphone rang.

"Run straight. I'm right behind you."

I checked the call—Muir's Princeton number; it was Gladys or Jessie. They could wait. The time read: 9:00 a.m. I let the call ring out and dodged after Lara. We came out of the trees and miniature jungle.

"Tom!" Lara screamed.

A 10-weight word. He turned, 500,000-ton weight of relief, another 500k of love escaping him at the sight of her, radiating outward like a shock wave as she collapsed into his arms.

Bishop.

My cellphone rang again.

Gladys again. 9:03. I ignored it. The words have not been invented to describe the wonderful-wonderfulness-wondrous wonder I was witnessing. Only then did I notice Tom's legs. His left leg, below the knee, was prosthetic, while his right leg was encased by a mechanical brace.

"Stop staring, Russell! I can still beat you in a race."

Muir had said the same about his foot. All was right with the world until, when my phone rang again, I answered it and it wasn't.

Pennies from heaven

Gladys informed me all of what she knew with the emotion-less calm of someone who'd worked her entire career as Nathan Muir's secretary at Langley. Two commercial aircraft, both

Towers; she advised me Jessie was in a panic for her mother and her brother. She was swearing at the television in Russian.

I got Jessie on the phone. I calmed her as best I could.

You remember the call? How foolish I feel now, how naive, how impotent. I told you Mom and Nate were on an entirely different flight. I told you not to watch any more TV and you told me you wouldn't. You said, you were going to climb the backyard tree and try to find a bird's nest. I said, stupidly—the stupidest thing I have ever said in my life, and I am horrified every time I remember, which is every day.

Words are everything to me. Their meaning gives me meaning. They are the width and breadth of my being. I operate on words; and after my operation, words were what I first recovered as they returned to me my thoughts. How could I in that crucial moment of life chosen my words so unartfully?

Before I disconnected the call, I told Gladys I would dial Madeline's airline and confirm where she and Nate were and that they were safe. If I could, I'd get a flight—if there were any. If not, I had the rental car. I'd drive. I wouldn't risk a wiretap, so I couldn't tell Gladys about Tom. Later, when I did, she said, "God still smiles on the faithful, even when some people do their worst against their faith."

Bishop and Lara were wrapped in each other's arms, deeply involved in their affection for each other. I would not ruin that. I slipped away, back into Muir's jungle alone with my heart of darkness. I left a note:

"9:30 a.m.—Check the news. It's unbelievably bad."

I took the car and I hauled ass out of there. I knew the flight they were on as both Madeline and I had taken it many times: me to Cedars, she, beginning a couple years before, to secretly rendez-vous with Nate's father. I couldn't get through to the airline, and at 9:38, unbelievably bad got entirely worse. American Airlines Flight 77, Dulles to LA, turned around and under the suicidal command of al-Qaeda terrorist Hani Hanjour—

By the Steeds that run, with panting breath,
And strike sparks of fire,
And push home the charge in the morning,
And raise the dust in clouds the while,
And penetrate forthwith into the midst of the foe en masse;
Truly man is, to his Lord, ungrateful;
And to that fact he bears witness by his deeds.

—the hijacked aircraft was flown into the Pentagon.

Madeline and Nate were murdered along with 2,975 other victims of the nineteen hijackers. This attack, like the three other hijacked flights, had been approved and ordered by Osama bin Laden at his Malaysia al-Qaeda summit. Of our activities in May, we will never know what bin Laden intended to do with the ATROPOS warhead, only that it had been headed for New York City's harbor and would have arrived in a Manhattan flooded with rescuers and responders, families of the dead and missing, aid organizations, military and national guard, and dignitaries, including the president.

The CIA cancelled the CBS red-carpet premiere.

I ARRIVED HOME twenty hours later. The radio played the entire drive. I'd spoken to everyone I needed to until my cellphone battery ran out. At one point before that, somewhere in Virginia along the I-95, Lara called. She'd grasped the flight Madeline and Nate had been on. She was horrified. We shared our grief. She hated how she could be so happy in the face of such tragedy.

I said her happiness was all I had right now to keep me together. While we didn't speak of Tom directly, indirectly she communicated that Tom Bishop was dead. That identity—the man who that was—had gone into the shadows once and for all and would never step back into the light. Tom Bishop had erased Tom Bishop for good. An escape hatch he'd meticulously built for four years. He now would only live for Lara. When we were ready, Jessie and I were welcome any time.

I asked if she needed any money or paperwork of any kind. She did not. Everything was taken care of—

"There's more than enough for two lives."

Gladys met me at the door. She wore a hijab and had been praying.

I checked you, Jessie, but you'd been up all night, had only recently fallen asleep. You were in peace, and I left you to your rest.

"I'll go climb the backyard tree and see if I find a bird's nest," you had said.

"Honey, be careful. Don't need you falling out of the sky. You're all I got."

The one time words had counted most. I filled with self-revulsion.

In the kitchen, on the L-shaped bench at Muir's—mine, now—breakfast table, built in to a paneled corner nook, I stared at a bottle of Macallan 25 next to Muir's starburst crystal tumbler of the liquid fire I'd poured myself. To drink it would be the foolhardiest thing I could do. I would never return from the bottom of the glass.

Gladys slid in beside me. "In Islamic writing of the *Qisas Al-Anbiya* and *Tafsir* we call the Hebrew prophet Isaiah, *Ashiya'*. He is notable in Islamic tradition for predicting the coming of Jesus and Muhammad."

I didn't know why she was talking. I didn't understand the words she was saying or why she spoke them.

"Are you afraid of what I think of you?" I said.

I wept.

"No, no, no, Russell, no." She pulled me in. I could feel her breastbone hard against my temple. She stroked my head. I felt the heat of her fingers massaging my scar.

She spoke: "Isaiah in the Bible says, 'Woe to those who call evil good and good evil, who put darkness for light and light for darkness, who put bitter for sweet and sweet for bitter.'

"We have much the same in the 'Surah al-Dhariyat'," she went on. "We say, 'By the heaven abounding in beauteous paths and beauties, surely you are perplexed in having different words. Turned aside from Truth is he who will be led astray in future. Down with the liars who are immersed in heedlessness and neglect. They inquire: "When will be the Day of Recompense?" It shall be a Day when they will be burned over the Fire! It is said unto them: "Taste you your trial! This is what you used to demand to be hastened!"'

"The words of our prayers are different, Russell, but our deepest identity is that we are one: good people of honest faith and peace will unite together and we will beat the evil and the lies."

"Yeah, maybe."

She released me. We both looked at the liquor. She said, "We must hope and trust life," and she left me.

I took the Macallan with me into Muir's study. I found an English volume of Muir's true mentor, Jacques Maritain. Muir's favorite book of his own professor: *The Range of Reason*. I opened it randomly and read out loud. Not Muir's one last Rule of Thumb, but double-underscored, perhaps, a warning:

"Having given up God so as to be self-sufficient, man has lost track of his soul. He looks in vain for himself; he turns the universe upside down trying to find himself; he finds masks, and behind the masks, death."

I was not myself. Could I ever be again?

I toasted the dead and tossed the whiskey.

ONE WEEK LATER, a young student of computer engineering, physics, and mythology presented herself at CIA headquarters, seeking employment and the opportunity to serve in the War on Terror. The Office of Recruitment had anticipated her arrival since the day in May when they had received Nathan Muir's final letter of recommendation; the day the dogwoods in the Memorial Garden dropped their first white petals into the koi pond.

The letter began:

> *"It is with immense pleasure that I share with you the perfect jewel of a candidate for Agency Service and duty to the United States of America, Miss Amelia Kim. Her suitability as an officer in the Office of Technical Services comes with my highest recommendation and utmost respect. With proper and vigorous training, and the most difficult challenges you can set for her, I see Miss Kim flourishing over a long and successful career superior to anyone I have had the pleasure to recommend, and, having said that, I include in that rare group myself.*
>
> *"Of truest sincerity, Nathan Muir."*

ABOUT THE AUTHOR

In 1989, Michael Frost Beckner's script for *Sniper* launched a military-thriller franchise now in production on its eighth sequel. Three consecutive record-breaking spec script sales and three films later, Tony Scott directed Beckner's original screenplay *Spy Game*. An international blockbuster that paired Robert Redford and Brad Pitt as CIA partners and rivals, it is now a classic in the espionage genre. Branching into television with his CIA-based drama *The Agency* for CBS, Beckner's pilot predicted Osama bin Laden's terror attack and the War on Terror four months before 9/11. In that series alone, Beckner would go on to predictively dramatize three more international terror events. Having penned more than twenty-five pilots for network and cable television, miniseries and docudramas, and dozens of original motion picture screenplays, adaptations, and rewrites, he is a Hollywood institution.

Now, in conjunction with the twentieth anniversary of *Spy Game*, Beckner returns to the world of Nathan Muir and Tom Bishop with the release of his trilogy of *Spy Game* novels: *Muir's Gambit*, *Bishop's Endgame*, and *Aiken in Check*.